About the Author

M. D. Charles lives in rural Lincolnshire. She graduated in 2000 from Loughborough University with a degree in Fine Art. Home is her favourite place together with her son and daughter, two cats and beagle, Maisie.

DRAPED IN DECEIT

M. D. Charles

DRAPED IN DECEIT

Vanguard Press

VANGUARD PAPERBACK

© Copyright 2020
M. D. Charles

A CIP catalogue record for this title is
available from the British Library.

ISBN 9781784655631

*Vanguard Press is an imprint of
Pegasus Elliot MacKenzie Publishers Ltd.*
www.pegasuspublishers.com

First Published in 2020

**Vanguard Press
Sheraton House Castle Park
Cambridge England**

Printed & Bound in Great Britain

Dedication

With love to my Mum and Dad

Acknowledgements

Thank you to my family and friends who have helped shape this story and of course my editing and production team at Pegasus.

Chapter One
Long Awaited

Lying on the grass, I was determined to soak up any summer sun I could get a hold of this year. I even allowed the noise of the kids, newly released from school for the summer break, to wash over me. The only drawback to all this was that, for the past month, Dan had been distant; in truth, it had been even longer than that really. I'd noticed he'd seemed distant weeks before his adopted mum died. Her death had hit him hard; he had always been so close to her. When she fell ill it came like a bolt out of the blue; only weeks later, she passed away, her health plummeting, finally succumbing to the ravages of her cancer, leaving her almost unrecognizable. She no longer looked like his mum, as he'd known her. It all seemed to happen so quickly. It was a shock to everyone, not least the family.

She had obviously been suffering for a long time and had ignored the signs, preferring to carry on, keeping everyone, including her own family, in the dark. 'Course, I don't suppose for a minute she knew it was cancer, but she had to have known something was wrong. Even Dan had said she seemed preoccupied about something, but he just couldn't get to the bottom of it, at least not until it all came out. That was when he distanced himself from me. In fact, not just from me, his girlfriend, Nicola James, but from Mallory Edwards, his best friend, from Tess Brinham and Jules Harvey and everyone else he was closest to.

After the last month or so of trying to get through to him, of texting him to let him know I was here for him, it seemed that things were finally shifting. Nearly a week after his mum, Fran, had died, my phone suddenly buzzed to life after lying dormant for so long. I had almost obsessively kept it by my side, hoping each day his name would pop up on my screen, signalling a return to just me and him, but there had been nothing for weeks on end. Nothing.

So, I sat there with it in my hands, listening to the buzzing, which I knew would end in a minute if I didn't answer the call. What would I say? Was it really him? It could be his sister, Charlotte, or even his dad. Maybe he was ringing to break up with me. If I didn't answer, then he couldn't. No, that was just stupid. There was only one way I was going to find out why he was ringing, and that was to answer it.

"Hey, Dan. You okay?"

He must have heard the apprehension in my voice, because I had. It felt weird, talking to him like this. He was my boyfriend after all, yet I was scared to say too much. Oh, I wanted to. I wanted to demand to know why he had ignored me for so long, even though I knew well enough the reasons for it. But I hadn't spoken to him for weeks, had I? Waiting on the end of the phone for him to reply seemed like forever.

"Hey, Nic," he mimicked, and then there was another pause. "I'm sorry, really I am..."

In my own head, I had already finished the sentence.

"... but I have to break up with you." Maybe he'd had enough of me with everything else that had been going on, but that wasn't what came out, much to my relief.

"... I haven't taken much notice of you lately, with all this, have I?"

I could imagine him smiling on the other end of the phone. My stomach did an unexpected flip at the warmth of his words.

"You've been through a lot, Dan," I consoled him.

"Will you meet up with me?" he suddenly asked.

"S-sorry?" My words tumbled out like they had tripped over my lips in a rush to get out of my mouth.

"It's all right. I understand. I didn't contact you at all, did I? All the time my mum was ill. It's only now she's gone — "

"No, that's not it at all. I just didn't know whether you would be ready to see anyone, Dan, and you caught me unawares, that's all. I'd love to meet up with you. I've really missed you…"

My words hung in the air for a minute. I wanted to kick myself. Had I said too much?

"Thanks, Nic. Can you make it today?"

"Sure thing," I responded.

My mum had asked whether I would go into town with her, but I could put her off. It was only the start of the summer break, and there was always tomorrow. If I told her it was to meet Dan, she would understand.

"How about two?" he asked.

"Sure. Do you want to meet in town, by the old theatre?" I suggested. It was half way from where I was now in Avery Park and where he lived on Morsley Road.

"Yeah, sounds good. I'll see you then, and thanks, Nic… I've missed you too… You do know that, don't you?" he added after another pause.

"Yeah, I do," I said, hoping he wouldn't guess from my voice that I hadn't been sure at all. "See you at two, then," I added before ending the call.

After taking his call I remained where I was as guilt began to creep over me like the clouds gathering in the sky. I wondered what he really must have gone through, all those days knowing his mum was going to die. It must have been horrible, and for Charlotte, his sister, it had been her real mum, and her dad too. All the time they had been going through that stuff, I had just been worrying about Dan not contacting me. How shallow did that make me? I made a mental note to ask him how they were both doing when I saw him outside the old theatre on Brompton Road at two.

As I got up and walked from the green towards the entrance gates, my steps had more of a spring to them. He had rung me to meet up; that was all I had been worrying about, that we were still

13

okay. Despite my shallowness, my stomach did another flip, and I smiled to myself. We were still okay.

We were all still at college. Dan and Mal (his proper name was Mallory), but none of us ever called him that because we only ever knew him as Mal, though when he annoyed Tess, it was Mallory. He and Dan were in the same classes. Both of them were studying business and finance. Tess, Jules and I were all studying different subjects, though we had some classes together. We were all friends which made me think about something else. Had he been in contact with any of them? Maybe Mal. I ought to let them know, but surely we could just have this afternoon together without anyone else? Yeah, I'll talk to him about them. Maybe he'll want to meet up with them all once we've spent some time together. First thing I needed to do though, was to get home, explain to Mum, and then make my way to meet Dan.

Leaving our house on Chievely Terrace just after one thirty felt more like I was going on a first date than just meeting Dan. I felt excited, and my stomach was in knots. I was actually nervous about how he would be with me. He was always so forward, but it had been so long. Would it be awkward with neither of us knowing quite how to be? Although we had only been together for a year, we had known each other for a few years. In fact, I had got to know him through Tess. She had known his family for most of her life, which made me wonder whether he had actually been in touch with her? I hadn't spoken to Tess in days. To be fair, it was quite a bit longer than that. But if he had, she'd have phoned me, definitely.

Maybe when I get home again, I'll ring her, even go round to her house on Baggley Crescent. It was in the same area as Dan, so maybe I could walk home with him and then make my way to her instead, just on the off chance. That was how she knew him. Her family had lived around there for years. I checked the time on my phone. I didn't want to be late. Looking around, I realised how close I was, about five minutes. How had I walked so far and not taken in anything around me? And why did I feel so nervous?

The streets were practically deserted, but it was Sunday. With the sun out again and the clouds having dispersed, I did pass a few kids playing and dog walkers, but nothing more than that.

My route to Brompton Road had allowed me to amble there instead of rushing, but I wasn't sure whether that had been best after all; it had given me way too much time to think things over. But I was here now; in the distance, I could see Dan waiting. As I drew a little closer, he looked up from where his head had been hunched in towards his chest, sensing my presence. He smiled, stood up, and began walking in my direction. I stopped, taking in everything about him that I'd missed since he had cut me off, but he was just as I had remembered and more.

At seventeen he had a muscular build; strange really because I'd never known him to work out at all. It often crossed my mind how he had such a great body but the hunger he stirred in me always seemed to block that more searching question. But with blonde hair that had the slightest wave to it, and the bluest eyes, I was easily swayed. But he was mine – he'd come back to me. Drawing closer, he immediately took me in his arms. I languished there, taking everything in. As I reluctantly pulled away, he cupped my face in his hands and kissed me. Everything I'd worried about melted in that second. It felt normal, good – more than good. It was like all the pieces that was our jigsaw puzzle, were slotting back into their rightful places.

"God, I've missed you, Nic."

"Me, too," I whispered.

He took hold of my hand and sat back down on the wall. But the elation that had initially greeted me now evaporated, giving way to what looked like despair.

"What's the matter? What's happened now?"

The way he'd succumbed to this mood so quickly made me wonder what had really happened. He must have realised what I was thinking. He put his arm around me and pulled me closer.

"It's nothing like that, Nic, really."

15

But he didn't offer anything more. Why? What could it possibly be that he couldn't share, or didn't want to?

"I'm sorry. It's not that I'm keeping anything from you." He guessed what I was thinking by the way I'd withdrawn. "It's just that I haven't really sorted everything out in my own mind."

"Try me," I offered. "Maybe we can work it out together."

"Okay, since my mum... since Fran... died," he amended, "I've been thinking about my real mum – my biological mother, I mean."

"Whoa! I wasn't expecting that. Have you told anyone else? And where's all this come from? It's a bit sudden, isn't it?"

"Not really, but after your reaction, can you imagine me telling Greg that I want to try to trace my real mother? Fran's body's barely cold. We haven't even buried her yet, and I'm running to someone else to replace her. How would that look?"

"But it's not like that," I defended.

"That's why I told you. I knew you would understand, Nic, but Greg won't. He's just lost his wife, and Charlotte's just lost her mum. While Fran was alive, they were good to me, but it's different now. No matter how close I was to her, even though they took me in when I was only weeks old, they're still not my biological parents. He would see it as some sort of weird betrayal. I never, ever felt as though I could broach the subject of my real mum and dad. I did once years ago, and it just sort of fell on deaf ears, like they didn't want to engage with what I was asking. From then on, the subject of my adoption seemed closed to me, and they never encouraged any more talk of it."

"I'm sorry, Dan. I never knew."

"There's no reason you would; no one did. After that initial reaction, I just sort of accepted that what I had was it... finished. If they didn't want to know, who else would?"

"Not even Tess?" I asked.

"No, not even her. No, that's not fair. She wasn't in the loop, even though our parents were good friends. It was just brushed under the carpet like some dirty secret. Everyone around us, including them, just assumed I was happy with just them, that I didn't want to know my birth parents."

"So, what happens now?" I asked, sure he would want my help in some way. Why else would he have asked me to meet him and then tell me all this?

"I'm not sure. The only thing I am certain of is that I want to find my mum. I need to know where I came from, who I look like, you know."

"Yeah, that's natural," I assured him. "Do you want me to help?" The last thing I wanted was for him to think I was trying to barge my way into something that was effectively his own business.

"I thought you'd never ask."

And at last he smiled.

"Want to go for a walk?" I asked reaching for his hand and pulling him to his feet. Facing one another, we both laughed at the awkwardness we had initially felt. I threw my arms around him. "I'm so glad you're back, Dan. I have really missed you."

"Me, too. I love you." And he kissed me hard, sealing his words.

"Come on," I urged. "Let's go to Avery Park. I was there when you rang this morning. We can talk some more about finding your mum and where we go from here."

"Do we have to? I don't want to talk any more." And before I could offer up any resistance, he grabbed hold of me and kissed me. I tried to protest, but he swiftly brushed my objections aside.

"I haven't seen you for ages," he murmured.

I answered him with my own hunger. I teased his lips with mine, but my breath was ragged, I wanted more. I think I knew all along that we'd both felt the same during our separation. When I finally pulled away, he continued to watch me.

"That's better. I thought for a minute you had gone off me."

"Did that prove I haven't?" I whispered.

"Oh, yes," and he smiled.

"So come on... Avery Park awaits."

I made a grab for his hand again, and this time he made no move to pull me back. Matching my steps, he remained by my side. Eventually he let go of my hand and lazily slung his arm around my shoulders.

Walking to Avery Park felt like old times; I felt comfortable again. All those weeks I had felt as though something was missing, and now it was back. I felt complete with him by my side.

"What has it been like at home since Fran's death?" I asked when we were almost at the park.

"The atmosphere's been rubbish. There have been a steady flow of visitors, Greg's friends and relatives mostly, but their attention has been aimed at him and Charlotte for the most part. I've just felt as though I don't belong. It's not Charlotte's fault. She still sees me as her big brother though, thinking about it, she has been distant since Fran died and Greg just doesn't really speak to me much at all now, and I don't know why. He's withdrawn completely. He spends a lot of his time with Charlotte, more than he used to actually. I hadn't thought about it before, but he does."

"Well, you've got me now. And I'm not going anywhere," I assured him.

"Is that a promise?"

"You bet it is!"

"You're coming to her funeral, aren't you?" he asked more seriously.

"Yeah, I'll come for you," I promised.

"Tess and her mum and dad haven't been round yet. I thought they would have come straight away, but I haven't heard anything. In fact, I haven't heard anything from Mal or Jules either."

"They probably wanted to give you some space, Dan. They'll be as keen to see you as I was – well, maybe not quite *that* keen."

He laughed. "I hope not."

"How about it? It would be good for us all to get together, wouldn't it? It's been too long, and it might be just what you need."

He gave no answer. Instead he seemed to mull the idea over, allowing it to settle.

Arriving at the park, we made straight for the open field and the shade of a huge oak tree. There were a few people milling around, but no one we knew. I felt Dan relax by my side. He lay down, stretching his arms back and turned his head towards me.

"You know what you said about us all getting together, that it might be just what I need. But it's not what I need right now. I just want to be with you, for us both to fool around like we used to before... Come on," and he patted the ground next to him. I playfully refused.

"Get down here, Nic!" he ordered playfully. I raised my eyebrows teasingly.

"Really?" I responded.

"Yes. Now. Get down here!"

I laughed at his insistence, but I obliged willingly. With his arms wrapped around me, I felt safe. I didn't need anything else. But our peace was interrupted. Both of us had closed our eyes, our thoughts immersed in each other and the warmth the sun was so readily providing. We didn't hear anyone, let alone see them approaching. We jumped at the voices directed at us.

I squinted up towards them.

"Hey, mate," Mal said, directing his greeting towards Dan. We both sat up uneasily, having been so caught out.

It was then I saw Tess. She was my best friend, though I'd seen nothing of her lately – my fault, not hers. When Dan had cut off ties because of his adoptive mum's illness, I'd effectively cut off ties with Tess, but that, I hoped, was about to change. I watched her curiously. It had been too long since I'd seen her. She was smaller in height than I was but around the same sort of weight, unfairly making her appear heavier. With very light-brown hair, she sort of matched Mal, though any similarity spectacularly ended there. He, on the other hand, was taller like Dan and just as lean. Jules, who was alongside, was different again. As dark as my hair was, hers was light, almost baby blonde with startlingly blue eyes, not dissimilar to Dan's; though the one thing we did share was hair that was both long and straight. She had all the confidence I didn't and the attention I preferred to shy away from.

"This is a surprise," I said to Tess. "I was thinking about coming around to see you later."

"We can all walk back my way, if you want," she offered. "Jules came round earlier, and then we hooked up with Mal and had a walk around here. Sunday's are so boring, there's nothing to do," and she rolled her eyes in Jules's direction, gesturing her annoyance at her presence here.

"No, there isn't, but it is good to see you all. We were just saying we should all get together, weren't we, Dan?" I remarked.

"Er, yeah, we were," he said, cutting short his conversation with Mal. "I was just telling Mal when the funeral's been arranged for."

"We've been meaning to come around and see you all, Dan," Tess told him. "My parents just didn't want to intrude."

"It's fine, Tess. Tell them they're welcome to come anytime."

"I will."

"So when is the funeral?" Jules cut in.

"It's Friday," Dan answered abruptly. "Friday at eleven at St. Thomas's. It's a burial."

"Okay," Mal answered. "Do you want to come with us, Nic?"

I looked at Dan. I didn't seriously think he would want, or be allowed, to take a plus one to a funeral service, but he nodded that I should accept Mal's invitation.

"Yes, thank you. I would appreciate it."

We all sat for a while longer, but the conversation between us faltered, and I think Tess figured it was all a bit early for the sort of playful banter that usually accompanied us as a group, so she steered the conversation in mine and Dan's direction.

"We had better get going." She glanced over at Mal for some support.

"Yeah, I think it's time. You ready, Jules?"

"I suppose I haven't got much choice. Can I have a lift home?"

"How can I refuse when you put it so eloquently?" Mal answered not so subtly.

"Come round a little later if you want, Nic. I'll be there, okay?" Tess told me.

"Yeah, I will. I'll walk with Dan, and then I'll to make my way to you," I responded.

We all said our goodbyes and that we'd see one another again on Friday. After watching them walk away and ensuring they were out of range, Dan let out a sigh. I turned to him.

"Was it that bad?"

"No, not really. I just can't be bothered making conversation at the moment. It's different with you because I haven't got to try. It's just comfortable."

"Oh, thanks very much!"

"It was meant to be a compliment."

"I know. I was just joking."

"I'll tell you what, though. There's something eating Jules. Have you seen anything of her lately?" Dan asked.

"No, why?"

"I just wondered. She wasn't very happy about leaving, was she?"

"No, she wasn't, and it surprised me that she had been around at Tess's. Though, from the look Tess threw me, she wasn't particularly happy about her being here. Jules was predictable as usual though, hanging on your every word," I said, half joking.

"Us is more like it," he corrected.

I wanted to correct him again but decided it wasn't really the time for all that.

"Actually, I thought she might get it on with Mal at some point. I always thought they would end up together."

"Nah, he's always had a thing for you, Nic."

"No, he hasn't. Me and Mal are just friends."

"Yeah, I know that, but he's always had a thing for you."

"No, he hasn't and anyway, we need to sort out where we start with this adoption thing, find out about your real mum?"

21

"You're changing the subject."

"No, I'm not. I just don't like you talking like that."

"I was just playing… Now, what were we doing?" and he kissed me, forcing me down.

I dodged him and sat up. "Adoption!" I berated.

"Yes, I know."

"Right, well social services would be as good a place to start as any."

He watched me intently before breaking out into a smile.

"Stop it, Dan!"

He raised his arms defensively. "All right, I'm sorry. What about going there tomorrow then?" he suggested.

"So soon?" I asked, surprised.

"Well, if we're going to do this we might as well do it sooner rather than later, don't you think?"

"Yeah, it's just that I thought you might want to get Fran's funeral out of the way first."

"Do you think I ought to?"

"It might be wise, Dan. But in the meantime, let me find out more about it, about what we've got to do and where we need to go, yeah?"

"Okay, but Greg's got his office at home. What about that as a starting point? See if there's anything in there that might help us."

"You mean, without Greg knowing what we're doing?"

"Yeah, I'll tell him we've got some college work to get done over the summer, see if he'll let us spread out in there."

"And you think he'll buy that?"

"You don't know how persuasive I can be," and he winked.

"Oh, I think I do," I commented, and we both started laughing. He was more like his old self now. I just hoped all this adoption stuff wasn't going to be too much and set him further back.

Chapter Two
Friends

We laid back down under the shade of the oak tree for another hour before we both agreed, reluctantly, that it was time go.

"Are you walking me home then?" Dan quizzed, but he was smiling as well.

"Um, really it should be you offering to take me home, don't you think?"

"No, I quite like it this way and besides, you're the one going to Tess's after you leave me." He laughed but then grew more serious. "I don't really want to leave you at all. Today's been great. Just the thought of going back into that house with that atmosphere just klls me."

"Meet me again tomorrow?" I suggested.

"No. I've got a much better idea. Why don't you come to me? Then we can escape after I've asked Greg about using his office to do our college work. He wouldn't dare refuse if you were there."

"I'm not sure, Dan. Will he even want me there? I know what you've said about friends and relatives coming and going but— "

"I want you there," he insisted. "And besides, he likes you. Please come," he added, his voice pleading.

"All right. It won't be until late morning though."

"That's great."

We carried on, ambling towards his house. Our conversation had more or less petered out as we sauntered along Morsley Road, to the far end where Dan's house stood, beyond a substantial pebbled driveway. Just before we approached it, leading to the this large, imposing, detached house, he stopped dead in his tracks, pulling me back sharply.

"Once you've finished at Tess's, give me a ring, and I'll walk you back home, okay?"

"You don't have to do that. I'll be fine," I assured him. "I was only joking earlier."

"I know you were, but I want to. Promise me?"

"Okay. I'll ring you," I promised. "Now, are you going to let me go?"

"Not until you've said goodbye properly." I smiled and obliged, but he responded a little too eagerly, his lips playfully lingering on mine, reluctant to let me go. I freed myself from his grasp. But I was reluctant as well.

"It's time you went in and I went to Tess's. She'll be wondering what's happened to me."

"Impatient to hear all the gossip is more like it," he teased.

"Of course," I agreed and I walked away a few paces. Catching up, he kissed me one more time.

"Don't forget to ring me when you're on your way back," he reminded me.

"I will."

"I love you, Nicola James," he called out. I turned and smiled, but I said nothing in reply.

When I turned back again, he'd gone, disappearing into that vast driveway.

Tess's house was just a couple of streets away from Dan's. It took me just five minutes to reach it, but the size of the houses, being only a short distance from his, were substantially smaller, although it was still detached. I had barely turned into her driveway when the front door swung open. She stood there waiting.

"I thought you had changed your mind," she called out.

"I told Dan you would be wondering where I was," I responded. "I'm sorry I've been so long. I just— "

"I know, Nic. Come on in," she said as I reached the front door.

It was nice in here, homely, and there was always a guaranteed welcome waiting. As I followed her into the kitchen, she grabbed two cans out of the fridge. Her mum appeared behind us.

"Hello, Nicola. You all right? We haven't seen much of you lately."

"Oh, hello, Mrs Brinham. Yeah, with Dan's mum passing away and everything, I haven't felt like going anywhere. But we're changing that now, aren't we, Tess?"

"Yeah, we're just catching up. You don't mind, do you, Mum?"

"No, of course I don't. It's good to see you, Nicola. Don't leave it so long next time. You both going upstairs?"

"Yeah, we just thought we would get something to drink first," Tess told her.

I couldn't wait to start questioning her about what had been going on in my absence and how come she and Jules were such good buddies, though I already knew that wasn't really quite so. I didn't say anything until we reached her bedroom. I was really just glad to be in her company again. After Dan had cut me off because of what was happening with his family, I had effectively done the same with Tess. Although there had been phone calls and text messages, I had seen little of her. I had missed my best friend, and I hadn't even realised it until now.

Closing her bedroom door behind me, it felt as though everything was truly beginning to get back to normal. I fell backwards onto the bed, allowing myself to just lie there before I turned my attention to my friend, who was watching me curiously.

"What?" I questioned.

"We haven't sat like this for ages, have we?"

"No, we haven't," I agreed, and then I remembered Jules. "You and Jules seemed close when we saw you at the park this afternoon," I commented, eyeing her curiously.

"You know we're not," Tess answered with a smile.

"Okay, I saw the look you gave me, but wasn't she at your house this morning?" I pressed.

"Yeah, she was," she said, and her smile broadened. "But don't be fooled. She only came round to try to find out what was going on at the Trennan place."

"How do you mean?"

"I think she was hankering after going round there with me," Tess confided.

"She didn't come right out and say that then?"

"I know Jules is our friend, but all of us know she'll only ever do what suits her. I certainly didn't invite her around here. That's how she came to be with me and Mal when we saw you both. And anyway, what would I have had to talk to her about except her? She's not interested in anything else, unless it's someone she's got her eye on."

"Dan," I blurted out. I hadn't meant to say anything, but I couldn't take it back now, not the way Tess was looking at me.

"I wasn't sure whether you'd worked it out."

"What? That she's interested in my boyfriend or that she might actually be getting somewhere?"

She laughed out loud. "Dan would never do that to you, Nic."

"Yeah, I know that." But the fact that Tess had come out with that still felt unsettling.

"What did she ask then?"

"Just how Charlotte and Dan were coping since Fran's death. Whether they would appreciate a visit. She asked more about Charlotte really than Dan."

"Oh, really?" I questioned.

Jules was the sort who relished attention, and if someone noticed her she played up to it all the more. As far as any of us were aware, that really was her strength. She couldn't get enough of being the centre of attention.

Although I got on with her, I was always acutely aware that if someone better came along who could further her aims, she would be off like a shot. It was different to the way Tess was, she never made a secret of her disdain for the way Jules hogged centre stage.

"She hadn't been here long anyway before Mal came," Tess added as an afterthought. I smiled.

"What?" she questioned.

"It's nothing really. I'm just glad I've got you on my side."

"And Mal," she assured me. I nodded in answer. I didn't want to respond any further to any mention of Mal remembering what Dan had said. What was he seeing that I had never, ever glimpsed? Mal was just my friend – maybe not my best friend as Tess was – but still my friend.

"What's the matter?" Tess asked, seeing my reticence after she'd mentioned Mal's name.

"Nothing," I lied. "It was just good getting together, even though it wasn't planned."

"He wasn't ready for it, though, was he?" she asked.

"No, not really, Tess. He just found it a bit awkward. I just think it was a bit soon. He didn't really know what to say with everything that's happened."

I wanted to say more, to tell her about what he had told me about how Greg was acting towards him now, about how isolated he felt there, and that I was going to help him find his real mum. But how could I? Doing so would betray everything Dan had confided in me.

"I think he's just going through a rough time at the moment, with what's happened to Fran and with the fact that it seemed to happen so quickly. Maybe once the funeral's over, things will get better."

"Yeah, I hope so," Tess agreed.

Mentioning the funeral brought on a welcome reprieve from questions about Dan.

"You're definitely coming with us on Friday, aren't you?" Tess asked.

"Yeah, it was good of Mal to offer," I replied.

"No, it wasn't. We're all friends, Nic."

I laughed at Tess's indignation.

"Are you laughing at me?" she rebuked.

"Yeah, what of it?"

Picking up one of the many cushions we'd both had to discard to be able to sit on her bed, she threw it in my direction. I tried to intercept it and failed miserably; it hit me squarely in the face. For a split second, Tess's face sobered as she waited for my reaction... until I grabbed hold of the same cushion and flung it back. We both fell about laughing, an easiness settling between us at last.

"I really have missed this," I said once our giggles had subsided. I had forgotten for how long I had closed myself off from her and Mal.

"Me too," she agreed.

"What time's Mal picking you up on Friday?" I asked, trying to keep our conversation away from any more talk of Dan.

"Well, he's picking Jules up first. I think that's because she lives nearest to him, and then it would perhaps be best to pick you up and then me because I live nearest to Dan and St Thomas's. So, if he picks you up at about ten fifteen, does that sound about right?"

"Yeah, sounds good."

"Well, I'll run it past Mal, and if it's any different, he'll ring you himself, yeah?"

"Yeah, thanks, Tess."

"Like I said, we're all friends. Are you seeing any more of Dan before Friday?" she added.

"Er, yeah, tomorrow. I'm going round to his house. We were going to try and get some college work done that had accumulated from last term that we really need to get sorted over the summer."

"There wasn't any extra in the classes we share, was there?" she questioned.

"No, it's just some individual stuff that we need to add to our work. It's just a bit of research really for when college starts again in September."

"Oh, okay."

"I'm a bit vague on exactly what it is that Dan wants to do, but he thinks we can muddle through it together. He thinks we might be able to use his dad's office at his house."

"Well, it sounds as good a place as any. We're going over there tomorrow, so we might see you."

"Oh, all right, though it depends what time. I'm not going to be there until late morning."

"Well, I don't think my parents will want to go until late afternoon anyway." But after a pause, she continued. "Tell me to mind my own business, Nic, but everything is all right, isn't it?"

"Yeah, of course. Why?" I asked.

"You just seem a bit on edge, that's all."

"No, I'm fine, really. Dan's having a bit of a hard time dealing with all this, and I'm just trying to help him, but there's nothing more than that."

"It's just that I haven't seen you for so long, and you don't seem your normal self," she explained.

If only you knew, I thought. I desperately wanted to tell Tess everything. She was my best friend in the whole world, and yet I couldn't tell her this. If I told her about the whole trying to find his real mum thing and it somehow got out, he would never forgive me.

"Look, it's none of my business. I just want to know you're okay, and I'm here if you need me, all right?"

"Yeah, thanks, Tess. What would I do without you, eh?"

"Just remember, we're friends, Nic."

"Best friends... always," I agreed. The atmosphere between us suddenly grew very tense. Could she see what was in my mind? No, I was just being stupid, and inwardly I laughed.

"What is it now?" She smiled, mirroring my obvious grin.

"Sorry, I was just thinking, that's all," I replied, bringing any more questioning to an abrupt halt, I hoped.

She didn't question it further; she merely brushed it aside, knowing she'd get whatever I'd been thinking out, eventually.

"Actually, Tess, when I met Dan earlier it struck me just how fit he is. I mean, really… obviously gym fit, I mean." I caught on when she started smiling. "He never even goes to the gym. In fact, he doesn't do anything remotely sporty."

"You're complaining because he looks so hot?" she responded, seeming completely confused.

"I know it sounds weird, I just got to thinking," I told her.

"Maybe he takes after his real father. Or, maybe he's just different, you know, like those Aryan races or Nephilim, wouldn't that be fabulous," and she looked suitably impressed with her assessment of him.

"That's just stupid, Tess."

"Well I was actually joking but…"

"Oh, I don't know, it just seems so odd."

"Is Jules going to go to the Trennans' then?" I asked, changing the subject.

"I don't know. She didn't say. She was just preening as she normally does about how awful it must have been and must still be. I don't think I can remember a time when she's been more concerned about someone other than herself."

"Oh, Tess, that's a terrible thing to say. I'm sure her words must have been sincere."

"I'm sure they were, but you can bet there's an ulterior motive in there somewhere."

I listened carefully to the words Tess had just spoken. I knew she was right, though there was a part of me that still felt it was a little unfair. Maybe Jules did just feel sorry for them. But even as my own words echoed in my mind, Tess's words rang out again about her asking about Charlotte. She had never been that close to her. So why was she asking after her now? That was the one thing that made no sense at all, making Tess's words about Jules having an ulterior motive way more credible.

"Maybe she wants to try and help the one person who needs it most of all – Charlotte," I suggested, though it wasn't what I was really thinking.

"Um, maybe," Tess answered, sounding totally unconvinced.

"You're not buying it, though, are you?"

"I'll reserve judgment," and we both laughed.

"Can I come round again soon?" I suddenly asked.

As I'd already said, it had been weeks since I'd spent any time with Tess. She knew just how to make me laugh. Dan was important too, but I had the feeling he was going to need as much as I could give and that maybe I was going to need Tess because of it.

"Sure, you're around at Dan's tomorrow, aren't you? Come here when you're finished."

"Do you want me to ring you first? Just to make sure you're in?"

"No, I'll be here. Just come when you're ready... Are you going now?" she asked, sensing my readiness to get off.

"Yeah, I should get back. I didn't tell my mum where I was going – after Dan, that is." I didn't say anything to Tess either about ringing Dan when I was on my way back. I don't know why. It just didn't seem important. Walking downstairs, I bumped into Tess's mum again as we reached the front door.

"Going already, Nicola?"

"Yeah, I didn't say how long I'd be out, Mrs Brinham. Mum will be wondering where I am."

"Well, best not keep her waiting."

"Nic's going to Dan's tomorrow, Mum. I was telling her about us going around there as well."

"Yes, sad business, isn't it?" Mrs Brinham replied.

"Yes, it is, for everyone," I agreed.

"Nic's calling around again tomorrow after she's been to Dan's," Tess informed her.

"Well, you might as well come back with us and have some dinner here. How does that sound?"

"Lovely."

"That's settled then. We'll see you at the Trennans', Nicola?"

"Yes, and thank you, Mrs Brinham," I answered. She seemed pleased with what she had accomplished and left me and Tess alone again to say our goodbyes.

"Sorry about that, Nic," she apologised. "My mum does tend to go on a bit sometimes."

"It's fine. It'll be nice to spend some more time here... I'm looking forward to it already." And I smiled as if reinforcing my words.

"Okay, we'll see you at Dan's then."

Walking away, I glanced back and waved. "See you tomorrow," I called back.

As I walked out of the drive and back onto the pavement, my mood felt lighter. It had done me good – spending time with Tess. I just had to get my head around me and Mal being friends, rather than him having a thing for me, as Dan believed. It felt a bit weird, what he had said, although I would have to get it out of my head by Friday, because Mal would be picking me up en route to Tess's and then St Thomas's. I had no desire to somehow accidentally pass on my troubled mind – and, more importantly, what was going on inside it – to him or anyone else.

Walking away from Tess's, I remembered the promise I had made to Dan about ringing him when I left. But I would be walking directly past his house, so I toyed with the idea of phoning him when I was more or less outside. I decided that would be best. It was early evening now, and being relatively quiet as it had been for most of the day, my path remained clear.

Dan's house was just around the corner, and even though I knew how stupid it was because I'd only left him a few hours ago, I was longing to see him again, even after Tess's suggestion of him being some sort of angel or even an alien, which was completely off the scale, even for her. But was it? Even so, as I turned the corner, my excitement was almost ready to burst at the thought of seeing him again.

My thoughts were abruptly halted though, as were my tracks. I stopped still before quickly backing up to the corner again. There was a stone column marking the corner where the path and road branched out onto another road, making up a low wall to either side with railings straddling it and a laurel bush hiding the property beyond. Settling behind it, keeping my presence hidden, I leaned against it, waiting. Right in front of me was Jules. What is she doing here?

Anger welled up inside me. She was just standing there on the edge of the drive. Should I go over to her? Ask why she was there? No, she would then know I was annoyed. Would she start questioning me if I did? I knew – or at least I had an inkling, like Tess had already said – that she had a thing for Dan. But why should all that matter? Dan had made me promise to ring him when I was on my way home. But had Jules arranged to go there? Did Dan know about it? No, all I was doing was trying to second-guess what she was doing. Why was she here though? I had to go over to her.

I finally made my move, and I was just about to call out to her when she obviously saw someone. She suddenly waved excitedly and hurried towards their house. Who was she greeting so warmly? I moved away from the corner but leaned against the railings, thinking about what might be going on inside now. But I was just making myself more miserable, so instead I walked as casually as I could past their house, surreptitiously glancing over. But the driveway was deserted, and no one came out for me as he or she had done for Jules. I carried on walking and took my phone out of my pocket. There were no messages or missed calls, which I knew there wouldn't be. I wondered for a while whether I ought to just ring Dan. But I couldn't get out of my head that it might have been him standing at the front door, waiting for her.

Scrolling through my contacts, I settled on Dan's number. Surely he wouldn't have said to ring him if he'd known Jules was going round there. If he ignored my call though, that would give me my answer, wouldn't it? No, even if there was nothing going on, I couldn't interrupt him now, so I closed it and shoved it back in my pocket. Shuffling forward, I miserably made my way home, still unable to get out of my head thoughts of what really must be going on in there.

As I walked over the threshold of 7 Chievely Terrace, my mood had darkened considerably because of what I had seen on Morsley Road.

"Had a good day, Nic? How's Dan doing?" my mum questioned before I'd had chance to say anything.

"He's fine. I'm tired, Mum. I'm going upstairs."

"But your dinner's in the oven."

"I'm not hungry!" I called back, hoping that would be enough to make her leave me alone. To my relief, she said nothing more, allowing me to seek the sanctuary of my bedroom.

Once I had shut the door, I took my phone out again. Nothing… Why would he insist that I ring when he hadn't even bothered to check where I was?

Another hour passed, and still there was no word. I was just about to scroll to Tess's number when a message came through. I checked who it was from before I read it. I stared at it for a minute; it was Dan. What would he tell me? There was only one way to find out. As I clicked on it, I just stared at the screen. I don't know what I had expected to read, but I found myself smiling, relief washing over me.

Where are you? Still at Tess's? Please text so I know you're safe and that you're still coming tomorrow. Love you x

Straight away, I set about answering his message.

Sorry, saw Jules going into your house, didn't know what to do so just came home. But yeah, if you still want me, I'll be there tomorrow x

His reply was immediate.

Yes, I definitely want you here x

I lay back on the bed, relief again sweeping over me. I didn't know why Jules had been there, and Dan hadn't volunteered an answer, but he wanted me there tomorrow, and for now that was all that mattered.

Chapter Three
Seeking Answers

I couldn't remember Dan changing the arrangements about meeting at the old theatre on Brompton Road, but who was I to question him? I arrived slightly early and felt strangely curious about what lay within. I'd never really taken much notice of it, and I'd certainly never ventured inside, but its appeal was overwhelming. I drifted up the steps and crossed its threshold, powerless to stop it. My eyes searched my surroundings while I waited for him. Looking down, the floor was laid out in a black-and-white checkered design, which in its day would have gleamed, its opulence welcoming its patrons of the day. But now, it was cracked and scuffed with debris all over, giving me only a subdued glimpse of its past glory.

Searching further, my attention settled on an elegant staircase, marble balustrades sweeping upwards, leading to an upper floor with more seating areas. The foyer, where I was standing, was oval in shape, with the staircase rising up from it. Part of the way up it branched out at each side, sweeping around the foyer below.

I took a step towards it when I sensed someone behind me. It was obviously Dan. I spoke as I turned around.

"I knew you'd be late."

But he wasn't there; no one was there. The atmosphere suddenly changed. It grew sombre, and I felt cold and alone.

"Dan!" I shouted, "Dan... please!" My fear rose quickly within me. Someone grabbed hold of me, but they remained concealed and yet, in the distance I could hear someone. Was it Dan, trying to reach me? "Dan... Please... Where are you?" I screamed. I could still hear him. He was calling out to me. I tried to reach him.

"Nic...Nicola! Wake up!"

I opened my eyes with a start and stared straight into my mum's eyes; she had her hands on my shoulders, shaking me.

"W-what's the matter?" I asked, barely lucid.

"You were having a dream. It seemed like a bad one. It was, wasn't it?"

"Er, no," I lied.

"Well, it's eleven thirty. Isn't it time you got yourself ready and into bed?" Confused, I looked down. I still had my clothes on.

"Er, yeah. I'll get undressed and get into bed." But she continued eyeing me curiously.

"You sure you're all right? You were really thrashing about."

"Yeah, I'm fine, Mum. It was just a dream." I got off the bed and held the door open. For a couple of seconds, she just stood there, she wasn't going anywhere. "I'm fine, really, Mum," I repeated.

She nodded reluctantly before leaving me to it and closed the door behind her. Getting undressed I then crawled into bed, hoping I didn't drift into that same dream.

Squinting into the sun streaming through the gap in my curtains, I stretched, yawning from the uninterrupted sleep I had just woken from. I peered leisurely at the clock on my bedside table; it was ten to ten. I lay there, thinking of nothing, until Dan suddenly resurfaced in my head and with him the dream my mum had shaken me from last night. I ran through the images I had seen of the old theatre on Brompton Road and why it had appeared in my dream in the way it had. But then it occurred to me. I had met Dan there yesterday. I had obviously been processing what had already happened and conjured up the inside from my own imagination. I certainly didn't think for a minute that it looked just the way my mind had painted it.

But neither had Jules, Tess or Mal been in it. So, I couldn't have confirmed it from them. Though maybe Dan had and I was simply confirming a memory.

Dan! I suddenly remembered. He'll be expecting me at his place in an hour. I jumped out of bed and ran straight into the bathroom and showered.

Descending the stairs, I realised my mum had already left for work, and she wouldn't be back until at least five thirty. On the worktop, I found a note from her.

Morning, Nic. Gone to work. Be back around five. Left you asleep after the dream you'd had last night. If you're going out, leave a note just to let me know. Love you,

Mum x

I stood there for a minute before diving into the bread bin. I hadn't realised until then that I was absolutely starving. Once I had eaten and washed the pots and left my mum a note to say where I was going and that I would be at Tess's for dinner, I left.

After locking up, I headed out towards Morsley Road and Dan. The roads at this time of morning had considerably quietened again from what they would have been earlier on. The sun was out, and the warmth on my bare arms felt good. Maybe I would get the answer to what I had seen last night. Jules's presence there had evoked such anger in me. I just hoped it proved to be as unfounded as my dream had.

As I neared Dan's house on Morsley Road, I grew unexpectedly nervous. Would Jules be there again? Had she ingratiated herself within the household so quickly? My pace slowed as I wondered what I would be faced with. Only several paces into his driveway, I caught sight of him at the front door. He stood there, watching my advance. My nervousness quickly gave way to a fluttering in the pit of my stomach. Every fear I'd held on to since I'd seen Jules there last night, even though I'd got that assurance through his text message, now evaporated into thin air.

I carried on walking, only too aware of his eyes scrutinizing my every move. As my steps took me closer, I averted my gaze, preferring to focus on the loose pebbles of the driveway.

"I've been waiting ages," he joked when I was within touching distance.

"Sorry," I apologised playfully.

"You will be," he teased. "Come on in," he urged.

Walking into the hallway felt really oppressive after being outside in the full sun, and the fact that it was covered from floor to ceiling in dark oak panelling didn't help either. In fact, the only relief from it all was the white ceiling.

"Hello, Nicola," his dad greeted me, making me jump. I had been so engrossed in mulling over the panelling that I hadn't even seen him there.

"Oh, Mr Trennan," I replied, conveying my unease. He'd caught me completely off guard. I hadn't expected to see him at that precise moment. "M-may I offer my condolences." He met my awkwardness graciously and smiled, though his eyes seemed to bore straight into me. He was tall, an attribute that gave him that authoritarian feel, and I felt unnerved.

"Thank you, Nicola. That's very sweet of you," he answered.

As he turned, I quickly glanced over at Dan and squirmed. He smiled as well, but his smile was completely different. It was encouraging.

"Dad," he said, calling him back after eyeing the large bag we'd decided I should bring and which was hanging from my shoulder.

"Me and Nic have got some college work we need to catch up on, and we need a bit of room to spread out. Any chance we can use your office? And Tess said she and her parents were going to come round a bit later... About the office, though, I just thought, if we could go in there, we wouldn't have to put all our stuff away again if they or anyone else comes around, and it would be quiet."

"Yeah, sure. Go get your stuff, and I'll make sure Charlotte doesn't disturb you."

"Thanks," Dan replied gratefully.

"Yeah, thank you, Mr Trennan," I echoed.

"It's fine," he responded. "I can't stand in the way of that level of commitment, can I? And call me Greg, please."

"Okay, thank you, Greg, it'll get it out of the way," I repeated.

"Well, it's got to be done," Dan said, as he made his way up the stairs. "I'll just be a minute," he called back to me.

While he was gone, Greg showed me in to his office. It was large, bigger than my bedroom at Chievely Terrace, though all the rooms I had seen in this house were bigger than any of ours.

"I haven't been in here since the morning Fran died," he confessed.

I wasn't quite sure how I was supposed to respond. It seemed weird being in here with just him, but I had to contribute somehow.

"We build walls around ourselves to protect us, and sometimes we steer clear of areas where that pain affects us the most," I told him. "Eventually, though, we have to face whatever it is to be able to lessen that pain."

"How very true that is," he agreed. But the need to contribute further was thankfully taken out of my hands with Dan's reappearance.

"Got my stuff," he said brightly. Greg responded with a resigned nod.

"Well, I'll leave you both to it," he said and walked to the door.

"Thanks for this, Dad," Dan called over. Greg nodded again before closing the door behind him.

"Wow! Have things improved between you two?"

"No, it's only because you're here. It's different again when we're on our own."

"Okay. Well, let's get started then."

"Where?" Dan asked a little impassively.

"You okay?" I asked.

"Yeah, I just feel a bit weird in here."

"All right, I think setting out all our work would be best. If your dad walks in again and we've got nothing in front of us, it's going to look a bit suspicious, don't you think?"

"Yeah," he answered, but then he smiled broadly. "Thanks for this, Nic."

"I want to help, Dan, so stop thanking me, and let's get on with it," I responded.

"Message received."

I ignored his sarcasm and the smile behind it and began laying out both my work and his.

Once it was spread out, I slumped back in Greg's plush, soft leather swivel chair. I looked around leisurely, perusing the whole room and the furniture in it. My eyes finally rested on the polished mahogany desk before me and the various drawers down either side.

"Maybe these drawers would be as good a place to start as any," I informed Dan. When I'd walked in here with Greg, I'd remembered the filing cabinet against the wall, to the right of where I was sitting and to the left of the front window.

"Dan, do you want to start by checking through that filing cabinet while I search through these drawers?"

"What am I looking for?" he asked.

"I don't know. Anything to do with the adoption – social services, anything like that, okay?"

"Okay," he responded and walked over to the filing cabinet. I tried the desk's top drawer to my right. It was locked. The next two below it opened, much to my satisfaction, though I quickly found they yielded nothing. I began on the other side, but the closed book before me, the one I had placed there, caught my attention. I leafed through it until I reached the last section I'd written. Taking the top off my pen, I gripped my fingers around it just in case Greg decided to make an impromptu appearance. I then carried on and opened the top drawer to my left.

Nothing, just office stuff – a hole punch, staples, stuff like that. I opened the second one down, but that revealed little more.

"Hey." Dan's tone sounded hopeful. I looked up, wondering what he had found. "I've got a name," he said, unknowingly answering my question. But right at that moment, the turning of the doorknob shook us. I closed the desk drawer quickly and poised my pen over my work. Dan, too, quickly closed the drawer of the filing cabinet he'd just taken the piece of paper from and stuffed it into the back pocket of his jeans.

"Sorry to disturb you both," Greg said. "I was just going to make a cup of tea. I wondered if you wanted one."

"I don't, Dad. I don't know about Nic."

"No thanks, Greg. We're just trying to get through all this, aren't we?" I said, turning to Dan for him to back me up.

"We are, yeah. We really want to get this bit done, and then we'll be about finished."

"All right, I'm sorry. I won't disturb you again." And he closed the door without another word.

"Phew, that was close," I whispered.

"Yeah, hopefully he won't come back again," he responded and took the crumpled piece of paper out of his back pocket. "There were loads of bits of paper in that second drawer, Nic, but I managed to find this amongst it all." He held it out. It was a compliments slip. I'd seen these before, a small piece of paper headed 'Social Services', yellowing from the years it had obviously been in there.

"A name as well, scrawled right across the centre," I uttered.

"Yeah, Gail Lassiter."

"It must have been in there a long time, Dan, and from the yellowing, it can only mean one thing, can't it?"

"It's got something to do with my adoption," he finished.

"My thoughts exactly," I concurred. "But we need to keep looking."

Stowing the paper away in my own pocket, we carried on, Dan continuing to search the filing cabinet while I continued searching through the last of the drawers on the desk's left-hand side. There were loads of papers in this last one, all in order, but they were just paid bills. I searched through them all methodically, thinking something else might have been hidden among them, but I found nothing. I looked up at Dan, hopeful that he had come across something more.

Hunched over the lower drawers, he looked as focused as I had been.

"Any good?" I called over.

"No, there's nothing. I think that slip must have been overlooked at some point. Maybe it had just been forgotten."

I swung around in the chair. When I had walked in here with Greg, I'd noticed a long, narrow mahogany table with matching lamps standing on either end behind the desk alongside the wall. There was a single drawer in the front of it. Pulling myself a little way in the chair towards it, I pulled on the drawer. Predictably, it was locked. Slumping back in the chair, I sighed.

"What's up? You had enough?" Dan asked.

"Not quite. Where does Greg keep the keys to this and that top drawer of his desk?" I questioned.

"No idea," he answered. "We might as well call it a day if they're both locked."

"You're not going to give up that easily, are you? If these drawers are locked, you can bet there's going to be stuff in there that he doesn't want seen. Otherwise, why would he lock them?"

"Well, what more can we do?"

"We can look for those keys."

For a minute I sat, looking around the room. Surely the key for the desk drawer, at least, would be hidden somewhere in here? I got up and walked around, in part to stretch my legs, but I figured as well that in doing so, it might bring some inspiration my way. Instead it was Dan who called out, excitement billowing from him.

"Nic, I've found it. One key, at least." I turned to see him holding it aloft like he'd beaten everyone to first place.

"Where did you find it?"

"It was inside his penholder, here on the desk."

42

"Which drawer does it belong to?" I asked.

"I don't know," he said and walked around to the chair. Sitting down, he tried it first in the desk drawer. Amazingly, the mechanism clicked, and he pulled it open. There, to both our delights, was the other key, pushed right into the front left corner.

"We need to try it in the drawer behind," I insisted.

From the way he looked at me, I knew he wasn't that keen, but he relented.

"Okay, but let's see what's in this one first."

I stood back a little and allowed Dan to sort through the papers in there. There was a lot of legal stuff that went right over my head, some bank papers, but also a plain white A4 envelope, which looked like it had been in there for some time.

"Take it out," I urged, but he seemed reticent. "What's the matter?"

"This can't be it, can it?"

"There's only one way to find out," I encouraged.

He nodded and carefully pulled it open. The seal came away easily. This obviously wasn't the first time the envelope had been opened. Reaching for the paper within, he pulled it out.

"It's your birth certificate," I said. We both looked at it intently, trying to take in the information there.

"Her name's here. Look, Nic. Her name was Paige Ellison. I never knew that. I never knew my mother's name.

"And look," he said, pointing out his own name. "I must have started out as Daniel Ellison. So they didn't change my first name."

I couldn't begin to imagine what was going on inside his head. For the first time, he was seeing evidence, real evidence, there on paper that his mother, his birth mother, existed. But looking at it, I noticed something else. It was a full certificate, and below where his details were, his birth date and place of birth, was a space for his father's name, but it just said, *Father not known.*

"Doesn't that bother you?" I asked. "Not knowing who he was?" I let my finger hover over those three crucial words.

"He obviously didn't care, did he? So why should I? Besides, it's my real mum I'm more interested in."

I nodded. I suppose I could sort of understand that. Although I had known my father, he had died nine years before. I knew my circumstances were different from Dan's, but my dad had worked away a lot of the time, so I had little memory of him.

"So what are you going to do now?" I asked.

"I want to find her," he replied decidedly.

"And what about the certificate?" But even as the question was coming out, I noticed him jotting down a few notes.

"Once I've got what I need, I'm putting it back. I don't want Greg to know we've seen it. Then I'm going to go to social services, like you said, to begin searching for her. You'll come, won't you?"

"Yeah, of course, but don't you think it'll be better to wait until after the funeral, like we agreed?

"I suppose so, yeah," he replied and his mood dipped a little.

"It would be better to use the photocopier as well. It's on. Look."

I pointed to where it was behind him, plugged in and ready. "Actually, Dan," I began, but his concentration was focused on the certificate and getting it printed just in case Greg made another unexpected appearance. But the question that had just popped into my head wouldn't budge.

Wouldn't the certificate say that he was adopted? I puzzled. Maybe now wasn't the time to bring it up. I made a mental note to broach it later. Maybe I could have a look online, I decided. I could do some research, get some idea of what sort of paperwork was involved in being adopted.

With that copy done and safely stowed away in my pocket and his actual certificate back in its envelope and back in the drawer, I turned my attention to the narrow table behind us, the one that really intrigued me. Taking the key from the front-left corner, I held it up like a trophy as Dan had earlier.

"Are we going to take a look, see what's in there?"

"There's not much point now, is there?"

"It's up to you," I offered. "But look what you found in this one. You might find more besides in that."

He took the key from me and began swinging its head between his thumb and index finger as if deep in thought as to whether he should unlock it or leave it well alone.

Without warning, he forced back the chair he was sitting in and stood up.

"Come on, then. I don't suppose it'll hurt, will it?"

I smiled victoriously. He unlocked the drawer and pulled it open.

To our surprise, there was only one letter in there. He took it out. It was addressed to Greg, and it was in Fran's handwriting. He turned it over. It had already been opened and obviously read.

"Wow! That must be some letter!"

"Why do you say that?"

"There's just one letter, Dan, and the drawer where it has been kept is locked. Doesn't that beg the question of what its contents actually contains?"

"I know how it looks, Nic. But it doesn't feel right to read it, not when it's addressed to Greg and particularly when it's in Fran's handwriting. I'm sorry. I can't read it."

"It's okay," I said as I took it from him and reluctantly placed it back in the drawer. Pushing it closed and locking it, I then placed the key where we had found it in the front-left corner of the desk drawer. Locking that, I then dropped the key back into the penholder where Dan had first found it.

"There. It's all done," I said, and I sorted our books into a pile. But that letter and – more intriguing – its contents still occupied my mind, and for me at least, it was infinitely more intriguing than the certificate in importance. "Well," I said mischievously while hauling myself up onto the desk. "What to do now?" I asked. He tried his best to remain unaffected by my question, but after only seconds, the corners of his mouth began to curl upwards.

"What do you suggest?"

"How about a walk?"

"I thought you were going to suggest something a bit racier."

"We can have a race if you'd rather," and I laughed.

"No, a walk will be good enough. Thank you."

I jumped off the desk and held my hand out.

Grabbing it, he pulled me to him. We were kissing when Greg appeared at the door again. On seeing him, I pulled away like a shot.

"Oh, sorry," he said. "I didn't mean to interrupt— "

"No, it's fine, Dad. Actually, we were just going out for a walk. We're all done here."

I gathered up my books, and after depositing them in my bag, I followed Dan out of the door.

"Won't be long," he called, taking the stairs two at a time. "I'll just leave these on my bed."

"Get enough done?" Greg asked while Dan was out of the way.

"Yes, thank you. It was just a bit of work that both Dan and I felt we needed to do. At least now it's out of the way."

"It was quite a coincidence that you both had work to do, wasn't it?"

"Yeah, it worked out quite well, and doing it together helps. How's Charlotte doing?" I asked, changing the subject.

"She's okay, though pretty much like you'd expect with losing her mum, but we're all coping as well as we can. Thank you for asking, Nic. What work were you and Dan doing anyway?"

"Er, just a bit of research." I had the strangest feeling that he had an idea what we'd really been doing by the way he was watching me, but at that moment, with a beaming smile, Dan came bounding down the stairs, saving my bacon.

"Right. You ready?"

I nodded.

He turned to his dad. "We won't be too long because Nic's meeting Tess and her family here in a while. She's going there for dinner, aren't you?"

"Yeah," I answered, but I suddenly felt very uncomfortable. There was no way he could have guessed what we'd been looking at, was there?

Being out in the open made the air feel far less stifling. I didn't say anything to Dan until we'd walked beyond the drive and out onto the pavement.

"Did you feel slightly uncomfortable in there?"

"How do you mean?"

"I got the distinct impression he knew what we had been looking for in his office."

"Nah, that's stupid. How could he?"

"He hasn't got a camera in there, has he?" I asked.

He laughed at me.

"Don't look at me like that, please. I feel stupid enough suggesting it." He put his arm around me, but I couldn't get the way Greg had looked at me out of my head. "He knew something, Dan. I'm sure of it. He also asked what work we'd both been doing in there."

"What did you tell him?" he asked.

"I just said we'd been doing some research, and then thankfully you came down the stairs, cutting off any more conversation."

"That's cool. If he says any more, I'll make something up to do with our work at college, okay?"

"Okay," I agreed.

"What time's Tess coming around?" he asked.

"I don't know. Around three, I suppose. Why?"

"Well, that's another hour. If you really were that uncomfortable in there, we can just walk around until she arrives."

"I'm not imagining it, Dan."

"I believe you. Do you understand how I feel now? I have to live there."

I didn't say any more. He was right, of course. I had endured only minutes of Greg, but still I couldn't escape the feeling that he knew something.

True to his word, we did stay out until we saw Tess and her parents arrive. We had been sitting on the bench down the road from his house and had a clear view of their arrival. After giving them a few minutes to get inside and exchange pleasantries, we slowly ambled back, with Dan's arm still resting protectively around my shoulders.

Chapter Four
Tempers Flare

As we walked in through the front door, the air felt slightly chilled. Our advance towards the back of the house and the sitting room felt like we were both being watched with too much interest, which I'm sure Dan felt too.

"Dan," Greg called out, waving him towards them. As he grabbed hold of my hand, his stride gathered momentum.

"Mr and Mrs Brinham, hello. It's nice to see you. Where's Tess? Didn't she come with you?"

"Yes, she's outside with Charlotte. Hello, Nicola," Mrs Brinham added, turning her attention to me.

"Hey, Mrs Brinham." I nodded to Michael, Tess's dad.

"Are you still coming home with us?" she asked.

"Yes, if that's all right?"

"Of course it is. You're always welcome."

"Actually, Dad, do you mind if we go outside and see Tess?" Dan asked.

"No, don't be long, though. We've got guests."

"Okay," he answered, but Greg's reaction to his request seemed way too clipped. I saw Tess's mum catch her husband's attention. Greg didn't notice; his focus remained firmly fixed on Dan. What is going on with him? I wondered. Dan's mood remained unchanged though.

Maybe he was just used to Greg speaking to him that way. It was certainly the first time I'd witnessed that sort of behaviour from him, though Dan had gone on enough about it. But he'd also said that Greg didn't say much at all when they were on their own, that he concentrated more on Charlotte, so it didn't really add up. But at that moment, I felt him squeeze my hand. Was he feeling it after all or just trying to make me feel more at ease? The atmosphere in here certainly did little to help.

Leaving them to talk amongst themselves, we headed out of the French doors and into the garden. High shrubbery flanked parts of the borders of it, but it was mostly just lawn. At the far end, Tess and Charlotte had settled themselves on the garden swing. I figured that was probably Tess's doing. She would want to get Charlotte as far from Greg's hearing and influence as was possible and she would have wanted Charlotte to feel comfortable. Tess had been close to her in the past, as she had been with Dan. All three of them had known one another long enough. But all through Fran's illness, Tess hadn't heard a thing from her, just the same as I hadn't heard from Dan. Over the last few days though, that contact had changed.

Charlotte, however, had seemed more distant than ever. Even during the couple of times I had been around to their house, she had been nowhere to be seen. I understood that she was grieving for her mum, but she was usually the first one there when any of us turned up, and this was the first time I had even clapped eyes on her. She looked tired, which, taking into account the grief she was suffering, wasn't that surprising. And now that she and Dan were together, the difference between them was easy to see. Charlotte looked very much like her mum, Fran. She had darker hair like mine and hazel-coloured eyes. Dan's colouring couldn't have been in more contrast if he'd tried, though there were slight similarities between them in facial features, but I figured that was just me. I imagined he looked more like his mum only because he shared no blood with his adoptive family.

"You all right?" I asked Dan, knowing we were far enough away now for Greg not to overhear us.

"You caught that, did you?" he inquired.

"What? The clipped tone? Yeah, and so did Tess's mum and dad, though Greg didn't realise they had noticed anything. He was too focused on you."

"It feels like I don't even belong here, like he doesn't really want me anymore. Do you know what I mean?" Dan seemed far away from me, his mind entrenched in that last dialogue with Greg.

"Unfortunately, I do, but forget about it for now, Dan. He'll probably realise he was wrong in the way he spoke to you once he's thought about it."

"I doubt it," he muttered, but he didn't get a chance to add any more; Tess and Charlotte were only just up ahead. I walked straight to where Charlotte was sitting and threw my arms around her.

"Hey! You okay?" I whispered in her ear. Pulling back, she smiled.

"Yes, thanks, Nic."

"How are you doing, really?"

"Okay, I guess. It's been really strange since… Mum. Hasn't it, Dan?"

"Yeah, it has." And he smiled, just for her. I could clearly see he had no problem with Charlotte, nor she with him. So what the hell was going on with Greg?

"I was just telling Tess that Jules came around to see us last night," she informed us. "She was really nice. She fussed over all of us. I think Dad enjoyed her company." I surreptitiously stole a glance at Tess, and she at me.

"That was nice of her," I agreed. "We saw her with Tess and Mal – didn't we, Dan? – the other day," I added.

"Yeah… She was full of it then, as well," he added in a low growl.

"Even if you didn't, I enjoyed her company," Charlotte hit back.

Busily searching through Greg's office for anything to do with Dan's adoption, I had completely forgotten about Jules's visit here last night. I had meant to question Dan about her when I arrived, but the topic had gone completely out of my head, and Dan was watching me, trying to gauge my reaction to what Charlotte was saying. I caught his eye and smiled, giving nothing away.

"You're going around to Tess's when she and her folks leave, aren't you, Nic?" Dan asked.

"Yeah, I'm going there for dinner. How about us all getting together and maybe asking Mal and Jules as well?" I saw Tess's smile wane at the mention of Jules. "It'll be good," I said, aiming my attention directly at Tess.

"I would like that," Charlotte agreed. "It's not been much fun cooped up here." And she suddenly looked back towards the house. Greg was ambling his way towards us.

"Charlotte, I think it's time we called it a day," he called.

She looked crestfallen at his suggestion, having to leave us.

"Oh, come on, Dad," Dan said. "She hasn't seen anyone for weeks. She's just enjoying the company. Let her stay with us a bit longer, please. We haven't been out here long."

Greg's face was like thunder; he looked like he was about to explode.

"Since when was it up to you to say what goes on here?" Greg asked.

"I was only saying." Dan laughed, obviously thinking that, with me and Tess sitting here, there wouldn't be any more said.

"Get inside, Charlotte!" Greg spat.

"Please, Dad, can't I just stay here a bit longer?"

"I said go inside… Please." And his tone softened a little.

"What the hell is the matter with you?" Dan said, rounding on him.

"I beg your pardon?"

"It's been like this since Mum died; it's just as though we're paying for it for some weird reason. What is it, Dad? Do you blame me for what happened to her?"

"Shut your mouth!" Greg growled.

"Why? Touched a nerve, have I?" And Dan jumped up to face him.

"Dan, please don't," I urged.

"Yeah, listen to your girlfriend, Daniel."

"What am I supposed to have done to you? Is it because I'm still here and Mum's not?"

He started to walk away without giving any reaction, but his silence had said it all. I looked over at Tess. She looked as relieved as I did that Greg had turned to leave, but Dan wasn't finished.

"Maybe I would be better out of here, eh?" Dan challenged.

With that Greg turned back.

"Yeah, maybe you can make a new life for yourself."

"You know, don't you?"

But Greg didn't reply; he just laughed at what Dan had asked.

"Answer me!" Dan demanded and pulled at his arm to turn him around to face him. Greg did swing around, but at that moment, he brought his fist up, landing it squarely on Dan's jaw. The force of it sent him stumbling back.

"How dare you? Your mum... She hasn't even bloody well been buried yet!"

And with moist eyes, he walked away, back towards the house. As he walked past Tess's mum and dad, who had come outside hearing the commontion, he exchanged a few words but then carried on, disappearing into the house.

"Tess, Nicola, are you ready to go?" Tess's mum shouted. Tess waved them over. They looked mortified at what had just taken place and were in a hurry to get out of here.

"We ought to get going," her mum said, but she seemed to backtrack on seeing Dan nursing his jaw.

"Are you all right, Dan?" Tess's dad asked. "Grief can throw up any number of emotions," he said, trying to make excuses for what had just occurred.

"Yeah, I will be, but thanks, Mr Brinham." He nodded and turned to go back into the house, following in Greg's wake.

"You know where we are, Dan," Mrs Brinham added. "If you want us, all right?"

"Thanks, Mrs Brinham."

"Right, you two, it really is time we were going." Tess got up and waited for me.

"I'm not leaving Dan like this," I answered.

"I knew you were going to say that," Tess responded.

"Yeah, so did I," Dan agreed, stopping in his tracks. "You're going to Tess's, Nic. I don't want you staying here, not with the atmosphere the way it's turned out. I know what you're thinking, but I'll be fine, really."

"I won't leave you, Dan," I told him.

"Nic, you are. You're going to Tess's house anyway. I'll be fine. Fran's funeral is on Friday. That's only another couple of days, and then we can get together again."

"Why can't we get together before that?" I questioned.

"I'll ring you, and we'll arrange something then. Is that okay?" He smiled.

"Okay," I finally agreed. I just hoped that things didn't kick off again after we had walked out.

"She'll be fine," Tess added after a grateful glance from Dan.

"I'll ring you when I'm on my way back home," I offered.

"No, Nic. Leave it for tonight. I'll ring you tomorrow. I promise."

I sighed heavily; I wanted to believe that he would. We had only just got back on track after Fran's illness and subsequent passing. Was Greg somehow annoyed that we had hooked up again? Maybe it was because we seemed happy. No, he had spoken – or rather spat – the words out that Fran hadn't even been buried yet. That just compounded my belief that he somehow knew what we had been looking for and what we'd found in his office – Dan's birth certificate. Was all this commotion due to the fact that he didn't want Dan looking for his real mum?

"I promise. I'll ring you tomorrow, Nic," he repeated. "I'm not about to stay away like I did before."

I nodded, allowing him to take my hand and help me up from where I was still sitting on the grass.

"Come on then," Tess urged. But my attention returned to Dan. He nodded, but all I wanted to do was throw my arms around him. He didn't resist, and I eventually let go, signalling to Tess that I was ready to leave.

"You will ring me tomorrow, won't you?" I asked again.

"I promise," he repeated a third time.

We left him standing there, watching us go. Tess's mum and dad were waiting in the hallway for us.

"Come on, Nicola. He'll be all right."

Resignedly I nodded, but I wasn't so sure, and my stomach was churning. I followed them out, back into the daylight and the unevenness of the pebbled driveway. I looked back suddenly, feeling someone's eyes on me. I expected to see Dan watching my retreat, distancing myself from him and all that lay unresolved within that house. But it wasn't Dan; it was Greg, and he made no move at all to hide himself. He just continued to watch me – no smile, no nothing. He was just staring; he seemed empty. I turned away from him and continued walking alongside Tess, linking arms with her. Because of that one gesture, I at least felt reassured and safe.

Back at Tess's, we went outside and made ourselves comfortable on their garden chairs while her mum fixed dinner. I couldn't stop thinking about what was going to happen now that we weren't there.

"He'll be all right, you know, Nic."

"Yeah, I know," I agreed. But Tess didn't know what I knew. Could I tell her? Should I?

Would Dan turn away from me if I did?

"Like my dad said, Nic, grief affects people in different ways. Greg probably finds it hard seeing you and Dan together at the moment. Maybe it's just compounding what he's lost."

"Yeah, that's what I thought earlier, but it's not that, Tess."

"Well, if I didn't know any better, I would say you know exactly why he was acting that way. What is it? What's happened?"

"I can't tell you, Tess. I'm sorry."

"I'm your best friend, Nic. You can tell me anything."

"I can't tell you this."

"Okay, but you know you can trust me, right?"

"Yeah, I do, and thanks." But before I could say any more, her mum shouted us both in.

As I walked back towards the house, the smell of pasta Mrs Brinham had just placed on the table drifted out to us.

"Wow! That smells really good," I admitted, feeling the pangs of hunger rumbling around in my stomach, where only a short while before that churning had been.

"Right. Tuck in. Nicola, take as much as you want," Mrs Brinham offered. "There's plenty to go round."

I did as she had offered and tucked in with gusto. I even had seconds. Pudding was equally as good, and I ate that with just as much enthusiasm.

"That was really good, Mrs Brinham. Thank you."

"It's a pleasure, Nicola."

I waited while Tess finished hers. I hadn't realised quite how hungry I was. I felt a little bad at how quickly it had taken me to demolish my plate of food plus my pudding when everyone else was still eating. Mrs Brinham seemed to sense what was going through my mind.

"It's nice to see you enjoying the food I've laid out," she said, and she playfully threw a scornful look at Tess. "You can definitely come again, Nicola."

Tess rolled her eyes irritably; she was still wading through her pudding.

"I can't eat any more, Mum."

"See what I mean, Nicola." And she laughed. "Go on then. I'll clear the pots, shall I?"

"Thanks, Mum."

"Yes, thanks again, Mrs Brinham," I repeated, echoing Tess's words.

"Do you want to go outside again, Nic?" Tess prompted.

"Yeah," I answered, though I figured maybe it was in Tess's mind that I might open up out there more so than if we had gone upstairs to her bedroom.

Out in their garden, the air was cooling just a little. It wasn't chilly, but the coolness was enough just to make it pleasant without the searing heat as it had been a few hours earlier.

"How are you feeling now?" Tess asked. I wondered whether she had figured that maybe I'd had time to mull over what she had said to me about being able to trust her. I knew I could; I didn't even have to think about that. The issue was just whether I could say anything about Dan, about what was going on with him.

"I'm feeling full," I responded, skirting the real issue. "Your mum's cooking is really great, Tess."

"Yeah, I suppose I'm just used to it." The conversation then petered out, and for a few minutes, we just remained there, pulling at blades of grass.

"You sure you're okay?" she asked again.

"No, not really," I replied.

"You can tell me, Nic. I know something's eating at you?" And she did. She probably knew me better than anyone, except my mum, of course. Maybe even better than her. Obviously, in a different way.

"All right," I decided. "It's Dan, Tess. But if I tell you, you've got to promise me you won't say anything to him or Mal or Jules or anyone else."

"You've got it. You know I wouldn't, Nic. I won't breathe a word."

"Now that Fran's gone, Dan's set his heart on finding his real mum, his birth mother."

"Well, that's natural that he would want to do that. Why is that so cloak and dagger?"

"When I went round there earlier, Dan asked his dad – Greg – if we could use his office to do some college work that we had needed to catch up on."

"Yeah, I remember you saying that the other day."

"No, Tess. I wasn't exactly being straight with you... We made that up just to be able to get in there."

"Okay." And she waited for me to elaborate.

"Dan wanted to go straight down to social services to begin his search for his real mum. I disagreed and persuaded him to wait until after the funeral. He said that Greg's office would be as good a place to begin that search as any."

"So that's what you did?" she pressed.

"Yeah, and we found something." Tess's eyes widened at this revelation.

"What?"

"Well, it was just an old compliments slip, you know, a small bit of paper you sometimes get in with other documents with their business name in the heading, with a name on it – Gail Lassiter – but we found Dan's birth certificate as well."

"Whoa! Where is it? Has Dan got it?"

"No, we put it back but not before we had taken a copy of it."

"So, when is he going to go to social services to try and begin tracing her? He is, isn't he?"

"Yeah, he wanted to go there straight away like I said, but I persuaded him that it wasn't a good idea."

"Yeah, I can see that. But this is good, isn't it? I know you've been occupied, but— "

"I think Greg knows. I think that's why he got really angry and kicked off in front of us in the garden. I'm scared for him, Tess – Dan, I mean."

"I've known him for a lot of years, Nic. He'll be fine, really. Fran loved him, and so does Greg, even though he's not his own."

"I don't dispute that, Tess. It's just what he said about growing up. His adoption was never talked about."

"But it must have been because Dan's always known he was adopted."

"No, I don't mean like that. He told me it was never discussed, like he wasn't bothered, that he viewed Fran and Greg as his only parents, that it was like an unspoken rule. He said there was always something not quite right. After telling me all of that, it's just the way Greg was with him today. I could have sworn he knew we were looking for something and had found it."

"You mean, he saw you in there, searching?"

"Yeah, that's exactly what I mean, like there was a camera trained on us or something."

"Do you know what you sound like?" And she laughed.

"Yeah, crazy!" I smiled like I was resigned to that fact.

"Did you see one in there?" she questioned.

"Not that I noticed, and Dan dismissed it like you just have."

"I'm not dismissing it, but why would he have one in there?"

"But if he hasn't, how do you account for his behaviour outside and even when we first entered the house? He was watching our progress through to the back really strangely, like watching us so carefully."

"I don't know – honestly, Nic. Just see how things go from here. That's all I can think of to say to you. But Dan will be fine. Don't worry about him." And she seemed to mull over something else.

"What now?" I asked, wondering what more was going on in her head.

"I've just remembered about Jules. You didn't say while you were here last night that she was going around there to see Dan and Charlotte."

"That's because I didn't know. I had meant to ask Dan about her when I was on my way there earlier, but as soon as I arrived, he asked his dad whether we could use his office to do some work, and it completely went out of my head. Though I admit I am more than a little curious myself. I watched her from the corner of Rosely Crescent just after I had left you. He wanted me to ring him as soon as I left you, but I didn't. I figured it made more sense to ring him when I was almost outside his house. It was then that I caught sight of her. I was going to shout to her and ask why she was there, but then someone obviously opened the door because she hastily made her way down the drive, checking both ways so that no one had seen her. She looked a bit suspicious to me, like she didn't want anyone knowing she was there. I don't know who it was at the door, but they were obviously pleased to see her."

"Um, I found it a bit curious too, when Charlotte was telling us. From what she said, she must have ingratiated herself pretty quickly, but then Jules always does," Tess commented.

I knew well enough what Tess thought of Jules, but I trusted Dan. I was as aware as Tess was that Jules was more than a little keen on him, but he didn't reciprocate her feelings. I had often wondered why both he and Mal seemed so immune to her charms, but maybe it was because we knew her better than others did. That wasn't fair though, and I said as much to Tess.

"We have to give her the benefit of the doubt. She may well have been there just to see how they were all doing. You heard Charlotte – "

"Yeah, but come on, Nic. You heard what Charlotte said about how Greg seemed to enjoy her company!" I laughed at the way her comment had spewed so bitterly from her.

"But she would have been careful with Charlotte being around, Tess."

"Yeah, but it sounded very much like she was using Charlotte to get to Greg."

"But he's way older than her. It may not have even been that way."

"Um… I get what you're saying, Nic, but I don't buy it."

"No. We both know Dan isn't keen on her, but I still think it's him she's trying to get it on with, not Greg."

"Well, until we get more out of Dan, we'll have to agree to disagree. And we won't see him again until Friday."

"Well, I might. He promised he would ring me tomorrow."

"Are you going to ask him?"

"Yeah, I think I will."

"Well, let me know, yeah?"

"Will do, and I had better be heading off. I haven't seen my mum at all today. I left a note to say I was coming here, but I still feel a bit bad about leaving her on her own so much. I know my dad's been dead nine years, but…"

"You've got your own life as well, Nic."

"I know. I just wish she would find someone."

"She will when she's ready."

"That's it, though, Tess. It's been nine years. How long is it supposed to take?"

"She'll get there."

I nodded in hopeful agreement. "Anyway, I've still got to go." And after hugging and making her promise again to keep that vow of silence I had held her to, she led me back through the house to the front door.

Shouting out my goodbyes to her parents, I left.

Chapter Five
The Funeral

The few days since I last saw Dan flew by in a haze. He rang me the next day, like he had promised after we'd found the birth certificate; the same day Greg had got really angry and kicked off in front of us all. Dan assured me that everything had been all right after Tess, her parents and I had left, but I still didn't know whether I believed him. He told me that Greg hadn't said any more to him, only the obligatory conversations he'd had no chance of avoiding. Dan seemed even more determined to begin his search, though we still agreed it would be on the Monday after Fran's funeral. I had wanted to meet up with him before Friday to put my own mind at rest really, but Dan's answer had been a resounding no. It wasn't worth chancing Greg exploding again at this point.

I asked whether he'd managed to find anything in Greg's office that might have proven me right about a camera being in there, but he hadn't set foot in there since that day. I couldn't blame him. From what he'd already told me, Greg was unstable enough; any small thing might set him off.

Not for a minute though, did I believe everything was fine, as Dan repeatedly tried to assure me.

Charlotte had crossed my mind quite a few times since Tess and I had left his house. How was she? Had any of the anger aimed at Dan that day been redirected at her later? But Greg had ordered her inside before he'd started on Dan. Thinking back, it seemed more likely that he had been protecting her from it. Was it because she was his biological child and Dan wasn't? What would Fran have made of this whole situation? Would it have escalated this far if she had still been here?

I doubted it; she adored Dan. They both had from what I remember – at least, when I was about.

The change in Greg seemed like a complete turnaround, even with the way he had watched me as Tess and I walked back down the drive, the day I'd gone home with her and her parents to join them for dinner – but even so, I mentally made a note to ask Tess about it when I saw her later.

As I thought about the events that were still to come this morning, my gaze drifted over to the outfit I had picked out to wear. I had decided on a deep-grey skirt, straight and simple, with a navy blouse – short sleeved because of the time of year. I had finally settled on black, opaque tights and black flats. I had wondered about the colour combination, but what I had in black certainly wasn't suitable attire for a funeral, so what was before me would have to do. Then I lazily looked over at the clock on my bedside table.

Quarter to nine! I jumped out of bed and into the bathroom. Reappearing in my bedroom after hastily showering, I decided to telephone Tess, though I felt really out of sorts because I was running late.

"Hey, Tess, it's Nic. How's things?"

"Okay. I'm not looking forward to this funeral, though."

"No, me neither. Look, is Mal still coming for me at ten fifteen?"

"Yeah, after he's picked Jules up. I did run it by him, and he was fine with it. Don't worry."

"I'm not worried. I was just running a bit late. I hadn't realised what the time was."

"Actually, Nic, did Dan say anything to you when he rang, about Jules going around there?"

"No... Well, he did mention her, but he said that he'd tell me all about it when he saw me again on Monday. That's when we're going to social services, like I told you. But he did say that she'd been there again that night, but when he was relaying it to me, he was texting, so, like I said, I'll know more on Monday. You haven't heard from Charlotte yet, have you?"

"No, I have rung like I told you the other day, but there still hasn't been any word. Look, I'm still getting ready myself, but I'll see you in a while. And if we get the opportunity, we'll talk some more about all this. And don't worry about Mal. He'll be there around ten fifteen."

"Okay." I ended the call. I stayed where I was, sitting on the edge of the bed, rehashing what Dan had said about Mal. It would be the first time I had seen Mal since they all bumped into us at Avery Park. I just prayed I wasn't any different with him. I still wanted him as my friend. I looked again at the clock beside me. It was half past nine, and he'd be here soon. Resolving to push all thoughts of Mal to the back of my mind, I finished getting ready. I wanted to be able to walk straight out of the house as he drew up. Although Jules would be in the car, it would prevent him from coming to the door to fetch me, thus minimizing the risk of any awkward silences.

At five to ten, I was standing by the kitchen window, looking out onto the road beyond, watching out for Mal's black Mini to draw up with Jules, en route to Tess's and then on to St Thomas's for the service before Fran's burial in its grounds. I wasn't leaving anything to chance.

He drew up with Jules in the front seat; she was preening herself from the mirror in the sun visor before her. It was a little after ten, and the service was due to begin at eleven.

Predictably he jumped out of the driver's side, but luckily, I was just coming out the front door.

"We've got a little while before we need to set off, Nic, but we can go straight to Tess's if you want," he suggested, seeing the swiftness of my pace from the front door to his car.

"Yeah, we might as well." I made my way to his side, seeing that Jules wasn't making any attempt to move. Even though I wasn't the slightest bit overweight, I was a bit taller, and I had to squeeze to get into the backseat.

"Sorry," Mal apologised, watching me as I tried with difficulty to squeeze myself into the impossibly small space.

"It's okay. I can just about manage, and I appreciate the lift, Mal." Pushing his seat back, he apologised again.

"It's fine, really," I assured him and then I turned my attention to Jules.

"Hey, Jules."

"Hello, Nic." But she stopped right there, didn't say another word, so I turned to Mal and tried to make conversation with him. I think we both felt a little awkward with Jules continuing to add to the glossy lipstick she had already copiously applied. I heard a giggle escape Mal's lips. She turned to him with a look of pure disdain.

"Don't you think you've got enough of that on?" he asked. "We're going to a funeral, not a nightclub."

"It'll be like casting a little brightness on an otherwise dull day," she quipped.

"I don't think that's quite the idea, Jules. You're not there to impress anyone. We're going to offer our support," Mal responded haughtily.

"It doesn't hurt to make an effort, does it, Nic?"

"Er... I don't know really." But I got the distinct impression she had involved me because I had very little make-up on. It didn't feel like the occasion warranted it, certainly not as much as she had plastered on, but I said nothing more.

"Nic's just exercising her right to be impartial." And Mal laughed again, easing any tension I felt but piling it all on Jules.

"Oh, shut up, Mallory!" she spat.

"Be glad to," he finished, cutting dead the chance of any more conversation.

The rest of the way to Tess's was thankfully clear, and we arrived far more quickly than even I had anticipated, and I think all of us were glad of it.

"Okay," Mal announced, neither particularly to me nor to Jules. "Let's get out for a few minutes. It's only quarter past ten.

We've got ten minutes before we need to get moving again." And he pulled his seat forward for me. I was glad to be getting out; my legs were beginning to go numb from being so cramped. As I escaped the confines of the backseat, Tess's parents were just leaving to drive to St Thomas's, and Tess was just locking up.

"What are you doing?" Mal asked. "We were going to stay here for a bit. We've got ten minutes till we really need to leave."

"Wouldn't it be better just to get there? We don't want to be turning up after the hearse, do we?"

"Sure," he responded, almost as if he didn't care. Of course, I had been in the car; Tess hadn't. She glanced over at me, a puzzled expression settling over her with the questions silently beginning to bombard me. I surreptitiously shook my head, signalling that I would fill her in later.

Standing by the driver's side door, Mal waited for us both to climb into the back. Tess clambered in first, positioning herself behind Jules who once again hadn't even bothered to move. I piled in behind her, pulling my legs in towards me in readiness for Mal to push his seat back so the cramping could begin again.

"Everyone okay then," Tess gushed.

"Yeah," Jules replied, but then she fell silent again, and Mal didn't even bother to answer.

"It's not really one of those sorts of days, is it?" Tess said to me; though neither Mal nor Jules seemed as though they wanted to engage.

"No, it isn't, Tess," I answered, and we too fell silent. That was the way it stayed for the remainder of the journey. No one uttered a word.

As we drove over the cattle grid into the field next to the church, which was obviously doubling as its car park, we saw that by far we weren't the first to have arrived. There was row after row of cars and many more people milling around, most of whom none of us knew. Of course, Dan, Charlotte, and their dad, Greg, weren't there yet. That was why people were milling around; they were waiting for them and the hearse before they filed into the church.

Getting out of the car, Jules marched straight ahead with Tess behind her, thinking we were following.

"You all right?" I asked Mal quickly, stretching my limbs after being cramped in the backseat again.

"I really hate her sometimes!"

"Mal, today's not about any of us."

"I know that, Nic." And he too followed in Tess's wake. I ran to catch up with him. I had worried about how I would be with Mal after Dan had made that revelation about him having a thing for me, but I felt comfortable. He was just Mal, my friend.

Keeping pace beside him, I tried to lighten the mood. "I do agree, you know? Jules's lipstick is definitely way too bright. It would look infinitely better in a nightclub." For a second, he watched me soberly but then laughed.

"I knew you did. You didn't do a very good job of being impartial." But our joking suddenly came to an abrupt halt. As we were walking towards the gate leading into the church grounds, we looked to the road beyond its main entrance. The hearse had just come to a smooth, silent stop. A small group had gathered just a short way from it. I made a move to walk over, breaking away from Mal, Tess and Jules, whom we'd caught up with and who had also stopped to watch proceedings. But I felt someone grab hold of my arm and pull me back.

"No, Nic. It's not the time." It was Mal's reassuring voice behind me. I looked back, almost imploring him to let me go.

"Please," I uttered, hardly realising the word had come from me at all.

"Not now. We have to go into the church. We can't intrude on them like that."

Reluctantly I agreed and walked over its threshold, passing the heavy oak doors into the porch. From there we entered the nave, our steps echoing on the flagstones, each one reverberating around its cool stone interior. Mal pointed to a row of unoccupied pews about halfway down on the right-hand side.

He whispered to me, "We don't want to be too close to the front, do we?"

"No," I agreed and glanced back at Jules and Tess. "This is okay, isn't it?"

"Yeah, it's good," Tess replied, ushering us in.

I sat down between Mal and Tess, my mind refusing to leave the church's front gate, where they'd all gathered waiting to follow the coffin into the church. I shuddered at the thought of having to go through such a thing at their ages. I know I'd lost my own dad, but this was their mum; at least the only mum Dan had ever known. I couldn't begin to imagine how they were coping. Feeling someone take hold of my hand I suddenly jumped.

"Are you all right?" Tess whispered.

I nodded, "Yeah, I was just thinking…"

"Do you want to tell me?" she asked.

"I was just thinking about them waiting outside. It's their mum, after all."

"All we can do is be here for Dan and Charlotte. We can't do any more than that, Nic."

"I know." But quietly I knew that wasn't all I could do or was doing, as Tess knew full well.

Maybe I could make sure social services would be open on Monday and decide exactly what time and where we needed to be. That would be a start, at least.

My mind must have drifted again because the next thing I realised was the organist striking up, and Mal nudging me to stand up. Fran's coffin was being carried down the aisle on the shoulders of six pallbearers, followed by Greg, Dan and Charlotte. Dan looked our way as they all passed, his arm slung around Charlotte's shoulders just like it had been around mine only days before. He nodded, but his mind was elsewhere, his eyes seemingly empty, his focus quickly returning to where it had fleetingly left to concentrate once more on the only one who mattered this day: his adopted mum. Once so bubbly and full of life, she now lay, silent and unseen. Once the pallbearers had reached the front they lowered the coffin onto a stand, leaving her family to take their seats in the front pew on our side.

The service proceeded like any other, emotional and sombre. The vicar spoke of Charlotte and Daniel's loss over their mother's death – and Greg's loss; she had been his wife, of course. It didn't seem long at all before we were all filing back out of the church after the coffin's procession, which Greg followed. His eyes were raw with emotion, as were Dan and Charlotte's, who had taken their places on either side of him, their heads bowed in silent respect, united in grief. I watched as they made their way past us. Greg had his arm around Charlotte, comforting her, but there seemed to be no such concern for Dan.

We waited until those ahead of us had filed out into the aisle, then took our places behind them to follow, exiting the church as unobtrusively as we had entered.

The coffin was carried away from the church to the rear of its grounds, where a grave had been newly dug and awaited its occupant to be lowered into its depths. We all stood back, observing from a distance, giving the main family their privacy. The only ones by the graveside were Fran's closest family. I had never seen a burial before, and at that moment, as the vicar began with the words: "We have entrusted our sister, Frances, to God's mercy", I knew I never wanted to see another one again. I watched Dan, Greg and Charlotte at the graveside. Charlotte was being supported on either side. She looked as though she might fall in headlong if her dad and Dan had let go. It was natural, I knew, to be grieving that much for your mother, but it seemed as if there was something else. When Tess and I had spoken to her outside at her house days ago, she hadn't seemed this bad, though I suppose this atmosphere didn't help. If we got a chance to speak with Charlotte and Dan afterwards, then maybe we would find out if there was something more.

As I stood there, the only thing going through my mind was escape. Watching only the backs of those at the graveside, I could see the ragged rise and fall of Charlotte's shoulders, the tell-tale signs of her suppressed grief. If she was crying, her tears remained silent. Though brief, that dignified resolve quickly gave way to deep, retching sobs; no longer was she trying to hold them back. They flowed freely like a torrent unleashed. I saw Dan's arm, which was now wrapped around her shoulders, pull her closer to him, trying to comfort her, but nothing could stop the pain she was now allowing to escape.

I moved back a little. I really didn't want to see any more. Instead I stepped directly into Tess's path. She moved sideways, allowing me to take my place beside her. She looked at me and smiled through the silent tears she, as I, had been shedding. She took hold of my hand again and squeezed it, letting me it was okay, that we were both there for each other. I was glad she was there. As she kept hold of my hand, the vicar's booming voice came reverberating back into my consciousness.

"And we now commit her body to the ground – earth to earth, ashes to ashes, dust to dust."

Tess squeezed my hand again, realising before I even had that I was openly crying. I couldn't stay here. Instead I broke free, attracting a few curious looks as I retreated, seeking the shaded sanctuary of an old yew tree further back from where we had all been standing.

The congregation of voices drifted back to me with the ending to the Lord's Prayer.

"For thine is the kingdom, the power and the glory, forever and ever. Amen."

Leaning against the trunk of the yew tree, I realised someone was standing before me. I raised my eyes to see Dan standing there, *my* Dan.

"Hey." I smiled.

"You okay?" he asked, his voice full of concern.

"Yeah, I suppose it just got to me."

"I know what you mean. Not very cheerful, eh?"

"Oh, Dan, I'm sorry. I didn't mean to sound so— "

"It's fine," he assured me. But he seemed as though he was waiting for something more.

"What is it? What's wrong?" I asked.

"Can we meet tomorrow, Nic? Just you and me?"

"Yeah, of course, but I thought we were meeting on Monday."

"As far as I'm concerned, we still are, but I need to get away from the house for a while. Please meet me, Nic. Same place, outside the old theatre?"

"Ten?" I offered.

"Thanks." And he quickly kissed me on the lips. I smiled. I wanted to throw my arms around him and run from here to somewhere, anywhere so none of them could reach us. But at that moment, Dan's attention was diverted, causing me to follow his gaze. I turned to see Mal and Jules approaching.

"Thanks for coming," he began. "Mum would have loved the fact that so many friends have turned up."

"We wouldn't have missed it, mate," Mal responded. "We all thought a lot of Fran. She was a good person."

"Yeah, she was. Thanks, Mal. Look, I..." But before he could finish, Greg walked up as well.

"Nicola, Mallory... Jules. It's good to see you all, and thank you for coming. We appreciate it, don't we, Daniel?"

"Yeah, we do," he answered. But his response seemed almost robotic.

"Well, you're all welcome to come back to the house, if you would like to." He then turned to Dan. "We'd better be going."

"I'll be over in a minute."

And without another word, Greg disappeared, leaving Tess amongst us once more after she'd had a quick word with Charlotte. Dan's eyes travelled to each of us in turn.

"Well, I'll see you all back at the house then." And he moved forward to kiss me. As he cupped my face in his hands, his touch was tender, lingering. He pulled away without another word and

71

followed Greg, who was with Charlotte and some other relatives who had been standing with them around the graveside.

With Tess in conversation with Jules and her parents, who had just walked over, Mal spoke, commanding my attention.

"That was strange, don't you think?"

"What?" I answered, still deeply entrenched in my own thoughts.

"Dan. He was about to say something, but when his dad spoke, he clammed up completely."

"It probably just went out of his head, Mal. He's all over the place at the moment."

"How was Charlotte?" Jules asked Tess.

"Missing her mum." Her reply was curt.

"It must be difficult. You never know what to say at these occasions, do you?" Jules said to anyone who was prepared to listen – and Tess definitely wasn't.

"No, you don't, and what you do say always sounds inadequate somehow," Mrs Brinham replied while scowling at Tess.

"Actually, she didn't say much at all. She seemed much quieter than she had been when we saw her a few days ago, Nic. That was it really," Tess said turning again to Jules. Mal raised his eyebrows in surprise while Jules remained strangely quiet.

"We've decided not to go to the wake," Tess's mum informed us, "so we'll say goodbye now." They then made their way over to Greg to offer their apologies and condolences.

"Well, at least we got an invitation to the wake," Mal quipped, looking towards me and Jules.

"Mal, that's a terrible thing to say!" Tess chastised.

"Oh, I didn't mean it like that, Tess. You're welcome to come as well."

"Oh, thank you, Mal."

Realising he'd upset her, he held out his arm to escort her back to his car. After she reluctantly took it, they both sauntered off just ahead of us.

"Don't you think that was a bit strange? Greg, I mean. But Dan was strange as well, wasn't he?" I overheard Mal say to Tess.

"Yes, they didn't really seem very comfortable with one another," she reluctantly admitted.

"So what are we going to do about going back to the house for the wake?" Mal said, turning back to me and Jules.

"Well, we won't get to find anything out if we don't go, will we?" Jules answered matter-of-factly.

"And besides, Dan and Charlotte are good friends of ours. You've known Charlotte the longest, Tess, and you're close to her too, Jules," I reasoned.

"And you and Dan have been together for over a year now, and he's my best mate," Mal said. "So we're agreed?"

"Yep, I think we should all be there, definitely," I concurred.

We all continued back to the car, more or less in silence. I looked back down at the entrance gate before we walked into the field, where all the cars were parked; many were still there. I caught Dan looking over in our direction. He smiled when our eyes met. But it was a look of resignation, like he had finally accepted something, but what? Maybe it was something about his birth mother he could only tell me. But what if it was something more, something about Greg or Charlotte maybe?

Lagging behind Mal and Tess, I wondered whether to tell them what Dan had asked me about meeting him tomorrow, but then I remembered Jules was beside me. He had also said just me and him, so I held back, even from Tess, until we were on our own.

It was just a fifteen-minute drive from Dan's house on Morsley Road to St Thomas's, with it being situated on their side of the town. Since leaving the church, no one had said a word.

There wasn't even any music blaring out from the radio, which, for Mal, was unusual. Normally he liked nothing more. He must have read my mind, because at that precise moment, he turned to me as I sat beside him in the front seat. Unlike on the way here, Jules had elected to sit in the back with Tess. She had remained ominously quiet since innocently asking Tess about Charlotte and receiving that curt reply for her trouble.

"You okay, Nic?" Mal asked.

"Yeah. Why?"

"Well, it was all a bit weird, at least I think it was, like there was something amiss."

"Yeah, I know what you mean, Mal, but they have both just lost their mum, and Greg has lost his wife."

"Yeah, but there was something more," he said and half turned to Jules and Tess in the back. "Don't you two think so?"

"I think Nic's about right," Jules answered. "Greg has lost his wife, and Dan and Charlotte, their mum."

"What do you think, Tess?" Mal asked. At first she just shrugged, thinking. Her mind was doing overtime just like the rest of us.

"I don't know," she answered. "It was a funeral, wasn't it? Grief affects people in different ways."

"Yeah, it does," I agreed. But that wasn't the sort of answer Tess usually gave. Her thinking, especially where her friends were concerned, was always more vocal. She was thinking something, and she wasn't voicing it only because there was someone here she didn't want to hear it, and that was Jules. I was sure of it. I remembered when Greg had come over to speak to us, Dan was standing with us. He'd addressed me and Mal and then seemed to stall for a second before he included Jules's name. I thought that had seemed a bit strange at the time, but now that Tess was being guarded as well, maybe she did know something more. Maybe Charlotte had confided something to her, maybe something about Jules.

"Well, let's see what you all think once this wake's over," Mal commented, bringing the car to a crawl, following the others as they made their way towards 115 Morsley Road. Passing those now parking, we found a space by the side of the road a few houses up. Getting out, everyone remained tight lipped about what they had initially been talking about in the car.

People were walking both ahead of us and behind us. Fran had been very popular, and her death had certainly confirmed that, bringing many family and friends, whether those who had been close during these last months or those who had known her from years ago. Walking amongst them back down towards the driveway of their house, I felt alien, as though I didn't really belong here, especially the way Greg had watched me walking away from the house only days before.

Tess, Jules and Mal were ahead of me. I stopped and turned to walk back to the car. As I turned around, it was just as if Mal had sensed my anxiety.

"Nic, what are you doing?"

"I can't go, Mal. I don't belong there."

"And you think the rest of us do?"

"No… I don't know."

"Come on. We've come here to support Dan and Charlotte. We all knew Fran, and we all got on well with her. She would want us all here, and Greg did invite us. Please." And he held out his hand. I took it gratefully before he let go and instead put his arm around me.

"It'll be all right," he whispered in my ear.

"Thank you," I whispered back, and I meant it. The friendship we all shared had always remained so constant. I didn't know why I had worried about seeing Mal again. Maybe Dan had just been joking.

"Are you coming then?" Mal questioned, grabbing hold of my hand again after realising I had slowed down. I nodded, allowing him to lead me back to where Tess and Jules were standing, waiting for us, and a few stragglers who were still making their way past us.

Relief swept over me as we turned into the driveway. I had imagined them waiting there by the front door, welcoming everyone in. But as we neared the house, we filed in, the same as everyone before us. Once inside we did find them mingling, but Dan, Charlotte and Greg weren't very far apart; Dan and

Charlotte were certainly near enough for Greg to hear what they were saying. Making our way amongst them, we each in turn offered our condolences before walking any further.

As I embraced Dan, he whispered in my ear, "I'll see you outside. It'll be a bit freer out there."

"Okay," I whispered back.

Even though I had been inside this house loads of times before, it always struck me just how impressive it was, both inside and out, standing grandly in its grounds as each one on this road did.

Following Mal's lead, we all wandered through to the back of the house and out into the extensive garden, seeking again the warmth the sun was providing. There were a few other people out here, but there was more than enough space to enable us to talk freely, and Mal seemed anxious to get something off his chest.

"I don't like this," he stated without a second thought to who was around us.

"What?" I asked, looking around to make sure we weren't being overheard, but we were missing someone. "Where's Jules?" I questioned.

"I don't know," Tess answered, "but I'm glad she's not here."

Ignoring her comment for the moment, I turned to Mal.

"What, Mal? What don't you like?"

"All this is weird. My mate's acting strange, and even Charlotte's not right. I know she's grieving, but... And Greg – he watches them like... Oh, I don't know. It just doesn't feel right."

"Yeah, I know what you mean," Tess agreed.

"Well, I'm going to try to find out why they're acting so weird, and please don't tell me it's down to the way people express their grief differently, either of you."

"We weren't going to," I protested.

"What do you think it's about, Nic?" Tess asked now we were on our own.

"Honestly, I don't know. But they're both quite distant."

"Yeah, I got that feeling from Charlotte at the church," Tess told me. I turned, seeing her look over my shoulder. Mal was returning with Greg and Dan in tow. "I want to talk to you about Jules later," she said and abruptly clammed up.

"Thanks for coming," Greg said. "Dan and Charlotte appreciate having their friends around them. It's a difficult time for us all."

"Where is Charlotte?" Tess asked pointedly.

"Charlotte's gone for a lie down. It's been particularly difficult for her. She and her mum were very close. She's not coping as well as Dan here."

I don't know whether Tess noticed, but I saw Dan's reaction when Greg explained to us how close Charlotte and her mum had been. He appeared separated from the conversation, ripped apart from what he was within this family, such as it seemed now. Greg lingered beside him.

"Are you going to stay and talk for a bit?" I asked, but Greg suddenly jumped in.

"There's still a lot of people we have to talk to, Dan." Then he turned to us. "If you'll excuse us…"

"I'm coming," Dan said with an edge to his voice before turning back to us. "I'll see you all soon, and thanks for making the effort, really," he added, seeing Mal watching him intently. Finally his gaze rested on me as if reaching through all barriers to silently remind me about tomorrow. I nodded and smiled but said nothing. There was nothing more that needed to be said.

"Well, I'll say goodbye then. See you soon, Mal, Tess." And he turned and walked away.

"Right, I'm off," Mal said indignantly. We all followed behind him like sheep being herded from one pen to another. He didn't stop until he reached the car.

"What was that for?" Tess demanded.

"We were treated as though we were nothing to him." And he looked around suddenly. "Where is Jules?" he asked.

"Ugh, leave her. She'll be preening herself to someone," Tess replied acidly.

"We lost her soon after we arrived," I told him.

"You mean, she shook us off," Tess corrected me. "She's probably chasing after Greg!"

"What?" Mal asked, disbelief echoing through his words.

"Oh, I'll tell you later."

"You'll tell me now, Tess Brinham!" Mal shot back.

"Later!" I told them both. "Don't look now, but Jules is coming."

"I was looking for all of you. It wasn't until I saw Greg that he told me you had all left."

"I bet he did," Mal growled in a low voice.

"Sorry?"

"We were all beginning to fret a bit, Jules. We hadn't seen you since just after we arrived," I told her, hoping she hadn't realised I'd covered up for Mal's comment.

"Until now," Mal interrupted. "And we're just about to leave. Are you coming with us?"

"Oh, yeah, thanks," she gushed and flicked her head back, ensuring her long mane of hair flowed out behind her, but it was wasted on Mal.

"Right, I'll drop you off first then. I'm meeting a mate on the other side of town."

"Wouldn't it be easier to drop Tess off first?" she questioned.

"No, I'm dropping both Tess and Nic off in the middle of Furham. You're meeting your mum, aren't you, Nic?"

"Yeah," I said. "Tess and I said we'd meet her for a late lunch because Tess wants to have a chat with her."

"Oh, okay." And she didn't question us any further. Instead Tess began to question her.

"You didn't happen to see anything of Charlotte while you were in there, did you, Jules?"

"Yeah, Greg took me upstairs to see her. He'd persuaded her to go and have a lie down. She was worn out, poor thing."

"She's all right, though, isn't she?"

"Yep, Greg was lovely with her," she gushed.

I glanced over at Mal as he was driving, but he was smiling broadly – sarcastically, I figured – at her response. I didn't dare turn around and look at Tess; I could feel her squirming from here.

Chapter Six
Trust

As Mal brought his Mini to a stop outside Jules's flat, I heard him give a small sigh, though I don't think anyone in the backseat heard it.

"There you go, Jules," he announced.

Since she was directly behind me and I was next to the kerb, I got out and pulled the seat forward, enabling her to climb out.

"We'll get together soon," I suggested.

"Yeah, lovely," she responded, though it was with little enthusiasm.

"Well, we'll be in touch soon," I reaffirmed.

"Okay." And without another word, she disappeared. Everyone in the car remained tight-lipped until I pulled the door shut behind me. Then both Mal and Tess started at once. It was chaos, both of them talking over the other.

"Whoa! Stop!" I yelled. "Can I just ask one thing first, please?"

"Yeah, shoot," Mal replied.

"Why did you say that to Jules, that I was meeting my mum? I didn't know what to say. Talk about dropping us in it!"

"Yeah, sorry about that, Nic. I didn't know what to say when she suggested dropping Tess off and then it would have been you. I had to come up with something quick and I didn't want her thinking we were cutting her out."

"I don't know whether you achieved that, Mal."

"Oh, well. We're going to my flat now, okay?"

"Er, yeah. Good job I hadn't arranged to meet my mum, eh?" Ignoring my jibe, he continued.

"Right. Let's go. You and Tess have got loads to tell me." After we dropped Jules off at her flat on Haran Street, we weren't in the car many more minutes. Mal's flat was no more than five minutes away on Risely Road.

On the stretch where Mal lived, opulent-looking town houses stood back from the busy main road, separated by a wider-than-average pavement. Climbing out of the car and craning my neck to glimpse his flat on the third floor brought memories flooding back of the first time we had been here, when we'd all pitched in to help him move. Jules had been there with us that time, but as had been so typical of her, she'd done very little in the way of helping out, though she'd always seemed to be exactly where Dan was, hanging on his every word.

That had been six months ago, just after New Year, before the start of a new term at college.

Mal had pestered Dan for weeks to move in with him, eventually managing to wear him down. He had been just on the point of agreeing when Fran fell ill, putting a stop to everything.

We both followed him in through the front door, at least the front door that led up to his flat on the third floor. There were thirteen steps on that first flight and another thirteen on the second. I think I lost count after seven on the third flight due to Tess's heavy breathing and continual grumbling behind me that there were too many steps to climb – not to mention more groaning that Mal could at least have moved somewhere that had fewer steps or preferably none at all. He just laughed and shouted, calling her Chubbs, his favourite nickname, and at the same time explaining that the exercise would do her good.

This was predictably met with a scowl and more grumbling. Although I didn't turn around to see the face she had pulled, I knew well enough it was there. When we reached the top landing, she was red faced and puffing.

"Jesus, Tess, you're in such bad shape," Mal commented but there was concern in his voice.

"Do you mind, Mallory? I don't normally have to trudge up three flights of stairs!"

"Well, you don't have to stay," he snorted.

While they had been trading insults, my eyes had wandered around my surroundings. Mal's front door was green, a real grubby green colour, but so were the skirting boards and the banister we had clung to, so stubbornly aiding our ascent; though, in Tess's case, it had been more like scaling Mount Everest for all the huffing and puffing she had done. From a distance, the paint hadn't looked too bad, but on closer inspection, it was peeling and dingy, obviously from years of the landlord's neglect; he'd obviously only bothered about the rent he managed to separate weekly from his aggrieved tenants, Mal being one of them. But my attention again returned to the insults flying to and fro between them both. Though not for a minute did I suspect they were throwing them at each other maliciously. They were enjoying their exchanges equally. That's how it came across to me anyway.

"Stop!" I yelled.

They stopped dead and stared at me. I didn't even think they'd realised how heated their bickering had become.

"Can we stop this now, please?"

"We were only joking, right, Tess?"

"Yeah, just playing," she scoffed, confirming my suspicions.

"Well, I'd hate to see it if you really meant it!" He pushed her away playfully, as though getting the last word in before unlocking his door. Throwing it wide open, he turned to us both with a beaming smile, along with a demonstrative outstretching of his arm, signalling for us to enter, he said, "After you, ladies."

As Tess followed me in, I heard him begin to say something. I figured it was another half-hearted insult he was ready to throw Tess's way, but he stifled it. Probably thought better of it with me and Tess being in such close proximity. After another throwaway comment, he'd have felt her annoyance for sure.

I slumped down on Mal's sofa, relieved to feel something else taking my weight instead of my own legs. The funeral had taken its toll on everyone, and I was certainly feeling it now.

"What are you thinking about?" Tess questioned, collapsing down next to me.

"I was just thinking about everything that's happened today. It's been a bit weird, don't you think?"

"I'll say," Mal said, setting our cups down on the coffee table before us. "Now, are you going to tell me what all this is about with Jules and Greg?" He made himself comfortable, dangling one leg over the arm of the chair he was slouched in.

"Well, I haven't actually got any proof. I just think she's maybe after Greg. You heard her in the car. She was gushing about him," Tess told him.

"Well yeah, I suppose she was a bit but it was Dan who bothered me more. He was acting like his dad's puppet or something, and he's never been like that. Never!" Mal responded.

I wanted to tell him about Dan asking me to meet him tomorrow, but I just didn't feel like I could. It didn't feel right; I would be breaking his confidence. I was going to tell Tess, but she was different, and if he had wanted Mal to know, surely he would have said, I thought, convincing myself more than anything.

"I don't think he's very happy there, Mal," I admitted instead. "I don't think it's so much that he's his dad's puppet; it's more that he's trying to keep things civil for Charlotte's sake."

"Why do you say 'civil'? Has something more been going on?" I looked at Tess, wondering what I could tell him without giving everything away.

"Well?" he demanded.

"He's not very happy at home, Mal."

"He wants to find his real mother, his birth mother," Tess blurted out.

"Tess!" I shouted angrily. She eyed me sheepishly and shuffled around uncomfortably on the sofa.

"I'm sorry, Nic. It just sort of came out."

"Dan wants to find his real mum?" Mal echoed.

"Yes," I conceded. "We've only talked about it, though." And I willed Tess not to say another word. "Mal, please don't say anything about it. Greg doesn't know anything about what Dan's thinking of doing."

"'Course I won't, but there's nothing really stopping him now, is there? And I don't suppose Greg will bother about it, will he?"

"I don't know," I answered. "It's early days, and with them only just getting the funeral out of the way, it could be misinterpreted. Greg especially needs time to adjust."

"Maybe that's why he was a bit shifty at the church and back at the house."

"I don't know. I think he's been a bit weird anyway. How do you mean, shifty?" I questioned.

"When we walked into the house, he kept watching us. He was just acting a bit shifty. Maybe something's already happened between him and Jules, and he was worried that we knew something."

"Don't be ridiculous, Mal!" Tess laughed.

"Well, it's not a million miles away from what you were thinking."

"I was just saying that I thought she was interested in him. That's all."

"Yeah, but he took her upstairs!"

"To see Charlotte!" Tess shot back.

"That's what Jules told us," he said and smiled. "She seemed pleased about something anyway."

"No... I don't think that for a minute. She would have been as concerned about Charlotte as the rest of us."

"Have it your way, Tess," he finished. "Anyway, what are you both up to tomorrow?"

"I'm not doing anything as far as I'm aware," Tess answered.

"Er, I've got some errands to run for my mum," I lied.

"When are you seeing Dan again?"

"Monday," I answered. "We're meeting in the centre," I said at the last minute. I wasn't sure what to say. I certainly didn't want to say we were going to begin searching for his mum.

"Shall we meet up tomorrow then, Tess?" Mal asked. "Seeing as Nic's too busy running errands for her mum?" he mimicked.

"I don't know. I'm not sure if I've got anything going on. Can I give you a ring?"

"Yeah, sure, but you just said you're not doing anything," he mumbled.

"As far as I'm aware," she repeated.

"Okay," he answered lazily. "What about Jules then?"

"What about her?" Tess questioned cuttingly.

"Well, she might want some company."

"You're joking, right? You only want to see if you can get anything more out of her, don't you?" Tess questioned.

"Well, it would be worth a try, wouldn't it? And don't say you wouldn't because you're as intrigued as me." Mal pointed out.

"You really are too much, Mallory Edwards!" Tess answered and looked my way. I laughed. "What?" She demanded.

"You're like an old married couple."

Mal grimaced, and she snorted and changed the subject.

"It's time I was going anyway. You coming, Nic?"

"Yeah." I hauled myself off the sofa. "Are you two meeting up tomorrow then?" I asked.

"Is it still all right if I ring you, Mal?" she said, looking a little ill at ease. I suddenly wondered whether I'd hit a raw nerve. Inwardly, I smiled at the thought of them being together.

"Yeah, okay, just don't make it too early," he answered soberly.

"Then, yeah, I suppose we are," Tess said, answering my question before leading me out. "'Bye, Mal!" we both shouted out as I pulled his flat door shut.

Outside we walked back down the hill together. At the bottom Tess would have to go one way and me the other.

"I really am sorry I told Mal about Dan, Nic. I didn't realise what I was saying until it was out."

"It's all right; it's done now. At least he doesn't know anything about us going to social services on Monday. If I tell you something else, you won't let this slip, will you?"

"No, I promise… Cross my heart and hope to die," she added for effect.

"Dan asked me to meet him tomorrow at the old theatre on Brompton Road. He needs to get out of the house."

"Are things that bad?"

"Um, I think so. That's why I said I had some errands to run for my mum."

"I think it would be a good idea to go back over to Mal's tomorrow then," Tess suggested. "It would at least keep him out of Furham, where you two are likely to be."

"You would do that for me? For us?"

"'Course I would. Dan's going through a lot at the moment, and he needs you, Nic. But give me a ring later tomorrow, yeah?"

"Yeah, 'course I will," I assured, and I hugged her. "Thanks, Tess."

"You're my best mate, remember?"

"Always," I promised. "Catch you later," I called back before heading home.

Most of what I passed on the way I didn't even see; my mind was still so full of Dan and what he had said, or rather what he hadn't, and Mal had planted even more in my mind than I really wanted there. Jules was a tough nut to crack, to figure out. Was Mal on the right track with what he was thinking? I wondered. He was definitely right when he said she was gushing a little too much when she talked about Greg. But she had never paid him the slightest bit of attention before Fran's death.

She was the oldest out of all of us at almost eighteen, though only by months. But even Tess thought she was chasing him, and Mal had been right about Greg watching us. I had also felt his eyes on us while Tess and I were following Mal outside. Maybe he was suspicious that we had figured out what was going on, if actually anything. But there were parts of what Mal had said that seemed perfectly feasible, but I just couldn't get the idea of Greg and Jules out of my head. She could have the pick of any of the guys at college and often did. That was why it seemed so inconceivable. But Dan suddenly ran through my head as well. Did he know something about it? Was that why he and Greg were so at odds with one another? Surely he would have mentioned something about it. But thinking about it, when Charlotte had been talking about Jules being around there and Greg seemingly enjoying her company, Dan was grumpy about it. Was he just thinking what we'd all been thinking? It was certainly possible.

My mind was buzzing with everything going on that I managed to get most of the way home and didn't even notice where I had walked, I was only about ten minutes away when my phone rang.

"Hey, Mum," I answered.

"Where are you, Nicola? I was expecting you back ages ago."

"I'm on my way home now. I'm just down the road."

"Okay. I'll see you in a minute." And the line went dead.

Walking in through the front door, I expected to be bombarded with questions about where I had been and what I had been doing that had caused me to be so late. But she was sitting there, quite calm, considering. I walked straight through.

"Hey, Mum."

"Hi, Nic. How did it all go?"

"Well, the funeral was like any other, I suppose. Sombre. I told Dan I would meet him tomorrow. That's okay, isn't it?"

"Yeah, 'course it is. He's welcome here, if you both want to come back."

"Yeah, we might do that. Thanks, Mum."

"Did he get upset? How's Charlotte doing?"

"They all were, but things aren't really very good between him and Greg, and poor Charlotte was beside herself."

"Why do you say things aren't very good with his dad?"

"Well, Dan wants to find his real mum, his birth mother."

"Well, there's nothing wrong with that, Nic. It's natural that he would want to. Is his dad not very happy about it?"

"He doesn't know."

"So, why are they so at odds?" she asked.

"I don't know," I said, and I began filling her in on what we had been doing in Greg's office and what we'd found there.

"Does he not feel able to talk to him about wanting to find his real mum?"

"It's complicated, Mum. Dan's never felt able to speak up about his adoption to either Greg or Fran, but now that she's gone, he just needs to know who she was and where he really came from, who he looks like, you know?"

"Well, like I said, Nic, it's natural he'd want to know, but if you want my advice, then try to persuade him to talk to his dad. It might save a whole load of grief later on."

"I'll see what he says."

"So, what else happened?" my mum probed.

"Jules was flirting... a lot."

"Well, that's just Jules, isn't it?"

"Yeah." I laughed. "I suppose it is... Actually, Mum, do you mind if I go up to bed? It's been a long day."

"'Course not, darling. What time are you meeting Dan tomorrow? Do you want me to wake you?"

"We're meeting at ten outside the old theatre. I'll need to be up by about eight thirty, so yeah, please, if you don't mind."

"Okay, see you in the morning then."

"Night, Mum." And I kissed her on the cheek before climbing the stairs.

I felt as though I was always here, sitting on this low wall opposite the theatre, waiting endlessly for him to appear. With him nowhere to be seen, my attention drifted over again to its dilapidated front as it now appeared from years of neglect after being closed down. Just like last time, my curiosity was too much, and I found myself getting up and walking towards it.

The main door was open, and the air around me felt warm and soothing. But the nearer my feet carried me to its entrance, the cooler the air became. Walking in over its threshold, I felt a shiver run through me, but I brushed it off because I was inside now with no sunlight for warmth. Again, its interior was elegant, like I had glimpsed last time, and I looked around, surveying its past splendour. But it didn't remain so. Darkness descended all around me, bringing with it a sense of unease, flooding me. I wanted to leave; I didn't like the feeling of what was around me, encouraging me on, but my feet wouldn't let me go. They kept me there, suspended.

"Please," I called out. It was then that I heard something, someone. I looked behind. I smiled. It was Dan. He was calling to me. I reached out, but still my feet kept me there, restrained by something I could not see.

"Nic! Nicola!" he pleaded, willing me to reach out further. I tried desperately, but the doors were pulling shut from where they had stood open, once welcoming its patrons. I called out desperately to him, but my voice was growing hoarse: weak. Slowly he was receding, still tantalizingly close yet too far for me to grasp. I was terrified and my shouting for Dan was giving way to frantic screams, the last one hanging in the air as the doors slammed shut...

"Nicola, Nic." My mum was standing over me. It took me several minutes to get my bearings, to focus on my surroundings.

"W-what's the matter?" I asked, confused as to why she was there, standing over me with that look on her face.

"You were dreaming again, Nic. Why are you having these nightmares?"

"I-I'm fine, Mum, really."

"You wouldn't be saying that if you had seen what I've just seen. You were thrashing about like someone demented, and you were screaming."

"It was just a dream, Mum. Everyone has them."

"Not like that, they don't... Anyway, it's eight thirty. You said you wanted to be up, to meet Dan," she added when I looked at her blankly.

"Oh, yeah." I remembered. "Thanks. I'll get up in a minute."

She left my bedroom without saying another word, but I knew she was worried about me. I must have been thrashing about wildly for her to comment like that. Sitting up, I tried to recall what the dream had been about. The image of the theatre and the feelings it had evoked immediately flashed through my mind. I had been trying to get to Dan, to escape the confines of the theatre. Now I realised how I must have looked to her. I must have looked like I was completely mad and screaming as well. No wonder she was looking at me like I'd gone crazy. But why had I dreamt of that place again?

Chapter Seven
More Questions

My mum said nothing more about the dream she had woken me from this morning.

Though all the time we spent in the kitchen together having breakfast, I could tell it was on her mind. She was just waiting for me to tell her what was really wrong, but there was nothing more than I had already told her. She wasn't the only one waiting for answers; so was I. Why had I dreamed about the old theatre? That's what puzzled me the most. It wasn't even like I had ever been in there.

However, I did search the internet for a meaning to my dream before I ventured downstairs, being careful to remain silent about it where my mum was concerned. It didn't make for cheerful reading. Under the heading of "theatre", it read,

To dream of a theatre is a sign you may shed many tears for some action which cannot be undone.

I sat there, going over everything that had happened over the last few days, including Greg's reaction to me after Dan and I had been in his office. Was he blaming Dan for us having been in there? It wasn't like we'd gone in there without his permission. He'd been happy enough about it at the time.

It was the only thing I could think of. Could my dreams really point to that? Maybe deep down I was feeling guilty for what we'd done, but we'd only searched around his office for some scrap of evidence to do with Dan's adoption. Surely that wasn't a hanging offence. Better that, though, than predicting something that was going to happen connected to the old theatre. No, I told myself, and I laughed at how seriously I was beginning to take all this. It was only a dream, after all.

I was still processing it and its interpretation when I saw Dan sitting on that low wall opposite the theatre. A chill ran through me as I allowed the memory of it to invade my thoughts yet again.

"You okay?" he called out. "You look really rough."

"Oh, thanks. You don't look so hot yourself!" I retorted as I sidled up to him.

"It's called concern, Nic. Maybe you're not familiar with that particular concept."

"Don't start. I had enough with Mallory yesterday."

"Why? What's he been up to?"

"Oh, he was just winding Tess up."

"And she was biting," he guessed.

"Yep," I confirmed.

"Do you think he's got a bit of a thing for Tess? Maybe he's moved on from you."

"Stop it!" But I laughed when I saw him smiling, realising he was just teasing me.

"You're just as easy as Tess to wind up."

I wasn't so sure about that, but he did have a point, at least about Mal.

"That has crossed my mind, but I'm not sure. He just seems to enjoy winding her up too much and succeeds every time. Anyway, forget about them two for now. How are you?" I asked.

"Um, okay."

"Liar… How are you, really?" I persisted.

"It was pretty quiet after everyone had gone. Dad… Greg… Jeez, I don't even know what to call him now… Anyway, he just shut himself away in his office. I spent the evening with Charlotte upstairs. We talked about Mum and stuff to do with her, but it wasn't long before she drifted off to sleep. I figured she was better off that way. At least, while she was sleeping, she wasn't thinking, eh?"

"Yeah, she's very young for all this to have happened. But at least she's got people around her who care."

"Yeah, she is lucky to have that."

"Oh, Dan, I'm sorry. I didn't mean it like that."

"I know, but she is lucky, more so than me."

"Oh, I don't know. Jules seems to care... maybe a little too much!"

"That wouldn't be jealousy I'm sensing, would it?" he mocked.

"Certainly not," I retorted. "That is, unless her charms are working on you."

"Jules has a great many attributes – none of which, I might add, interest me."

"Well, I'm very pleased to hear that, and while we're on the subject of Jules, you didn't tell me what happened that evening when I saw her walking down your drive that night. You wouldn't like to elaborate on it now, would you?"

"Do I have a choice?"

"No." And I smiled, waiting for him to begin.

"Right, well. I was in the garden when Charlotte shouted through that she could see Jules at the top of the drive. She waved to her from the front door because she thought she was going to walk away again."

"I did wonder who had waved to her," I cut in.

"Well, it wasn't me. I stayed outside. Only they both came out to me."

"Am I supposed to be pleased about that?"

"Do you want me to tell you what happened or not?" And he gave me that look that commanded my attention.

"Okay," I replied meekly.

"Out of the corner of my eye, I saw Jules more or less dragging Charlotte outside towards me. It was the last thing I wanted, Nic, but for Charlotte's sake, I played along with being happy to see her. She took notice of my sister, but I could tell she really wanted me."

I laughed at the conceited manner with which his words came across.

"What's the matter?" he asked in all seriousness.

"Fawning over you, was she?"

"No, I'm just trying to explain." But I think he realised at that point what he had said. "When I said 'wanted me', I didn't mean literally. Just that she wanted to be in my company." And he laughed too. "You did want to know, didn't you?" he questioned.

"Absolutely. Carry on," I responded.

"Well, she was a bit over the top, but it was all in vain because I've got you. But Charlotte did enjoy her being there, so much so that she turned up the night after as well."

"What about Greg? Didn't Charlotte say that he enjoyed her company?"

"Yeah, he came out eventually and joined in with her and Charlotte. I was on the sidelines, as always."

"So how was Greg around her?"

"I think he was a bit flattered. I think it took his mind off Fran for a while. To be honest, I didn't take an awful lot of notice. She gushed here and there when he was talking and the same the next night. It was all a bit repulsive, listening to her. You know what Jules is like."

"Yeah, I do," I agreed, thinking back to yesterday when she, Tess and I had been in Mal's car. I remembered the way she had been going on about Greg then.

"So she wasn't all around you then?" I asked, trying to sound unaffected by the way I was steering the conversation. But he laughed again, knowing exactly why I was asking.

"How many times am I going to have to tell you, Nicola? You're the only one for me. However, she was sort of trying to flatter both of us when I was actually bothering to listen. That's about it, though. Charlotte was soaking it up a bit too much. She's the one who worries me the most. She seems as though she's growing too close to her. Being the concerned brother that I am, I decided to check her phone. She's got Jules's number in there."

"Has she got Tess's and mine?" I asked.

"Yeah, but she hasn't contacted you or Tess, has she?"

"No, she hasn't contacted me, though I don't know about Tess. I could ask her, and if she hasn't, then I could get her to text or something. That any good?"

"Yeah, that's not a bad idea. When we're home alone, she's becoming a little withdrawn. I know she's missing Mum, but it feels like more than that. I think she's brooding about something, and I haven't got a clue what it is."

"Have you tried asking her?"

He looked at me as if I had just asked the most stupid question in the whole world. "Yeah."

"I'm just trying to help, Dan."

"I know. I'm sorry. It's just that I'm worried about her, and I worry more that she's getting in too deep with Jules."

"I'll have a word with Tess. See what we can sort out, okay?"

"All right. Thanks."

I looked over at the theatre, standing directly before us, with the high-wired railings protecting the passing public from its derelict state.

"Do you ever wonder what it's like in there?" I asked him.

"No, it's just an old theatre. Passed its best, obviously from the state of it." Involuntarily, like I was in one of my dreams, I felt myself being drawn towards it. Before I knew it, I was standing before the railings, looking at the entrance – the ornate hardwood double doors, faded and cracked, that even in this state still gave a glimpse of the splendour that had once welcomed its eager community. I felt Dan's presence beside me.

"Changed your mind?" I asked.

"Not really, but I couldn't leave you here on your own. It's about time they knocked it down, don't you think?"

"It could be restored," I suggested, remembering its opulence from my dreams – whether only in my imagination or how it had really been, I didn't know. "It needs someone with vision and plenty of enthusiasm to restore it to its former glory. Someone who really cares," I finished.

"I need that," he responded.

"You already get it, Daniel Trennan!"

"You can never have too much." And he squeezed my waist. "Come on. Let's walk around for a bit."

"Oh, before I forget, my mum said we can go back there if we want," I suggested.

"Yeah, maybe later, eh?"

"Yeah, whatever you want." And we left the theatre and the many questions that still buzzed around my head concerning it.

Walking around the centre of Furham, I was suddenly glad that Tess and I had spoken about my meeting Dan today. I felt a lot easier knowing Mal wouldn't be anywhere near. After all, I had blatantly lied about what I was doing. With that in mind, I relaxed and I felt happy with Dan's arm around me, just ambling along through the shopping precinct. It was pretty busy, as most Saturdays were, but thankfully there was no one around we knew.

Sitting on a bench, we settled to share the chips he had just paid for. Everything seemed like a world away; it was sunny. I was with Dan. I looked up. The word just seemed to slip from my mouth as if I had seen a ghost.

"Mal."

"Hey, mate," Dan called out after me.

"Yeah, hey, mate... Nic. Fancy seeing you here."

Dan picked up on the tone immediately. "What's the matter, Mal? There's no need to be like that with Nic. What is it?"

"You should ask your girlfriend that. Wanted him to yourself, did you?" he almost spat.

"Mal, I'm sorry. It's not what you think," I said, but that just sounded lame.

"Oh, really. I thought we were friends, Nic. You could have told me you were meeting him instead of lying to me. I would have understood that you would have wanted to be with Dan."

"What's going on?" Dan asked, again thoroughly confused by what Mal had just said.

"Ask her," he said, and without waiting for me to explain, he began walking off.

"Mal!" I called after him and I got up to follow, but Dan grabbed hold of me.

"Let him go," he urged. "I'll have a walk around there and see him later."

"He's angry with me, Dan. He asked me and Tess if we wanted to hang out today, and I told him I had errands to run for my mum. You said you wanted to meet me today, just you and me."

"It sounded more like he was jealous to me."

"Oh, don't start that again, please."

"Okay," he answered defensively. "But you didn't say anything to anyone else?"

"Only Tess, but she wouldn't have said anything... No, she wouldn't have," I repeated after he looked at me quizzically.

"You sure?" he questioned.

"Yes, I am. She's our friend and my best friend."

"Exactly. She's Mal's friend as well and she's got a thing for him." I couldn't argue with that but no, she would never have said anything after promising me to keep quiet about me meeting Dan.

"No, Dan." I protested. Tess said she would keep Mal away from the town centre, and I trust that she meant that."

"Well, she didn't do a very good job of it, did she?"

"Please."

"Okay," he stressed, holding his hands up as if labouring his point.

"You have a walk around to Mal's later, and I'll speak to Tess. Deal?"

"Deal." He laughed. "How were they when you all left our place yesterday?"

"Mal and Tess think that Jules is after Greg." He laughed out loud again at that suggestion.

"Mal seemed to think you were a bit uneasy yesterday as well because you were following Greg around, although I would think it was the other way around, wasn't it?"

"Yeah." And he laughed again. "He kept his eye on me and Charlotte all day, at least until we were on our own again. It might have been his way of caring where Charlotte was concerned, but it certainly wasn't where I was."

Leaning my head against his shoulder, I relaxed again. There wasn't anything more that could happen now that Mal had seen me and confronted us. But my mind was turning again.

What was Tess doing? She had told me last night that she would keep Mal away from where I was going to be with Dan. Had she forgotten and not rung him to arrange to go around there?

Had she decided to have a lie-in and decided not to go and, worst of all, hadn't meant what she'd said to me?

I started to wonder whether Dan was right when he'd said Tess was Mal's friend as well as my best friend.

"What are you thinking about? It's not still Mal, is it?" he asked.

"It's all of it really. How did we get to this point?" I questioned, not only Dan but me as well.

"Well, it's only Mal. He's thrown a hissy fit. That's all."

"But what if it's not just Mal. What if it's Tess as well?"

"But you said there's no way she would have said anything. Are you changing your mind now?"

"I don't know, Dan. There's no reason to it. Only yesterday, we were so solid."

"Well, it's probably best to just wait until you speak to Tess later. When I've been to see Mal, I'll give you a ring, let you know what he said."

"Yeah, perhaps you're right." As I looked around, I realised my enthusiasm for Furham's centre had waned considerably since Mal confronted me, so I turned again to Dan. "I've had enough of it here. Do you want to walk back to my place?"

"Yeah, I don't mind." And so we ambled away from the centre, and I allowed myself to relax once more.

Chievely Terrace was coming into view, and I was glad of it. I think we'd both spent long enough in Furham, especially with bumping into Mal.

Walking in through the front door felt just like I had been set free. Here there could be no risk of running into anyone I had no wish to.

"Hi, Nic. Everything all right?" my mum shouted from upstairs.

"Yeah, Dan's with me," I shouted back.

"See what's in the fridge for dinner for you both. I've got to go out," she answered as she made her way downstairs.

"Going anywhere nice? You didn't mention anything earlier."

"I'm just meeting a friend. It didn't come up until this afternoon, but I won't be late. You'll be okay, won't you?"

"Yeah, sure. You don't mind Dan staying, do you?"

"No, make yourselves something to eat, like I said. Everything all right with you, Dan?"

"Yes, thank you, Mrs James."

"Okay, 'bye then… And I'll see you later, Nic."

"Yeah, 'bye, Mum."

"Um, we're alone," he remarked, eyeing me curiously.

For the first time since Mal had confronted us, I laughed out loud at his observation.

"It's just nice to be alone again and not for any other reason than that," I chastised.

"Have it your own way." And he shuffled along the sofa away from me.

"And I didn't mean like that either!" And I pulled him back, caressing his face, kissing his eager lips. Pulling away, I held his gaze. "Right. You hungry?"

"Only for you," he answered playfully.

"That is way too cheesy!" And by the time we had finished fooling around, getting something sorted to eat was a rushed affair and not long before he'd had to leave.

"You'll ring me later and tell me what Mal's had to say, won't you?"

"'Course I will, and the same goes for you with Tess. Agreed?"

"Yeah, 'course."

"So we'll meet at the same place, same time, on Monday morning to go to social services, yeah?"

"Absolutely. But I'll get Tess to text Charlotte in the meantime."

"Thanks, Nic. What would I do without you, eh?"

"I know… It's unthinkable, isn't it?"

"Oh, yes," he answered and gave me one last lingering kiss. "Until tonight," he whispered teasingly.

After I closed the door, I stood there for a minute, leaning against it, thinking only of him. After little more than a week since he'd got back in touch, it felt like we'd never been apart.

My stomach did a little somersault thinking about it all, but someone else entered my head as well… Tess. I had assured Dan that I would ring her. I needed to ask her about Charlotte and tell her about Dan's concerns that she was growing too close to Jules.

With the phone in hand, I settled myself on the sofa, ready for the long haul. I tapped out her number.

"Hey, Tess," I greeted.

"Oh, hey, Nic. Everything all right?"

"Yeah, you?"

"Um, yeah."

"I met Dan earlier; he's quite concerned about Charlotte. He seems to think she's getting a bit too close to Jules. He wondered whether you would text her, see how she is. He thinks she's becoming a little too withdrawn."

"Yeah, of course, I will. I might even ring her, see if she wants to meet up."

"That sounds like a great idea. Actually, Tess, Dan and I saw Mal in Furham earlier this afternoon, around lunchtime. Didn't you go and see him?"

"Yeah, I did, and I'm sorry. He did say he had seen you both. I ended up not going around as early as I had hoped because he had things to do. I've arranged to go around again in a bit."

"I had no idea he was going into town and he's mad as hell with me now."

"He's just really upset that you lied about what you were doing, Nic. He thought we were all mates and that we didn't have to keep anything from each other."

"But I haven't kept anything from him, not really."

"Just give him time to get over it."

"If you say so. Anyway, Tess, if you can try and get in touch with Charlotte…"

"Yeah, I will," she assured me.

"Well, I've got to go. I'll speak to you soon."

"Okay, Nic, 'bye." And the line clicked off. Wow, that had not been my imagination. She was definitely being cagey. But Tess was my best friend. Even so, she had seemed really cool. I wanted to ring her back and demand to know what else was going on that I clearly didn't know or wasn't included in. That would just make matters worse though, wouldn't it? Our conversation hadn't been as long as it normally was either. It made no sense.

Maybe when Dan rings me later, I'll learn more. Maybe it'll all be sorted out by then.

Chapter Eight
Shock Find

I looked at the clock. It was eight thirty. My mum still wasn't home though I wasn't particularly worried. She had said she was going out with a friend for a drink, so I didn't expect her that early anyway, but Dan hadn't rung me either. Had something happened? Had he forgotten that he'd said he would ring? No, he'd only left here a few hours ago; maybe he was still with Mal. Yeah, maybe he'd got it all sorted out with him, and he was still there, catching up.

I decided to wait until nine. Three hours were long enough. Since I was on my own, the time dragged on forever. I found myself going over again what Tess had told me and how she had seemed. Distant. Cool maybe. Those were the only words I could find to describe the way she had been on the phone. How different our conversation had been from days before, even from yesterday. I had sunk so far into my own thoughts that the phone's sudden bleeping startled me. From the caller display, I could see it was Dan.

"Hey," I answered brightly, belying the anxiety I had imposed on myself.

"Sorry it's late, Nic, but I haven't been able to get hold of Mal. After I left you, I went straight around there, but there was no answer. I hung around for a bit, but there was no sign of him. Did you manage to get in touch with Tess?"

"Yes, I did, but I didn't really get much from her either. She seemed really cool with me. When I told her that Mal was angry, she just said that he was upset that I hadn't told him what I was doing... and that he thought we were all mates, that we didn't keep things from one another. Her solution was that I should just give him time to get used to it, I guess."

"Get used to what?"

"Quite," I agreed. "But I did explain about Charlotte and that you were worried that she was getting too close to Jules. She said she would text her and maybe even ring her, see if she wants to meet up sometime. That was shortly after you left me, around six."

"That's great, but Charlotte's not here... It's going on nine now, and I've no idea where she is, Nic. I'm going to leave it a little longer and see if she turns up of her own accord. I know she's just turned sixteen, but she's still my kid sister, and Greg's out. I haven't got a clue where he is. I can't even reach him on the phone."

"All right. Give it half an hour and ring me back. If she's still not back, then we'll go and look for her. It's still light yet, okay?"

"Yeah, okay," he answered, but the apprehension in his voice was unmistakable.

Ending the call, I then reactivated it with another to Tess. It usually rang several times before she answered, but it kept ringing. When the call went to voice mail, I quickly ended it without leaving any message. Where was she? I toyed with the idea of ringing Mal as well, but being subjected to this afternoon's tirade, I thought better of it. Maybe Tess was with him. Maybe they had already arranged to meet Charlotte. Maybe that had been in Tess's mind while we were talking about her. I slumped back onto the sofa and brought my knees into my chest though that still brought little comfort.

How had it all come to this? Why couldn't I just meet Dan without being accused of lying?

Maybe he was right about Mal after all. Maybe he was jealous that I had been with Dan. But immediately that little voice inside my head was having none of it and instead began conflicting with my train of thoughts already circulating. What was I thinking? They were both my friends. I looked over at the clock on the mantelpiece, expecting it to be at least twenty past nine. It was still only ten past. If I felt jittery, how must Dan be feeling? It crossed my mind to ring him earlier than we had arranged, but what would I say? That I'd rung Tess and that there hadn't been any answer? Would he read more into it than I intended, or was that the whole idea?

Where was she? She didn't even know that Charlotte hadn't arrived home yet, or did she? I was beginning to arrive at the same conclusion that I had earlier – that maybe Tess was already with her. But if she was, wouldn't she have rung Dan or Greg just to let them know she was okay?

But Greg didn't know, did he? Dan had already told me he was out. I looked again at the mantelpiece. Quarter past. I sprang from the sofa to check the time on the microwave in the kitchen; it had to be wrong. The time felt far later than it was displaying. But it wasn't – it read sixteen minutes past nine. I sauntered once more through to the sitting room at the back of the house, feeling strangely nervous. Charlotte hadn't ventured far since Fran's death. Dan himself had said as much, saying that Greg spent more time with her and more or less cutting him out. Perhaps it's just a case that lately she's felt a bit swamped by everyone's attention, I thought; maybe she just needs a bit of time on her own. Though she could have made it another day to do a disappearing act, I thought selfishly and felt myself inwardly berating her for causing me and Dan so much hassle. I felt annoyed that just as thoughts of Tess and Mal were being forced upon me, so too were thoughts of Charlotte and I suddenly caught myself pacing the room. When had that happened? A longing to just get out of here, to escape the confines this house was imposing, engulfed me. I walked to the kitchen again and looked out the window. But that did nothing to ease the feelings of captivity.

I strode straight to the front door and pulled it open. The feeling of relief was immediate. I inhaled deeply, feeling freer somehow. But it was short lived.

My phone, which I had left on the sofa, was bleeping again. I hoped it was Dan, calling me a little early to say Charlotte had just arrived back and that he would meet me as we had arranged – to go to social services to find out about his real mum.

"Hey," I greeted, equally as brightly as I had the first time he'd rung.

"Hey," he echoed, though less enthusiastically. "I can't wait any longer, Nic. She's still not back. I'm going to go out and look for her. She's not usually this late, and she's not answering her phone either."

"All right. I'll meet you," I responded.

"Thanks. Walk towards the centre, where we were earlier and I'll meet you there. Keep your phone on you, won't you?"

"I will," I assured him. "She'll be fine. She's probably just got caught up and forgotten all about the time."

"Yeah, I hope you're right." And he cut me off.

I stood there for several seconds just trying to process what he had said. She still wasn't home. I suddenly felt ashamed of what had been going through my head only moments ago. How could I have thought that about her? I also now remembered my mum. She would be home at some point, and she would be expecting me here. I hurriedly scribbled a note, saying that Charlotte had done a disappearing act. I quickly re-read it deciding it sounded a bit callous and scribbled it out, writing instead that she hadn't arrived home and that I was meeting Dan in the centre of Furham to look for her.

I made sure to let her know that I had my phone on me. Those thoughts brought me back again to Tess. Perhaps she would help, and Mal as well. Surely we could put our own squabbles aside, whatever they were, to look for Charlotte. Making that decision, I set the call in motion as I stepped out of the front door.

I hadn't made it to the end of the terrace when the voice mail again kicked in. Where are you? I yelled out in my mind, but outwardly I just decided to leave a message.

"Tess, where are you? Charlotte's disappeared, and Dan and I are out looking for her. I know it's quite late, but can you help us – Mal as well – if you can get hold of him? Dan went around earlier, but he wasn't there." The phone bleeped again, telling me the time span for leaving a message was up and had cut off.

Stopping, I took one last desperate look, hoping she would call me back before I shoved the phone back in my pocket. I looked around quickly, just in case, before continuing on to the shopping precinct in town where Dan and I had been earlier this afternoon. It would take me at least half an hour, but maybe I would catch sight of Charlotte while I made my way there.

Another thought suddenly occurred to me. What about Jules? Maybe Charlotte was there. Carrying on walking, I brought up Dan's number. It had barely begun to ring when he answered.

"Nic, have you found her?"

"No, but I've just had a thought... about Jules. Charlotte might be with her. I was just thinking it might be worth going around to her flat before we do anything else." My heart sank as I heard him sigh.

"I've already been there, Nic. There was no answer. I've tried Mal and Tess as well. Neither of them are picking up."

"I know. I've done the same – with Tess, at least."

"All right, I'll see you in a bit." And he ended the call without saying another word.

I walked down street after street, and there was nothing, no sign of her at all, but neither was there any call back from Tess. What was going on? Why was all this happening? I questioned for the umpteenth time.

I figured I would just have to wait until she called me back. I was fast approaching the centre of Furham, and thoughts of Dan began to occupy me once more. Five minutes more, and I would be with him, and with a bit of luck I would find out more – that is, if Dan knew any more. Had he been in touch with Greg yet? Was Greg out looking as well? And would he blame Dan for this as well as everything else he seemed hellbent on laying on him.

As I turned into the precinct, there were a few people milling about, as I had expected. It was Saturday evening, after all. My eyes searched for Dan. I saw him straight away. He was pacing around the same bench we had been sitting on only hours before.

"Have you heard anything from her?" I asked as I walked over to him. All I wanted to do was fling my arms around him, but all he had on his mind was Charlotte, and rightly so; I couldn't imagine how he was feeling. His answer was immediate.

"No, and I don't know where to start, Nic."

My phone started bleeping, cutting out the need for my response. I quickly looked at the screen.

"It's Tess," I said as I opened the call.

"Tess, thanks for getting back to me."

"Nic, I've just got your message. I contacted Mal straight away, and he's just picked me up. We're going to drive around and see if we can spot her. Where are you?"

"I'm with Dan in the precinct, where we were this afternoon. We're going to have a look around here."

"Have you been in touch with Jules?"

"No, but Dan tried. He went around there, but there was no answer."

"Okay, for now we'll just carry on. We'll call if we come across anything, all right?"

"Yes, thanks, Tess – and Mal as well." Cutting off the call, I turned to Dan.

"Yeah, I heard," he said before I had a chance to say anything.

"They're driving around to see if they can spot her. She asked if we had been in touch with Jules. I told her that you'd been around there, but there had been no answer."

He nodded.

"We need to start looking, Nic. She could be anywhere!"

I followed him through the precinct, my eyes scanning every inch of it for a glimpse of her. Jules ran through my mind again. Maybe she was there now. Taking my phone from my pocket again, I set the call to her in motion. Still following Dan, I willed her to answer.

"Hello," a softly spoken voice answered.

"Jules, is that you?" I questioned.

"Yes," she answered nonchalantly.

"Jules, it's me, Nic. Charlotte hasn't come home yet, and Dan's worried sick about her. We're in the centre of Furham looking for her. You haven't seen her, have you?"

"No, I've been out." Unlike Tess she made no attempt at offering any help.

"Will you help us look?" I asked pointedly. Though she tried to stifle a sigh, I heard it plainly enough.

"Yes, of course. I'll make my way in. I'll ring you again when I get nearer."

"All right, thanks. We appreciate it."

And she cut the call off without so much as a goodbye.

"She's really strange, Dan," I called to him. He'd walked a little way ahead of me.

"She's helping, is she?"

"Yeah," I answered. No more than that needed to be said, and I started calling out Charlotte's name in case she'd had an accident and couldn't get out from wherever she was.

In every street and road we walked down, I continued to call out, but all that ever returned to me was silence. Dan, too, joined in calling out to her, but that same emptiness met even him.

I wrapped my arms around myself, feeling a chill run through me. Even though it was midsummer, the light was now beginning to fade, and with it thoughts of the old theatre on Brompton Road entered my mind. I was just about to say something when my phone bleeped again. It was Tess.

"Hey, Tess," I answered, hopeful.

"Hey, Nic." But her tone was less enthusiastic. "I'm sorry. We've looked all over. We've been to Avery Park. We even stopped and asked people if they've seen a young girl matching Charlotte's description, and we called out to her, but there's been nothing, no sign anywhere. We were going to come to you and Dan. Where are you?"

"Canley Street." But just as I said it, I realised how close we were to Brompton Road.

"Okay," she said, interrupting my train of thought, which had settled uneasily within me. "Stay there, and we'll be with you in a few minutes."

"Will do," I answered, and I turned to Dan.

"Yeah, I got it," he answered impatiently, cutting any more conversation dead.

"We'll find her," I reassured him, but we'd been looking for ages, and I didn't know whether even I was that convinced that we would. Dan said nothing. I don't know whether he was in silent agreement, but his mind had wandered off elsewhere, somewhere I wasn't invited. I desperately wanted to do something more than I was doing right at this moment, but there was nothing I could do for him short of telling him exactly where his sister was and depositing her safely in front of him.

Instead, I retreated into my own head as Dan had already done. But immediately Brompton Road pushed its way to the forefront of my mind yet again. Thoughts of that old theatre flooded my senses as though reaching out to me. No, and unwilling to allow it to proceed further, I mentally pushed the images floating around me out of view.

When I heard a car slowing up, my mind released me, and my eyes searched in its direction. They rested on Mal's black Mini. I watched as they got out of the car, but I averted my eyes as they drew closer. Dan's gaze met their advance, never flinching from them.

I felt a world away from my friends. Even though Dan made no attempt to back away, I don't think he knew quite what to say. It was Mal who spoke first.

"We've looked all over, mate, and we'll carry on looking until we find her, but we just don't know where else to go. Did she have any special places she liked to go?"

"No, not really." His mouth was moving like he was in full flow of a conversation with Mal, but inside he was somewhere else, somewhere away from me and them as I'd glimpsed only minutes before they'd arrived. His eyes looked closed off to everything but Charlotte. Mal suddenly looked at me for more help. Momentarily, I too, withdrew inwardly, fighting my own battle with the invading images of the old theatre, which refused to be banished.

"What is it, Nic?" Tess noticed immediately.

"Er... nothing. It's just that I keep getting images of the old theatre on Brompton Road." I said nothing more about it, and Tess didn't pry. Instead, I turned to Mal.

"The only thing I can think of is that she's recently grown very close to Jules." Dan nodded, almost absentmindedly, confirming what I had said.

"Have you spoken to her?" Mal asked.

"Yes, she's looking as well," I told him. "She's making her way towards the centre. She's going to ring when she's nearer to us."

Having half turned to speak to Mal, I could now feel Dan's breath on the back of my neck. He harrumphed loudly, almost making me jump out of my skin, forcing his way back into the conversation.

"Why are you going on about the old theatre?" he demanded.

I looked immediately at Tess.

She was the only one who really knew about this except for my mum, of course – well, only the fact that I'd been having dreams. I had spoken to Tess about them after I had gone around there.

"What are you looking at Tess for?" Dan asked with an edge to his voice. "Has this got anything to do with when we met there earlier? You were preoccupied with it then?"

"I've been having dreams about it, Dan. Being trapped in there, vaguely feeling as though there's some sort of danger in there."

"What? You think that Charlotte might be in there?" And he laughed. It was almost mocking.

110

"I'm just trying to explain, Dan." I knew he was worried but he was making me feel like an idiot and it hurt. I don't know what I had expected, but it certainly wasn't that.

"Maybe it's worth a walk there," Tess calmly suggested. "We're not far away, are we?"

"If you want," Dan scoffed, "but it'll be a waste of time. Charlotte's never even mentioned that place. I don't even think she knew… knows… it's there," he quickly corrected himself.

"So we're going, yeah?" Tess asked.

"Sure," he responded and waited for me to lead the way. Now I felt sidelined not only by Tess and Mal but by Dan as well, although they had greeted us both warmly enough, I still felt like I was being edged out.

"Look, Dan," I said. "They're just dreams I've been having lately. They don't mean anything, and we certainly don't have to go, not if you don't want to."

"I said I would go," he answered abruptly.

I shrugged, not really knowing what else to say. "Okay." And I began to lead the way.

Tess sidled up to me, leaving Mal to walk alongside Dan. I don't know whether Tess had joined me just to allow Mal and Dan to talk or whether she genuinely wanted to be here, but things remained pretty strained between us.

The sight of the old theatre gave me goose bumps, though I had no idea why. It was situated about halfway along Brompton Road, just a short way from the town centre; it was on the left. It was a wide road with land to either side. I had never seen the theatre as it would have looked with gardens on both sides. The land was still reminiscent of how it must have been laid out, with part of it laid to lawn with borders fringing it. That blueprint was still very faintly there, but it looked more like a wasteland now, awash with weeds and wildflowers.

With Tess still by my side, I made my way towards the railings, looking through them at the theatre's entrance as I had been doing when Dan and I were here earlier.

"So, what are we supposed to do now?" Dan grudgingly asked.

"We find a way in," Tess retorted.

I looked at Dan for his response, but Tess caught my eye first. "What?" I questioned.

"Well, it's the logical thing to do, isn't it?" Tess shot back.

I heard Dan sigh.

"Look, if we take a look in there, then it's one more place we know that she isn't, yeah?" And Tess glared at Dan. "We want to make sure she's safe, just the same as you do, Dan!"

"Yeah, I know," he relented and looked at me.

I smiled and nodded my understanding, realising just how worried he really was. "Let's find a gap then and get in there." I looked around just to make sure there wasn't anyone who would see us entering. The sign on the railing further down strictly forbade any trespassers, probably due to the fact that the building was deemed unsafe.

Finding a suitable gap, Dan led the way, followed by Tess. Mal allowed me in before him, though he remained uncommunicative where I was concerned, only with the obligatory questions when they were needed. I followed along the side of the theatre to a single door. The lock had been broken and lay discarded several feet from us, further down the path, close to the building. It had obviously been thrown there with the hope that it wouldn't be noticed.

"Someone's definitely been in here," Mal observed.

I looked Dan's way. I knew Mal hadn't said it intentionally and Dan would realise it, but right now, by the look on Dan's face, he had clearly hit a nerve where Charlotte was concerned.

"It could have been anyone," I suggested.

"Yep, it could have," Tess concurred.

"Come on then. We won't find out if we don't go in, will we?" Dan responded gruffly.

I followed as before, with Tess in front of me and Mal behind. The street lamps shone a little light into the corridor before us, highlighting the whitewashed walls, peeling and flaky.

Closing the door behind him, Mal plunged us back into the dank, cold darkness. It at once limited my vision and heightened my other senses. I heard only our own tentative footsteps gingerly inching forward. As we felt our way along the walls, the first door appeared on our left. Mal put the light on that was on his phone. He walked around with it, trying to make out what was actually there.

"Sorry. It's all I've got," he apologised.

"It's better than nothing and better still than some of us have," I answered gratefully.

As he walked around, I could make out only a little in there. There were hangers along the opposite wall and mirrors down this side, where we were now standing, with work surfaces below.

Many of the acts must have got ready here before waiting to go on stage. "Charlotte?" I called out, but there was no answer. I turned to Dan, Tess and Mal. "There's nothing here, and there's still far more of this place that we've got to search through."

"Yeah, you're right," Dan answered, and we followed him back out. There were five smaller dressing rooms like the one we had just exited. Then we climbed the steps up to the stage. It became slightly lighter as we reached the top, but still we made our way by feeling along either side of the walls of the corridor. The only sound around us was our footsteps on the concrete steps, ascending one after the other. We remained silent as we listened for any sound that Charlotte may be here.

The stage was a vast area, beginning right back at those steps we had just climbed. I looked up into the roof space. Ropes hung everywhere as well as pulleys that would have been used for the curtains and background scenes, which had long since been discarded, as were many fixtures and fittings used in this theatre.

All around us was wide open space, and beyond that was the stage that the public saw. My imagination conjured up stagehands running around, trying to get ready for each performance, and those working the pulleys and lighting system backstage.

"Where do we start?" Tess asked, forcing my attention back.

"We could start up there and work down," I suggested.

"All of us?" Mal questioned.

"Yeah, we all stick together," Tess ordered.

There were three viewing boxes on either side above the stage. We searched the left side first and then took one row at a time, moving together around the circle before finishing in the final three viewing boxes. We found nothing, which was much, I think, to all our relief.

Moving down to the stalls, we all felt lighter, having found no sign of Charlotte, even though we'd been calling out to her constantly.

"Can we get this over with and get out of here, please?" I asked, turning to Tess, who was nearest to me.

"Yeah, there can't be many more places to search. Besides, she's probably at home now."

"No, she's not," Dan stated. "I keep ringing, but there's no answer."

Taking a row each, beginning with the one furthest back from the stage, we followed Dan's lead, moving forward side by side, searching all before us. Thankfully again, we found nothing, finishing at the last row directly in front of the pit where the orchestra would have been positioned. That brought another thought from Mal.

"We haven't checked beneath the stage yet, have we?"

"I don't know how we'd even get down there," Tess commented.

"I think I saw some steps when we were in the wings, so there must be some on this other side as well," Mal answered, and he got up from where we had all been taking a rest in those front row seats. "Come on then," he urged us.

Dragging myself out of my seat, I followed Dan and Tess. She looked back at me. I could see something in her eyes, something I had no desire to think about. I smiled guardedly and continued to follow in her wake. The little bit of light we had from the stage faded as we descended some wooden steps on the right-hand side of it. At the bottom, we found ourselves plunged into almost total darkness. It felt eerie with a musty, dank smell. We stopped right at the foot of the steps, allowing our eyes to adjust to the darkness around us. Shadows… Outlines of objects slowly began to take form as our eyes adjusted. This must have been where props were stored, I figured, and at that moment, Mal echoed just what I had been thinking. Having walked forward a few paces, he immediately hit something with his foot.

"What the….? He questioned. Tess and I took several paces towards him. I bent down, my hand brushing against the object he'd walked into. I stifled a scream desperate to escape.

"No," I uttered and inched back further towards Dan, who was just standing there, statue still. I wanted to get away from here, but I couldn't move any further.

He was staring down, as I was, from where I remained on the floor.

"What's the matter?" Mal laughed, thinking it was the darkness that was bothering us. Tess, too, now felt her way to what or who lay there. Feeling the softness of hair and the skull it covered, she too jumped back, her voice reduced to little more than a hoarse whisper.

"We've got to get out!"

I could hear the tears breaking in her throat and the scream rising up, trying to find its voice.

"Dan, come on," I urged, with that same desperation as Tess, rising up within me. I grabbed hold of his hand and instead tried to pull him away.

"No," he whispered, standing his ground. "I'm not leaving her here. She's my sister."

"We've got to." But before I could say any more, Mal was back on his feet and propelling Dan towards the steps. Not even stopping at the top, he forced Dan's feet to move over the stage and back down the stone steps, where we had first entered.

At the bottom, with the exit in view, Mal continued to push him along the corridor.

Remaining close behind Tess, I couldn't think of anything, not yet. As we pushed through the door, the dimness of the evening greeted us like an old friend. Mal kept hold of Dan until we got beyond the wall opposite, where we all finally collapsed on to the softness of the grass. The place seemed a world away from how it was during the day, a magnet for congregating groups. Seeing Dan there, outwardly quiet but inwardly chaotic, I reached out to him. He took my hand gratefully, allowing me to wrap my arms around him. His tears came slowly at first, but quickly gave way to deep, retching sobs.

Chapter Nine
Fallout

It felt like we were there, languishing, thinking for ages, and yet only minutes had passed. No one uttered a word, certainly nothing referencing Charlotte. No one could; the tears we all seemed unable to stem explained everything. But the bleeping of my phone, demanding my attention, shattered our silence. I thought of ignoring it. Dan was the only one who needed me right now. But I felt him pull away.

I ashamedly took it out of my pocket and opened the call.

"Nic, it's me, Jules."

"Oh, hey! Where are you?" I asked, keenly aware that Dan was beside me.

"Near the town centre."

"We're outside the theatre now, if you want to make your way here."

"Oh, why? You've found her?" she said, almost as an afterthought.

"I'll explain when you get here."

"Oh, all right. See you in a minute then." And she ended the call.

"She's on her way," I explained, but nothing was said in reply. I reached out again for Dan, who welcomed me into his arms. But it was Jules who continued to occupy my thoughts. She hadn't said anything about Charlotte. She had only asked whether we had found her, and that had been as an afterthought. I looked over at Tess, who was still being comforted by Mal. He met my gaze.

"We ought to ring the cops," he suggested. "We can't just leave it like this."

"Do what you want," Dan answered.

I suddenly thought about Greg. With everything that had happened, he'd completely gone out of my head. But what if this wasn't Charlotte? What if it was some stranger?

"Dan… Your dad," I said. "You've got to say something. He doesn't even know that she's missing." But he didn't say anything. Instead, it was Mal who I heard speaking.

"Yeah, police please."

I heard him tell them that a body had been discovered, and he gave them our location, but once I heard the word *body* from Mal's end, I didn't want to hear any more. I didn't want to believe it was Charlotte, even though we all knew it was a possibility. I wanted to be strong for Dan, not just break down at the first thing to happen. But there was no stopping them. I tried to stem my tears, but Dan must have realised my anguish and squeezed my shoulder. As his tears had only moments ago, my own welled up like a torrent unleashed, and I openly wept for what seemed like ages; we were still clinging to one another when the cops arrived, followed immediately by an ambulance.

I was still leaning into Dan when I saw not only the cops but also Jules out the corner of my eye. She was dressed as though she'd been out somewhere, and she had heels on, so there was be a man involved somewhere. But who? My eyes followed her advance from the corner where she had momentarily stalled, watching as events unfolded. I whispered quickly to Dan and then raised my voice a little so Mal and Tess would hear.

"Jules has arrived." We all stayed where we were on the grass, waiting for her to reach us. I don't think any of us would have had the strength to even get to our feet anyway.

"What's happened?" she asked without a single reference to Charlotte. No one else even tried to speak.

"We were searching in there and stumbled across a body." *Literally*, I had wanted to say, but I held back.

"Who is it?"

"We're not sure yet," I relayed.

"Yeah, we are," Dan disputed. "It's my sister who we're waiting out here for." He turned to me again. "I didn't want to leave her there."

"It's better this way," I consoled him.

"Why is it, she's in there on her own, surrounded by all that darkness?"

I looked back at Jules, who I could see had another question on the tip of her tongue. I shook my head very slightly so that Dan wouldn't realise. He didn't need this, not yet and certainly not from her. It was enough that the body in there might be his sister's. At least, that's what we all thought. No, it's what we were all sure of.

Two cops appeared alongside us, both male. They both dipped their heads in our direction but at no one particular person.

"I'm Police Constable Howley," the cop directly before us announced, "and this is Police Constable Larriman," he said, introducing him after a slight pause. "We received a call that a body has been found."

"Yeah, I made the call," Mal told him. "We'd been looking for Dan's sister, Charlotte Trennan." And he looked over at us. I could see the pity in Mal's eyes before he fell silent again. Tess remained strangely quiet too. Her concentration was firmly fixed on the grass.

"Can you tell us any more?" Howley asked.

"I know we shouldn't have been in there, but we'd searched all over for her," I said.

"We searched the whole place before we even went down there. I think we're all pretty certain it was Charlotte," Mal explained, and he looked to me and Dan for confirmation.

"Yes, I thought it was," Dan agreed in little more than a whisper.

"All right. We'll go down and take a look. But you knew this girl, did you?"

"Er… yeah," Mal began awkwardly. "She's Dan's sister, like I've just told you," he repeated, and he inclined his head in our direction.

"So you're Daniel Trennan?"

"Yeah." And the word caught in his throat.

"When did you realise she was missing?"

"I don't know. Most of the afternoon, I think. It was… What time was it when I rang you, Nic?"

"Initially, it was nine, but you rang back just before nine thirty to say you couldn't wait any longer and that you were going out to look for her." I turned to the policeman. "She's only sixteen."

"So what was she doing out at this time without you or her parents knowing where she had gone?" Dan was still holding my hand. His grip tightened as the questions were being asked. I quickly intervened; I could feel from how tightly he was squeezing my hand that he wasn't coping well with this.

"Dan and Charlotte's mother died just over a week ago, and it's still a very difficult time for all of them."

"Well, I'm sorry," he apologised, "but I have to ask these questions. Where's your father? Is he out looking as well?"

"I don't know whether he's at home now, but he wasn't earlier. I've left a message on his phone, but he obviously hasn't picked it up yet." Dan looked shattered, and I could still feel the tension in him.

"Look. I'm sorry, but I've got to ask this. If we can't get hold of your father, do you feel up to identifying her?"

Dan immediately looked at me. "Will you come with me?"

"Of course," I responded, and I turned back to the cop. "We can show you where she is."

He nodded. "Okay, I'll be back in a minute."

"Are you sure you want to do this, Dan?" Mal asked.

"She's my sister, mate. I can't do anything else for her now, can I?"

Mal nodded, just the same as the cop had done. There was no more he could say, no more anyone could say. We waited, none of us uttering a single word. Even Jules had been sensible enough to remain silent. Because Jules had been so close to Charlotte of late, I had thought she would have contributed something, but now wasn't the time to start questioning her. She wasn't the only one, though; what about Tess and Mal? I hadn't been able to get hold of Tess. Where had they been, and why had Greg still not answered his phone?

Before anything else occurred to me, three cops, including Police Constable's, Howley and Larriman, who had been questioning us, approached, taking me and Dan to one side.

"Now, do you want us to inform your father if this does turn out to be your sister?" Howley asked.

"Charlotte," I finished.

"Yes, Charlotte," Howley echoed.

"Er... please," Dan answered falteringly. "Actually, he's my adoptive father."

"Okay, it's not a problem," he answered. "Now, are you both still okay about going back in there to identify her?" Again Dan's attention settled on me. I nodded and smiled encouragingly.

"Yeah, it's the least I can do for her," he answered.

"All right, if you both want to follow us?" We both nodded. My mouth was so dry. Answering anything was the last thing I wanted to do, and I figured Dan was no different.

Although outwardly I had been careful to appear sure enough about our entry back into that shadowy void when I'd encouraged Dan, that it was the right thing to do, I now felt entirely different as we edged towards it. I looked back at Tess and Mal. Mal seemed lost in thought, but Tess returned my smile. It was as unenthusiastic as mine had been, blending perfectly with the horrid circumstances from which we had all found ourselves. I could feel Jules's presence close by, the sickly sweet-smelling perfume she always wore was a dead give-away. Dan must have sensed my unease at passing by her so closely that he quickly squeezed my hand.

"Don't leave me in there, will you?" He said the words a little louder than I would have thought was really necessary, but then I remembered Jules. Had he said that just to let her know we were too strong to be broken apart? But those thoughts now drifted into insignificance, where they belonged, only to be replaced by a deeper, darker fear that what we'd all believed as we had rushed out was now about to be realised. That Charlotte, that young, inoffensive, beautiful girl that she was, was lying there, alone and cold and still. No one comforting, no one there to watch over her.

Other cops were busy cordoning off the whole place as we walked closer to the side entrance.

The third cop – Sanders, who had been introduced to us by Howley – pulled the tape up so that all of us could proceed underneath it. I nodded my thanks as I followed Dan through. Howley and Larriman remained at the front, with the third cop continuing to follow me. As we came to that side door, I tugged on Dan's tee shirt.

"You are sure about this, aren't you?"

"Yeah, I have to do it, Nic, but you can stay out here if you really want."

"No, I'm not leaving you to do this on your own."

He smiled sadly and nodded before following the police in, led by their torchlights, which shone our way ahead. Every step was bringing us closer to that terrible realisation.

My eyes followed the path the light traced. We were soon out on the stage, where the police stopped and checked with us again.

"Right," Howley said. "Where now?"

"She's below the stage," I said. "That's where we all ended up, over there in the corner. There's some wooden steps leading down to it."

Although we had managed without much torchlight, Sanders obviously deemed it necessary and shone the torchlight over to where I had pointed.

"Okay, do you want to stay here?" he asked me. "My colleague and I will take Daniel down to identify the body."

"No, I'm not leaving him." And I turned to Dan. "Unless you would rather go alone."

"No, I want you with me, Nic." And he turned to all three cops. "She's coming with me."

"Fair enough. Come on then," Howley answered casually, as though this were just an everyday occurrence. It was anything but to us. As they led the way, we followed them back down the steps, the wood creaking beneath our combined weight as we descended. At the bottom I reached out for Dan's hand. It was shaking. Mine wasn't much better, but I gently squeezed it, trying to reassure him that I was here, that I wasn't about to bail on him.

The torchlight marked out the body, but they were careful not to flood her face in light. The cops approached her first, making sure the find was as we had said. I saw Howley nod to Larriman and Sanders. He then turned to us.

"Daniel, are you still all right to do this?" Dan nodded his reply and inched slowly and falteringly forward at their say so. I hung back with Sanders, not wanting to intrude on what was harrowing enough. With Howley by Dan's side and Larriman standing on the other, Howley slowly shone the torchlight up to her face. Even though I was sure it was her, I gasped as I caught a glimpse. Dan, too, flinched. I thought he was going to collapse until Howley grabbed him. Both cops looked at one another.

"Is it your sister, Daniel?" Howley, who was still holding him up, asked.

"Yeah, it's Charlotte," he whispered. His voice was almost breaking.

"I'm sorry, but I need you to verify her name for us please – and speak clearly."

"Oh, for pity's sake!" The words escaped my lips before I even realised what I'd said.

Howley, who had just spoken, glared in my direction before concentrating his attention on Dan once more.

"I'm sorry. I know how hard this must be, but I need you to verify her name, Daniel," he repeated.

"It's Charlotte… Charlotte Trennan," Dan mumbled, and he tried to break free from Howley to kneel down by her side. But Howley's hold on him just tightened more.

"I'm sorry," he said. "I can't allow you to touch her. We need to preserve the scene."

But Dan angrily pulled himself away and continued. He leaned over her, kissing her on her forehead, quietly sobbing, "Why you, Charlotte. Why?" As he turned his attention towards me, his eyes implored me to do something.

For a second I just stood there, not knowing what to say or do, wary of making a move towards him in case of Sanders, who was still standing beside me, keeping me where I was. But I didn't care; Dan needed me. I broke free and knelt by his side, easing him away from Charlotte.

"We can't help her any more by staying here, Dan. We'll find out what happened to her. I promise."

He said nothing and allowed me to lead him away. I looked at Howley who had been standing behind me. Taking his place on the other side of Dan, he led us both back up the creaking steps to the stage. The wide open space washed over me, replacing the oppressive atmosphere from where we'd just ascended. Dan looked dreadful. I could sense how raw his pain was. Mine was little better, but Charlotte was his sister. I don't think what either of us had been faced with had really sunken in. I remembered the enthusiasm she'd shown in their back garden when, only a few days before, I'd suggested we all get together. Never again would I hear her voice.

"We have to go now," I heard Howley beside us say. I looked ahead, towards the other side of the stage, and realised why. More cops, about four of them, were walking towards us with a couple of other men in white overalls.

"They're coming for my sister, aren't they?" Dan questioned.

"Yes. They need to check the body… Sorry," he added, seeing both our pained expressions. "They need to get an idea of the nature of her death and any clues that might help in the area surrounding her. Come on. Let's leave them to it. It's best that you're not present for that."

"They will treat her gently, won't they?"

"They will," Howley responded, trying to somehow make it all better, but how could anything make that better? I knew, as well as Dan did, that Charlotte was just a body now, at least to them anyway.

As we exited the theatre, a few people had begun to gather. I couldn't help but watch those just standing there as they watched us, trying to gauge what had been going on, trying to fill an insatiable lust for the macabre. I wanted to scream at them, and maybe in my head I already had or was, but outwardly both of us remained silent, allowing Sanders, who had accompanied us out, to lead us back to where Mal and Tess were still sitting on the grass, where we'd left them.

"Oh, God, no," Dan whispered just as I squeezed his hand. We had seen them both in that same moment, like magnets being drawn to one overwhelming force. Neither Mal nor Tess gave away our impending presence.

"Dad." Dan spoke at last.

Greg turned, breaking away slightly from Jules. Though she stepped away as if we had interrupted something, Greg's expression was broken like nothing could ever fix him, not even the sight of his son, who stood alive before him.

"How could you?" he accused.

"What?" Dan asked, bewildered as to why Greg had just responded like that.

"I go out for the first time since we first got the news that your mother was dying, and this happens? You allowed this."

"No, I didn't. We've all been looking for Charlotte for ages, all of us." But Greg simply ignored all of Dan's protests, ignoring him, and instead spoke to Sanders, who was beside us.

"I want to see her. I want to see my daughter."

"I'm sorry, sir, but I'm afraid that won't be possible. Identification of the victim has already taken place, and forensics are in there now. Of course, you'll be allowed to see her as soon as they're finished."

"I want to see her now! I want my daughter." I could hear his grief catching in his throat, threatening to overwhelm him. He looked like a different man – broken, shattered, just as Dan had been, still was. Sanders who was still beside me and Dan quickly signalled to two others, one of them being a policewoman.

Dan suddenly took a step towards his dad.

"Get away from me!" Greg spat venomously.

"Come on," the policewoman said gently. "We'll get you home. We'll arrange for you to be able to see your daughter tomorrow." And she nodded to Dan before turning to the rest of us. "What about all of you? There's nothing you can achieve by remaining here, you know."

"I'm not going anywhere yet," Dan responded abruptly.

"I'm staying as well," I agreed.

"Yeah, me, too," Tess answered.

"So am I," Mal agreed, uniting us all and leaving the policewoman no alternative but to focus again on Greg.

As she guided him away towards a police car, Greg didn't turn to say anything more to Dan.

"'Bye, Dad," Dan called after him. I didn't think Greg was going to, but he did stop and turn, though he said nothing. There wasn't any more said between any of us until Greg was safely settled in the backseat of the police car.

"I'm going to be welcomed back with open arms, aren't I?" Dan said miserably. "He thinks I'm responsible for her death."

"You can stay at my house. My mum won't mind," I offered.

"There's always mine if you get stuck," Mal interrupted.

"Thanks, both of you, but I need to face this tonight, at some point anyway. For now, though, I'm not going anywhere. My sister's still in there, and I'm not going anywhere until they bring her out."

"Well, we're all with you, mate," Mal reassured him.

"Actually," Jules spoke up, "I'm going to go. There's nothing I can do, but I'll come around in a couple of days, Dan, if that's all right. But if there's anything else you want before that, you know where I am," she added huskily.

He nodded. "Thanks," he answered without even a glance in her direction.

No goodbyes were offered. It didn't seem right somehow, though Tess did catch my eye, raising her eyebrows at Jules's quick departure after Greg had left. She was flirting, unashamedly, even in the situation we'd all found ourselves. Was there nothing she wouldn't do?

"It was good of her to stay as long as she did. She was obviously a comfort to your dad," I heard myself saying even though I'd been thinking the exact opposite. His response wasn't what I'd expected at all.

"Yeah, maybe. If he'd have come home earlier after being with Jules, then Charlotte would still be here!"

"You can't say that, Dan. You've got no proof," Tess responded.

Her defence of Jules surprised us all, I think. But now wasn't the time to make further comments.

"Well, she was obviously somewhere because she said herself that she'd been out, didn't she, Nic?" Dan asked.

"Yeah, but we don't know where, Dan."

"Well, you all think what you like." And that finished the conversation between us all.

Chapter Ten
Consequences

Half an hour passed, and still there was no movement from inside the theatre, but neither was there any out here. No one had made even the slightest attempt at conversation since talk of Jules and Greg had put a grinding halt to it. I think all of us had withdrawn into ourselves and our own thoughts. They were the same thoughts, I was sure, only different memories of her. It seemed wrong somehow to be thinking back to how things had been, how they used to be and would never be again. I was just about to say as much when I saw some movement coming from the side of the theatre and the two forensic guys leaving. A couple of cops followed them. They were heading in our direction.

"Dan," I prompted.

He looked to where I had inclined my head. He made a move to get up as they drew closer, but they just walked straight past us.

"Excuse me," I called out. Hearing my voice, they both turned.

"Can you tell us what's happening?" Dan asked.

"Sorry, we can't give out any information."

"But I'm her brother," he responded.

"I'm sorry, but we still can't. We have to see her next of kin, her father."

"Yeah, right, thanks." And he sat down on the grass again. "That's what you get for not being proper family, blood related."

"That's not it at all, mate," Mal said. "They have to inform your dad first of anything they've found."

"That's just it, though. He's not my dad, is he?"

"You're still family."

"No, I'm not. In Greg's mind, he and Charlotte were family. I didn't even come close, and I certainly don't figure now." He turned to me.

"Can I come to your house instead of mine, Nic?"

"Yeah, 'course. Do you want to wait until they bring Charlotte out?"

"Yeah, then we'll go." I caught Mal's attention as he was turning again to Tess. Their expressions were guarded, as if they were thinking something neither Dan nor I were part of. My focus remained fixed on Tess until she met my gaze. Her eyes settled on me for only half a second before she averted them again; she'd realised I had seen the exchange between her and Mal. I had hoped that things had begun to thaw a little between us all after meeting them on Canley Street when we were still searching for Charlotte. For a while, I think it did, but now it just seemed as though we had settled back into that same old pattern, each keeping his or her own distance.

And I was beginning to wonder whether we'd be here all night when some more cops appeared at the entrance. Behind them, a stretcher was being carried out. It was Charlotte, wrapped in a black body bag. I nudged Dan.

"They're bringing her out," I told him. Tess and Mal turned around as well. We watched in silence as she was carried to an ambulance that was waiting to take her to the mortuary. I stole a glance at Dan. His expression gave nothing away; there was no clue at all as to how he was dealing with this. As the ambulance silently pulled away, he spoke at last.

"Come on then, Nic." He then turned to Mal and Tess, who were still sitting on the grass. "Maybe we can get together tomorrow sometime. And thanks for what you've both done tonight. I know it's been tough on you two as well."

"Yes, it has," Tess responded before Mal got a chance to answer.

"Do you both want a lift?" Mal offered at the last minute.

"Thanks but no. I need to walk, to think some more, you know?"

"Okay, mate," he answered.

"Maybe see you tomorrow then," Dan answered, and with his arm slung over my shoulder, we slowly walked across the grass and away from them and the theatre, stopping momentarily to speak to Howley and Larriman who were in our path.

"We will need a statement from you both and your two friends over there," Howley announced.

"Surely it can wait, at least until tomorrow," I protested.

"Yes, of course. Tomorrow will be fine." I signalled our agreement and urged Dan forward, away from this place. I shivered, feeling the cold of the night air for the first time.

"That's something to look forward to," Dan replied despondently.

"Come on," I encouraged. "Let's get you away from here."

"It won't make me forget, though."

We continued walking most of the way to my house in silence. The night air felt still and dense, heavy, equalling Dan's morose mood. He was in a place where I wasn't permitted, and yet physically he was right there by my side, his arm still draped around me.

Taking the keys from my pocket, I carefully unlocked the door, acutely aware of the squeak it always made as I pushed it open, sure that my mum would have gone to bed and be sleeping soundly by now.

"Nic, is that you?" she called from the sitting room. I turned to Dan and smiled reassuringly.

"Come on. It'll be fine," I said, and I led him through to where my mum was waiting. Seeing our faces, she knew instantly that something was wrong.

"What is it?" she asked. "What's wrong? You have found her, haven't you?"

I looked back at Dan before I answered. He nodded, his silence signalling for me to continue.

"Yeah, we found her, Mum, but she's…" I couldn't say it. The tears were stuck in my throat, holding fast any sound escaping.

"What?" my mum questioned. "Please start talking. You're beginning to frighten me."

Taking a deep breath, Dan began. "She's dead," he uttered. "My sister's dead."

"Oh my, no… I don't understand? What on earth happened?"

Finding my voice again, I continued, saving Dan from having to explain any further.

"We couldn't find her anywhere, Mum, and eventually we ended up at the old theatre on Brompton Road. We only went in there to be able to discount it. In all our minds, it was to be one more place we would have checked where she wasn't. After searching inside, we decided to go below the stage before we left there to resume searching for her away from there. But that's where we found her."

"Was it an accident?" my mum questioned. "Did she fall?"

"We don't know any more than that, Mum. Mal rang for the police once we were out of there, but they wouldn't say anything, although Dan and I went back in to identify her…Well, Dan did," I corrected.

"What about your dad, Dan? He must be beside himself."

"Mum, can we leave the interrogation until the morning? And can Dan stay here, just for tonight?"

"Er, yes, of course, but— "

"He's fine on the sofa, aren't you, Dan?" I said, cutting her off.

"A-Are you sure you'll be all right, Dan?"

"Yes, thank you, Mrs James. Things are just a bit difficult at the moment." She didn't pry any further into what he'd said. But all sorts must have been going round in her head now just as they were in mine and Dan's.

"Go and get Dan a blanket, Nic. He can't just lie there like it is. Do you want a drink, Dan?"

"Er, no thanks, Mrs James."

"Something stronger, for the shock?" she persisted.

"No, really. I'm fine as I am."

"All right, but Nic, don't forget that blanket."

"I won't," I promised, and neither of us said any more until she had discreetly disappeared upstairs.

"I've still got to face Greg tomorrow, haven't I?" he said miserably.

"Everything will look a little better in the morning," I tried to say brightly, but inwardly I winced at how much like my mother I had sounded.

"Charlotte will still be dead though."

"Yes, she will," I answered. What else could I say? "But maybe your... Maybe Greg will be a little more amiable. He'll have had the night to think it all over."

"I wouldn't bet on it."

"Let's not worry about that now." And I went to fetch him a blanket. Saying good night and leaving him there alone seemed totally wrong, but what more could I do? "I'll see you in the morning, yeah?"

"Yeah," he answered, but even that response seemed like a huge effort. I hadn't expected some grand gesture, but he didn't even reach out to me before I left his side. I turned back at the door.

"Try to get some sleep."

"You, too," he answered but followed it only with silence.

I jumped into bed straight away and was just about to turn my light out when my mum crept in.

"What's the matter?" I demanded, though I kept my voice to little more than a whisper.

"What's going on with Dan? Why isn't he going home?"

"Can we talk about this tomorrow, after he's gone?"

"No, not a chance, girl!" And she sat down on the bed beside me.

"Okay," I relented, and I began to explain. "Dan rang Greg loads of times to tell him that Charlotte was missing, but for some reason, Greg didn't answer any of them. Then when we came out of the theatre, after Dan had identified her, Greg just seemed as though he didn't want to be around Dan. He was horrid to him, blaming him for Charlotte's death and everything."

"Why? Why would he do that?"

"I don't know, but it's rubbish. Dan was really worried about what had happened to her. He was beside himself."

"But surely his dad wouldn't say that for no reason."

"He's been really off with Dan since his mum's death."

"You don't think you're getting in a bit deep here? You're not even eighteen yet, Nic?"

"What...? No I don't. Look, please, Mum, can we leave this for tonight? I just want to sleep; too much has already happened today. I've lost a friend, and Dan's lost his sister. I just want to try and forget for a few hours, at least."

"All right. You win, but we'll talk some more tomorrow, yes?"

"Yeah, okay." And she kissed me on my forehead, just the way she always had when I was young.

I heard the light being switched off, leaving just my exhaustion to overtake me, which it did almost instantly.

With a sudden jolt, I was no longer in my sunny, yellow bedroom. There wasn't even any brightness surrounding me. I wondered whether I had woken up again, and I was still in my bed. I patted the mattress around where I lay, but there was nothing there. In fact, I was sure I was standing up.

I looked around, but I saw nothing. Maybe it was just another dream, but then why was I still in darkness? If I was dreaming this, then surely this blackness would evaporate from around me as fast as it had appeared, but it didn't. Instead something was forming from the shadows of my mind, or at least where I had found myself. I caught my breath. Someone was approaching... I could feel my heart pounding... It couldn't be, but it was. It was Charlotte standing there. Relief swept over me, seeing her there. She was okay.

But how? I reached out, but she remained detached. She watched me as if she was waiting for something, but then she just smiled and urged me to move closer. I felt elated, doing as she'd gestured. But as I did, she walked further away, maintaining that distance. Realising she wanted me to follow, I complied, desperate not to let her go. As we moved together in sequence, my surroundings began to form out of the shadows just as she had done.

Before me there were stairs winding down, luxuriously carpeted, deep red in colour. Its softness cradled my feet. Every few steps, she would look behind to make sure I was following. Brushing my fingers along the marble balustrade, I stepped onto the staircase, sweeping down to the lower floor. Each step I descended, I could feel anger matching it, slowly rising. Inside my head, intentions were forming until I had reached that final step, and I knew exactly what I wanted to do.

Looking around again, I knew exactly where I was. I had never been on the staircase before. I had only ever looked up from the foyer, where I was now standing. I was in the old theatre with all its splendour. When she gestured again for me to keep following, I took a step forward but was immediately plunged into that same dense black void. The fear of not seeing anything rooted me to the spot. A flash of light suddenly danced around me, illuminating my surroundings. It settled low towards the ground a short way from me. The light worked its way along until it found its target. A face stared back, fear was etched in his features, eyes glassy and fixed. Terror ran through me, rendering me cold as ice. It was Dan, *my* Dan.

She was still standing there. I met her gaze; she smiled.

"No!" I screamed. "No!" And I dropped to my knees. Leaning over him, I pulled him into my arms. Someone was calling to me. I looked up at Charlotte again, she was gone.

"Nic!" The voice was growing closer, louder, but all I could see was Dan.

"Nic!" Almost absentmindedly, I looked down at the hands clutching my arms, digging into me, hurting me; but the voice was growing more urgent, reverberating all around me.

134

"*Nic!*" The stark light blinded me, disorienting me. Nothing felt real; everything was disappearing. The light was fading, and then there was nothing.

I don't know how long the darkness claimed me, but voices were again calling out to me. I stretched my arms out to grab hold, but still that darkness clung to me.

"Nicola, it's okay. It's Mum." Shafts of light were shining down on me. Where was I?

Wherever I was, she was with me. The light, white light. But no...

"Nic."

I turned my head towards the voice. "Dan... I... How?"

"You looked like you'd gone crazy or something." And his expression confirmed it. My mum's face came into view.

"You must have been sleepwalking," she explained.

"The light," I said. She looked up to where my eyes were directed.

"It's just the ceiling," she assured me. "You passed out after..."

"After what?" I questioned, trying to raise my head off the ground, but I immediately submitted to the pressure my mum was exerting on my shoulders to keep me there. She quickly glanced at Dan.

"You were trying to attack him," she answered.

"What? No."

"I don't know what you were thinking, Nic, but I know what I saw."

I looked at Dan. Now I realised why he'd looked at me the way he had.

"I must have been sleepwalking or something," I confirmed, repeating what my mum had already said. "But I've never done that before, have I?" I questioned, searching her face for answers.

"No, Nic, not to my knowledge. What were you thinking?"

"Well, I obviously wasn't, was I? Not if I was sleepwalking."

Dan looked at my mother. "I had better be going."

"No, it's still… What time is it?" I asked as I looked at the clock on the mantelpiece.

"Half past seven," she answered.

"At least have some breakfast first, Dan," I offered. I was sure he was about to refuse when my mum spoke up.

"Yes, that sounds like a very good idea. Toast and a cup of tea, Dan?"

"All right, thanks," he accepted.

When she left us alone, I felt the tension between us – on Dan's part, anyway.

"I'm not going to hurt you," I assured him.

"What was all that about, Nic? You looked like you wanted to kill me. You had your hands around my neck for Christ's sake."

I watched him for a minute. Was this really the time to tell him that I'd had a dream about his sister, that she had been urging me to follow her to where he was lying… dead? That his idea of my wanting to hurt him had just been me trying to pull him up into my arms, to feel him close to me one last time? At least that had been what I was doing in my dream, but obviously not in reality.

"Nic!"

"S-sorry. What?"

"You were staring. Thinking how to have another go?"

"No, Dan. That's not it at all. Where's all this coming from? I would never hurt you. Surely you know that."

"I'm not sure of anything anymore, Nic." I fell back into the chair; every bit of fight had left me. This felt like the end. "Are you going to tell me then?"

"About what?" I questioned.

"About what happened, about why you had that crazy look about you and your hands around my neck."

"It was a dream," I answered as honestly as I could, but even as I was explaining it, it sounded worse than lame.

"A dream," he echoed. "Nic, you don't try and attack someone when you're having a dream!"

"It depends on the manner of the dream," I retorted.

136

"Which is?"

"Dan, this is stupid. It was a bad dream, one of a few I've had lately. The content isn't really important."

"Doesn't sound stupid, you clearly believed it. But it's obviously something you don't want to talk about, at least with me. Why don't you want to tell me, Nic?"

"Because I don't want to hurt you any more than you already are."

"Sounds like rubbish to me."

"Can you not just trust me?" I asked.

"No!" And just then my mum walked back in with a plate full of toast in one hand and our cups of tea in the other.

"I'll just be in the kitchen," she said, walking away as quickly as she could. She'd heard us, and the awkwardness between us. That had been plain enough.

"Okay," I relented. "You want to know? I'll tell you." With the plate of toast firmly in his grasp, he settled himself further back in the chair, waiting for me to begin.

"My mum came into my room just when I was settling down to sleep. As she went out the door, the last thing I heard was the light being switched off. It must have been a while after that that I thought I had woken up. I thought I was still in my bed. I felt around for something solid like the bed I was laid on, but I couldn't feel anything, and then I saw something growing clearer out from of the shadows." I swallowed uneasily, wondering how he was going to take this next bit. "It was Charlotte, Dan. I saw Charlotte."

"What is the matter with you, Nic? What are you trying to do to me? You were the one person out of everyone that I could trust. Christ, how wrong could I have been?"

"Dan, no. You don't understand. It was her. It was Charlotte."

But he didn't wait for any more explanations. He brushed past me. I put my hand out to try and stop him, but I held back. That was the last thing he wanted, at least from me. My mum rushed through, hearing the front door slam.

"What's the matter? Where's Dan?"

"I said something he didn't like," I answered and withdrew further into the sofa and my own thoughts. Where do we go from here? I wondered. Tess and I weren't exactly what you could call friends, and Mal was even less so, and I'm sure Jules put up with me only because of Dan. Well, that won't be a problem any more, will it?

Chapter Eleven
Building Bridges

My mum looked at me aghast. "What do you mean, you said something he didn't like? He's just lost his sister for God's sake. What's the matter with you, Nicola?"

"Nothing. Don't you think I know he's just lost his sister, Mum? I was there, in case you had forgotten. And he wanted to know why I had done it, why I'd tried to attack him. I simply told him that I hadn't, that it was just a dream."

"Well, it must have been one hell of an explanation to make him walk out like that. Want to tell me about it?"

"I saw someone, okay? She wanted me to follow her."

"Who?" she asked, but from the look on her face she already knew.

"Charlotte," I answered.

"Um, I thought you were going to say that. So why did she want you to follow her?"

I knew she didn't believe me, but I also knew she wasn't going to let this drop, so I figured it might be easier just to get it over with.

"It was pitch black," I began. "She led me down a staircase to the foyer of the old theatre... That is the dream I had," I told her, seeing her looking at me dubiously.

"Okay, carry on."

"It wasn't like it is now, though. It was all new, everything sparkling. Then I was plunged back into that darkness. I carried on, following her until a light illuminated a body. It was Dan." She just sat there, from the way she was looking, I was sure she was at last beginning to believe me.

"Nic, I do want to believe you, but— "

"But what, Mum? I'm telling you what happened in my dream, exactly as it happened. I didn't want to tell Dan, but he just wouldn't let it drop either."

"Well, telling him that the body you saw was his – and on top of seeing Charlotte and expecting him to take in that she wanted you to follow her. That probably wasn't your smartest move, especially after all he's been through over the last few hours."

"I didn't say anything about him or the body. I didn't get that far, and I stupidly thought you were beginning to believe me." I got up to walk away.

"Where are you going?" she called after me.

"There's not much point in staying here, is there?"

"And why is that?" she questioned.

"Because you don't believe me either."

"Is that right? Actually, Nic, I think I do. How could I not when you've been thrashing about and calling out the way you have? I just think there could have been a better time and place for it to be brought up. That's all… With Dan, I mean."

Those four words – "I think I do." They were nothing remarkable when separated, but together they were the lifeline I had been hoping for. I thought it would have come from Dan, but they were music to my ears nonetheless.

"Thank you."

"What for?" she uttered and walked over to me. "You're my daughter, Nicola, and I love you, and I know you would never say anything just for its effect. Even though you have managed just that." She wrapped her arms around me and held me there long enough to make some difference compared to how Dan had left me feeling.

"I should go after him and explain."

"No," she answered firmly. "It's too soon. Just let him be for now. He still needs to deal with the fallout from the way his dad reacted to him at the theatre. Ring him a little later, this afternoon maybe."

"Yeah, you're probably right." I resigned myself to that and trudged off to the kitchen. I looked out the window at the occasional car passing by. I wondered where Dan was. Had he gone home to face Greg and the accusations that would surely follow? Or had he decided to bypass that option and gone straight on to Mal's? After all, Mal had offered to put him up, hadn't he? But what would they talk about? That wasn't hard to figure out at all. It'd be me. I was the one he'd walked out on, the one who had stupidly brought up Charlotte.

Maybe in Dan's world, I had allowed her to take the blame for what he thought I wanted to do to him. It wasn't as though he hadn't got enough images of her rolling around in his head. I suddenly felt really bad again, and I started to pace. It was getting stifling in here. I needed to get outside, to feel the air.

"Now where are you going?" my mum questioned, seeing me heading for the front door.

"I just need some air."

"You're not thinking of chasing after Dan, are you?"

"No, Mum," I answered sullenly. "I just need some air. It's stuffy in here." She didn't say another word; she just left me alone outside, sitting on the wall watching the world go by. I had nothing else pressing, did I? Sitting here, I just felt like I needed to reconnect. Any one of my three friends would be a start. But I'd lost Dan, Tess and Mal in one fell swoop.

Dan had been gone a good couple of hours, and no one had so much as tried to contact me. I certainly hadn't expected Mal to get in touch, but I did think Tess might. I know me and Dan had left them on dubious terms last night, but ordinarily we were best friends. Then something else occurred to me. We were all supposed to be going to the police to give our statements.

Would anyone ring me to ensure we all went together? But it was going on ten now. I certainly wasn't going to ring Tess on that pretext. Maybe if I waited until lunch… If no one contacted me by then, I would walk to Dan's.

"I don't know if that's a very good idea, Nic," my mum said in reply to my suggestion on my way back into the house.

"But you said to wait until the afternoon!"

"Yes, I did, but ring him; don't go round there. What are you going to do if Greg starts on you?"

"Why would he?"

"Well, Dan stayed here all night, for one thing."

"It'll be fine, and I can't stay cooped up in here forever."

"Fine. Do what you want." And she walked back into the sitting room to read the paper.

What would I do if he was there and didn't want to speak to me? Maybe I was just being stupid. Perhaps he just wanted time alone. But thinking back, it wasn't the timing as much as me trying to attack him. Who was I trying to kid? I couldn't leave it though, and I was fidgeting for the next hour and a half until the clock turned twelve.

Strenuously arguing, trying to get my point across, I finally managed to get out of the house with my mum grudgingly mumbling, "Good luck." At least getting out felt less restrictive from the lack of space in our house I had been pacing around in. For a while my stride quickened, rapidly distancing me from home. But once it was out of view, I slowed, thinking again about Greg.

What if Dan wasn't there? Should I go to Mal's first? But if I did and he wasn't there, what would I say to Mal? What excuse could I make? I certainly didn't want to make Mal aware of the spat we'd had, so I carried on to Morsley Road. Taking my phone out of my pocket, I checked it again. How many times in the last twenty minutes had I done that? I had honestly lost count. I still clung to some hope, no matter how futile, that Tess would ring me. I even toyed with the idea of going around there after I had been to Dan's. After all, she, Dan and Mal were on this side of Furham. But what sort of welcome would I get if I did go round?

I had been so wrapped up in my own thoughts that I hadn't even noticed where I was walking; I had no memory of my route at all to this point, and this hadn't been the first time. I was just short of Morsley Road. There was a bench just up ahead, right at the start of his road. I sat down on it, mulling over my options. I looked up Morsley Road to see if I could see anything going on. There wasn't anything, of course. All of these houses, without exception, were detached and imposing; they weren't giving any indication of what lay within, particularly not inside number 115. I knew well enough that its occupants were suffering, their grief over Charlotte deep and aching. And the longer I put this off, the worse I would feel as well.

Butterflies fluttered in my stomach, and my nerves jangled with the anticipation of what surely lay before me. I almost turned and walked back the way I'd come. But something moved my feet, one in front of the other, picking up pace and propelling me forward. At the edge of the driveway and still hidden by the huge conifer hedge, I again weighed up my options. Was I really doing the right thing?

Pushing those nagging thoughts to the back of my mind, I forged ahead, not stopping until I arrived at the front door. I knocked and waited, but no one came. I knocked again, wondering whether Dan and Greg had gone to the police station together. I knocked a third time, just to make sure there really wasn't anyone there. I caught a fleeting glimpse of someone before the door swung open violently.

"What?" Greg raged at me.

"I-I'm sorry, Greg, but I just wondered whether Dan was home."

"Does it look like it?" he spat, slightly less venomously than when he'd first opened the door. And by the smell of him, I could tell that instead of sleeping last night, he'd been drinking for most of it.

"Well, I'm sorry I disturbed you, Greg, and I am truly sorry about Charlotte."

"Huh," he mumbled, throwing scorn my way.

"Goodbye then." And I turned to go. The noise of the door slamming heavily behind me made me jump. I scooted out of the driveway quickly, wanting to get as far from him as possible.

At the edge of the drive, I turned left out of habit, as though I was going to Tess's, but I heard someone calling to me from down the road. I turned because of the familiarity of the voice as my butterflies fluttered with more urgency.

"Dan," I said to myself. I made a move to head in the opposite direction. I had no desire to be subjected to more of what Greg had spat or what Dan might have to say.

"Wait up, Nic!" He caught up with me on the other side of the drive, out of view of the house, though I doubted Greg would be the slightest bit interested anyway. I figured, from the state of him, that he was probably still drinking. I'm not sure why, but it bothered me slightly. I understood that he alone had to navigate his own way through his grief, but he had only just begun the battle, and already he was losing himself in it.

"I wanted to clear the air after what happened earlier this morning," Dan said.

"I'm sorry for what I said, Dan. Can you forgive me?"

"There's nothing to forgive. It was just a dream, wasn't it?"

"Yeah," I answered, though I wasn't quite so sure. It felt more like a warning to me.

"I take it you've been there?" he asked, directing his attention to his house.

"Yeah, your dad doesn't look like he's doing so well."

"Well, he'll have to wait a bit longer. We've still got to go to the police station and give our statements, or have you already been?"

"No, I've just been worrying about where you've been and the fact that I upset you."

"It's done, Nic. Forget it, please."

"Where have you been anyway?"

"I did think about coming back here, but I went to Mal's instead. I rang him first to make sure. I just needed to talk… to talk to someone not quite so close, just a mate," he added, seeing my reaction. "We talked about you," he commented, waiting for my response.

"Oh," I replied, denying him my interest.

"He just wondered how you were. I didn't talk to him about what you said this morning... if that's what you're thinking. Actually, Nic, what you said this morning... You didn't tell me everything, did you?" I swallowed hard, trying to moisten the dryness in my throat.

"No," I admitted.

"And you're not going to tell me now, are you?"

"Dan, Charlotte's been gone barely a day. I'm not sure you would want to hear it."

"I was wrong earlier. I should have let you continue, but instead I bulldozed you. Please, tell me."

"I'm not sure it's a good idea."

"Please," he continued.

"Okay, let's go and sit down." And I led him to the bench back down the road from where I'd been sitting only ten minutes before. Settling down, I began. "Right. Where did we get to this morning?"

"Why don't you start at the beginning? I didn't exactly give you a chance to speak then, did I?"

"You were upset, Dan."

"Even so."

"Okay. Well, my mum had come into my room, wanting to know more of what had happened... about Charlotte. In the end, I just asked if we could go over it in the morning. I was just so tired. The last thing I remember was hearing the light being switched off. I thought I must have woken up some time later because I was still in the dark. I couldn't say where I was, but obviously I thought I was still in bed. Then Charlotte appeared from out of the shadows and wanted me to follow her." I looked at Dan to make sure he was still okay.

"Go on," he urged, realising why I had stopped.

145

"I started to follow her down some stairs. It was then that I knew I wasn't home because the stair rail was cold, concrete or rather marble. I was in the old theatre again. I could see the foyer from where I was on the staircase. As I walked down though, I was plunged again into that black void. Still though she urged me to keep following her. She then led me along even ground, all the time keeping a comfortable distance until she finally stopped. A light began marking out a body. I had no idea who it was."

"Well, go on," he prompted.

For a few seconds, I said nothing. I just kept eye contact. "It was you, Dan."

For a few seconds, he just sat there, staring. "What's that supposed to mean? I thought you said it was just a dream."

"Well, yeah, but... I don't know," I finally admitted.

"You're lying," he said. "You've thought about this. I know you have, Nic."

"All right, all right," I repeated a little more quietly. "I thought it might be a warning. I think Charlotte was warning us about something."

"About me, you mean?"

"Not necessarily. It could be anything. The fact that I saw you doesn't necessarily mean that it is you. I could have thought your image there, not Charlotte."

"Um, I'm not sure I'd agree with that, but thanks for telling me, I think."

"Any time," I answered more light-heartedly, but he felt distant. "What are you doing now?" I asked.

"We're all due at the police station to give our statements, if you'll come with us."

"I will as long as it's what you want."

He took hold of my hand. "Why would you think otherwise?"

"Well, after you walked out this morning, I figured I'd blown it completely. I thought you wouldn't want anything more to do with me. And you don't seem particularly happy with me now."

"Would being told by your girlfriend that she'd seen you dead fill you with the joys of spring?"

"No, I don't suppose it would."

"Well, then." And he kissed me softly, pressing home his point. "I was angry, Nic, not really at you, but at everything else that's happened."

"Charlotte."

"Yeah, it still hasn't sunk in." And his mind seemed to drift somewhere only he knew.

"When do we go then?" I asked.

"We're calling for Tess and then walking to Mal's. I'd been for a walk just to try and clear my head when I saw you, and I did think the walk to Mal's might do all three of us some good."

"Then what would have happened if I hadn't seen you here?" I suddenly wondered whether he'd made all this up, that I hadn't been included at all.

"Simple," he answered. "I was going to call for Tess. Then we'd walk to Mal's, like I've just told you, and then Mal was going to drive to your house to pick you up. The fact that we've bumped into one another just makes it easier."

"And Tess is okay with me coming with you all?"

"Yeah," he answered but didn't elaborate any more than that.

"Come on. It's time we were moving." With his hand firmly clasped around mine, we walked around to Tess's.

Standing at her front door, I felt a tremor of nerves wash over me. I could feel sweat forming in the palm of my free hand, so I knew the other must be as bad.

"You all right?" he enquired.

"Yeah," I lied, but it was too late anyway. Tess was at the door. Without addressing either of us, she called back to her mum before pulling the door shut behind her. She smiled at Dan.

"You okay?" she asked.

"Yeah. Nic decided to meet me. We can all go to Mal's together."

"Okay," she answered.

I turned to her. I didn't want to feel like we were mortal enemies all the way to Mal's and beyond that. "Tess, it was all a bit strained yesterday. We're okay, aren't we?"

"Yeah, sure," she answered, but her response just left me feeling more miserable. There wasn't much more conversation between us except for what Dan contributed, which made the walk to Mal's only slightly more bearable.

With all our attentions focused on getting to Mal's instead of gossiping between ourselves, we made it there more quickly than I'd ever have done. As Dan pressed the buzzer, Tess and I waited behind him.

"Hey, mate. It's us," Dan replied to Mal's greeting.

"Come on up," he answered. Striding up the stairs two at a time, Tess and I rushed to keep up.

At the top, she was puffing just as she had the last time I was here with her.

"You're gonna have to get some exercise, Tess," Mal commented. I saw her shoot him a look that defied him to say anything more. And to my shock his obedience was immediate.

"Nic." He smiled as I followed Tess in. I nodded in reply. I still felt alien to this group, which only days ago had felt more like my family.

"Sit down, Nic," Dan said, offering the seat next to him on the sofa.

"Actually, can I have a word with you, Nic, outside?" Tess asked.

I noticed Mal's wary glance towards Dan, a silent but curious question hovering between them.

"It's all right," Tess responded. "I just want a quick word in private, away from you two."

"Yep, it's fine," I agreed, but inside my stomach was churning with questions of my own.

What was she going to say? What was she going to accuse me of? But instead I obediently followed just as Mal had. As she pulled the door shut, I expected her to start ranting at me, but why she would I was totally at a loss to counter.

"Nic, I just feel – or, at least, I did feel – that you held me responsible for Mal bumping into you and Dan in town," she explained. "With everything else that's happened, we haven't had a chance to really sort it out."

"I know, and maybe fleetingly I did blame you, but I know you wouldn't have told him, Tess. I was hurt that he thought I had lied to him when really it was Dan who'd wanted us to be alone. And only because his mum had just died. He just didn't want to be in a crowd. That's all. I'm sorry. You're my best friend, Tess. I've hated not talking to you."

"So have I. I've known all the way from my house that I was going to ask to talk to you alone, and I was dreading it."

All at once, I rushed at her, throwing my arms around her.

"How stupid have we been?" I asked.

"Monumentally," she answered, and we both laughed. But she suddenly grew serious again.

"Charlotte," I said.

"Yeah, it seems wrong really, doesn't it, to be laughing?"

"Yeah, it does," I agreed as Mal opened the door.

"All done?" he asked, looking at Tess.

"Yeah," she replied, relief spreading across her face. I followed her in to where Dan was waiting.

"Hope you don't mind. I had a word with Mal about him bumping into us in town."

"Dan explained why you didn't say that you were meeting him that day, Nic," Mal said. "I'm sorry I had a go at you."

"It's all right. I probably would have done the same thing in your position."

"Right. Now that everything's cleared up, are we going to the cops to make our statements?" Tess asked, and she looked at Dan. "You okay with that?"

"I will be."

She looked like she was about to throw her arms around him but then backed off and instead ushered us all towards the door.

Out on the pavement, Tess and I climbed into the back of the Mini, leaving Dan to sit in the front with Mal. The drive to the station wasn't far, and I think all any of us wanted now was just to get it over with. There was still social services tomorrow as well. I wondered whether it had gone completely out of Dan's head now. Or did he even care with everything else that was going on?

Chapter Twelve
Statements

As predicted, the drive to the police station was made in record time, probably due to the fact that it was early afternoon, but on parking, no one was in any hurry to get out.

"Right. We should make a move, don't you think?" Dan said to us all collectively and was the first to exit the car, followed by me and Mal, who let Tess out his side. "I'm not looking forward to this. It makes it all, my sister I mean, seem so final somehow," he muttered sombrely.

"It'll be one more thing out of the way, Dan, and then you can concentrate on what's important," I told him.

"Charlotte, you mean?"

"Yeah," I agreed.

"But why would she care now?"

"I meant your grief." He nodded despondently and left my side, making his way to the double glass doors leading to the reception. Mal caught him up. He was saying something out of my hearing, but whatever it was, he'd obviously hit the spot because their conversation was animated.

Most of the reception area was made up of glass, which on a day like today did nothing to calm my nerves. I felt apprehensive anyway, even though I had no reason to; these sorts of places always made me feel uneasy. The place felt stuffy and overbearing. The cop standing at the desk behind yet more glass watched our advance intently. He inclined his head.

"Can I help you?"

No one made a move to speak, leaving Mal, who was leading the way, to explain why we were there.

"We've all come to make a statement about what happened last night – about the body that was found in the old theatre. She was our friend and Dan's sister, Charlotte," he said, urging Dan to step forward to help him out.

"All right. Wait here. I'll go and fetch someone." And he disappeared.

"They obviously know all about it," Dan commented.

"They will do," Tess agreed. "I bet that was the highlight of their night."

Dan half looked around, clearly disapproving of the remark she had just made.

"If I can just take all of your names," the cop said, "someone will be with you in a minute. In the meantime, take a seat." After giving our full names, we all dutifully did as he'd suggested and sat down.

The bench was much like any other, except it was upholstered in a grubby-looking mock leather and defaced with varying degrees of obscenities. They'd actually been scrubbed out, or at least an attempt had been made, but the writing was still clearly visible, if a little faint. I was sitting on the far end, next to Dan with Tess next to him and then Mal nearest to the cop, who surreptitiously stole a glance at us from behind the duty desk every few minutes. I reached my hand out to take hold of Dan's. He squeezed it as if making sure I was okay, but I jumped – not from Dan's touch but from the opposite door being swung open so forcefully. It was the two cops from last night, Howley and Larriman.

"Okay, if you'd all like to follow us, we'll show you to the interview rooms, where both of us and two other officers will take your statements."

"They're taking individual statements," Tess whispered to me.

"Well, yeah. They won't take a statement from us as a group. Don't you watch TV?"

"Yeah, but I thought they would take it from all of us together."

"Maybe they think something more went on in there, eh?" I suggested.

"No, that's horrible!" she hissed.

"Well, we found her, didn't we? Let's just hope they're as thorough in finding out what really happened and who did it if that's how it turns out."

"Oh, God, Nic, I don't want to do this."

"Tess, it'll be fine," I told her, keeping my voice low. "Just tell them what happened in there, the same as the rest of us." I put my arm around her. She was close to tears. I had been close to Charlotte, but Tess had known her for most of her life. We remained like that until two others came and separated the boys from us. They were led down another corridor, leaving us to be led into rooms opposite each other on this same corridor. Howley led me into the one on the right, and Larriman led Tess into the other. I glanced back over my shoulder as I walked over its threshold; unable to hold it in, she was openly crying.

"Please, sit down," Howley said to me. I sat down uneasily. My mind was a jumble. What was going to happen now?

"Okay, Nicola... It is Nicola, isn't it? Nicola James?"

"Yes," I answered. Even in my hearing, I sounded sheepish, like I was hiding something. I kept my head down in case he saw something in my eyes that betrayed me and yet I hadn't even done anything; that didn't stop me feeling a sense of guilt though.

"Look, all we're going to do is have a chat about what happened, and I'll write it down. Just start from when you realised that Charlotte Trennan was missing. Are you all right to do that?"

I nodded. "Yeah," I answered more quietly than I'd intended. I cleared my throat before I began. "Dan and I had been in town, and we'd gone back to my house."

"And where's that?" he asked. "And what time?"

"Er, 7 Chievely Terrace. I'm not sure about the time, maybe around six." But I wanted to ask why he needed that information. Surely all I needed to do was stick to the facts. My mind must have wandered because I caught him studying me curiously.

"And then what?" he urged.

"S–sorry, I was just thinking. Um, we were there, at my place, yes, until about six. He went straight home from there."

"You're sure about that?" he questioned.

"Well, I wasn't with him, but…"

"No, that's fine… Carry on," he said after a short pause. But I didn't like the way this was going, and I decided to say so.

"Look, what is this? Dan had nothing to do with his sister's death. You're making him sound like… like you're trying to put words in my mouth about him!"

"Nicola, I'm just trying to ascertain what happened from what you're saying. I'm sorry if you think I'm trying to put words in your mouth, but I can assure you that's not my intention. I just want to get to the bottom of this. I'm sure you want the same, don't you?"

"Of course, I do," I responded.

"Then can we begin again?"

Resigned, I nodded. "I spoke to Dan about nine. He was really worried because he hadn't seen her for most of the day, and she still wasn't home. I told him to leave it until nine thirty, and if she still wasn't back then, I would go out looking for her as well… same with Tess and Mal," I added as an afterthought.

"Why nine thirty?" he asked.

"Because the nights are still light. I figured that wherever she was, as long as it wasn't getting dark, then she'd be okay." But my voice trailed off. "I know I should have said that we'd go straight out when Dan first called me, but with her mum dying only a few weeks ago, I thought she might have needed a bit of space." My throat constricted with the tears that were threatening to break free, just as Tess's had done as she walked into that interview room opposite. Howley awkwardly handed me a tissue from the box on the table.

"It's okay, Nicola. Carry on in your own time."

Wiping my tears away and clearing my throat, waiting for the emotion to subside, I began again. "If we'd have gone out looking for her earlier, we might have been able to stop whatever happened."

He didn't add any more to what I had just said or assure me that I wasn't at fault. Was that really true? Had our reluctance, or rather mine, to go out sooner not directly caused her death but maybe been a contributory factor to it? But could I have prevented it? Howley's continued silence did little to confirm or deny such thoughts. Would that very question be put to Dan? Would it also be put to Tess and Mal? Maybe all the cops involved in interviewing us had made this a strategy to pull our friendships apart. Maybe that was the idea – to pick each of us off, one by one.

"Are you all right, Nicola?" The tone seemed genuine enough, but I still had the feeling that he was looking for something, or rather someone, to pin Charlotte's death on.

"Yeah," I answered. I carried on with what had happened – about meeting up with Tess and Mal and about the decision we took that paved our way to the old theatre on Brompton Road.

"I know it was supposed to have been out of bounds," I said, remembering the sign that barred our entry into the grounds of the theatre, "but we all agreed that if we checked in there, then it was one more place where we knew for certain she wasn't. We figured that she might be in difficulty somewhere, unable to call out for help or get up, that she might have broken her leg or something. It never occurred to any of us that the reason for that would be so final."

"So whose idea was it to go there, to the theatre?"

I had to think for a minute. I couldn't remember whether it was me or Tess, but then it came to me.

"We had been talking about some dreams I had been having about the theatre."

"What dreams?" Howley questioned.

Reluctantly I explained that I'd been having them for a while. That they were just really random but that I always seemed to be in some sort of danger there.

"You're some sort of psychic then?" he asked, an air of mocking accompanying his question, at least that's how it came across to me. But he was also watching me, maybe weighing me up, deciding if I was hiding something.

"No, they were just dreams and I'm only trying to explain."

"Okay, Nicola, carry on."

"Dan asked what they had been about. He was worried about Charlotte, and I think he thought we were trying to push him in that direction."

"And were you?" Howley quizzed.

"No, not at all. I didn't even want to tell him about the dreams. I didn't want to upset him any more than he already was or have it appear as though we were being flippant when Charlotte was still out there somewhere."

"Okay." And he waited for me to continue.

"With talk of the theatre, Tess suggested that we go and have a look since we were so close."

"And Daniel agreed?"

"Yeah, well, grudgingly... I-I don't think he really wanted to go, but like I said, we all agreed that it would at least be one more place where we knew she wasn't." I was sure Howley would make more of what I'd just said.

"What happened when you were inside? Did you all split up?"

"No, we all stayed together." Had he thought that Dan's not wanting to go into the theatre was relevant? It certainly seemed that way with moving on to his next question.

"Who suggested that you search below the stage then?"

"I don't know. Mal, I think. Why?"

"I just need to cover every angle," he answered. I nodded, understanding what he was saying, but I didn't understand why. Was it just that he was going to check my story with that of the others? I didn't doubt that at all. All our accounts would be checked against each other in the hope of finding some discrepancy. Which one of us were they hoping to trap? Jules suddenly popped into my head. I hadn't even mentioned her; I had been so focused on myself, Dan, Tess and Mal that she hadn't even occurred to me.

"There was someone else with us, though she didn't turn up until after we had come out of the theatre," I belatedly told him.

"Who?"

"Jules... Jules Harvey," I answered.

"Julie, you mean?"

"No, her actual name is Julia Harvey, but we've always called her Jules."

"And what was she doing while the rest of you were searching for Charlotte Trennan?"

"I don't know," I admitted. "I rang her because she had grown close to Dan's sister in the days since their mother's death, and I thought she might have seen her or at least know where she might be. That's why I initially phoned her."

"And did she know?" Howley persisted.

"No, she said she hadn't seen her, just that she'd been out."

His focus immediately seemed to hone in on what I had just said. "Do you know where she'd been?"

"No, just that she'd been out. She said she'd make her way in towards us, to the town centre, where we were at that point, to help look for Charlotte." I omitted the fact that she didn't seem the least bit keen to help, though why I couldn't say. I just figured I had given Howley enough for now.

"If you can just tell me one more thing, Nicola... How was the body discovered?"

"We all made our way down the steps. I followed behind everyone else. Mal was at the front. He tripped over something. Dan held back, but Tess and I rushed over to help him. It was pitch black down there, and I remembered a musty smell as well. I don't know why, but I brushed my hand over the object that he'd tripped over. Tess did the same. We both recoiled at the same time, realising what it was. It was just a reaction, knowing it was a body, not Charlotte especially, but we dragged Dan out of there as quick as we could to save him the pain. Once we were outside, Mal rang the cops, but you know that, right?"

"Yes," he agreed. "Is there anything more you want to tell me, Nicola? Anything you've forgotten?"

"No, I don't think so." I wondered what he meant by that question, asking whether there was any more I wanted to tell him. Did I look like I was withholding information that might point the finger to the real perpetrator?

"That's fine then, and thank you for what you've been able to tell me."

"Can I go now?" I just wanted to get away from here.

"Yes, of course. If you can just read through this again though, to make sure there are no discrepancies and then sign it?" I nodded and took the two sheets of paper he was holding out to me. I re-read the words I had relayed to him, not just reviewing them but also reliving them. I could picture each person there still and our pain too. On top of that, I could feel Howley's eyes boring in to me. Maybe he was trying to work out whether everything I had told him was true or whether I was that possible person behind Charlotte's death.

The very idea made me shudder. I didn't even have the first clue who could possibly have wanted to harm her. The only one who came remotely close was Jules, but that just seemed ridiculous. Even her friends at school became suspects. She had never even spoken of any sort of bullying. But maybe it was another option; it wasn't like it was beyond the bounds of possibility. Nothing else made any sense. Putting the second sheet of paper back down on the table, I looked at Howley. I had one last question.

"Do you know how she died?" Even though Charlotte's death had happened barely twenty-four hours earlier and though the chance of him telling me anything was, at best, slim, I wanted to know. I wanted to know she hadn't suffered.

"I'm sorry. I can't say anything at this point."

"Please… She didn't suffer, did she?"

"I'm sorry, Nicola. I really can't say anything at this point." And he pushed his chair out, standing up. I followed his lead and also got to my feet.

"I'll show you out to reception," he said.

I thought again about the dreams I had spoken of to him. I really shouldn't have said anything. Maybe he'd use it. Oh, God, if he did what would happen now? I watched guardedly and followed him.

Once outside, Tess smiled awkwardly as I appeared from behind the door we had first entered. Being in that reception area felt quite different than it had when I first arrived. I felt freer. I hadn't realised quite how stuffy it had felt sitting in that interview room either. Tess stood up as I drew closer and threw her arms around me.

"Oh, Nic. That was awful."

"It's okay, but let's talk about it once we're away from here, all right?" I suggested quietly in her ear.

She nodded. "All right."

"Where's Mal and Dan? They still in there?"

"Yeah, I haven't been out that long, maybe a few minutes before you appeared."

"They won't be long," I assured her, only too aware of the cop still standing at the reception doing his paperwork. He looked engrossed, but maybe that was just a ruse, and really he was trying to listen to what we were saying. But any further fears I might have been holding onto dissipated with the appearance of Mal and, behind him, Dan. Mal looked over at us both.

"Come on. Let's get out of here."

Dan looked at me guardedly as Tess and I followed behind. I looked at Tess. From the look she gave me, questions were flying around in her head just the same as they were in mine.

Waiting to get into Mal's car, we were still no more the wiser than when we'd been inside the police station.

"What's up? What happened in there?" I asked after we were all settled in the car.

"Did any of you get the impression that you were being drawn in, like they were trying to blow us wide apart and then pick us off one by one?" Mal asked.

"Yes," I answered. "I did feel a bit like that, though Howley was careful to explain that he needed to cover every angle."

"Yeah," Tess joined in. "I was asked who found Charlotte, if we all stayed together, or if we separated. Larriman asked me if any of you seemed less surprised at what we discovered – you know, Charlotte. I know it seems unfair, but I did tell them that Jules only turned up after we had left the theatre, that she was nowhere to be seen before that. Sorry."

"Don't be," I responded. "I said much the same."

"Yeah, I did as well," Dan echoed.

"Well, maybe they'll be knocking on her door," Mal commented a little too smugly. Starting the engine, he turned back to us. "Do you all want to come back to my flat for a bit?" Both Tess and I nodded eagerly, pleased to be getting away from here.

"I'll come back for a bit," Dan said. "Then I'd better make an appearance at home and face Greg."

"Okay, mate. I'll drop everyone off when you're ready. That all right?" Mal asked me and Tess in the back. We both smiled gratefully.

"Thanks," Tess answered, and her voice hovered for a second as if unsure whether to say anything more. But any more conversation was swiftly lost as he turned back to concentrate on the job at hand and the route back to Risely Road. I think all of us, for the moment, had said enough. The silence was a welcome reprieve to what we'd each endured while being interrogated. At least, that's how we all saw it. Parking up, Mal's voice broke through the elected silence.

"Come on. It'll be a bit more comfortable up there." He pulled the seat forward for me, just as Dan was doing for Tess.

Chapter Thirteen
Bust Up

Falling back against the softness of the sofa felt good and comforting after the stiffness imposed by the unyielding plastic of the chairs we each sat on while we gave our statements. Tess collapsed beside me, still puffing from the climb up the stairs.

"I'll help you exercise if you want, Tess," Mal offered teasingly.

"Oh, give it a rest, Mallory!"

I smiled at the contentiousness between them. I looked over at Dan, who was thinking the same. I leaned over to Tess.

"He's just playing with you. You shouldn't let him wind you up so easily." She scowled at him, causing laughter around us.

I wondered again where Mal and Tess had been last night when I had rung to say that Charlotte wasn't back. Even when Dan had gone around to see Mal, nothing had been mentioned.

Certainly if Dan knew anything, he wasn't telling me. But this wasn't the time to broach such things. Maybe I could stop off at Tess's when he took Dan home.

Focusing my attention back on Dan, I asked, "What did you say to the cop who took your statement?"

"He was on with the same thing as with the rest of you, trying to find something that might stick, I reckon. I don't know whether he thought I might have had an argument with Charlotte with me being adopted, but he kept questioning me about any jealousy that might have been simmering over our status within the family, or rather mine. It was all stuff like that. Then it wasn't until I was reading it through that I forgot to say anything about Jules.

"He had to add it on at the end. I suddenly remembered you, Nic, saying that she was coming over while we were sitting on the grass after we'd found Charlotte. Then he started throwing questions at me about her."

"Like what?" Mal asked.

"He asked what my relationship was with her. I told him I didn't have one – that she was just a friend. I told him she had spent quite a bit of time with Charlotte since our mum's death. He asked what they had talked about. I got a bit annoyed at that point I told him, 'How the hell should I know?' He warned me to calm down and questioned whether I always reacted so badly when faced with questions I didn't like. That's when I said I wanted to go. I think he wanted to keep me there, but after standing my ground, he relented, said they might need to talk to me again."

"Yeah, I got that as well," Mal confirmed.

"I didn't," Tess replied.

"Me neither," I added. But then I admitted that I told Howley about the dreams I'd been having and that was sort of why we'd gone into the theatre in the first place.

"That's fine, Nic, don't worry," Mal reassured me. "I think we've all said stuff that might in hindsight have been better left alone. Like I said, I left myself open a bit, enough for them to say they might need to speak to me again."

"So, what did you say to warrant them saying that, Mal?"

"The same as the rest of you as regards Jules. But I got a bit miffed, same as Dan. They wanted to know where I had been that afternoon. I told them I had taken my car to a mate to be fixed. They asked if I had stayed there while it had been worked on. I said I had most of the time, and it was then that he started acting like he was accusing me. Like I said, I got annoyed, same as you, Dan. Before he allowed me out the door, he made it clear that they might need to have another chat. I was glad to get out of there, to be honest."

Neither Tess nor I said any more, but I did wonder where else Mal had been. It made me feel easier, knowing he had, at least, openly accounted for most of the time he had been away from home, but Tess still wasn't giving anything away. She was the last person I would have said had anything to hide, especially from me.

Tess and I had settled into our own conversation about what had gone on while we were giving our own statements that I didn't even realise Dan and Mal had wandered away. They had only moved a few feet away into Mal's kitchen, but they were talking quietly, almost secretly, between themselves.

"Nic!"

"Oh, sorry, Tess, what were you saying?"

"I said don't worry about him. He'll be fine. Dan just needs time."

"Yeah, I know, but he just seems a little too together, don't you think? It's barely been a day, and she was his sister, after all." But then I remembered Tess and how long she had known Charlotte. "Hey, I'm sorry. You must be feeling it, too."

"No more than the rest of you. I just wish I had forced contact with her, instead of leaving Jules to muscle in. Look how that ended!"

"Tess, we don't actually know she had anything to do with it."

"I know, Nic, but even so, I should have done more."

"I suppose any of us could say that after the event. None of us could have predicted what happened."

"Someone did." I didn't reply to her last comment. Her dislike of Jules was growing more bitter by the minute, and I sure didn't want to inflame it any further. I tried to divert the subject of our conversation to Dan and Mal.

"What do you think they're talking about?" I asked, brightening my tone.

"No idea," she replied, but her mind seemed firmly fixed on Jules. I sensed an uneasiness settling between us when Dan and Mal broke away from whatever they had been engrossed in and wandered back to us.

"What have you two been talking about?" I asked, directing my question at Dan.

"From now on, if you want the pleasure of my company, you may have to come here." And he smiled.

"Really? You're moving in with Mal?"

"I might be. I'm going to go back home and see what sort of reception I get. Mal's said I'm welcome to share the flat."

"That's good, Dan, and I'm not trying to put a dampener on things, but I just hope things get sorted with Greg."

"Yeah, I agree with Nic, even if you do still move in here. Hey, I've just wondered. If you do, will there be a party?" Tess asked eagerly.

"Is that all you think about, Chubbs?"

"Don't call me that!"

"Mal, stop it!" I berated, but he just laughed and sat down in the only available chair.

"So, what do we do now?" he said, lounging with one leg draped over its arm.

"I go back home and face Greg," Dan replied solemnly. Mal immediately jumped up.

"Right, I'll drop you off then."

"No, I have to do this on my own. Thanks and all that, but I think the walk will do me good. It'll give me a chance to clear my head."

"Do you want me to walk back with you?" I offered.

"No, you live in the opposite direction, Nic. I'll go on my own."

"Well, I was going to ask Tess if I could go back to hers for a bit." And I looked at her. She smiled, reassuring me that I could.

"Why don't we all walk together?" Tess suggested.

"No," I said. "You go on ahead." I knew he just wanted to be alone. I figured he had to have a lot going on in his head that he needed to sort through before he faced Greg.

"Do you two want a lift back in a while then?" Mal asked.

"Yeah, that would be great. Is it okay if I come to your place for a bit, Tess?"

"Yeah, that'll be nice."

Dan got up and inched towards the door. "I'll be off then."

"I'll come down with you," I said, giving him no chance to refuse.

"Okay... See you later," he called back to Mal and Tess.

Outside, I flung my arms around him. He seemed as if he had already accepted defeat.

"It'll be all right," I told him brightly.

"I hope so," he responded, but he remained as downcast as anyone facing a life sentence. I just hoped Greg had pulled himself together and wasn't still in the state I had seen him in earlier.

"I'll ring you later, whatever happens, right?" And he kissed me quickly before walking away.

"You better!" I shouted back. He turned and smiled. I stood there in the doorway until he disappeared from view. His whole stance worried me. He couldn't be as together as he was making out.

Wearily, I made my way back up the stairs to Mal's flat. Their conversation was in full flow when I opened the door. I think I heard the last fragments of it, which included Jules.

"What's she done now?" I asked, thinking they were still talking about her appearance outside the theatre last night.

"We still think she's up to something." Mal answered.

"Like what?" I questioned.

"With Greg," Tess relayed.

"I seriously doubt that, Tess. Greg was in a right state earlier when I went there to see if Dan was there. He's completely immersed in his own grief. I wouldn't think he even realises Jules exists."

"Then why had they been so close outside the theatre?"

"We didn't want to say anything while Dan was here, Nic," Mal explained. "But while you were both inside the theatre... Actually he hadn't been there that long before you came back out. Anyway, Jules walked straight up to him and kissed him on the cheek. He seemed pleased to see her until he saw me and Tess. Then he distanced himself a little, but we had already seen them.

Like Tess said, Nic, he definitely looked like he was with her. Doesn't it make you wonder where she was while you and Dan were trying to get hold of her, and Greg as well? We still don't know where he was, do we?"

"No, I suppose not." But I still didn't know where Tess had been either. Mal's whereabouts had partly been explained, but hers remained annoyingly secret.

"What do you both propose to do about it then?" I asked. "What can you do?"

"We, you mean?" Tess stated.

"Okay, we. But that still doesn't explain what you propose to do about it."

"We could talk to him," Tess suggested.

"Tess, he's a grown man. You seriously think he's going to allow us to dictate who he spends his time with?" I responded.

"But he may be spending time with someone who killed his daughter!"

"Oh, please! We don't know that, and we certainly can't prove it. At best, he would laugh us out of the house."

"Well, have you got any better suggestions?" she asked.

"Why don't we try and talk to Jules?" I suggested.

"Yeah, that might work," Mal agreed.

"All right," Tess concurred. "But I'm going home now. You still coming, Nic?"

"Yeah."

"I'll drop you both off," Mal said, jumping up.

Outside Tess's house, we both said our goodbyes to Mal after agreeing that we would meet up again at his flat late tomorrow morning. Then we would try to get in touch with Jules to see whether she would come over and join us.

On Tess's back lawn, I relaxed like I never thought I would have done again only hours ago.

"I'm glad we're back on track," I commented.

"We never left it, not really." Knowing that all that awkwardness was now behind us, I thought again of last night when I had tried to get hold of Tess when Dan and I were searching for Charlotte. I couldn't contain my curiosity any longer and decided to broach the subject.

"Where were you last night when I tried ringing you? I tried quite a few times."

"Oh, just out." She didn't elaborate any more than that.

"Where?" I questioned.

"Why do you want to know? I did ring you back as soon as I got your message. Mal and I came to help search for Charlotte. What's the big deal?"

"You've never kept anything back before."

She laughed. "What is this? Where's this suddenly coming from, Nic? You don't honestly think that because I haven't told you my exact movements that I must have had something to do with Charlotte, do you?"

"No, of course not. I just don't understand why you won't say where you were." Her focus on me was so concentrated that I broke eye contact.

"Oh my God. You do, don't you?"

"What...? No. I told you I just don't understand why you won't tell me."

"I thought we were past all this... How could you think that? I think I want you to go, Nic!"

"But Tess, I was just asking – that was all. Please don't be like this. I didn't mean anything."

"Nicola, just go!" And she stood her ground, eyeing me suspiciously. I shook my head before getting up to walk away.

"And don't bother going round to Mal's tomorrow morning either if that's what you think!" she spat.

"It's not," I said, trying to defend myself but I knew I wasn't going to alter anything by what I said now. I walked away, through the house, calling out goodbye to her parents as I went. Thankfully no one crossed my path, and I didn't stop until I was some way down the road.

How had that happened? Only hours before Tess and I had made up, and now I was in exactly the same position as before. But why wouldn't she just tell me where she'd been?

Surely she had told the police her whereabouts in her statement. So why couldn't she tell me? But the sound of someone arguing in the distance interrupted my train of thought. As I neared the corner where I had seen Jules hovering only days before, I wondered whether my worst fears had been realised. It all seemed to have gone quiet again after a door slammed, bringing the noise to a swift close.

I tentatively walked towards Dan's house. I had no option but to head that way; it was the only route home. When I was level, I stopped in my tracks. Dan was bent over, trying to gather up his stuff in a pile where it had obviously been dumped, strewn everywhere. I rushed across the road and into the drive towards him.

"What happened?"

"Don't ask, but I think I'll be stopping at Mal's tonight. Have you got your phone?"

"Yeah, want me to ring him and get him to pick you up?"

"Please, but can we get away from here first?" I helped him with all his gear, carrying it to the top of the drive and out of sight of the house; now with less chance of Greg coming out and starting on him afresh. Having rung Mal and now waiting on the roadside for him to turn up, Dan suddenly asked whether I would go round to the flat tomorrow.

"I don't think I'll be welcome somehow."

"Why?" he asked.

"I had arranged with Mal and Tess that we would do that very thing, late morning, but Tess and I have had words again, while I was at her place."

"What about?"

"I asked where she had been when I couldn't get hold of her last night when we were going to look for Charlotte, so I don't think it's going to happen."

"What did she say?"

"She wouldn't tell me. In the end she accused me of thinking that she'd had something to do with what happened to Charlotte."

"Right. As soon as Mal arrives, I'll stick what stuff I've got in the car, and then we'll go around to Tess's and sort this out."

"No, Dan. I just want to go home. You wait for Mal, and I'll go."

"But I don't like leaving you like this."

"I'll be fine, and besides, you've got enough on your plate right now. Ring me tomorrow, okay?"

"Okay, but will you just text me when you get back home?"

"Yes, 'course." And I kissed him before rushing off ahead of Mal making an appearance. I really didn't want to have to explain again why my best friend didn't want me anywhere near her for the second time in as many days. And I had forgotten all about meeting Dan tomorrow. It had completely slipped my mind when Mal suggested we meet at his place. We were supposed to be going to social services to begin searching for his birth mother. But it was too late now, even if he was still there, waiting, Mal was sure to pull up before I left again.

Maybe I could put it in the text message he'd been so insistent I send. I could query whether he still wanted to go. After all, I wasn't going anywhere else, was I? Though maybe it had slipped his mind as well with asking if I'd go around there.

When I reached Chievely Terrace, it was still light, it was just going on eight. I shouted to Mum as I walked in through the door.

"Hey, stranger!" she called out. I walked through to where she was, in the sitting room.

"You all right?" she asked. "You look a bit upset."

"Not really, no."

"What's happened now?"

"Oh, Tess and I had a bust up."

"Want to tell me about it?"

"No, because you'll probably say the same as she did."

169

"Try me." I told her about the phone call I had made to Tess and that she hadn't answered it until quite a bit later. Then where she had been when she hadn't answered the call.

"And you say she wouldn't tell you at all?"

"No, she wouldn't."

"Then maybe it was something she's too embarrassed to tell you. You can't assume though, Nic, that because she hasn't told you whatever it is she's keeping from you that she could be involved with what happened to Charlotte."

"I didn't. She jumped to that conclusion herself."

"It didn't run through your mind then?"

"Well, fleetingly, but I know Tess. I know she'd never do anything like that."

"But that's obviously not what she thinks, is it?"

"No," I admitted.

"Then you have to tell her."

That was all well and good, but she didn't want me at Mal's tomorrow so telling her, or rather explaining it to her, wasn't really an option.

Maybe Dan would say something.

"Oh, no!" I exclaimed.

"Now what's the matter?"

"Dan... He wanted me to text him as soon as I got home," I explained, taking my phone out of my pocket. I frantically began tapping out a message.

Dan, sorry forgot to text earlier. Have you forgotten about tomorrow, social services or do you want to set up another day x

"Why don't you just ring him?" she asked. "It would be quicker."

Ignoring my mum's jibe, I waited for his reply, which was almost immediate.

Yeah I had. Got loads on now. We'll go later in week, okay? Glad you're home safe, see you tomorrow x

I replied once more to let him know I was fine with that, omitting the fact that I would see him tomorrow, or rather I wouldn't.

I held on to the phone for a few minutes more as if by doing so I could keep that connection with him. How could everything be going so wrong again? How could Dan and I even spend that much time together now he'd moved in with Mal? I couldn't deny Tess her time at the flat, and as she had so vocally told me earlier, she didn't want me there. I looked over at my mum, who was watching me intently.

"What?" I demanded.

"Nothing. I was just thinking."

"Well, I'm going to bed. I've had enough of today. I'm not going anywhere tomorrow, so you can leave me to have a lie in." There will be nothing to get up for, I thought, not after Tess had had her say.

Chapter Fourteen
Remorseful

I woke, feeling strangely refreshed, though my dreams had remained a constant companion.

Charlotte had again been a part of them, but what direction it had taken had evaporated as the sun streamed through my curtains, filtering through my closed eyelids. I stretched, feeling rested for once, and then I remembered… Tess. Had she already rung Mal? And had he in turn relayed what had been said between us or rather how I had questioned her? Would any of them welcome me there now? How would Dan react when Tess told him her version of events, or had he already thought better of what he had said to me last night and was already preparing to distance himself? I know I had told him what had been said, but would Tess embellish it, preferring to play it out sadistically just for my benefit? I inwardly chided myself for even thinking such a thing. I was still trying to get my thoughts in some sort of order when I heard my mum's steps reverberating up the stairs.

"Hey, sleepy head, it's eleven, and you've got visitors." My mind raced as to who it could be. Maybe it was Tess, making sure I wasn't going to be anywhere near Mal's flat. But no, it was Mal and Dan's flat now, wasn't it? But surely if it was Tess, then my mum would have had a word first and smoothed things out between us. But why would she be here? She'd told me not to bother going to Mal's flat today if that's what I had been thinking. But then it occurred to me, my mum had said 'visitors'.

"Are you coming down then?"

"Who is it?" I questioned, not even bothering to raise my head from the pillow.

"You'll find out if you come downstairs, won't you?" And she promptly walked back out of my room and down the stairs.

Who on earth could it be? It certainly couldn't be Dan, though he had said he would see me tomorrow. But Tess was going around there; maybe she was already there.

But that still left the question of who was waiting for me downstairs. My mum had been no help. No, there was nothing else for it. The only way I was going to find out was to go down there myself. I pulled on an old tee shirt and some jog pants; then I tied my hair up in a loose bun. It wasn't as though I was going anywhere and if she wasn't going to tell me who these visitors were, I would please myself how I dressed.

At the top of the stairs, I listened for any familiarity in the voices rising up from our sitting room, but they weren't loud enough for me to be able to distinguish between them. Halfway down, I caught my mother's attention; she was just walking back into the sitting room from the kitchen.

"Oh, Nic. Come on through."

I dutifully followed.

"Dan? Mal? What are you doing here?" It was only then I remembered what I had thrown on to greet my unknown guests. I looked down self-consciously, realising what a frightful mess I must have looked.

"Planning a lazy day in, were we?" And Dan smiled smugly at my obvious embarrassment.

"Like I said yesterday, I wouldn't be there." I didn't want to go into the details any further with Mal sitting there.

"And I said in the text I sent that I would see you tomorrow," Dan stated.

"In your text, yes, I know, but you know how things are, Dan. I don't want to make the situation any worse."

"Oh, by the way! Mal knows all about it."

"And more," Mal added, smiling mischievously.

"I just don't want to make her feel any worse by being there."

"You won't. We're going to sort it, aren't we, Dan?"

"Yeah." He smiled.

"Unfortunately, we can't do it without you, so you've got to come with us." And Mal smiled too, like they were harbouring some sort of secret deal.

"You're not going to leave here without me, are you?" I asked.

"No," they both answered in unison.

"Um, are you coming like that, or do you want us to wait while you get changed?" Dan asked.

"Why? What's wrong with it?" I demanded playfully, feeling like part of the weight had already been lifted. I still had to face Tess though, and I was really unsure about that, but at least these two were okay.

"There's nothing wrong with what you're wearing," he answered.

"Are we staying at Mal's? Sorry. It's both of yours now, isn't it? Are we staying at the flat?"

"Um, sounds good, doesn't it?" Dan remarked, turning to Mal.

"Yeah, you should have moved in sooner."

"Well?" I asked, joining in with this new-found alliance.

"What?" Dan mumbled.

"Are we staying at the flat?" I repeated.

"Oh, yeah. We are, aren't we, Mal?"

"Yeah, and Tess will be getting grouchy if we don't get a move on."

"Come on then," Dan urged me. "You'd look great in anything, honest." And he winked.

"Okay, what are we waiting for?" I responded.

"At last!" And he threw his arms up in mock exasperation, waiting for me to follow Mal to the front door.

"I'll see you later, Mum," I called back.

"Play nicely, all of you." Did she know something I didn't? Had Dan and Mal explained everything, or had my mum had a word about what I had told her last night? I had little time to think about it anyway, because those two didn't shut up all the way back to their flat.

I had half expected Tess to be standing on the pavement outside the front when we pulled up, but thankfully there was no sign of her. It would be bad enough when I walked in with them; the last thing I wanted was another argument outside for all to see. At the door Dan waited for me to go ahead of him.

"No, you go first." I wanted both him and Mal in front of me when I saw Tess. I felt uneasy as it was, and my stomach was in knots, standing testament to that.

"It'll be all right," he assured me before making a move to follow Mal. We tramped up the stairs. The noise must have alerted Tess, but as I looked up, there was still no sign. What if she immediately stormed off when Mal and Dan revealed my presence? What if she stayed but refused any explanation and wanted nothing more to do with me? Would I be forced to leave, making it too awkward for me to linger? Reaching the top, Mal turned back.

"Ready?"

I reluctantly nodded. He threw the door open, but still there was no sign of her. For a second, relief swept over me until I took a few paces inside. She was standing by the sink. She turned.

"What's she doing here?" she demanded.

"We need to sort all of this out," Mal explained.

"No, we don't. I don't want her here!"

"And it's mine and Dan's flat, Tess."

"All right, I'll leave!"

"Oh, no, you don't. We're going to talk about this, and if you're still adamant when we're finished, then you're welcome to leave." She glared at him for reasons I assumed were because of what he had just said, but I sensed something deeper between them.

"Right, sit down, Tess, and you, Nic."

I did as he said without question. Mal seemed in no mood to be messed with.

"I don't know quite how to begin— " I said.

"Right," Mal spoke, thankfully interrupting what I had no idea to say.

"You didn't mean what Tess thinks you were accusing her of, did you, Nic - about Charlotte, I mean?" Mal asked.

"No, of course, I didn't. I— "

But Mal cut me off again. "So do you want to tell Nic where you were, Tess?"

"No, I don't." And the look she gave him dared him not to say another word.

"Well, if you're not going to tell her, I will!" Mal warned.

She got up to leave, but he barred her way.

"Please, Tess," I said. "I would never have asked if I'd have thought it would cause this much trouble."

She looked at me and glared again at Mal before taking her seat once more. Before she said another word, she looked again at Mal. He nodded as if encouraging her to begin.

"I was with Mal," she mumbled.

"So why was that so secretive?" I questioned.

"Because I made a fool of myself. That's why."

"Ah."

"Yes, ah," she echoed, and she scurried from the room, slamming the door behind her.

Bounding after her, I found her out on the landing.

"Do you want to tell me about it?" I asked tentatively. Knowing now why she had refused to say where she'd been and with whom, I didn't want to pry too far. I think I had already pushed her far enough. "Look, I'll understand if you want me to go. I am sorry, though."

"I know you are. But my stupidity's out there now for all to see, isn't it?"

"No, it's not stupid to misread the signals, if that's what you did."

She turned to face me. She must have been crying because her mascara had bled all the way down her cheeks. I took a tissue from

176

my pocket and handed it to her, pointing to where the streaks of black had run.

"Thanks," she said, taking it. "I should have just told you, Nic, but I felt so stupid when he didn't return my feelings. He said there was enough going on. I think maybe he likes you more than he likes me."

"Now that is stupid," I told her. "I must admit – I thought there was something there. I still do. He teases you unmercifully. Why would he do that if he didn't like you? Give it a bit of time, and he is right about there being enough going on at the moment. Maybe what he needs most at this moment is his friend... you!" I added when she looked at me blankly. "Talk to him. Ask if you can both go back to being friends. Tell him that you miss that."

But I had no need to say any more; the door opened, and Mal stood there.

"Everything okay?" he questioned warily.

"I'll leave you to it." And I coaxed him away from the doorway nearer to Tess. "I think maybe you two need to talk now." And I left it there, walking back into the flat to rejoin Dan.

"Made friends again?" he asked.

I nodded. "Yeah, but I think they've got even more to get sorted."

"Yeah, I think so too."

"I've told her to just go back to being friends."

"Do you think they can manage that after Mal rejected her so forcefully?"

"Was he that brutal?" I asked.

"He was a bit forthright," he explained.

"Well, I don't intend losing either of my friends, so they had better get themselves sorted."

I relaxed a little and leaned against Dan, thinking about last night and all the unnecessary angst I had put myself through, believing that Tess hated me so much for what she thought I had thought of her, though fleetingly I must admit I had. Pushing that to the back of my mind, I listened intently for the sound of anything happening outside.

"They'll be all right. Relax," Dan encouraged and pulled me closer.

"I hope so." I wasn't as sure as he seemed to be, but from the look on Tess's face as she walked back in through the doorway, I believed I had my answer.

"Everything okay?" I asked hopefully.

"Yep, everything's sorted, eh, Chubbs?" Mal responded.

"Don't call me that!" she warned, though I was sure I could make out a very slight smile as she said it.

"Anyway you two, now that everything's sweet again, I really need to go back to my dad's and get the rest of my gear," Dan announced. "There's still some stuff in my room that he didn't grab hold of that I need."

"Want me to run you over there?" Mal offered.

"Nah, you stay here. You've probably got better things to do."

"You mean like talking to Tess."

"Oh, thank you!" she grumbled.

"I was only joking," he laughed.

"You'd better be," she teasingly scolded.

I don't know what had been said between them, but it had obviously had a good effect on her.

"In that case, I'll go with you," I elected.

"Won't there be too much stuff to just carry back?" Mal questioned.

"Well, if there is, I'll ring," Dan responded.

"Okay. Tess and I will wait here for you both."

"Okay, you ready then, Nic?"

"Yep." And I followed him out. "See you both in a bit," I called back.

"You okay about doing this?" I asked, following him down the stairs.

"Yes, why?" he questioned.

"Well, with everything that happened yesterday," I responded, "and the fact that we left the flat a little too hastily, yet now you've slowed right down. I just wondered if there was something wrong."

Out on the street, he laughed. "I'm that transparent, am I?"

"Probably not to anybody else... Want to tell me about it?" And I took hold of his hand as we walked. We hadn't left Risely Road before he stopped again and sat down on a wall, urging me down next to him.

"Now what?" I joked.

"You remember Jules was standing with Greg when we came out of the theatre."

"Yeah," I answered and waited for him to elaborate, but I was sure he would just be confirming what was already in my mind about what Mal and Tess had told me the other day.

"Well, it was the same. She was there when I walked in yesterday, acting like she owned the place, and they were both drinking. My sister was barely cold, and he was acting like that."

"What did you do?" I pressed.

"I completely lost it, blaming him for Charlotte's death and her for befriending her just to get to him. I took a swipe at him. I couldn't help it, Nic. Of course, she rushed to his defence. That's when he told me to get out. I just stood there. I couldn't believe what was happening after everything we had been through over the last few weeks. First Fran and then Charlotte.

"I didn't think things could get any worse. I wanted to help him up, but he managed on his own... well, with a bit of help from her. He fumbled and cursed his way past me and disappeared up the stairs. The next thing I knew, he was coming back down with a load of my clothes bundled up in his arms. He shouted to Jules to get the door and unceremoniously threw them out. Even though he'd had a drink, the way he looked at me – he hated me, Nic. Why would he look at me that way? What have I actually done?"

"You haven't done anything, Dan. It's just the grief. It affects everyone differently."

"No, it was more than that. He blames me."

"They say we hurt the ones we're closest to," I tried to console.

"Not in this case." And he smiled ruefully.

"Maybe he's calmed down now," I said hopefully.

"I doubt it. What he feels for me isn't going to go away easily, even if he hasn't had a drink today. I just hope Jules isn't still there. If she had any sense, she would have left soon after I did."

I wondered just what she was up to and what she hoped to get out of this. Was Greg a substitute for Dan? Had she turned to Greg when she realised Dan wasn't going to return her advances? Or had it always been Greg? Maybe she'd wanted to get close to Dan to get to Greg?

"You've gone very quiet," he murmured, catching my attention.

"I was just thinking about Jules."

"What about?"

"Just what she's hoping to get out of this. I don't understand it. I had thought it was you she was after, not Greg."

"You're not the only one who's said that, and I'll tell you something else. That night we were looking for Charlotte, how many times did I ring my dad?"

"Loads. Why?" I asked, puzzled as to why he had brought that up.

"Haven't you wondered? We couldn't get hold of Jules either, could we? We don't know where either of them were. Could they have been together?"

"That has occurred to me," I said, remembering talk of it at the flat with Mal and Tess. I remembered as well seeing her watching momentarily from the shadows that night before she made her way towards us. Had she just left Greg when I saw her? I wanted to be able to explain, though there was no other explanation I could give. But if that was the case, it made Jules's friendship, which she had suddenly struck up with Charlotte, seem all the more cold and calculated.

"You're thinking the same thing I am, aren't you?" Dan asked.

"I don't know what I'm thinking, Dan. Come on. Let's get around there and get it over with, and then we can get back to the flat."

"Wow, you've changed your mind from this morning."

I smiled despite the uneasiness of my thoughts. "Well, you live there now, don't you?"

"Um, and long may it last."

"Come on then," I urged, and I dragged him to his feet from where we'd been sitting on the wall. "We've got somewhere to be."

I stopped him just before we reached his driveway. He'd been dragging his feet ever since I hauled him away from that wall.

"Look, we're just going back to get the rest of your stuff, and then we'll be out of there, right?" I said, trying to bolster him.

"Okay." He smiled and grabbed hold of my hand. "Ready?"

"Ready," I agreed, and we walked forward, down the drive together. Making our way towards his house felt better this time, I felt stronger with Dan by my side.

He already had his keys in his hand, ready in case Greg was out and the place was locked up.

Everything seemed peaceful enough. Maybe Greg wasn't there, or if he was, hopefully he was alone. I figured that had to be the best outcome; it would at least give Dan and Greg a chance for a long overdue talk, obviously, if Greg was willing. He turned the doorknob to see if it was unlocked. It opened.

"He's obviously in," he murmured. "We'll check in the back. That's where he was last time, with her."

I tentatively followed, the silence creeping over me like coldness rippling over my skin.

He called out, "Dad? Dad?" But he stopped abruptly. "Oh, God!" The shock momentarily rooted him to the spot. Finding his feet, he rushed forward to Greg.

It was then that I saw him. He was lying just beyond the door; from here only his legs were visible. I rushed to where Dan was kneeling, his form reminiscent of that night in the theatre where he'd knelt over the body of his sister. Only now it was his dad.

"Dan," I said. I could hear the echo of my voice from the emptiness of the house around us. He said nothing. His left hand was placed beneath Greg's head, cradling it. There was blood all over, on Dan too.

"No. No. Nic… Please…" The words escaped unhindered, and his body seemed to sink over Greg's still form, his shoulders heaving, giving way to those same deep retching sobs.

Chapter Fifteen
Isolated

Immobilized, I stood there in the doorway, processing nothing. Only the stillness of Greg's body.

"Nic. Do something. Please," he pleaded through desperate sobs, shaking me out of my own trance. Taking hold of my phone in my shaking hands, I tapped out an all-too-familiar number.

"There's been an accident," I tearfully relayed. I gave out the address and whatever else they demanded of me. I don't even remember what had been said, and I remember only the grim sight before me, with Dan still cradling his dad in his bloodied arms.

"Dan, they're coming. You've got to leave him now." I grabbed hold of him and tried to pull him away. Blood was everywhere, and it was on my hands as well now. Inside I was screaming, terrified of what lay before me and for Dan. I wanted him to leave Greg; I wanted both of us to get away from here before anyone turned up.

"Please, Dan, we have to go." And I tugged at him again. He shrugged me off.

"No! I can't leave him."

I wanted to run, to get as far away from here as I could, while I could.

In the distance I heard the wailing of sirens. A sudden realisation hit me. It could be either the ambulance or the cops, maybe even both. I pleaded again with Dan.

"Please. There's nothing more we can do for Greg."

But he wasn't listening. No amount of pleading was making any difference. I weighed up whether I should go and get out of here before anything else happened. What would this look like when they did turn up? But the sirens were getting closer, louder.

I turned; I could see through the front door, it was wide open. I thought about trying to leave that same way, but how could I leave him…? It was too late. The ambulance had just turned into the drive, and I was going nowhere. Seconds after it another vehicle followed, its lights also flashing. It was the cops.

"They're all here, Dan." But he heard nothing of what I had said.

The paramedics were rushing forward, knowing much of the situation already from what I had told them over the phone. Their expressions were grim and movements purposeful as they neared the door.

Their closeness seemed to break through a barrier, and I heard myself calling to them.

"Please, he's in here." Their gaze immediately settled on my hands, smeared with blood, and then on Dan.

"Please, sir," the first paramedic said. When Dan made no attempt to acknowledge them, he was forcibly moved away from Greg's side, only to be replaced by a cop hovering by ours.

"It would be better if you came outside," he said, "and left the paramedics to get on with their work."

"What are they going to do? Perform a miracle and bring him back to life?" Dan spat. He looked at me. I wanted to say something, anything to help, but I couldn't. As Dan had already more or less said, Greg was far beyond anyone's help now, and instead I encouraged him to back off and walk with me through to the front of the house and then outside. The cop followed. Out there, my heart sank.

Another car had pulled up. Howley and Larriman were standing there.

"Nicola," Howley greeted. I nodded before he turned his attention to Dan.

"What happened here?" he asked, but I already knew exactly what he was thinking. There must have been some sort of argument, a scuffle maybe, resulting in this… Was that really how it would begin? Instead, it was me who spoke first.

"Dan and I came back for the rest of his stuff… We found Greg…" But as I was saying the words, they sounded unconvincing even to me.

"I would rather Daniel told us," he said, cutting me off.

"It was like Nic's just said," Dan answered. "We came here to get the rest of my stuff. Greg – my dad, I mean – threw a lot of my clothes and other things out here on the driveway yesterday, and we just came back to get the rest of it."

"And no one else was here?" Howley questioned.

"No one," Dan answered.

"And you were here the whole time, Nicola?"

"Yeah, what is this? What are you accusing us of?"

"We just need to find out exactly what happened. I'm sure you want to know what's happened to your dad, don't you, Daniel?"

"'Course I do," he answered. "But this has nothing to do with me or Nic, and it's Dan, not Daniel."

Howley said nothing.

"Can we go now?" Dan asked.

"We'll need to take a statement from both of you, but if you can wait until the paramedics have finished, we'll drive you both to the station and get it down while it's still fresh in both your minds, okay?"

"No, actually it's not okay," I said. "His dad's in there. How do you think he's feeling? His mum and sister are both dead as well. They're all gone. Can't you just leave him alone?"

"It's all right, Nic." And Dan turned to Howley. "We might as well get it over with." I looked at him, astounded that he was happy to do this. "I'd rather just get it over with, Nic."

I nodded, reluctantly agreeing though I did wonder whether this really was as wise as he seemed to think. Seeing something out of the corner of my eye, my attention was diverted to one of the paramedics appearing from out of the shadows of the house.

"I'm sorry, he's gone," he said to Dan. "There was nothing we could do."

Dan nodded. That particular piece of information was of no surprise to either of us. There was only the fact, I supposed, that they felt they needed to say it at all.

"We're waiting on the forensics team now," he said to Howley and Larriman.

"Okay, well, there's not much more we can do here," Howley said to us both. "So, would you like to accompany us to the station now? Then we can get your statements sorted."

"Yep, that's fine by me. What about you?" Dan asked.

"Yeah, as long as you're okay with it."

"That settles it then," Howley finished.

Pulling away from the house in the police car, I wondered what would await us at the station.

My memory of being there only the day before held very little to smile about. My attention strayed to where Dan was sitting beside me. He met my glance with a wry smile, knowing neither of us could talk with Larriman and Howley in the front. So instead I watched what was going on around me outside. It was sunny again as we passed numerous people coaxed out by the weather, their smiles and laughter matching the warmth around them, though it all belied the dark, foreboding rumblings inside of me. Our route around the back of the station seemed to confirm that feeling.

Walking away from the car towards the back of the building, I could feel a concentrated stare from behind us, aimed right between my shoulder blades. Larriman was leading us, while Howley remained behind. I mulled over what he might be thinking. Was he getting ready to pounce as soon as we entered the interview room? Or would we be taken into separate rooms like before, giving them an opportunity to then go through our individual statements, looking for discrepancies? Larriman turned to me, breaking through my thoughts.

"Nicola, come in here, and we'll take your statement." I looked back at Dan and then at Howley.

"I thought with us both coming here in the same car that you would be taking our statement together."

"I'm sorry, but we have to take a statement from each individual person involved in that given situation," Howley answered. Although I hadn't meant to make my feelings quite so clear, I sneered at Howley.

"It's just the way things have to be done," he answered.

Making no attempt to reply, I walked in through the door Larriman was still holding open for me.

"Sit down, Nicola." My defences shot up immediately. Was this just his way of taking a statement, or did he actually think we had something to do with Greg's death?

"Now, if we can start at the beginning." And he looked at my blank expression. "From the time you arrived at..." – and he looked over his notes – "115 Morsley Road."

"Yeah, Dan's," I answered. "We walked there from their flat – that is, Dan and Mal's flat on Risely Road... 210 Risely Road," I corrected.

"And was his flat mate there when you both left?"

"Yes, both Mal and Tess, our other friends. Mallory Edwards and Tess Brinham," I added a little awkwardly.

"Did you see anyone you knew near the property?"

"No," I answered. "There was no one there when we arrived."

"So you checked the whole house before you discovered the body then?"

"No, of course we didn't, but there was no sign that there was anyone else there."

"And you both entered together?" he asked.

"Yes," I confirmed.

"And what happened after that, after you both entered?"

"Dan called out to his dad and carried on to the back of the house, to the sitting room. That's where we found him, just as he was when your lot arrived."

"You had blood all over your hands. Dan did too. Can you explain that, Nicola?"

Inwardly I laughed at the absurdity of his questions. "Is all this really necessary?" I asked.

"Yes, it is. Now please, Nicola, can you explain the blood?"

"Dan knelt by his dad, realising what had happened, that he was gone. He took him in his arms and cradled him. I think it was his way of saying goodbye. He was bereft; he had just lost his dad as well as his mum, and his sister before him. I don't think he was actually imagining how the blood might look when the police arrived!"

"Okay, thank you for that, Nicola," he responded, completely oblivious to what I had just said. Though I doubted it had gone unnoticed. "Now yours - can you explain the blood on your hands?"

"I tried to pull Dan away from his dad. I didn't think it was doing him any good, holding on to him the way he was. It was just after that, you lot turned up... If this, what's happened to Greg, had been our doing, do you seriously think we'd have waited around for you?"

"At this point, Nicola, I'm just taking your statement."

"So can I go now?"

"Yes, if you can just read through this to make sure everything's correct and that there isn't anything else you want to add." He passed me the paper. It was then, again, that it occurred to me that I hadn't mentioned anything about Jules. I broke off from reading any more.

"When Dan went around there yesterday to try to talk to his dad, Greg already had a visitor. It was Julia Harvey. Dan said they were both drinking. I don't know whether that's relevant."

"Well, we'll check it out. Can you give me her address?"

"Yeah, it's 23 Haran Street." He took the paper from me and began adding more to the statement I'd already given. Satisfied, he handed it back for me to continue checking.

"Yeah, that's fine," I responded. "Is that it?"

"Yes, for now. We may need to speak to you again, though."

"Yeah, sure," I answered, but I really hoped that was the end of the questioning. When I saw Larriman pushing his chair back and getting to his feet, my thoughts strayed once more to Dan. How had he got on with giving his statement? Was he out yet, waiting in reception for me? I didn't even know how long I'd been in here or even what time it was.

As Larriman opened the door for me to pass through to reception, my heart sank when I saw no one there. Dan must still be giving his statement. There was no way he'd have left here without me. I went and sat down on the grubby bench we'd all been sitting on while waiting to give our statements the day before. I couldn't relax. I dug my fingers into the leather to detract my attention, but it was no good. My mind was fixed. Nothing could enter, and nothing could escape. I jumped up from it, no longer able to just sit around. I approached the front desk and the cop who had surreptitiously been watching me ever since I appeared there from the interview room.

"Can you tell me what's happening with Daniel Trennan, please?" I felt jittery. I didn't even know whether he was still here.

"As far as I know, he's still giving his statement. He certainly hasn't come out here yet, and he will come out this way."

"Okay, thank you," I replied. At least I knew he was still here. But why was it taking so long?

I knew I couldn't ask him that. I looked nervous enough and felt it too. But it was stifling in here, just like last time. I approached the desk again.

"I'm just going outside. It's hot in here. Can you tell him I'm out there when he comes out, please?"

"Sure," he answered, swiftly dismissing me.

Finding a shaded spot on the steps leading up to the station's glass frontage felt infinitely cooler and a little calmer. But Dan still didn't show. I must have been sitting there for about twenty minutes. I was just about to go back in and ask why it was taking so long when I saw him talking to the cop at the desk. I stood up as he turned. He looked relieved to see me, and I definitely felt the same to see him. He came out, and I rushed into his arms.

"I don't want to go through that again," he said.

"Why? What happened?" I questioned.

"He wanted to know everything. Every slight detail. He was going on like maybe we had cooked it up between us."

"Yeah, Larriman wanted an explanation as to how you were covered in your dad's blood and why I had got it on my hands."

"That's just stupid. Don't they realise he was my dad? Adopted, yeah, but he was still my dad. What was I supposed to do? Just stand there and watch him? That's just what I said to Howley. As regards to the blood on you, Nic, I told him you tried to pull me away from my dad... Greg."

"Yeah, that's exactly what I said."

"Then we've got nothing to worry about, not that we have anyway, but they're going to want to stick this on someone."

"What about Jules?" I asked him. "Did you say anything about her, about her being around at your dad's place yesterday?"

"Yeah, I told them she might have been the last one to see him alive."

"But you can't know that, Dan."

"Yeah, I can. She got close to Charlotte, and then she died. Then she got close to my dad, and now he's dead. Who's next, eh?"

I didn't know what to say. Was he thinking that maybe he would be the next one? No, Jules was calculated, cruel even. But a murderer? No, no way.

"All of my family's gone, Nic, in only a matter of weeks. I'm the only one left. Am I next?"

"No." And I gave a feeble laugh. "Dan, we don't even know that Charlotte or your dad died at the hands of anyone else. For all we know, their deaths could have been the result of accidents, terrible tragedies."

"It seems strange though, doesn't it? All my family wiped out, okay, separately, but it still only leaves me."

I wanted to tell him it didn't, that he wasn't alone. That agreement we had made about going to social services to begin the search for his birth mum was still playing on my mind. But would he thank me for going on about it now? Probably not. I wondered whether it was worth holding off until both Charlotte's and Greg's funerals were out of the way. Maybe now there would be a double one. They'd died separately, but they were still father and daughter. Would Dan be left to arrange everything? I wanted to say something more, but I figured it was probably prudent to get him back to Mal and Tess. At least there we would be with our friends. Maybe there it would be easier to talk this over. Maybe we could all help him through this.

When I suggested we go straight back to the flat, he eagerly agreed. I think he was thinking along the same lines. There we could talk openly where we knew we would be supported.

Taking his keys out of his pocket, Dan unlocked the door leading to the flats. We managed to get halfway up when we heard the flat door being opened and both of them calling to us over the banister.

"Is that you, Dan… Nic?"

"Yeah, won't be a minute," Dan called back.

When we reached the top, they both looked worried sick.

"Where have you been?" Tess asked. "What happened at your dad's, Dan? You've been gone so long."

"And where's the rest of your stuff?" Mal added.

"Can we sit down first?" he replied. "I'm a bit tired." And he did sound really exhausted.

They followed us into the flat and loitered, waiting for me or Dan to put them out of their misery and explain what had happened. Dan looked at me, wondering whether I'd kick things off. I shook my head.

"It's best coming from you, Dan."

"My dad's dead," he blurted out. Just like that, no build up, nothing.

191

"What?" Mal said, disbelieving. Tess was just as dumbstruck.

"He can't be," she responded.

"Why?" Dan asked. "We found him when we went around there, didn't we, Nic?"

"Yeah, he was just laid there, still as the... Well, you know."

"W-what happened?" Mal questioned.

"We don't know," I told him. "We just found him. There was no one else there. I phoned for an ambulance, and the cops turned up seconds after them." Both of them were shaking their heads almost in unison, unable to process what we were telling them.

"It's hard to believe, isn't it?" Dan said.

"Yeah," was all Mal could manage to say.

"I'm really sorry, Dan," Tess said at last. "What about the police? What are they doing?"

"We went with them to give our statements. At the house they were waiting for forensics to turn up, so we went back with them. It was Larriman and Howley again."

"Don't tell me they suspect you both," Tess questioned.

"I hope not," Dan responded. "Our statements were the same, so they shouldn't, but like I said to Nic, they'll want to pin it on someone."

"We mentioned that Jules was there with Greg yesterday," I said. "I think they'll be going around to have a word before long."

"Why? What did you say?" Tess asked.

"Just that she was with Greg when Dan went around there yesterday... and that you said they were both drinking," I said to Dan.

"Yeah, they were." Dan nodded. "And I told them she might have been the last one to see him alive."

Tess's mouth was agape at the enormity of what Dan had just said. "Do you really believe that?" she asked excitedly.

"Enough, Tess. We don't know when he died let alone in what circumstances or who, if anyone, was actually there... Now, can we change the subject?" I asked, seeing the drained and dejected expression on Dan's face.

"Yeah," Mal agreed. "That is enough for now."

"I'm sorry, Dan, truly I am," Tess said. "We've just been so worried about you both. We couldn't figure out what had happened, why you were taking so long."

"It's all right." He turned to Mal. "I'm gonna go and lie down for a bit. Are you two staying?" he said to me and Tess.

"Yes, absolutely," I assured him.

"Definitely, me too," Tess agreed.

"I'll see you in a bit then," he said and walked out of the room.

Once he'd left, I began relaying to Mal and Tess the sort of questions Larriman and Howley had bombarded us with.

Chapter Sixteen
Unexpected Visitor

We all talked long into the evening about what had happened, not just about Greg but also about me and Dan; and we discussed what, if anything, was going to come of the statements we'd made earlier. I managed to broach the subject of Charlotte and Greg's funeral arrangements. What was Dan going to do about them?

"Sounds stupid, but I hadn't thought about that," Mal answered.

"I suppose it is reasonable to assume that it'll be a double funeral now, don't you think?" Tess suggested, agreeing with what I had openly wondered about.

"Well, it would certainly follow, but we'll have to wait until Dan gets up to confirm. It's at least a possibility though."

"How is he, really?" Mal asked. "He seems to be taking all this a little too well."

"Yeah, that's my worry," I agreed.

"So we need to address it with him. It's not like he's got anyone else, has he?" And Tess quickly looked my way. "Everyone he's ever counted as family is dead; within a few short weeks, he's been left completely on his own. That's got to have left some sort of mark on him. Has he said anything about it to you, Nic?"

"Only what I've told you two – that he's convinced Jules must have had something to do with Greg's and maybe even Charlotte's death as well. His mind's fixed on the fact that she got close to Charlotte and then she died, and the same happened with Greg, and now he's dead. I know you're of a similar mind where Jules is concerned, Tess, but none of us can know she had anything to do with Charlotte or Greg's death, or as yet how they actually did die."

"Yeah, I know, and I do take your point, but we don't know she didn't either."

"So what happens now?" I asked.

"Well, it's getting late," Tess said, "and there's no sign that Dan's about to make an appearance anytime soon, so I'm going to make a move. What about you, Nic?"

"Yeah, maybe it would be better to let him sleep through. I think enough's happened today without more questions from us."

"Do you want me to drive you both home?" Mal offered.

"No," I replied. "The walk will clear my head." Tess refused as well, saying much the same.

"Come around again in the morning, whenever you're ready," he said. "He'll probably need us all then, and I'll try to broach the subject of what's going to happen regarding both funerals, though until they release both bodies, nothing can happen."

After I left Tess, my pace picked up, and I was home a lot quicker than I had ever made it before. It was after nine, and my mum was once again pacing the kitchen.

"I didn't think they would keep you out this long," she said. "Where have you been?"

I'd completely forgotten about my mum since I'd walked out with Mal and Dan this morning.

"You should have rung me," I said, hoping that would reassure her, even though it was a bit late in the day to be saying it.

"I tried, Nicola, but your phone was switched off!"

"Oh, God, yeah!" I had completely forgotten to switch it back on when we came out of the police station, and Tess and Mal hadn't mentioned it when we got back to the flat. "I'm sorry, Mum."

"So... where have you been? What have you been doing?" she pressed. I took a deep breath.

There was more than one thing to tell her.

"It's Dan's dad, Greg, Mum... He's dead."

"What?"

"After I had made up with Tess, I went around to Greg's with Dan to give him a bit of moral support and to get the rest of his stuff to take back to Mal's, because they agreed that Dan would move in there. I did tell you what happened the day before, didn't I?"

"No, I don't think so. I don't know. I can't keep up with you."

"Well, Greg more or less kicked Dan out, with Jules listening from the sidelines."

"Oh!"

"Yeah, well, that's another story. I saw Dan when I was walking past on my way from Tess's, after she had asked me to leave. You remember – we fell out."

"Yeah, that bit I remember."

"Well, when I got back here, I obviously must have told you all about Tess but omitted what had gone off with Dan."

"So what happened to Greg then?"

"Well, like I was saying, after Tess and I had made up, I walked over with Dan to fetch the rest of his stuff. As we walked in, Dan called out to his dad. He didn't want the arguments and recriminations that had taken place the day before starting up again. We began to walk through the house to the sitting room at the back, as Dan had the day before; that's where Greg had been with Jules, and he naturally thought that was where he would be again. We were about halfway through when Dan saw Greg's body slumped by the door, just inside of it. He was already dead."

"Oh, God, Nic." She rushed to me, pulling me to her. Her embrace felt good, reassuring. "Come and sit down." I hadn't realised until now how utterly worn out I felt.

"So what happened?" she persisted. "Did the police come...? The ambulance?"

"Yeah... Mum, can we talk about this tomorrow? I'm really tired."

"Of course, we can," she said and ushered me up the stairs. "I'll be up in a minute." If she did, I wasn't aware of it. As soon as I was horizontal, I didn't remember another thing.

I woke to the light just beginning to filter through my curtains. It felt really early. I peered out the window. There was still dew on the grass. I sat back on my bed with the intention of trying to get back to sleep, but thoughts of Charlotte suddenly flooded me – and with her, Greg, lying there still as the grave. It felt creepy, but I couldn't push the image of him slumped on the carpet like that out of my head.

Deciding a lie-in was the last thing I needed, I headed downstairs and ate my hastily prepared breakfast. I hadn't quite finished when my mum joined me at the kitchen table.

"Do you want to talk now?"

"Not really. I want to get back around to Dan and Mal's."

"I would rather you took it easy today, Nic."

"I will. We're just hanging out at their flat."

"Who's we? You and Tess?" she asked.

"Yeah, there's nothing wrong with that, is there?"

"No, I just want to know that you're okay – really okay."

"I am, Mum. It was just the shock of seeing him like that. I'll come back home earlier, all right?"

"Well, this time I want you to sit down and talk to me, yes?"

"Yeah, okay." And after the obligatory hug, I snuck out the door before she found some other reason to keep me there.

Deciding to walk instead of calling Mal to pick me up, as he'd offered, made me feel better.

The morning sun was still subdued. It felt good, fresh. I rang Tess on the off chance that she was still home.

"Hey, Nic. Yeah, actually I'm ready now. I was just thinking of setting off. There's nothing to do here."

"Do you want to meet up half way? I'm on my way too," I said.

"Okay, wait for me at the junction down the road from Mal and Dan's."

"Will do." And I hung up.

Dan was still very much on my mind. Both Tess and I had left before he had surfaced last night, and he hadn't rung me at home either. Maybe he had slept straight through; it wasn't like he didn't need it.

It took me a little over half an hour to reach the junction, but Tess was still nowhere in sight. I leaned against the wall across from it to wait for her. I had been there about ten minutes when she came into view.

"I didn't think you would be about this early, especially with what happened yesterday," she commented.

"I couldn't sleep. I had images of Charlotte and Greg going around in my head."

"Oh, Nic, why are you here? Wouldn't you be better off at home?"

"No, I want to see Dan, Tess. I want to make sure he's okay."

"Yeah, I can understand that. Come on then. I'm famished. I've had no breakfast. They can at least supply us with that, eh?"

"Um… burned toast and a cup of tea," I commented, not really feeling it.

"Don't knock it. I'm starving!"

Arriving at Risely Road, Tess pressed the buzzer to their flat.

"You going to let us in?" she questioned.

"Give us chance. We've only just surfaced, but yeah, come on up." And Mal buzzed the door open, allowing our entry. Giving a quick rap on the door to let them know we were there, I opened it. We had barely got in through the door before we were bombarded with questions.

"So what are we going to do about Jules?" Mal asked. "We still don't know where she was, do we? And I for one would like to try to find out. Wouldn't you two?"

"Yeah, I'm in," Tess replied enthusiastically.

"Great," Dan joined in as he walked through from his bedroom. "I'm glad we're doing something."

"Well, I don't think that's quite been decided," I responded.

"Are you in agreement, Mal?" Tess asked, bypassing me.

"Yeah, I'm sorry, Nic," he apologised, forcing his attention back in my direction. "But we need to try and find out – for Dan's sake, if nothing else. It's not that we believe she had anything to do with either of their deaths, but she's offered no explanation at all as to where she was when you tried ringing her when we were looking for Charlotte, or even when Greg died."

"To be fair, has anyone tried to contact her?" Everyone's head dipped in response. "Tess?" I asked.

"No, I haven't," she said, keeping her voice low. Mal shook his head in answer, and Dan shook his head too.

"Then shouldn't we be trying to bring her back into the fold and give her a chance to explain things?" I asked.

"You really think she will?" Tess asked.

"It's at least worth a try, isn't it?" I asked.

"Okay," she agreed at last. But I had no chance of saying any more since the intercom was buzzing from the main door downstairs.

"Who's that? You're not expecting anyone, are you?" Tess questioned Mal and then Dan.

"No one," Dan answered.

"Me neither," Mal said.

"Is someone going to answer it then?" I asked impatiently. Dan got up and took the handset from its casing on the wall.

"Yep?" he inquired.

I looked at Tess, amused by his choice of greeting. She had been having the same thought and returned my smile.

"Er, yeah, come on up," he answered, buzzing the door open before replacing the handset.

"So?" Tess butted in. "Who is it?"

"Jules," he answered. "She's coming up."

"What?" she responded.

"Now's our opportunity to bring her back into the fold," I suggested.

Mal stood up and was about to open the door when she knocked on it. Opening it, she made no attempt to walk through. Instead, she looked only at Mal.

"Can I come in?" she asked. He made an attempt to look back at Dan for his agreement, but his face gave nothing away. He turned back quickly to Jules.

"Sure, come in." He smiled. Walking past Mal in amongst us, she was acting really weird, like we were strangers to her, ready to pounce or something.

"Sit down," Mal suggested, offering his own chair. The air felt electrically charged, as though something was about to blow.

"H-how are you?" I asked a little too tentatively.

"I'm tired, Nic," she answered evenly. "I'm tired from all the questions the police have been throwing my way about your father, Dan."

"What did they want to know?" he asked, deliberately not making eye contact with her.

"They kept going on about the day before yesterday when you came around and saw me there. They asked me what time I left him and whether I had seen him again later. They also asked about how we got on. They seemed to be under the impression that you didn't like me very much, and they wanted to know why that might have been. Had you fallen out with your dad because of me?"

"I told them you were there. So what?" Dan responded.

"Jules," I began, "we've no idea where you were the night we were searching for Charlotte, and you've never offered any explanation— "

"What's it got to do with you anyway where I was? The police know where I was, and they seem satisfied with my explanation, so isn't that enough?"

"Jules, it would help everyone if you would just tell us. We all need to move on from this. We all need each other. We're all friends, aren't we?"

"All the questioning felt like you had hung me out to dry. You two found Greg, didn't you?" she said, focusing on me and Dan.

"Yeah, we found my dad," Dan pointed out.

"I'm sorry, Dan, about Greg," Jules responded. "It must be hard losing not only him but Charlotte and your mum as well."

I could feel him tensing at Jules's words. I touched his arm, hoping it would defuse any reply he was about to shoot back in her direction. He turned slightly, acknowledging me before addressing her.

"Thanks," he said. "I appreciate that."

She smiled like he had suddenly given her the world.

"Maybe we could talk about your dad sometime," Jules suggested.

I felt him tense up again.

"That might be good, Dan," I concurred. "Maybe in a few days, when the rawness has lessened a little."

"Er, yeah, maybe." And he nodded to Jules for her agreement.

"Okay, it's a date then!" she said.

"Er…" Dan sounded lost.

"We're all right now, aren't we?" Tess jumped in, realising the conversation was about to stall. She also wanted to divert Jules's attention away from Dan. Her attention, as both Tess and I had hoped, switched, giving me a chance to quietly smooth things with Dan. He met my gaze and shook his head.

"Later," I whispered to him. He seemed to understand what I was saying and took a deep breath, maybe letting me know he still wasn't happy about it.

"I hope so," Jules replied to Tess.

"Well, it's good to have you back," Mal said, his tone warm and welcoming. Although the thought that had suddenly jumped into my head was completely bonkers, it nonetheless occurred to me what a good actor he would make, seeing this performance in full flow, if his future financial career were ever to crash and burn, and inwardly I laughed at the absurdity of it. That is, until Jules began speaking again.

"So, Dan, do you want to give me your mobile number now? I think it's changed and I can ring you in a few days when things have had a chance to settle down," she said, smiling and glancing my way.

"Er, yeah, okay." And he fumbled for his phone.

"I'll tell you the number, Jules," I offered after collecting myself. It was already safely stowed away in her contacts section before Dan had managed to get to his. She ran through the number just to make sure I hadn't changed at least one digit and then rang it just to double-check.

"It is right," Tess said as his phone bleeped in confirmation. "Dan won't know it anyway. He doesn't even know Nic's, let alone the numbers of the rest of us," she told her, making her point.

"Okay, that's fine then." And she got up.

"Where are you going?" Tess questioned.

"I've got a lot to do, Tess. I was only ever nipping over here for a short while," she explained and then turned to Dan.

"I'll speak to you in a couple of days, and we can get together." And I'm not sure whether it was for my benefit or just for Dan's, but she squeezed his thigh. He instantly grabbed my hand, but she ignored that gesture and carried on as though his attention were solely on her.

"Speak soon then," she added huskily and then turned to the rest of us, gushing her goodbyes. Mal accompanied her to the door, telling her not to leave it too long next time and said we would ring soon to arrange a get-together.

After Mal closed the door, Dan almost busted a gut with excuses as to why he couldn't possibly meet up with her.

"I don't think you're gonna have much choice, mate." Mal laughed.

"I'm not meeting her!" he said finally.

"Dan, he's only playing with you," I said. "You're going to be the only one she's likely to tell where she was that night when we were looking for Charlotte."

"Yeah, but at what cost?"

"Your body, it looks like." And Mal chuckled again, knowing how much Dan must have been squirming.

"Please, haven't I been through enough?" Dan implored.

I looked at Mal for a bit of support.

"Look, mate," Mal responded. "I'll come with you when you meet her, but I'll stay out of the way. If she comes on too strong, then I'll step in, yeah?"

"I suppose that's as good as I'm gonna get," he replied, backing down.

"Don't complain. I haven't even got one woman after me." And then he sheepishly looked over at Tess, remembering what had happened with her.

"You don't deserve anyone, Mal" I rebuked. Tess stayed in the background, both physically and by staying well out of the conversation.

"Go and make a cup of tea, Mal," I light-heartedly ordered. But he knew why I had said it. Once he was out of the way, with Dan helping him, I sidled up to her.

"You okay?"

"He doesn't see me like that at all, does he?"

"No, he doesn't." Her expression dropped even more than it had when Mal had made that last comment. "Hey, cheer up. I haven't finished yet. He thinks a whole lot more of you than that. I told you last time – give it time. He'll come round, and besides, there's so much more to you. Everyone knows that despite what Mal protests; it's just you who doesn't."

"Thanks, Nic."

"Anytime, buddy."

"Right, there you go, and you can make the next one," Mal teased.

"Actually, Tess and I are going after this cup, and then I'm going to make my way home," I told them both. "But if you're lucky, I might make one if I come back over tomorrow."

"If?" Dan quizzed.

"Neither of us have been asked back yet."

Dan looked crestfallen as if he'd done something to upset us, but then Mal jumped in.

"Nic's just trying to be funny, Dan… and failing miserably!" he added and then turned to me.

"It's not working," he said triumphantly.

"Okay," I replied and turned to Tess. "You ready once we've drunk these?"

"Sure," and she smiled.

"You are coming around tomorrow, aren't you?" Dan asked in all seriousness.

"'Course I am." I threw my arms around him, kissing him full on the lips.

"Phew," he exclaimed. I smiled at his relief. We all stayed like that for the next hour, and we would have, for longer, but I remembered my mum, the assurance I'd given her, and what I'd already said to Tess about our departure after finishing our drinks. I turned again to Dan.

"I had better go. I'll see you in the morning, okay?"

"You could stay," he whispered. My smile broadened.

"I really can't," I answered. He sighed but reluctantly released me from his arms.

Mal harrumphed. We both looked back at him and Tess sheepishly before smiling broadly. It was good to get back to some semblance of normality.

"So I'll see you in the morning." I smiled and bit my lower lip at what had been clandestinely suggested. Extricating myself, I turned to Tess.

"You ready then?"

"Yes," she said, exasperated. "I thought we were going ages ago."

"Um, sorry," I apologised.

"And you two had better start making plans about how you're going to extract that information from Jules because, as well as Mal, we won't be far away either, Dan," Tess told them both before following me out of the door.

"How about us spending the afternoon in town?" I suggested.

"Yeah, I could do that." So, on leaving Dan and Mal, we headed straight into town and did a spot of clothes shopping – or rather Tess did. Mine was more along the lines of window shopping. Following her around the rails did feel a tad tedious, but it took both our minds off everything and everyone connected with what had happened over the last few weeks. Tess's mind was firmly fixed on what she was searching for. Mine, however, had wandered. My attention drifted over to a woman who had been watching us for several minutes, though Tess remained oblivious to her. I raised my eyes and turned to Tess.

"Do you – ?"

"What? Do I what?" she questioned, looking back at me.

"There was a woman..."

But before I could finish, she interrupted. "There are quite a few in here, Nic."

"No, there was a woman over there, watching us, but she's gone now."

"Who?" she said, looking around. "What did she look like?"

"I didn't get a good look at her. I think she had light-brown hair."

"What? She probably just thought she recognised us. We are pretty unforgettable, you know."

"Oh, never mind. It's probably just my mind working overtime."

"Just probably?" she questioned, and laughed.

Chapter Seventeen
Arrangements

"Wow, you were serious, weren't you? I didn't quite expect you back this soon," my mum called as soon as I opened the front door.

"I spent part of the afternoon with Tess, just me and her in Furham, clothes shopping. It's been nice for a change."

"Did you buy anything?"

"Tess did, but I didn't have any money. Saw a lot of things I'd like to buy though." I had expected her to say that she'd give me some money or take me into Furham to have a look, but I didn't get either.

"What are the boys doing?" she said instead.

"Mal was going to try and broach the subject of the funeral arrangements with Dan after we left last night, but nothing's been said, so I would think he's still working on it, though, to be fair, maybe it would be easier for him to talk with us out of the way."

"Um, good thinking," she agreed. "Now, are you going to tell me what happened with Greg, like you said you would first thing this morning?"

"Can I sit down first?"

"Of course. I've put your dinner aside. Do you want a cup of tea as well?"

"Please, Mum."

Giving me chance to finish the last of my dinner, I spied her watching for her chance to begin questioning me.

"You want me to tell you what happened now, right?"

"You make it sound like I'm waiting to interrogate you." I laughed at her half-hearted attempt at humour, but my expression sobered when I saw the seriousness that accompanied her words.

"So?" she said, waiting.

"Well, after Tess and I made up, Dan said that he still had some stuff he needed to pick up from home that Greg hadn't thrown out onto the drive the day before. I said I would walk around there with him. When we arrived, it seemed peaceful enough. Dan tried the door because he thought it might be locked, but it wasn't. Maybe that should have told us something, but it didn't. I followed him in. He called out to his dad straight away, but there was no answer. He figured he would be in the same room at the back of the house as he had been the day before when he walked in on him and Jules."

"He walked in on them?" And her eyes widened.

"Not like that, Mum… She was just there." I think she had expected something a bit juicier before the main event; it certainly seemed so by the tone of her voice.

"Oh… Go on then. Sorry."

"Yeah, um… Where was I?" I had completely lost track with how my mother had reacted.

"Dan thought Greg would be in the same room he and Jules had been in the day before," she recapped.

"Oh, yeah. Well, I followed him through; he kept calling out to him, even after the way Greg had been with him. A little way in we saw him by the door. He was just lying there." My thoughts strayed back to the image of him slumped there, so still, so final.

"Are you all right, Nic?" Her voice slowly penetrated through the fog of my thinking. I turned to her from somewhere deep within, reacting to the comforting tone.

"Yes, I was just thinking back to — "

"Have you had enough? Don't you want to talk anymore?"

"No, it's not that. I just keep getting glimpses of Greg's body slumped there." A cog in my mind suddenly clicked, snapping me back to my surroundings. "Dan rushed to him, wouldn't leave his side until he was pulled away by the ambulance crew, and then I led him away outside, accompanied by the cops."

"So what happened after that?"

"Well, we had to wait a while, and then they suggested we go down to the police station with them to make our statements while the events were still fresh in our minds."

"And you just accepted that?" She seemed shocked and horrified that I'd done such a thing. I rolled my eyes, an act that only served to inflame her further. "Nic, even if you were still level headed after what you had seen, I'm sure Dan wasn't. That shouldn't have been suggested at all!"

"I did say it wasn't right. I said that Dan wasn't in any fit state to give a statement, that it was his dad lying there, but he said it was okay. He said he just wanted to get it over with. What more could I do? And besides, we just told them what happened, exactly what happened," I added when she gave me that look. "We made sure to check with each other about what had been said, and we both said the same things. Actually, Mum," I said, thinking back to Greg. "Did you know much about him? Greg, I mean. What was he like? You know, his character?"

"I didn't know him very well, but from what I did know, he wasn't a very nice man, certainly not to his wife anyway."

"Fran."

She nodded.

"I thought they were really happy as a family. It hit them all really hard when she died." Though after what Dan had already told me, that happiness hadn't extended to him, at least where Greg was concerned.

"I'm sure it did," she agreed. "But not when Greg was younger." But she stopped at that.

"That's not all of it, is it?"

She had begun to tell me something I had no intention of allowing her to cut short.

"He just had a number of affairs, that's all," she said.

"And?"

"Isn't that enough, Nic?"

"He had more than enough then," I guessed.

"Well, like I said, I didn't know him very well. I knew a couple of the women he had affairs with – that's all. He and Fran adopted Dan, as you know, and that seemed to make things a lot better. He seemed to settle down after that. They had been unable to have any children. Maybe that's why he did what he did – the affairs, I mean. But then Charlotte came along naturally. That's all there is really. From my point of view, that's all I can really give you. He just wasn't a particularly nice man, and I still hold that view, even though he's dead now. That's why I didn't attend her funeral. From what I knew of her – and it was very little – she seemed decent enough. Why do you ask anyway?"

"No reason really. It's just that when I went around there to do some college work with Dan and we worked in his office, he seemed suspicious somehow when we came out. I asked Dan if he had any cameras installed in there. I know it sounds really stupid, but it's just a feeling I got."

"Well, you don't have to worry any more, do you?"

I nodded. She was right. He wasn't going to do me any harm from where he was now. But something else bothered me.

"Why didn't you tell me any of this about Greg before?"

"It never came up, and you always seemed to get on all right with him. And besides, it would hardly have been fair on Dan, would it? Or Fran come to that. After all, she was still alive when you both got together."

"Yeah, I suppose you've got a point," I agreed. "I was – "But at that point my phone rang.

"What's he ringing for?" I puzzled out loud.

"What's the matter?" my mum asked. "Who's ringing?"

"It's Mal," I answered as I opened the call. "Hey, Mal. There's nothing wrong with Dan, is there?"

"No, don't worry, Nic. He's fine. Actually he's gone back to bed – he's exhausted. But he's had a phone call from the funeral directors. Both Greg and Charlotte's bodies are going to be released. He's going down there to arrange everything in the morning. He wanted me to ring you to ask if you would go down there with him."

"Yeah, 'course I will. What time will he be there?"

"Well, I'm driving him into Furham, so I'll pick you up. His appointment's booked in for ten. We'll pick you up between nine thirty and nine forty-five. Is that okay?"

"That's fine. Thanks, Mal."

"Any time. Are you coming back here afterwards?"

"Yeah, I would think so. But I'll see you in the morning, and thanks again."

"I'll leave him to sleep now, but I'll tell him that we're picking you up in the morning. He'll be really pleased. I think all of this is beginning to take its toll. He's going to need us all more than he realised. Anyway, Nic, see you in the morning," he said before ending the call.

I put my phone down by my side. I knew Dan seemed to be handling all this a little too well. I sighed heavily, immediately alerting my mum. She was getting ready to bombard me with questions again. I wasn't wrong. They began immediately.

"What was Mal saying?"

"The funeral directors have been in touch with Dan. He's got an appointment to sort out all the arrangements tomorrow morning. He asked Mal to ring to see if I would go down there with him."

"And?"

"Well, I'm going, of course."

"Nic, don't you think Dan should be doing this on his own?"

"Oh, yeah. He's got people queuing up to help him, hasn't he?"

"That's not what I mean, and you know it!"

"I'm sorry, but he wants me there, Mum, and I'm not going to let him down." I got up and walked through to the kitchen. She followed me.

"Look, I'm sorry, Nic. I'm just worried about you. You've been through so much over the last few weeks. I know it's Dan's parents and sister, but you're my daughter, and I hate to see you going through all this."

"I know, but I need to be there for him."

"I know, but just remember I'm here if you need me, okay?"

"I do know that." And I put my arms around her. She was concerned about how much I could handle – I could see that. But Dan needed me, and I wasn't about to turn my back on him now.

"I'm going to go to bed, Mum. It'll be a hard enough day tomorrow anyway, and I need to sleep."

That sleep came quickly once I got settled down. Immediately I closed my eyes everything went blank, every thought just drifted away and I felt myself sinking into unconsciousness. But too soon I saw something jump from the shadows. At first I felt too tired to care, to even raise a flicker of interest; but it remained, continuing to shift from my field of vision. My focus eventually concentrated on what appeared to be a sphere of light. Very slowly it moved, but as it did, it left a trail, an outline of someone. I remembered seeing the image of Greg lying there. I tried to shake it off, but the light only grew stronger. The theatre again came into view, and I saw Charlotte lying there. I looked more closely at the sphere of light. From it she came into view in my mind.

The surroundings were changing. From the darkness, wood panelling was appearing; I was in their house on Morsley Road. Charlotte shot across my eyeline once more and disappeared into Greg's office. I wanted to follow, but I didn't want to be there, anywhere, in that house. I tried to get back to the front door to see daylight, but I couldn't reach it. My feet were rooted. I was unable to put one foot in front of the other. She reappeared, holding something. I couldn't make out what it was. She was holding it out to me and smiling. I was so close and yet she was willing me to break free and walk towards her. I reached out... I did it. I had taken that first step, but I couldn't understand. Was I outside? Light flooded my senses. I didn't want to open my eyes though; the power it radiated felt blinding until I heard someone...

"Nicola!"

Sleepily I looked up. It was my mum. "Where... What?"

"Oh, my God, Nic, you've fallen out of bed! What are you doing?" The look on her face seemed to confirm everything she'd said to me earlier. "You were calling out to Charlotte, I think. This has got to stop, Nic. I don't want you to go tomorrow. He's not being fair to you. He's expecting too much!"

"Mum, I'm fine. Everyone dreams," I told her, and I got myself back up and into bed.

"Not like this, they don't."

"Please, will you just let me go back to sleep?"

"Okay, but please have a lie-in tomorrow."

"Um," I responded sleepily. I heard her close the door. I quickly switched my lamp on.

Setting my clock for eight, I slumped down again and closed my eyes. Sleep came quickly though Charlotte thankfully didn't return.

The shrill cry of the alarm shook me from my sleep. I grabbed it and silenced it before my mum could come in and demand I stay put. I sat on the side of the bed, trying to ward off the urge to jump back in and lie there for another ten minutes. I knew if I did, I would still be there way after nine thirty when Mal and Dan were due to pick me up. Wearily I left the comfort of my bed and wandered into the bathroom for a shower. The feel of the cool water cascading over my body refreshed me instantly.

Switching it off, I heard my mum moving about downstairs. She wouldn't be happy that I was getting ready for when they were picking me up. Once I was done, I headed straight down. Better, I thought, to face her wrath now than to wait upstairs and head straight out as soon as I saw Mal's car. I'd still have to face her later when I got home. Otherwise she would only be on my mind for the rest of the day.

"I thought you were having a lie-in?" she demanded.

"I didn't say that, did I?"

"Well, not in so many words, Nic, but you were dog tired at two this morning when I came in.

"Well, at two in the morning, I would have been!"

"I didn't mean tired. I meant about having another dream – or rather a nightmare."

"Loads of people do, Mum."

"Not the way you were, Nic, and they're getting more frequent."

"Please, can we just drop this? They'll lessen with the more time that passes."

"What are they about anyway?" she asked.

I looked out of the window, hoping the appearance of Mal's Mini might save me from this, but he was still nowhere in sight.

"Charlotte and the old theatre on Brompton Road," I said instead.

"What? All the time?"

"Mostly, yeah, but not entirely. The inside of the theatre is predominant in most of them."

"So what happened in your dream last night?" my mum questioned. There was no way of avoiding this; maybe by telling her, she would begin to understand.

"My sleep came quickly, I drifted into it, and I could feel myself falling, and then everything went blank. I don't know whether any time had passed, but I saw something come from out of the shadows. I can't explain it any better than that. But a ball of light appeared, and as it moved, it left a trail like someone walking, a figure."

"And you think it was Charlotte?"

"It was," I corrected. "Eventually I saw it was her. Then we were in the theatre, and I saw where she was laid, where we found her. But then the surroundings changed, and I was surrounded by the wood panelling in Dan's hallway at his home on Morsley Road. Charlotte was still there, but she disappeared into Greg's office. I didn't want to follow; I didn't even want to be in that house again. I tried to get back outside into the light. I could see it. I remember taking a step, that first step towards her. She was holding something out to me, but I couldn't quite reach her. I

213

think it means something," I told her. But I could tell, from the way she was looking at me, that she thought I had finally gone completely mad.

"So, when are Mal and Dan picking you up?" she asked, completely ignoring what I had said about the dream meaning something.

"About half past nine," I answered. I really thought I was beginning to get to a place where she was finally starting to understand where I was coming from.

"Please, just be careful, Nic." But at that moment Mal's car pulled up.

"I've got to go." I looked at her. "I'm fine, really, Mum."

She nodded, but she didn't look convinced.

I made my way outside before Dan had a chance to get to our front door. I looked back before I reached the car. She was watching from the kitchen window. I waved, but she just nodded.

"Hey," I said to Dan, throwing my arms around him. He waved to my mum who, at least this time, made an attempt at a smile.

"Is she okay?" he asked as we turned to get into the car.

"Yeah, she's just worried about me with what's been happening." And I rolled my eyes.

"She's right to be, Nic. I worry about you as well."

"I'm fine… Really," I added when he threw me the same look my mum had only minutes before.

"Hey, Mal," I greeted breezily as I climbed into the backseat, ignoring any more concern Dan was casting in my direction. I looked back at the house as we pulled off, thinking Mum would still be there at the window, but she had disappeared from view.

"Hey, Nic. You both still coming back to the flat after you've finished at the funeral directors?"

"We will, but there's something I want to do first," Dan answered. "We'll be a while, so don't expect us anytime soon, yeah?"

"Okay, mate."

I wanted to say that I had said all that without even moving my mouth once.

Hadn't Mal just spoken to me? Dan had got something into his head to do, but what it was, I had no idea.

"Will Tess be coming around?" I said instead.

"I've no idea," Mal answered. "She often just turns up, though I am working for a few hours a little later at the golf club, so, depending on what time you're back, you'll probably have a bit of time to yourselves."

"I'll see you again some time today though," I said, trying to keep the conversation light.

"Yep, you probably will," he responded, smiling through the rear-view mirror before bringing the car to a stop.

Having freed myself from the confines of his Mini, I waited until he had pulled off again before I turned my attention to Dan.

"Where are we going after the funeral directors?"

"Can we just get this over with please, and then I'll tell you?"

It all sounded a bit cloak-and-dagger, but what other choice did I have? Reluctantly, I agreed. He seemed preoccupied this morning, but I didn't have time to venture into that any further before the funeral directors came into view.

From the oak surround of the reception desk, we were led up the stairs and into an office to make the arrangements for Greg and Charlotte's funerals. Whether they would be joint ones or separate, I had no idea, but I guessed I would find out shortly.

"Sit down, please," we were encouraged by a man of medium height; he was very solemn in his gestures. I figured he was one of the more senior members of this firm or maybe even the most senior. Why do all funeral employees have this persona? I thought, losing myself in yet another daydream. It's almost as if there's a manual they all follow for the stuffy and solemn – to the letter of the law – and I inwardly laughed at my inner monologue running away with me again.

"Nic... Nic!" My eyes shot straight to Dan.

"S-sorry. What?"

"I said it would be better to have a double funeral for Charlotte and my dad, don't you think?"

"Yes," I answered, and I looked at the guy before us, conveying my apologies. "I think that would be nice. They'll be together." But then I immediately regretted saying what I just had with Dan sitting there. After all, he had been part of the family too.

"Obviously there will be separate coffins," the man explained in all seriousness.

"Oh, yes, I know. I didn't mean…" And my mind started to drift again, though I was careful to remain looking as though I was actually listening. I heard bits and pieces and agreed with Dan where he needed me to, and finally the guy stood up, signalling that we were finished with all the arrangements in place. We both again shook hands with him before he led us back down the stairs, where he held the door open and shook our hands once more, again offering his condolences, before saying goodbye.

Walking a little way up the road, I took my phone out. It was going on twelve.

"We've been in there two hours?" I said, amazed at how long we'd actually been there.

"It went quick, didn't it?"

"Yeah," I agreed, though most of it had been lost on me.

"Are you hungry?"

"Ravenous," I replied.

"We'll grab a sandwich on the way then." I stopped. I had forgotten about the conversation I wanted to have before we went in to the funeral directors.

"On the way where? Where exactly are we going, Dan?"

"Home. I just want to go back there… I need to, Nic. Please?" He added, noticing my reticence. I reluctantly agreed, figuring he would go with or without me.

Chapter Eighteen
Messages

My apprehension grew more acute the closer we approached Morsley Road. I had to hasten my pace just to keep up. Dan had gone quiet as well, withdrawing again somewhere I wasn't permitted. I wanted to ask why we were going there, but what would be the point? It seemed obvious anyway. He needed to feel close to them again. Even with the way Greg had been with him during those last days, Dan must still miss the pull of his family.

"Do you want me to come back to the flat with you after we've done here?" I asked for no other reason than to make conversation, and I was beginning to wonder why I was here at all.

Nothing had been said between us since we'd finished the sandwiches we had picked up before leaving Furham on the way to his house.

"Yeah, 'course. Why?"

"Because you've been really quiet since we left the funeral directors. I just wondered whether you'd rather be on your own."

"It's just everything that's happened. I can't get my head around it. I don't even feel as though I can grieve, not for Greg anyway. Charlotte's different. To be honest, I'm trying not to think too much about her." I knew what he meant. If you didn't think about her, then it wasn't quite real, and maybe nothing had happened. But then again I saw her in my dreams.

From where in my imagination my dreams came from, I wasn't quite sure. Was I the one bringing her in? Was everything that was going on in my head while I was asleep real? But I had followed her. Didn't I already have my answer?

"Now who's drifting?"

"Sorry," I responded, my attention snapping back into place. "Are you going back home for anything special?" I asked, my curiosity finally getting the better of me.

"No, I just wanted to go around there while I can still get in."

"What do you mean? The place will be yours now, won't it?"

"I doubt it. You're forgetting that I was adopted. There'll probably be other family members that'll lay claim to it." Although I'd assumed the house would now be his, with Dan being the only surviving member, his status within it hadn't crossed my mind or the implications of it.

"Has something happened?" I asked.

"No. I don't care what happens to it. I just wanted to come around here, to think. Besides, it wasn't just the funeral directors who rang yesterday. Greg's solicitor also rang. His will is being read next week, after the funeral, on Wednesday at ten."

"Oh... well, maybe this will do you good, to be close to them," I added.

"No, I don't think so. It's not even about the will. Maybe it's just to lay ghosts to rest." I didn't make any attempt to reply. Instead my mind drifted again to Charlotte. Why was she in my dreams? I think that was why I was growing more apprehensive.

"Right," Dan stated. "Are you still okay about coming in? I know what we were greeted with the last time we came around here. That's why I'm asking, Nic," he said, seeing my expression.

I looked around. I hadn't realised we'd even arrived. I had been so engrossed in what Dan had been saying and in my own thoughts that I hadn't taken any notice of anything around me.

"Yeah, I can't say that I'm looking forward to it, but I'll come in." Maybe it will lay to rest a few ghosts of my own as well, I thought, remembering the image of Charlotte in that house last night.

He took hold of my hand and reassuringly squeezed it before moving forward. When we were only a few paces into the driveway, I heard the clinking of keys.

"We won't get far without these, will we?" He had no idea what was going on in my head any more than I did in his. I surreptitiously stole glances at all the windows, feeling eyes boring into me.

"Are you sure you're okay, Nic?"

"I'm fine," I lied. "Let's just get this over with, eh?"

"Yeah," he agreed, but I sensed an uneasiness with him as well. I wanted to tell him to turn around, to tell him I really didn't want to go in there, but something was pushing me forward, keeping me from speaking my truth.

As he inserted the key, I could still feel trepidation running through him. I placed my hand on his back, trying to ease any anxiety away. He turned and smiled uneasily, feeling the apprehension bouncing off us both.

"Here goes nothing," he said, turning the knob, and he pushed the door open. An eerie silence greeted us like an old, unwelcome friend. I wanted to turn and run, but instead I matched Dan's faltering footsteps as he entered. Waiting for me to step over the threshold, he made a move to close the door.

"No," I responded. "Please, just leave it open a little way."

"What? Just in case we need to make a quick getaway?"

"Don't joke, Dan!"

"I'm not laughing," he replied without the hint of a smirk. But then his focus shifted. "Can we go into the sitting room at the back first, Nic? I just need to see it one more time."

"Yeah, I'll come with you." I didn't wait for him to agree. I had no intention of leaving his side. It wasn't just the silence that was unsettling or even the smell. The stale remnants of alcohol that Greg had consumed, trying to fight off the grief that must have been overwhelming before he succumbed to his death in whatever manner it had happened, continued to drift over this place. But even with that, I felt something more, even before we had entered.

Though I had seen nothing at the windows to stop me entering, my eyes searched them vigorously, sensing we were being watched. I laughed inwardly at the images I was creating in my head. After all, couldn't I just be recalling how Greg had watched my departure from their house on several occasions, his eyes boring into me? But we were in here now, and I had agreed to us going through to the back, so I stayed as close as I could.

As we walked nearer to the sitting room, Dan stepped to the side as though Greg were still lying there. We could clearly see the blood stain on the carpet from the wound to the back of Greg's head. I stood there, to the side, while Dan moved over to the sofa to sit down.

"I just want to spend a bit of time in here," he explained when I glanced over. My expression must have looked puzzled.

"That's fine," I responded. I figured anything was good as long as it helped. "Do you want me to leave you to it?"

"No, please stay," he said and patted the space on the sofa beside him. I sat down. "It feels weird being in here again, don't you think?" he asked. I didn't need to think at all.

"Just a bit," I agreed, and nothing more was said.

"The cops seem to think it was just an accident," he suddenly announced.

"Oh," I responded. "Jules is off the hook then?"

"I don't know. As far as I'm concerned, she's still got some explaining to do."

"Have they said any more about Charlotte?"

"No, they're still making enquiries, but they've done a post-mortem, same as Greg. That's why they're releasing both bodies."

"Maybe if the cops have said Greg's death was just an accident, don't you think it would be better just to let it go?"

"No." And he gave a hollow laugh.

"I'm just trying to help, Dan."

"I know that, Nic, but I can't just let it go. They've all gone. Fran's the only one who died from something we know – cancer. I know her mum's death hit her hard, but Charlotte was unusually withdrawn before her death, and Greg – well, what can I say? And are you really trying to tell me that he just fell and hit his head?"

"I don't know. But he was drinking really heavily, Dan. That might have been a contributing factor. Maybe he collapsed because of the drink. These are all ifs and maybes. We don't know exactly what happened, do we? All we can do is assume."

"But I need to do this."

"I know… Do you want to stay here or wander around? Maybe go out to the garden?"

"In a while. I want to go to Charlotte's room, sit there for a while. Do you mind?"

"No. You want me to come?"

"Do you mind if I go up there on my own?" he asked.

"No, I'll wait down here, but I'll stay around the hallway." He smiled, knowing exactly what I was thinking. If I was there, I could make a quick getaway if I got spooked.

"Come on then." And he followed me out. I can't say I wasn't pleased to be leaving that room behind, but being left downstairs while he went upstairs wasn't filling me with much joy either.

"Right. You sure you'll be all right?" he asked, planting one foot on the bottom of the staircase. But something seemed to hover around him. I looked at him hard, trying to figure out whether I had seen something or imagined it, because it was gone again almost instantly.

"You sure you're all right, Nic?" he asked, watching me curiously.

"Er, yeah. Yeah, I'm fine," I assured him, but I wasn't so sure. "I'll just stay here." He nodded, but I don't think he was any more convinced than I was.

"I won't be long," he assured me and bounded up the stairs two at a time, demonstrating his point. But as soon as he disappeared, that light reappeared in the same spot. The dream I'd had about being in this house suddeny flashed through my mind, and I inwardly shivered. The light began to diminish in its intensity, but it was growing in size, and from it a sense of familiarity was stirring within me until the figure I had seen in my dream appeared.

"Charlotte," I whispered. My fear at seeing her image so close rooted me to the spot, stopping any movements forward or back.

Making no move towards me, she smiled and made her way to the bottom of the stairs, towards Greg's office, just as she had in my dream. I made no move to follow her, but again that was just as it had been in my dream. Barely a minute lapsed before she reappeared, holding something. Again it was exactly as it had been in my dream. But what was she holding? It looked like an envelope, but what? And then, taking just one step towards the stairs, she disappeared again as though she'd never even been there. I looked up towards the stairs; there was no sound at all. I looked again at Greg's office and the letter… That's what it must have been, I suddenly realised. The letter in the drawer Dan wouldn't look at. She was holding on to a piece of paper similar in size to a small envelope. I looked again at Greg's office door. I really didn't want to go in there. But what choice did I have? How could I ask Dan if we could go in there? What excuse could I give? That I wanted to have a nose at that letter? I could hear myself saying it. *It's all right, Dan. All your family's dead now. What does one small letter matter?* I cringed at the thought of it. But what if that was what Charlotte had been trying to tell me? That what she was holding was important, and it was in that office. I listened for any movement upstairs, it was still quiet. I wondered how long it would take me to get in there to have a look.

Taking a step towards it, I was pushing the door open before I realised I had even moved. Getting the key from the pen holder, I unlocked the drawer quickly to get the other key to open the drawer behind me. It was there but in the opposite corner. I was trying to remember whether we had put it back in the right place. But we had – I know we had. It had to have been Greg. Maybe he'd gone back in there to check whether it had been moved. Maybe I was right after all. I had been sure he'd known something at the time Dan and I had been searching for stuff to do with his adoption. He'd seemed off with me. Yeah, that had got to be it, so I put the key in the lock and pulled the drawer open.

It was empty. Where had the letter gone? I thought again about Charlotte. Hadn't she been telling me to go and get it? What else could she have meant? I closed the drawer, locked it again, and put the key back in the drawer in the same place I'd found it. I quickly flicked through the papers in there, wondering whether the other key had been moved.

Sitting in the swivel chair, I thought about Dan upstairs. There had been no sound, but I was sure it wouldn't be that way for much longer, so I closed that drawer as well and replaced the key. I exited the office, quickly closing the door behind me and resumed my position just several paces from the front door. I had been there only a couple of minutes when I finally heard some movement upstairs and saw Dan appear shortly after.

"Have you been there the whole time?"

"I've wandered around a little but yeah, mostly. Have you done what you wanted to do?"

"Yeah. I've been sitting in Charlotte's room. I felt closer to her there. Does that sound stupid?"

"No, not at all." I remembered all the times I had seen her in my dreams as well as only a few minutes ago. As he stepped off that last step, I followed him through, into the kitchen.

"It feels so empty of anything now, doesn't it?" I nodded my agreement. I knew what he was getting at. Not only was there a distinct lack of love here, but the resentment that had pervaded as well – at least, on Greg's part – was gone. Everything seemed to have been forgotten, good and bad.

I wanted to say something about the letter or the lack of it, but what would he say? He would know I had been rooting around, looking for it. But he wouldn't know it was missing. Would he care? And should I? But I did for reasons I just couldn't fathom. Why couldn't he just have read the contents of it when he'd had the chance?

"Right. Are we ready to go?" he asked.

"What?" I asked snappily, shaking me unwillingly from my thoughts.

"Whoa! What's wrong with you?"

"I'm sorry, Dan. I didn't mean it that way. My thoughts were somewhere else entirely. Do you want to go?"

"Yeah, if you're ready."

"Yeah, I'm fine."

"After you then." And he waited for me to lead the way.

After locking the front door, he grabbed hold of my hand and my attention. "Thank you for this, for coming here with me, Nic."

"Has it laid some ghosts to rest?" I asked, remembering his reason for coming.

"Yeah, it has." I only wished I could have said the same. Why was Charlotte lingering around me? While walking away, I turned back. I saw something fleetingly at the upper window, the last one on the right as I looked back.

"What is it?" he asked.

"I'm sure I saw something at that window on the right, the last one."

"It's probably just the reflection of the sun. Besides, that was Charlotte's room."

"'Course it was."

"Sorry?"

"I just said, 'Course it was.' I had forgotten it was hers while looking at it from the outside." I shuddered inside though. That was no reflection.

"Come on. Let's go to my flat. Mal should be at work for at least another hour or so."

Together we walked out of the drive and towards Risely Road. Half of the way back, we walked in silence. Both our heads full of our own thoughts, though there were only two things occupying mine – Charlotte and that letter. I know I had seen her at that window. Who else could it have been? There was no one in the house; it certainly wasn't the reflection of the sun, as Dan had been quick to dismiss. And where was that letter? Had Greg destroyed it after we had been in there? And how was I going to find out anyway? I thought about Tess. It would be good for us

224

just to relax together, just me and her. Maybe she knew something, I only hoped she wasn't going to fly off the deep end as she had last time which made me more cautious about sharing this at all. I hoped Dan was wrong about Mal still being at work. If he was at the flat, then the odds were that Tess would probably be there as well.

"What are you thinking?" he questioned.

"Sorry, what?"

"You've been really quiet since we left my house."

"Oh, I was just thinking about that very thing, your house. It wasn't quite as bad as I had expected it to be," I lied.

"That's good," he commented. "I'm looking forward to us being on our own for a bit, away from the house and everything connected with it, aren't you?"

"Yeah, I am." And I was. Any time that involved just me and Dan was fine by me. It was just that Tess remained stubbornly on my mind.

"I could do with a car like Mal's, couldn't I?"

"What?"

"You're not with me at all, are you?"

I laughed. "I am. You just caught me off guard. That's all. Anyway, you don't drive."

"I know, but I thought that might get your attention back from wherever it's been."

"Maybe I'd be better off with Mal, seeing as he's got a car, eh?"

"Are you playing with me?" he joked.

"What if I am?" And we both laughed, an easiness settling between us at last. He paused to kiss me.

"Hey, you two… That sort of thing's not permitted in public!"

I slunk away from his hold and looked to where the booming voice had originated. "Mal!"

He laughed at my response.

"Sorry, didn't make you jump, did I?"

"You wish." Dan laughed. "Anyway, I thought you'd still be at work."

"I have been. You're just late back. Sorry. Have I spoiled your plans?"

"No," I shot back. But he just laughed again. "Actually, Mal, Tess isn't coming around, is she?"

"She is a little later. Why?"

"Oh, no reason. I just wondered."

"Nothing to do with Jules, is it?"

"No why?"

"Dan told her he would ring, didn't he?"

"Oh, yeah." And I looked over at Dan, I'd completely forgotten, but he had already opened the front door and was climbing the stairs.

Chapter Nineteen
Reluctant Date

He was already in the flat, sitting on the sofa, when Mal and I reached the door. I smiled at his relaxed manner.

"Comfortable?"

"I was waiting for you." So, I settled myself down beside him.

"Don't get too comfortable, you two."

"Why not?" Dan questioned.

"Don't tell me you've forgotten about the call you said you would make to Jules to set that date up."

"It's not a date and I'm not sure I said I'd ring her."

"We know that, Dan. Mal's just playing with you." And I glared at Mal just to make my point clear.

"Yeah, I'm sorry, mate, but you've still got to ring her, it's courtesy and she'll love it!" But he was given a reprieve with the door buzzing. "Maybe that's her, eh?" And smiling, Mal made a move to answer it. "Okay, come up," he said before replacing the handset. I looked at Dan. That obviously hadn't been Jules, and the relief on his face showed it.

"So who is it?" Dan questioned.

"Who do you think?" he answered. After a couple of minutes, I heard her grumbling about the trek up the stairs again. I looked over at Mal; he smiled on hearing her complaining.

"Now, don't put her in a bad mood as soon as she walks in," I said.

"I wouldn't dream of it." He laughed.

"Hey," Tess greeted as she walked in through the door. "What's occurring?" she said through breathless panting.

"Dan here is just about to ring Jules. Obviously he'll wait until you get your breath back." She glared at Mal together with me and Dan.

"Good, I came just in time then," she said, directing her smile towards Dan.

"Don't sound too pleased about it, Tess!" Dan responded.

"Oh, I'm sorry, Dan. I didn't mean it that way, just that we might now get to learn a little more from her, not— "

"He knows what you meant, didn't you, Dan?" I interrupted.

"Yeah. I'm just not looking forward to speaking to her. She came on a bit strong last time."

"We'll all be with you, won't we?" she said, glancing in mine and Mal's direction.

"We will," we both agreed, but Mal looked like he was enjoying this a little bit too much.

"Give me one of your phones then," Dan responded.

"No, mate. It'll come across better if you do it on yours."

He looked at me, terrified at the prospect, but this time I had to agree with Mal.

"He's right, Dan. If you ring her on my phone or even Tess's or Mal's, she'll know we're with you. If she thinks it's just you and her talking, she'll be more likely to open up. And besides, she already thinks I'm invisible."

"All the more reason to use a different phone," he argued.

"Please, Dan, it's better this way." He looked at me, pleading not to have to do this. I wanted to tell him to forget it, that we could try to talk her around some other way. But this was the best chance we had of getting anything from her. We all knew she had the hots for Dan and had for as long as I could remember; Dan knew it as well. I think that's what was frightening him the most.

"Okay," he finally conceded and scrolled down to her number. Taking a deep breath, he set the call in motion.

"H-hello, Jules. It's Dan, Dan Trennan," and he immediately clammed up. I signalled, urging him to give a little bit more, to talk to her.

"Er, sorry. H-how are you?" he enquired. She obviously must have become a bit more responsive because Dan was now filling voids with yes and nos. I looked at Tess, who was having trouble containing her laughter at Dan's awkwardness over the phone, at least with Jules anyway. In fact, she got up and walked out onto the landing. Mal smiled as well, amazed at how much difficulty Dan was actually having. Finishing the call with "All right. I'll see you tomorrow afternoon," and assuring her that he was looking forward to it as well, he ended the call. With a groan, he threw his head back against the sofa.

"Tess, you can come back in now!" he shouted. She walked back in really sheepishly.

"I'm sorry," she apologised, "but you were so bad," and she laughed again. She glanced my way, starting me off, which just left Mal, who was openly laughing as well now.

"It wasn't my idea anyway!" Dan blustered.

"We're only joking, mate," and he smiled. "Though I have to say, on that performance, it does make me wonder how the hell you got Nic in the first place!"

"I hated every bit of that," Dan responded. "And for your information, with Nic, it was easy."

"Oh, thank you!" I responded.

"I didn't mean it like that. I just meant that you were easy to talk to."

I smiled. "Good."

"Anyway, what did she say when you said it was Dan Trennan?" Tess questioned.

"She said she knew who I was." And he laughed at his own awkwardness. "I felt a bit stupid after that."

"I bet," Mal agreed, still laughing. "So when is this date taking place?"

"It's not a date!" Dan repeated.

"Okay, okay. So when are you meeting her?" he added. "And where? And is she looking forward to seeing you?" he teased.

"Give it a rest, Mal!"

"All right. We're only messing… So when and where are you meeting her?"

"Tomorrow afternoon at two. We're meeting outside the old theatre on Brompton Road."

"Really, and she suggested that?" I questioned.

"Yeah. She thought it would be a good idea."

"What? Because of the night we found Charlotte?"

"Yeah, I think so."

"A bit weird though, don't you think, mate?" Mal commented.

"Well, yeah, but it was her idea, and you are all coming, aren't you?"

"Yeah, we said we would, but we'll stay out of sight," Mal assured him.

"That's cool, as long as you're there," Dan answered, feeling a bit calmer with the assurance Mal had given him.

"You're okay with this, aren't you?" he asked, turning to me. I think in his mind he thought I might be feeling awkward.

"Yeah, I am, but thanks for asking."

"You know I'm only doing this to try and find out where she was that night and whether Charlotte said anything to her.

I smiled. He was still going through so much, and the funeral was still to come, and yet he was concerned about what I might be thinking.

"Yeah, I do, Dan."

"So what's the plan?" Mal asked, cutting in.

"Wouldn't it be better if Dan walked there on his own?" I said. "We don't want Jules seeing us by chance, do we?"

"Yeah, that's a good point, Nic. What if I leave a little earlier and pick Tess up and then you?" Mal suggested.

"Yeah, we could hang out at my place until it's time for you to meet her, Dan," I said.

"I don't like the idea of that."

"But she needs to think that we're not all in on this," I responded.

"Well, that's not going to happen, is it? You were all here when she came around. She knows that you'll know we're going to meet up."

"But she doesn't know we were in on you ringing her, does she?" Mal added.

"So you're saying I haven't got any choice?"

"Don't panic, Dan. We'll be close. She just doesn't need to see us dropping you off."

"Fine." And the room fell silent. Tess and Mal went to make a drink.

"We're all there for you," I assured him.

"I know, Nic. I just don't like it. I know what Jules is. I think I do anyway. In one sense, she's supposed to be our friend, and yet in another we're being underhand in trying to get information from her."

"But why wouldn't she tell us where she was that night we found Charlotte?" I asked.

"I don't know. I don't know what I think any more. It's all such a mess."

"It'll get better," I assured him.

"Will it?" he asked.

"Yes, I know it doesn't seem like it at the moment, but it will, Dan," I assured him, finishing the conversation.

Joining us again with steaming mugs of tea, Tess caught my eye. "What?" I asked.

"I just wondered how you both got on this morning. You went to the funeral directors, didn't you?" I looked at Dan. I had completely forgotten. Had he even told me when the funeral was? I had been listening when I needed to; I was sure I had.

"Yeah, the funeral's a week from Monday afternoon at one. It'll be a double one, and they're both being buried. At first I opted for cremations, but I remembered Fran... Anyway, the guy who was arranging it said there was enough room for them both to be buried in the same plot if I preferred that. He said it might be a good idea with them all being family. I wanted to say he didn't realise how right he was."

"Don't do this, Dan. You were family too," I said.

"No I wasn't, not the way Charlotte was."

"Charlotte never thought that way," Tess interrupted. "You were her brother. A little thing like blood made no difference to her, Dan. She thought the world of you."

"That makes me feel worse than ever."

"Well, it shouldn't," Tess stated. "You were family, Dan. Obviously more than you realise."

"Thanks."

"You're welcome," and she smiled. "Anything else happen?"

"No," Dan jumped in before I could say anything. Why had he done that? Why not just say we went to the house after going to sort out the arrangements for the funeral? I didn't add anything; that was possibly the worst thing I could have done, so I remained quiet. Instead, Tess forged ahead.

"So, what are we doing about tomorrow, about meeting Jules?" she added when we all looked at her blankly.

"How long will it take you to walk to Brompton Road, Dan?" Mal asked.

"Um, maybe give me forty-five minutes."

"And you're meeting her at two. So you could leave here at one, yeah?"

"Yeah, okay."

"Well I think that would be better than dropping you off," and then Mal turned to Tess. "So, if I pick you up for one, Tess, and then we both drive to Nic's, we'll be at Chievely Terrace by about quarter past."

"Yeah, that sounds good, but where are we going to hide out so we can watch proceedings?" I asked.

"To make sure he's not doing something he shouldn't, you mean?" And Mal gave me a wink.

"Oh, grow up, Mallory!" Tess scolded.

"I'm sorry; I was just having a bit of fun."

"Well, it's not. Now, Nic's got a valid point. Where are we going to wait?" We all sat in silence, wondering where we were actually going to hide out, but no solution was forthcoming.

"What about around the side?" Tess suggested.

"We would be too far away," I pointed out.

"Well, we're only watching. We're not listening to them, are we?" Tess answered.

"No, but what about you, Mal?" I asked. "We need to be somewhere that you can just wander out from and see them there. You said you'd be there for him in case she comes on too strong."

"Yeah, you're right, Nic, I did… If I remember rightly, there was some ground that was part of the theatre, to the left of it, wasn't there?" he asked, aiming his question at me.

"Yes, there is, but I can't think whether there was anywhere we could hide amongst it. It was pretty flat."

"Weren't there some buildings to that side attached to the main entrance?" Tess wondered aloud. I closed my eyes and tried to search the image of it in my mind. I could see the waste ground, the outline of the path, and the grass that had long since died off, leaving only weeds growing in its place. Imagining myself walking along that path, I saw seating areas, or rather the place where they had been used as such. There was an area tucked away by the main building that was hidden from the road. I said as much to Tess and Mal.

"I know where you mean," Tess agreed, "and that seating area is raised in one part. It might enable us to watch what's going on, and Mal could get back onto the pavement, which would take him around to the front entrance again without being seen."

"And we'd have a clear view?" Mal asked.

"Yeah."

"That's settled then, yes?" he prompted.

"Seems like a good solution to me," I finished.

"And me," Tess agreed.

"Happy with that?" Mal asked Dan.

"Yeah, but if she does get a bit heavy, don't waste any time, will you?" Mal laughed.

"There are some who would envy you in your position, mate."

"Want to trade places?"

"No thanks."

"Right, well, now that's sorted out, I'm going to make my way home," I told them all.

"Let me give you a lift," Mal offered.

I looked at Dan before I answered. I knew we were just messing about earlier, but I just wanted to make sure he was okay with it. He smiled and nodded.

"That's a good idea. You've done enough walking for one day."

"You make me sound ancient."

"Well, you're almost eighteen. Time's moving on." I smiled sarcastically and turned my attention to Mal, completely cutting him off.

"That would be great, Mal. Thanks."

"Okay, whenever you're ready."

"Now?" And I waved at Dan.

"Oh, no, you don't!" And he stood up before I had a chance to get away. "I'll see you tomorrow, afterwards, yes?"

"Yes." And I kissed him quick, saying goodbye to Tess as well before Mal pushed me out of the door.

We made our way down the stairs and out to the car in silence, but as soon as I slammed the car door shut, the questions started.

"Where did you go after the funeral directors?"

"Why do you want to know?"

"He seemed a bit secretive."

"Maybe he wants it that way."

"Oh, come on, Nic. Tell me, please?"

"He'll probably tell you himself later."

"Please."

"Oh, Mal. We went to his house, all right? Nothing more sinister than that. He just felt as though he wanted to be there again, to lay ghosts to rest, if you like. I think it was finding Greg there. His way of coping with it."

"I can understand that."

"Now, can we go?" I asked with a smile.

"I'm just looking out for him, you know."

"I know, but don't say anything, will you? I'm sure he'll talk about it later. He didn't say much to me."

"Sure." And the rest of the journey was uninterrupted silence, replacing the chatter, much to my relief. I got out of the car, saying I would see him and Tess in the morning and reminding him not to say anything to Dan about what I had told him. After he assured me that nothing would escape his lips, I said a final goodbye and walked towards my front door.

"Hey, Mum," I called out as I walked in through the door, expecting her to be standing there, still as put out as she'd been when I walked out this morning.

"Hi, Nic. How did things go at the funeral directors?"

"A bit sombre, but the funeral's next Monday at one."

"How did Dan cope with it?"

"Yeah, he was okay. It's going to be a double funeral, a burial."

"Oh. Are they not looking for anyone in connection with either of their deaths then?"

"They're still looking into Charlotte's death, but they reckon Greg's was an accident, that he fell."

"Well, I suppose they know what they're doing."

"Dan's not so sure. He thinks Jules knows more than she's letting on. He's meeting her tomorrow."

"Oh." And she eyed me curiously.

"No, not like that. He just wants to get her to talk, about Greg and Charlotte. She was the one who spent the most time with her, and yet Jules was probably the last person anyone would have expected. We're all going, but Tess, Mal and I are going to stay out of sight."

"Okay."

"You don't approve, do you?"

"No, it's not that. Though I would question the wisdom of it."

"Well, either way she'll get him to herself."

"That's a good idea, is it?"

"Dan's not interested in her, Mum. If anything, he's more scared of her."

"Okay. Do you want your dinner?" she asked, changing the subject entirely.

"Um, please. I've only had a sandwich and a cup of tea."

Leaving me alone while she fetched it from the kitchen, I had time to mull over what she had said. Would Jules be able to get through to Dan? Was he really that opposed to her, or was he just acting that way for my benefit? After all, there were always guys at college flocking around her.

"You look deep in thought. Here." And she placed the tray with my dinner on my lap.

"I was just thinking about tomorrow, whether we really will find out any more," I lied, which really meant I was as worried as hell in case Dan ended up quite liking her.

"Oh, Mum. What if I've pushed him into this, and he does begin to see her in a different light? What if he does start to like her?"

"I can't see that happening, Nic." And she came over and sat beside me on the sofa. "If he did, he would be a fool. And besides, he thinks the world of you. You tried to attack him the other morning, and he's still here, so I can't see Jules getting the chance to muscle in. Can you, really?"

"No, not when you put it like that."

"Anyway, what else have you been doing?"

"Dan wanted to go back to his house. I think it was maybe a way of coping with what's happened."

"Yes, it probably was. Did it help?"

"A little, I think."

"And what are you doing tomorrow? Ah, yes, you're all interrogating Jules, aren't you? What time is it all taking place?"

"Dan's meeting her at Brompton Road, the old theatre, at two. Why? Do you want to join us?"

"You've got to be kidding. I'll be at work, so you will have to get yourself up."

We remained like that pretty much for the rest of the evening. For once, unlike the last few weeks, the atmosphere seemed easy, relaxed. After spending several hours talking, I was getting tired.

"Mum, I'm going to bed. I'll see you when you get back tomorrow night."

"No, Nicola. I'll see you when you get back tomorrow. You're bound to be home after me and play nicely with Jules." At the door I looked back and smiled.

"I always play nicely."

"Good night, Nicola," she replied.

After waking from another dream in which Charlotte was again a dominant feature, along with the interior of 115 Morsley Road, or more precisely the bottom of the staircase, I drowsily fell back to sleep. I'd had no idea what the time was; my bedroom had been pitch black.

Waking a second time, I could tell from the sun's rays streaming in through the gap in my curtains that it was another warm, sunny day. I lay there, thinking about Charlotte and the dream that had continued as I had drifted off again. She had started to climb the stairs, but there was nothing in her hand this time – which reminded me of Tess. I hadn't said anything to her about the missing letter. In fact, I hadn't had a chance even to really talk to her, and my head felt fuzzy from lying in. I was meeting Mal and Tess. No, they were picking me up. It felt late. I spun around to look at the clock. I fell back against my pillows, shielding my eyes from the brightness outside. It was just eleven. They weren't coming until one. I rolled over with the intention of closing my eyes again, but my brain had already kicked into gear, thinking about that letter and Tess. But Jules took over – and Dan. He was meeting her. I thought again about what my mum had said last night. I smiled, thinking about it; she was right. Dan wouldn't fall for anything Jules had to offer.

Even though I knew I had nothing to worry about, this morning I took my time getting ready.

I had wanted to text Dan several times but resisted the urge. He would have enough going on in his head without me. I had already had breakfast and checked the clock in the room numerous times. At the last check, it was half past twelve. I was still pacing when they pulled up shortly before one.

"Sorry, Nic. We're a bit early. Dan was driving me crazy. He's been pacing the flat for hours."

"So have I," I admitted.

"Will you text him just to calm him down? He'll be on his way now."

"Okay." And I led the way back in.

Hey, Dan. Just to say I hope it goes okay. Thinking of you x

His reply, as I had hoped, was immediate.

Missing you. Glad when this is over x

"He's okay. He said he'll just be glad when it's all over. I've been itching to text him. Thanks, Mal. I would still be worrying if I hadn't have done that."

"Why?"

"It was going around in my head all last night and most of this morning that Jules might just get around Dan."

"That she might muscle in on your territory, you mean?"

"I wasn't going to put it quite so eloquently, Mal, but yes."

"That's just stupid," Tess scoffed. "He would never do that to you. He's mad about you, Nic."

"Thanks, Tess."

"Right. Now that we've established that, shouldn't we get going? We don't want to be finding this hiding place when Jules turns up, do we?" I smiled to myself at the image I had conjured up.

Picking up my bag and keys, I followed them both out the front door and to the car.

"Where are you going to park?" I asked from the backseat.

"I thought maybe a few streets away should do it. What do you think?"

"Yeah, she'll reach the theatre from the direction of the centre, I would think. Make it the streets on the other side of the theatre, and we should be safe."

"Yeah, that sounds good," he agreed.

Pulling off, I thought of Dan again. It was almost quarter past one, and he would still be making his way there. I wished I could speak to him, but he had enough to think about. I had to put him out of my mind and, together with Mal and Tess, watch proceedings as we had assured him we would.

"It'll all be all right," Tess said, sensing I had drifted again.

"I know. I'll just be glad when it's all over."

"You and me too," Mal agreed. "I won't have to listen to Dan griping about it anymore."

Making good time getting into Furham, Mal navigated the roads around the pedestrianised shopping area with ease, guiding us away from the hustle and bustle of the centre and into the side streets we had all agreed upon. Bringing the car to a crawl, he found a parking space alongside the pavement.

"It could easily get lost amongst the rest of them here, don't you think?" he said to me and Tess.

"Yeah," we both agreed. It felt safe enough here.

"Right. Come on you two. Our hiding place awaits." And he led us through the streets that lay between Mal's parked car and Brompton Road. We walked along the road that led directly to the main entrance of the theatre. Before crossing, we were careful to check that Jules was nowhere in sight. Mal glanced quickly at his watch.

"What time is it?" I whispered.

"Twenty-five to," he answered. "Right, it's clear," he said, checking one more time. We followed him to the left side of the theatre, not pausing until we reached the spot. The seating area was just as Tess and I had remembered. We were crouched down behind the raised wall, which shielded us from the road and any prying eyes. We all had a bird's-eye view. My eyes darted to the low wall just across from us and the theatre. Dan had just arrived. His eyes were scanning, trying to gauge our position. I popped my head up above the wall and gave him a quick wave. He nodded in my direction and smiled. Mal immediately grabbed my arm, thrusting it down hard onto the wall.

"Ow! What are you doing?"

"I might ask you the same thing! We're not here to play around, Nic."

"I wasn't. I just wanted him to know we're here."

"For all you know, Jules could have been walking along there and seen you."

"She wasn't!"

"You didn't know that though!"

"All right, that's enough, Mal. I think Nic gets the point."

"I hope so," he retorted, looking my way.

"She's here," Tess whispered. Both my eyes and Mal's darted back to where Dan was sitting. Jules had taken her place beside him. She kissed him on the cheek. I felt both Tess's and Mal's eyes settle momentarily on me.

"I'm fine!" I lied and kept my eyes stubbornly fixed on her and Dan. But I didn't like this, and Tess had already figured that out.

"She's just playing up to him." But her words crumbled like the stonework on the theatre's walls because she'd taken hold of his hand, and Dan hadn't even tried to pull away. I felt Tess's hand clutch mine. Just the same as Dan, I made no move to pull away from her either.

"He looks comfortable with her," I commented.

"He needs to get some information from her, Nic. That's all it is," Tess assured me. She tried pulling him to his feet, but he stayed stubbornly fixed to the wall. I wondered what they were talking about. Whether she really was telling him about Greg and Charlotte or whether she was just trying to worm her way into his affections, I wasn't sure, but she certainly looked comfortable with him from where I was. She even had her head resting on his shoulder.

"Oh, I've had enough of this!" And I made a move to get up and leave, but Mal dragged me back down before I managed to get anywhere.

"I knew this was a bad idea!" Tess whispered to Mal.

"I know. I told Dan not to let her come," Mal agreed.

"Oh, really!" I hissed.

"Yeah, really, but he said you and he were strong enough for this, that you'd be fine with it. But that last little show certainly blew that one out of the water, didn't it!" Mal shot back.

"I'm sorry," I whispered.

"Don't apologise, Nic. Let's just not have any more theatrics, yeah?" and he glared. I looked at Tess and smiled sheepishly. It felt like ages since we had taken our place here, and my legs were starting to go numb from having to stay knelt down.

"I think she's getting ready to leave," Mal informed us. After all I had seen, I thought it was better not to watch, but I turned to catch a glimpse on hearing Mal say it was almost over.

"Nic, don't!" Mal ordered, but it was too late, I'd already seen. She was just pulling away from him. I stayed quiet, what could I say that would possibly make this any better.

"It was just a kiss, Nic," Tess responded, sensing my angst.

"Maybe," I answered, but I had already withdrawn.

Chapter Twenty
Explanation

Waiting a few minutes to make sure Jules was out of sight, I also took my chance to make a move.

"Where are you going?" Mal demanded.

"I can't do this. I shouldn't have looked. I shouldn't have come. Tell him I'm sorry." And my tears finally broke.

"Oh, Nic," Tess sympathised.

"Oh, Christ!" I heard Mal curse, and through my tears, I saw him signal to Dan.

"Please don't bring him over here," I pleaded. But it was too late; he was already making his way across to us.

"What's happened?" Dan asked as soon as he reached us.

"It's Nic. She saw Jules kiss you."

"I can explain," he said. "Let's go back to the flat, and I'll tell you everything. That will explain what happened."

"I want to go home, Dan," I responded.

"No, not until I've explained. Come on, Nic. You owe me that much, at least. Please?" I looked at Mal and then at Tess.

"Please come back, Nic," Tess said. I finally nodded, more for her than for anyone, even Dan.

"She has definitely gone, hasn't she?" Mal asked.

"Yeah, but I can go on ahead if you like," Dan said.

"Yeah, I think that would be best," Mal replied. "We parked up on Kettleby Street. We'll see you back there."

"I will see you there, won't I, Nic?" Dan asked.

I nodded, but I remained by Tess's side. I felt no compulsion at all to make any move towards him. He knew it as well. Although I could feel his eyes on me, I made no attempt to meet his gaze and, as he walked away, Mal rounded on me.

"What was that for?"

242

"Sorry?" I asked.

"Nic, she kissed him, not the other way around."

"But he didn't pull away, did he?"

"Yes."

"Not soon enough."

"Oh, come on!" Tess must have signalled something to him because he cut off abruptly and walked away from us, across the road.

"Come on," Tess said. "It'll be okay, Nic. Jules is devious, and you know that. It'll be her, not Dan."

I smiled resignedly. I knew what she was trying to do. But I already knew what Jules was capable of. I knew Dan hadn't instigated the contact. But when I'd seen her kiss Dan, even though it had been for just a second, he'd still lingered. To me, his response had said everything.

She put her arm around me and led me across the road. I glanced over in the direction Jules had walked. I suddenly stopped and did a double take.

"What's up?" she questioned, searching the direction my attention had gone.

"Jules. She was over there against the wall."

"Where?" But now there was no one.

"She was there, Tess. I saw her."

She smiled at me. "Nic, we gave her long enough before we made a move. Are you absolutely sure?"

"Yes, of course I am!"

"Okay," she responded almost apologetically, and her eyes searched again where I had pointed her out. Why would she do that? I asked myself.

"Come on," Tess said, shaking me out of my reverie. "Let's get across the road." Having little choice and with her hand firmly gripped around mine, I allowed her to lead me across. I looked back one last time before it disappeared from view. Though there was no sign of her, I knew Jules was still there, watching.

Catching up with Mal and Dan at the car, I remained quiet. I wanted to be able to turn back the clock, but how could I when I'd already seen him and Jules being that intimate?

"Right. Nic and I are sitting in the back," Tess told them.

"Straight back to our place then?" Mal asked.

"Yep," she said before turning to me. I nodded, but I wasn't sure how good an idea that really was. While I was in the car though, I said nothing.

"So what did you find out?" Mal asked.

"Can we talk about it back at the flat, Mal?" Dan asked. "I don't really want to talk right now."

"Yeah, sure." And silence settled over us all. It felt uncomfortable all the way back.

When Mal eventually parked up, he got out of the car and pulled the seat forward for me but said nothing. I thanked him, but he only nodded. Dan, too, seemed just as withdrawn. Only Tess remained cheerful, and that display was put on, I think, for my benefit. I walked past Dan and briefly acknowledged him, but again, I said nothing. Out of the corner of my eye, I saw Tess put her arm around him comfortingly. I knew what that was all about; she wasn't about to take sides. I suddenly envied her. Every part of me wanted to forget what had happened and fling my arms around Dan, but I couldn't. Something or someone was stopping me, namely Jules. I trudged up the stairs after Mal, leaving them to it. Following in, Dan went to stand by the sink in the kitchen. He didn't turn towards me, so I sat down on the sofa and waited for Tess. I felt so alone. Mal was certainly acting like I was being totally unreasonable, and I just couldn't decide about Dan. Tess was the only one I felt I could speak to with any sort of frankness.

"Hey, Nic," she called out as she walked in through the door and flopped down on the sofa next to me. I noticed Dan sidling over to Mal without a glance in my direction. Getting Mal's agreement, he then turned to me and Tess.

"We've just got to nip around to the shop. We'll just be a few minutes." I nodded but remained quiet.

As soon as they had left the room, I rounded on Tess, figuring she had to have had something to do with this.

"What was all that about?"

"I thought we needed to have a chat."

"Let me guess what about – oh yeah, Jules."

"It wasn't at all the way you've built it up, Nic. He was just trying to get information out of her about Charlotte and Greg."

"And he needed to kiss her to do that, did he?"

"Oh, come on, Nic. It wasn't like that, and you know it!"

"I don't know what it's like any more, Tess. Jules has been after Dan for as long as I can remember, way before we got together."

"And that doesn't tell you anything?"

"This is not about the fact that he's never had anything to do with her in the past, Tess. It's to do with what he did about half an hour ago."

"Precisely, but he didn't, Nic. That was down to Jules, not Dan. I agreed with Dan about you being there this afternoon, that you were strong enough to cope with what she threw at him and you. But maybe his faith in you was misplaced, eh?"

"I'm sorry, Tess." And I got up to go.

"He thinks the world of you," I heard her say as I closed the door. Walking down the stairs, I wanted to be back there, but I had already made my stand; I couldn't turn back now. The door to the street was ajar. I figured they'd left it like that to get back in without having to buzz up to us. But they'd gone nowhere. They were both sitting on the step.

"I'll leave you to it," Mal said to both of us.

"No, it's fine," I answered. "I'm going home."

"You can't," Dan cut in.

"I'm sorry?" I questioned.

"I'll see you in a bit," Mal muttered and disappeared.

"Please, Nic, sit down." And he patted the space next to him. I wanted to ask, 'Why? What's the point?' But reluctantly I did as he'd asked.

"Will you let me explain?" he asked.

"Why did you leave the flat?" I responded, shooting another question his way.

"Tess wanted a chance to try and talk to you first. Will you let me?" he repeated. I nodded and waited for him to begin.

"I think Jules wanted more from me."

"Well, I think that was pretty obvious!"

"Please, Nic, I'm just trying to explain." I nodded, I felt a bit ashamed.

"I'm sorry. Go on."

"I think she's jealous of what we've got. She said she spent a little time with Greg, but she wouldn't say whether she was with him or not that night we found Charlotte. She seemed genuinely sorry about her. She told me that she spent a lot of time with her after Fran died and particularly since her funeral. A lot of the time when I wasn't there."

"But she can say anything now. Charlotte's not here to prove or disprove anything she says."

"Yeah, I know that, and I still think she was having a fling with Greg, and, like you said about Charlotte, he's not here to disprove it either, is he?"

"No," I agreed.

"I know what you're thinking, Nic."

"And what's that?"

"That I didn't pull away from her kissing me soon enough."

"It looked heartfelt enough from where I was."

"Then you weren't looking hard enough. I love you. I have no feelings for Jules Harvey at all. I just want to get to the bottom of what happened between her and my sister and my dad – well, Greg. I want you to believe what I'm telling you, Nic, because it's the truth, but I can't make you."

For a minute I said nothing. I did believe him, but Jules was already in my head, chipping away at me.

"It was hard," I said, "watching you like that."

"I do understand that, but I wasn't doing anything. You've got to believe me."

"I do believe you," I said finally. Before I had a chance to process what had come out of my mouth, I was wrapped in his arms, and his lips were searching mine. I made no attempt to protest. This was how it was supposed to be. But for how long would it remain? Would she yet break down the barriers that held her at bay?

"Thank you," he whispered, interrupting imagined events my mind was already playing out. Pulling away, I remembered her standing there, watching as Tess and I crossed the road from the theatre. I explained to him what I had seen.

"It couldn't have been Jules, Nic. I watched her for long enough. She disappeared from view."

"But she could have come back and hidden, watching to see if anyone followed you," I pointed out.

"I suppose," he answered.

"I know what I saw, Dan. Tess said the same thing. Is this just me being paranoid because my boyfriend kissed her?"

"No, it's not, and I didn't. She did the kissing."

"But you still don't believe me?"

"Yes, I do, damn it! Look, I know how devious she is, Nic. I haven't forgotten either how long it took her to get to us when we were waiting for Charlotte to be brought out. I don't trust her any more than you do, but to get anything from her, I've got to play by her rules. And that doesn't mean what you think it does," he reiterated, seeing the pained expression on my face. "Come on. Let's go back upstairs." Taking my hand and helping me up, I allowed him to lead me back up to the flat and to Mal and Tess.

"I hope this means you've both sorted it all out now," Mal blurted out as soon as we walked in through the door.

"He's explained everything," I told him. "I still don't like it, but I don't suppose there's any other way."

"Right. Well, next time, don't take it to heart so much, eh?"

"What do you mean, 'next time'?"

"Oh, God, you haven't told her, have you?" Mal sighed.

"Told me what?" I demanded.

"She's invited herself over here tomorrow," Dan explained.

I looked at Mal, who bolted for the door, barring my exit. "Just cutting off your escape route."

The annoyance that had built within me evaporated in that moment of his idiocy. I raised my eyebrows at his failed attempt at humour and I sat down next to Tess.

"Are you okay with it?" Dan asked uncertainly.

"Well, I didn't think she'd be making an appearance quite so soon, but yeah, I suppose I've got to be. Do you want me here, or would you rather I stayed away?"

"No, I want you here. I want all of us here," Dan insisted.

"Oh, what? Me as well?" Tess asked.

"Yeah, we're all here most of the time anyway, aren't we?"

"Yep, sounds good to me," Mal commented.

"Okay," I joined in. "I'll be here then."

"Actually, Nic," Dan said. "I was going to ask if you wanted to stay over tonight."

"I don't know. I'll ring my mum later, okay?"

"Okay," he agreed. I could see in his eyes that he hadn't expected my answer to be quite so accommodating. I smiled, mirroring the fixed grin plastered over his face.

"I did only say I would ring my mum later."

"I know."

"You're all right with it, if I do stay, aren't you, Mal?" I asked. The last thing I wanted to do was rub him up the wrong way again.

"It's fine. You're welcome to stay whenever."

We stayed like that pretty much for the rest of the afternoon, though there was little of it left.

Once Dan realised I was pretty much okay about what had happened at the theatre, he began to elaborate a little more on what Jules had spoken to him about.

"I think she's trying to get me on side by talking about Charlotte. She said Charlotte talked a lot about Fran."

"Well, she would, wouldn't she?" Tess reasoned. "She knows she's on safe ground with that. Charlotte would still be grieving for her mum. Are you sure she didn't say anything more about her relationship with Greg or whether he had said anything about Charlotte?"

"No, that's why she's coming tomorrow," Dan said. "She said it wasn't private enough where we were."

"Ah, she wants it more private?" Mal grinned.

"No, not like that," Dan protested.

"You sure about that?" Mal remarked. But before Dan could react again, I jumped in.

"I'm just going outside to ring my mum, Dan, about staying over."

"Okay," he answered and he smiled before turning again to Mal. "She can't get up to anything too bad, not with all of you here."

Once outside on the landing, I tapped out my mum's mobile number and set the call in motion. She had already told me she wouldn't be home until later.

"Hey, Mum."

"Hi, Nic. What's up?"

"Dan's asked me to stay over tonight. Do you mind?"

"No, 'course not. Will you be home in the morning?"

"No, it'll be later than that. I don't know exactly what time."

"Okay, well, I'll see you sometime tomorrow then. Don't be too late, will you?"

"Okay, see you. Love you."

"Yeah, love you too, and be careful." Ending the call, I winced at her use of the word *careful* and all the connotations it carried.

"Everything okay?" Dan asked as I walked back in.

"Yeah, it's fine. I said I would see her tomorrow sometime. Exactly what time did Jules say she was coming over?"

"About eleven. You are going to stay while she's here, aren't you?"

"Yeah, but she won't like it."

"I don't care. You're going to be here as well, aren't you?" he said, turning his attention to Tess, remembering the slight reticence in her when he'd brought it up a few minutes before.

"Yeah, 'course."

"Right, I'm going to go out to get some food. You coming, Tess?" Mal asked.

"Yeah." After we'd all agreed on a takeaway, they disappeared, leaving me and Dan on our own.

"I'm really glad you're staying tonight," he said. "I really thought I had lost you earlier."

"Me, too." Maybe tomorrow Jules would realise just how hard it will be to come between us. But was I staying here just because of that? I questioned. No, we had been together for ages now, and I think I needed Dan just as much as he needed me.

The rest of the evening was easy, light. Our talk never extended to Jules again, and all thoughts, at least those spoken, stayed well away from events of the last few days and weeks.

It was good just being amongst friends. Tess left shortly before ten, and Mal drove her, leaving me and Dan alone for a second time.

Chapter Twenty-One
Unwelcome Intentions

Waking up next to Dan, I felt free of any doubts that had been lingering since yesterday. It wasn't like this had been the first time for us; Dan had stayed over at my place a few times before Fran had died, but I truly felt like we were now back on track.

But thoughts of Jules were never far away and with them snippets of last night's dream, with Charlotte again being the focal point. Rousing around, Dan sleepily opened his eyes.

Languishing, his gaze rested on me. He smiled.

"Hey, you," I said as he pulled me back into his arms.

"Morning," he whispered and settled back against the pillow. "You tired?"

"No, why?" I asked.

"Because you were tossing around like mad. You were dreaming of Charlotte, weren't you?"

"Yeah. How do you know?"

"You sort of called out to her. At least, it sounded like her name. Want to tell me about it?"

"There's nothing much to tell. She was in your house again. That's all."

"Again?"

"Yeah, there have been several dreams where I've seen her there." I omitted the bit about where she had wandered and what I thought she had been holding – in fact, what she was holding most times when I saw her now. Tess – I still hadn't said anything to her about that letter, and I wasn't sure whether I would get the chance when she came around again this morning, not with Jules coming over at eleven. Just thinking about her fawning over Dan again made my insides groan.

"You okay?" I asked, because I must have kept him awake.

"Yeah, I'm just happy you're here. I watched you for ages last night, just sleeping."

"I'm glad I stayed."

"So am I. I feel like everything's back to normal, almost anyway. You're not bothered about Jules coming over, are you?"

"A little," I conceded. "There's nothing I can do though, is there?"

"There's nothing you *need* to do. Like I've said, I've got everything I need right here."

"You need to know what she knows though."

"What if she didn't do anything to cause Charlotte's or Greg's deaths? What then?"

"You changing your mind about her?" I asked.

"I don't know. I don't know what to think."

My mind was already drifting, not only about Jules but about Tess as well – Tess and that letter. I had to say something to her about it. Maybe Greg put it somewhere else before he died; maybe he thought we had read it. But if he did, did that mean there was something incriminating in it? God, I wish we had read it. My mind wouldn't be turning at the rate of knots, trying to figure it out now, if we had.

"You look deep in thought," he commented, brushing a stray hair from my face.

"I was just thinking we should get up," I lied.

"Why? We've got plenty of time."

"Well, it wouldn't look very good if Jules turned up and I came wandering out of the bedroom, would it?"

"I wouldn't mind."

"Well, I would." And I made a move to get up.

"Oh, no, you don't. Stay a little longer, please." My resolve had already weakened and I fell back into his arms willingly.

I must have drifted off again, because I woke with a start to Mal's voice. "I'm just making a cup of tea. You two want one?"

"Oh, please, Mal," I answered gratefully, and I nudged Dan.

"Yeah, that'd be good, mate. We'll be with you in a minute." And he reached for me again before Mal had even closed the door.

"Come on, Dan." And before he got a chance to pull me back again, I shot out of bed, trying to dodge all his gear he'd brought back from Morsley Road, which was still strewn all over, exactly where he'd dumped it, and started getting dressed.

"Spoil sport!"

"You don't want Jules to see you like this, do you? It's not hard to imagine what ideas she might get." He obviously had a change of heart because he too shot out and hurriedly began to dress. We had both just made it out of the bedroom when the buzzer sounded from downstairs.

Mal looked back from where he was standing in the kitchen.

"Can you answer that, Nic?"

I picked the handset up and falteringly answered, "Hello."

"Hey, Nic, it's me, Tess. Let me in, will you?"

"Oh, okay." And I buzzed her in. I turned to Mal and Dan. "It's okay. It's just Tess. They both breathed a sigh of relief at the same time. I laughed. "This is stupid; it's only Jules who's coming around."

"You've changed your tune, haven't you?" Mal questioned. "Last night did the trick, did it?" And he smiled teasingly.

"Mal!" Dan reprimanded.

"Let's just say it put things into perspective," I said, ignoring Dan's disapproval.

"Good," he answered, going back to stirring the tea.

"Oh, thanks, Mal. I'll have one as well," Tess chimed in as she walked in through the door.

"Oh, thanks," I said as he handed me my cup.

"Where's mine?" Dan responded. Mal duly passed him a cup as well.

"All we need now is Jules Harvey!"

"Oh, Jules, how did you…"

Mal spun around. He was just about to say something when he saw Tess smiling smugly. "Gotcha!"

"You wait, Brinham!"

"Ha! Bring it on, Edwards." And laughing, she fell back into the sofa. Sneering, he turned his attention back to making his own tea.

"What time is it?" Dan asked.

"Ten thirty," Tess answered.

"Oh, good," I said sarcastically. "Only half an hour."

"I hope she's not here too long." Dan muttered.

"I bet she'll want to see you again," Mal commented, setting his tea down on the table in front of us all.

"Remind me why I have to go through all this again?"

"Because we need to know if she had anything to do with Greg and Charlotte's deaths," Tess told him. But none of us got a chance to reply, because the buzzer from the main door downstairs sounded.

We all looked at one another, wondering who was going to get up.

"Go on then," Mal urged. "I don't think it will have the same effect if Nic answers it, do you?"

Reluctantly Dan rose from the chair he was slouched in.

"Hello... Oh, yeah, come in, Jules." And he buzzed her in. Replacing the handset, he took his place next to me again and reached out for my hand.

"It'll be all right," I assured him. I didn't have time to say any more with Jules knocking on the door.

"Get up!" Mal hissed.

"Come in, Jules," he called out instead, giving Mal a disapproving look at the same time.

"Oh, hello!" she said, seeing us all sitting here. "I didn't know you would all be here. I thought we would be on our own." She looked pointedly at Dan.

"I didn't think you would mind, and Nic stayed over last night, didn't you?" And he smiled.

"Oh, well, no matter. You do look a little rough, Nic. Are you not well?"

I smiled at her feigned concern for my welfare. "Thank you for your concern, Jules, but I'm fine." I felt Tess's eyes boring into me as she took her place, perching on the arm of Dan's seat.

"So, what have you got planned for me?" she purred, eyeing him seductively. I surreptitiously stole a glance at Tess and then at Mal. Mal shook his head ever so slightly from where he had moved over to the sink, warning me not to say anything he knew I would regret.

"I'm sorry, Dan," I said instead. "I wouldn't have stayed so long if I had known you were planning something."

"Don't let us keep you," Jules delighted in saying. I could sense Tess was fighting to keep whatever she was about to say back when Dan jumped in.

"I hadn't got anything planned for you, Jules. I just want us to talk, and Nic is welcome to stay for as long as she wants." His focus never moved from her.

"That's okay. I just said that because I thought she might have somewhere she needed to be." And she smiled in my direction. "I'm sorry if it came across differently to the way I had intended, Nic."

"It's fine, Jules." And I smiled back in that same sickly way she had. "Actually, we've all just got a cup of tea. Would you like one?" And I got up to walk over to the kitchen, where Mal was still standing.

"Yes, thank you. That would be nice," she called over.

I caught Mal's eye. He was smiling.

"What are you up to?" he whispered.

"Just playing the game. Do you approve?" I responded likewise.

"Oh, yeah," he responded, keeping his voice low.

Walking back over with her tea, without speaking, I carefully placed it on the coffee table in front of her.

"Jules was just saying how strange it seems without Charlotte," Dan said, filling the void that had quickly descended.

"Yes, I bet it seems even more so without Greg, doesn't it, Jules?" I caught a suppressed giggle escaping Tess, and keeping my focus on Jules, I saw I had certainly hit the intended spot. She looked furious.

"I think we're all missing both of them, Nic," Dan said, trying to smooth things over.

"Yes, I'm sure," I answered curtly, but he had already returned his attention to Jules.

"Do you fancy going out for a walk, Dan?" she asked.

"Yeah, but after we've finished these," he answered, referring to the teas we were still drinking.

"So," Mal began, "where were you the night the rest of us were searching for Charlotte? Or are we to assume you were with Greg?" All eyes immediately settled on Jules.

"Why do I need to tell you?" she spluttered.

"It's up to you," Dan cut in.

"Now wait a minute, mate. We asked Jules this last time, and she wouldn't give us an answer. I think we all deserve one now." And he turned to her. "You are supposed to be our friend, Jules."

"All right, I was with Greg, and all I was doing was trying to help him get over the death of his wife, the same as I was trying to do for Charlotte."

"All right. That wasn't so bad, was it?" Mal asked.

"I didn't for a minute think it was going to be. I just don't like other people knowing my business – obviously except you, Dan."

"Weren't you aware of where Charlotte was going that night? After all, you did say you were trying to help her get over the death of her mother. It sounds like you spent a lot of time with her, so I would have thought she'd have confided in you," Tess questioned.

"She didn't tell me everything, Tess," as she drank the last of her tea. "Are you ready then, Dan?"

"Er, yeah." And he turned to me. "I won't be long."

"Okay, I'll wait here for you." And I went over and kissed him long enough for Jules to begin huffing. Pulling away, I immediately turned to her.

"Bye then."

"Oh, I'm coming back as well," she sneered. I smiled and nodded. By the time he had closed the door, my jaw was aching from the fake smile I'd been keeping in place.

"I don't know how I kept my mouth shut!" Tess admitted.

"Nor do I, Tess, and I'm knocked out, Nic, the way you handled her. That was just brilliant," Mal congratulated.

"It didn't do much good, though, did it? They've still gone out," I pointed out.

"They won't be long, and maybe Dan will get more out of her," he responded. I wasn't so sure.

She had him to herself now, and that meant she would be working on him without any resistance, at least from us. I felt completely deflated and plonked myself back down on the sofa next to Tess.

"He won't succumb to her charms, you know," Tess assured me.

I smiled. Tess never failed to see the bright side, for my benefit anyway.

"And I think she realises you're no pushover now," she added.

"She's right, Nic. Dan's not stupid, and you've given her food for thought. He knows she fancies him, and he was thinking just what I was, about Greg. Besides, you didn't see his reaction when you said something about it being strange for her without Greg. He was smiling in your direction; only your attention was focused on Jules.

"Really?" I asked Mal, and I turned to Tess. "I heard you doing your best to suppress a giggle and failing miserably."

"I know. I couldn't help it. She was mad as hell. She didn't like you kissing Dan goodbye either."

"Yeah, I caught that."

"So what do we do now?" Tess questioned.

"We wait until they get back. There's nothing else we can do," Mal told us.

We all remained like that for the next hour. Mal was making us a second cup of tea, and I was beginning to get fidgety, wondering when they were going to make an appearance, when I heard the bottom door slam.

"They're coming," I called over nervously to Mal and Tess, who was standing by the window, looking out aimlessly over the back at more flats and offices spread out down over several streets.

She stayed where she was, leaving the seat next to me vacant for Dan.

He came in through the door first and aimed straight for the sofa; only Jules followed him and plonked herself down on the arm next to him.

"There's a spare chair there, Jules," Tess pointed out.

"Oh, it's okay. I'm fine here... Done anything interesting while we've been away?"

"No, not really. We've just been chatting – you know, catching up," I told her.

"Yes, so have we, haven't we, Dan?" she spoke seductively, again her attention was fixed in his direction.

"Yeah," he replied nonchalantly, though he looked very uncomfortable between the two of us.

For a second I wondered why. What had happened while they'd been away? Then I felt his fingers touching mine. She might have tried to worm her way into Dan's affections and in the process cutting me out, but it wasn't working, he was still with me. I silently answered him by entwining my fingers around his. I caught sight of his head turning very slightly in my direction.

My stomach fluttered in answer before I turned, seeing Jules move away.

"You're not going already, are you?" I asked.

"Yes, things to do."

"Well, hopefully we'll see you again soon."

"Oh, you will, Nicola. I've told Dan I'll ring him and set up another date." She then walked over to Mal and hugged him, kissing him on the cheek. Then it was Tess's turn, which looked a bit awkward and standoffish on both their parts. Dan didn't bother to get up at all, leaving her to lean over to get to him. He turned his head for her to kiss him on the cheek as she had done with Mal, but she caught him off guard and planted one full on his lips.

"See you soon, Dan. I've enjoyed this afternoon." Then she turned and walked the few paces to where I was standing by the open door. She hugged me closer than she had Tess, and I felt her breath close to my ear.

"Don't get too attached to Dan. Well, I'll see you soon," she said more loudly for the others to hear and then glanced over her shoulder. "Bye then," she trilled before focusing on me again as she walked out.

"Bye, Jules," I called out before gratefully pushing the door shut. I turned, with her words still ringing in my ears. Neither Mal nor Dan seemed to have noticed anything, but Tess looked directly at me. She knew something was wrong. Ignoring her and focusing on Dan, I sat down on the sofa.

"I'm going to go home soon, Dan," I said. "I haven't seen much of my mum. If I leave in a while, I'll make it home before her."

"I'll take you home," Mal offered.

"No, it's fine."

"I'll walk part of the way with you," Tess offered.

"No, I would rather Mal took you," Dan answered.

"Okay," I relented. "Half an hour?"

"Yeah, that's fine. I'll take you later, Tess."

"Oh, all right."

"Well, you might as well stay with Dan while I take Nic." She grudgingly agreed, but I was sure she wanted to question me. It was a bit of a relief really. I was still processing what Jules had said. I wasn't ready yet to share it. She wasn't getting away with it though. I had already decided I was going round there to have it out with her, but it would have to wait until tomorrow.

"I wish you were staying," Dan whispered. "You will stop again, won't you?"

"Yeah, 'course I will. What did Jules have to say?" I asked, bringing Mal and Tess back into our conversation.

"She was trying to tell me that Greg loved me." And he laughed. "Whatever else he was doing with her, it didn't include that, did it?"

"What else did she have to say?" Mal questioned.

"She just talked about Charlotte – nothing new really. To be honest, she was more interested in me, what I was thinking. How me and you get on," he said to me. "She's jealous of you, Nic."

"Yeah, I got that."

He put his arm around me. "She's got good reason."

"Why?"

"Because I love you."

"Well, make sure you keep reminding her of that."

"Oh, I will." He turned to Mal. "Are you ready?"

"Yeah, sure." And he got up.

"I won't be able to get around tomorrow, but I'll ring you, okay?" I said to Dan.

"No, I'll ring you, tomorrow night, yeah?"

I nodded.

"What are you doing anyway?" he asked.

"Oh, um… Tess is coming around. She wants to go through some work we're going to be doing when we go back to college. Then we're going into Furham. Just a girlie day really."

He looked over at Tess.

"Yeah, what Nic said." And she looked at me. "I'll ring you later to let you know what time I'll be there." Mal looked at us both curiously. It was only Dan who suspected nothing. I felt as though I'd sort of dropped myself in it with Tess a bit. I was going to have to make my excuse to Tess a good one. If I wasn't careful she'd see right through me.

"Right, come on," Mal said. I kissed Dan and looked again at Tess. I had no choice now but to tell her; she wouldn't let it drop until I did.

Mal started to question me even before I had managed to get into the car. As soon as I had said that Tess and I were meeting tomorrow, he'd known something was wrong.

"Is it anything to do with Jules? Actually, no, don't tell me yet. There's something else I need to talk to you about."

"Can I get in the car first?"

"Yeah, hurry up."

Once I was in the car, I turned to him. "Right, what's up?"

"You know when we went to Fran's funeral?"

"Yeah, what of it?" I certainly wasn't expecting that.

"I saw a woman there. It was difficult to put an age to her because she was made up. I had never seen her before."

"Christ, Mal. I thought you were going to tell me something really bad."

"No, you don't understand. I've seen her since. I saw her that night when we found Charlotte and since, near our flat. I didn't think much of it before, but I'm beginning to wonder now. She was hanging around down the road yesterday when Dan and I were sitting on the doorstep."

"Maybe she lives around here," I suggested

"Um, maybe, but it just gave me a bad feeling."

"Well, just see how things go. It could just be a coincidence."

"Um," he answered, but it was clear she was really bothering him. In a way I was pleased. With that on his mind, he wasn't about to start questioning me. Though it did bring me back to that woman I had seen when Tess and I were shopping.

"What colour hair did she have?" I asked.

"Er, brown, I think, light brown. Why?"

"Oh, no reason. I just wondered." But could the woman Mal had seen have been the same woman I saw?

Chapter Twenty-Two
Return Visit

I suddenly felt very alone as I walked in through the front door. Jules's words, *Don't get too attached*, rang in my ears again. Kicking my shoes off, I padded through to the sitting room and curled up on the sofa. I must have fallen asleep because the next thing I knew was my mum shaking me awake. She was looking at me pitifully.

"What's wrong? What's happened? Is it Dan?"

"What?"

But then I realised why she was questioning me the way she was. I must have cried myself to sleep. My eyes were probably puffy from crying so hard, they certainly felt like it, and they were stinging. I sat up from where I had curled my body into a ball.

"Come on, Nic. What's happened?" she repeated.

"I don't want to talk about it."

"Oh, no. You're not playing that card again. You're going to tell me. From the look of you, you've done quite a bit of crying." She sat down beside me and held me in her arms.

"It's not what you think, Mum."

"He'd better hope it's not!"

"It's not. It's not Dan; it's Jules. Jules Harvey." I could see her mind processing what I had just said, wondering just where Jules fitted into it all and whether I was just covering for Dan.

"So what's she done?"

I explained how she had been at the flat and what she had whispered to me before she left.

"But you've told Dan what she said to you?"

"No."

"What? Why on earth not?"

"He's got enough going on at the moment; and besides, if I told him that, he'd go storming around to Jules's flat to have it out with her."

"And what's wrong with that?"

"I can sort this out myself, Mum."

"Oh, really? That's why you've been curled up here crying, is it?"

I wanted to get away from her, and I made my move.

"Oh, no, you don't." And she pulled me back.

"Please, Mum, I just want to be on my own."

"I'm just trying to help you, Nicola."

"I know that, and I'm sorry. But I just need to think through what I'm going to do." But the phone bleeping stopped me in my tracks. I didn't need to look at who it was; I knew.

"Are you not going to answer that?"

"Yeah." And I took it from my pocket. "Hey, Tess." I looked to my mum and signalled my route through to the kitchen. "What's up?" I asked once I was out of earshot.

"You know what's up, Nic. What did she say to you?"

"Nothing I can't cope with."

"That's not an answer. I know she said something, and I'll come over if you don't tell me. And what about what you said to Dan about me and you going into Furham and having a girlie day? We've only just had one, remember?"

"I know, but I had to say something. Please, will you just trust me?"

"Not a chance, Nic. Now spill, or I'm coming straight over!"

"Okay, Jules *did* whisper something to me. She told me not to get too attached to Dan."

"What?"

"Well, that's it. You've heard everything else."

"So I've been right all along. She's out to get him. Have you spoken to Dan at all since you left?"

"No. He's going to ring me tomorrow night. Do you believe me now about seeing Jules down the road from the theatre?"

"Yeah, I'm sorry, so what happens now?"

"What do you mean?"

"Tomorrow. I'm coming over."

"No, it's fine, Tess. I just needed an excuse for Dan. I've got a few things I've got to do."

"And that's it? You don't need me anymore?"

"Tess, it's not like that. I've got something to do that's boring. You wouldn't enjoy it."

"You mean you don't want me there. And I wonder why. Got anything to do with Jules?"

"No." But my tone suggested otherwise and I knew she hadn't missed it.

"You're going around there, aren't you?"

"No," I answered feebly.

"Nic?"

"Okay! Yes! I'm just going over there to ask why?"

"Why?"

"You know why," I answered.

"No, I mean, why are you bothering to ask that? You know why she's doing it."

"I just want to know why she's putting us through this when Dan's obviously not interested."

"Why don't you just tell him?" I could hear my mum's voice again, her constant questions. Only it was Tess speaking. "Well?"

"He's dealing with enough, Tess. He's lost every family member. He sure as hell doesn't need me obsessing about someone who might or might not fancy him, resulting in my jealousy."

"But we all know she fancies him."

"And he doesn't need me stressing about it or her, does he?"

"Maybe not, but you could to me."

I sighed, getting ready for the inevitable invitation she was working up to. "So…"

"You want to come with me, right?"

"Two's better than one."

"You reckon?"

"Absolutely. Now what time do you want me?" she questioned.

"I was going to take a walk over there in the morning. About ten?"

"Okay. I'll be around your place in plenty of time."

"All right. I'll see you in the morning." And I ended the call, sighing heavily.

Walking back into the sitting room to my mum, I could tell she had been listening. I smiled resignedly before falling back onto the sofa.

"What did she say?"

"She wanted to know what was up with me."

"So she knew something was?"

"Yep. I wanted to go over to Jules's tomorrow on my own to have it out with her, but Tess has decided otherwise."

"Good. You need someone to back you up." I wasn't so sure about that, or that I could count on her keeping quiet to allow me to do the talking.

"I still think I would be better on my own, but she won't back down."

"You need your friends, Nic, and I'm here most of the day tomorrow as well, okay?"

"Yeah. Thanks, Mum." I felt washed out from everything that had happened today, and my mind was beginning to return to Jules and Dan and what I was going to say to her when I knocked on her door. Would she back off, or would what I had to say to her just compound what she was already thinking, that she could take Dan from me?

"Nicola… Nicola!"

"W-what?" I answered.

"You're falling asleep. Go to bed."

"Yeah, I think I will." I had woken up a little with walking up the stairs, but now I had crawled into bed, sleep again began to claim me. Thoughts of Jules were still floating around inside my head, but I was rapidly sinking, willingly falling into unconsciousness away from everything that hurt. Even Charlotte didn't make an appearance. Did she know I needed nothing more than that, just that quiet, peaceful lull? When I did surface, it was with a simultaneous yawn and leisurely stretch. I lay there, thinking. I suddenly ached for that sinking feeling I'd had whilst falling to sleep last night, where nothing could reach me. The last thing I had thought about before I fell to sleep was Jules, and it was her who was returning now. I felt a dread in the pit of my stomach just thinking about later. I looked at the clock. It was eight forty-five. I figured I had plenty of time, so I rolled over and tried to get back to sleep.

But she stubbornly stayed in the forefront of my mind, goading me from within.

A loud bang from downstairs forced my eyes wide open. I sat up, wondering if I had dreamed it. Another round of banging confirmed I definitely hadn't. I rushed down the stairs, wondering where my mum was.

"I thought you were going to be ready," Tess said.

"What time is it?"

"Nine thirty."

"That's why I'm not ready," I answered sleepily. I turned, allowing Tess to follow me into the kitchen.

"So, what time are we going?"

"Is that why you're here so early? So I wouldn't already be gone?"

"Not exactly, but it did cross my mind. Does it bother you?"

"No, course it doesn't. Actually I'm quite pleased you're coming. It's not as if I'm looking forward to it."

"What are you going to say to her?"

"I haven't got a clue. I'm not even sure it's a good idea any more."

"Then it might be a good idea for you to get changed so we can get out of here before you change your mind completely, don't you think?"

"Yeah, okay." And I disappeared back upstairs, sneaking around my mum's door to make sure everything was okay.

"I'm just going out with Tess, Mum."

"Okay, be careful and good luck."

"Whoa. I think that's the fastest I've ever seen you move!" Tess said sarcastically.

"I thought you'd be pleased... Now, shall we go?" I smiled just to let her know I wasn't being serious. Allowing Tess to go ahead of me, I locked up. I was quite happy walking without any conversation, but Tess obviously had other ideas.

"Have you spoken to Dan at all this morning?"

"No. Why? I told you he was going to ring me tonight." My suspicions about something that might have been said or done were immediately alerted.

"Oh, nothing. Dan was his usual self last night, but Mal was very quiet when he came back. I just wondered what you had both talked about when he took you home." Was she really on the ball and had sensed that something really was bothering him, or was she just fishing, knowing we must have at least conversed a little with being in such close proximity with one another? Or maybe she wondered whether he had been talking about her.

"He has said something, hasn't he?"

"No."

"Why hesitate then?"

"I didn't. I was thinking about something else... Jules," I lied, hoping she wouldn't see through me. I didn't even know who this woman was that Mal had been going on about. Did he have some notion as to her identity? And I was almost certain that Tess wouldn't have, or that Mal would have said any more about the matter to her. Tess would have said by now if he had.

She continued to chat while we walked, and though I just gave the occasional word or nod in reply, being preoccupied with what was going on in my own head did nothing to distract her from ploughing on. We were three-quarters of the way there. We had already turned off away from the direction of Mal and Dan's flat when she finally stopped.

"Crickey, I don't even remember getting this far." I wanted to add that I could quite believe that with her incessant talking, but that wasn't fair. Tess was here for my benefit. She wanted to support me, and to be fair, I couldn't even have told her what she'd been talking about. Most of it had gone straight over my head.

"Well, it's not far now," I said, covering up what was really going on in my own head.

"Are you all right?"

"Yeah. I'm just wondering what I'm supposed to say to her."

"Well, why she said what she did at the flat would be a start. It's not as if she doesn't know you and Dan are together, and then there's the theatre, when you said she was watching you and me crossing the road. Be careful of her, Nic. I know she's always had a thing for Dan, but it sounds like she's getting some sort of weird kick out of all this." I looked over at the street name we had just turned in to – Haran Street.

"Well, we're here. I don't suppose there's any point in turning back now, is there?"

"Certainly not," Tess answered decisively. "We've got to let her know she can't do this, right?"

"Right," I answered just as resolutely, but my stomach was telling a very different story. It was churning horribly.

"Well, come on then." And she pulled me forward. It was about halfway down the street, and I now really wished we hadn't come. "It'll be fine. I'm not leaving you." Reluctantly I nodded and walked with her.

Reaching number twenty-three, I looked up. She lived in the first-floor flat, but from here, I couldn't see any sign of her.

"Maybe she's gone out," I murmured to Tess.

"Well, we won't know until we knock on her door, will we?" She was still acutely aware of how uncomfortable I was. With an air of decisiveness, though inside I was anything but, I walked into the passageway and knocked on her door. I waited with Tess standing behind me like some burly bouncer, though the picture I was painting in my head was altogether unfair; she was nothing like a bouncer. Though slightly smaller than I was in height but no bigger in build and with short, very light brown hair, she was really pretty, attractive, but she just didn't know it. With no apparent answer, I was just about to suggest we give up and go back home when I saw Jules through the square panes of frosted glass in the top half of the door; she was walking down the stairs. I anxiously waited, wondering what reaction I was going to receive.

"Nicola! Oh! And you've brought Tess along as well. What can I do for you?" she sneered.

"I want to know what all that was about yesterday, about what you said to me about Dan."

"I don't know what you mean, Nic. What am I supposed to have said to you about him?"

"Don't play games, Jules. You know very well what!"

"Look. I'm sorry, Nic, but you seem to have got the wrong end of the stick," she responded a little too sweetly, which prompted Tess into action.

"You've always fancied him, Jules. Why can't you just lay off?"

"Why should I?" she answered, lowering her voice. "It's not as if he won't get over you eventually, Nic." And she smiled in Tess's direction as if she had already won the game. I barred her way, feeling Tess take a step towards her.

"Just stop this now, Jules." But she didn't answer me; she suddenly slapped herself hard on her cheek and began to cry, loudly. She kept her hand there.

"What are you doing?" And I reached out for her, but I found myself rooted to the spot.

"Dan... What?" I cried out.

"I could say the same thing. What are you doing...? What's happened?" he said, turning to Jules. She was still crying for all she was worth.

"It's not what you think," Tess blurted out.

"Oh, and what's that?" Dan demanded.

"She slapped me," Jules answered weakly.

"No, she didn't!" Tess shot back.

"Shut up, Tess!" Dan snapped.

"Why are you here?" I questioned him.

"I came over to help out with something, and it's probably a good thing I did; otherwise, there might have been even more trouble. And I see you're not denying it, Nic!"

"Dan, I didn't do anything. Please, Jules, just tell him."

"I don't know what I've done to you, Nic, but I didn't deserve that."

"Oh, you so did!" Tess shot back.

"Tess!" And I looked again at Dan. "I didn't do anything, honestly."

"I'm sorry, Nic, but I think you had better go, both of you." And he put his arm protectively around Jules and closed the door on us. For a few seconds, I remained there, stunned before my tears finally began to fall.

"I wish I had slapped her!" Tess complained.

"Please, I just want to get out of here." And I turned around to go.

"Oh, Nic. He'll come around. He'll realise what she's up to."

"Will he? You've more or less told him that she deserved to be slapped."

"Yes, he will, and I'm sorry. That just sort of slipped out. I'll straighten it out with Dan." And she ushered me out of the passageway and back up the street. I remembered nothing about our walk back. Tess must have rung Mal while we were on our way, because we had barely reached my front door when my attention was diverted to the beep of his car horn.

I didn't turn to acknowledge him. All I wanted to do was to get into the house and try and forget the events that had just ripped my world in two.

I wanted to tell them both to go. The last thing I wanted to do now was to go over it all again, dissecting events for someone else's benefit.

"Sit down, Nic."

"Tess, please. I know you mean well, but I just want to be on my own!"

"Sorry, no can do. We're not going anywhere, not until I know what's happened and made sure you're all right," Mal interrupted.

"You mean, she hasn't told you?" And I looked at Tess, immediately regretting my tone. "I'm sorry. I didn't mean it like that. I just thought you would have told him on the phone."

"I was too worried about you."

"She was, Nic. She didn't know what to do for the best. That's why Tess asked me to come over. Now, are you going to tell me?"

"Can I have a drink first?"

"Sure, I'll go and make it. You want one, Mal?" Tess asked.

"Please," he answered, and for the first time in weeks, his smile for her was genuine without any hint of sarcasm he generally brought in to the mix where Tess was concerned, or maybe it was just because of the situation I now found myself in.

As she left the room, he began, "I had no idea you were going round there this morning. Why didn't you say anything?"

I relayed to him what Jules had said to me about my not getting too attached to Dan.

"When did she say that?" Mal pressed.

"When she hugged me at the door, just before she left. She whispered it to me, so no one else would hear. I guess she knew I would want to have it out with her and that I would go over there first thing. But after she had said that, my head was all over the place. I just wasn't thinking. Anyway, why was Dan there?" I asked, almost as an afterthought.

"I don't know. He rushed out earlier, said Jules needed some help. That was it. I don't even know whether Dan knew what was wrong."

But just then Tess reappeared with three drinks.

"Have you told him what happened?" she asked.

"No, I'm still at the beginning. I was telling him what she whispered to me yesterday." And I turned again to Mal. "I don't know what's going on. Why would she do that?"

"I'll tell you why."

"Please, Tess. Let Nic tell me." I could feel her shrinking back into the sofa. I reached over to her just to let her know it was fine, and my attention returned to Mal.

"Tess figured out immediately that something was wrong. That's why you came with me this morning, isn't it?" She nodded without saying anything, so I carried on. "I just wanted to know why she had said that to me when I hadn't done anything to her. At least, I didn't think I had. Anyway, she opened the door to us and was quite civil at first, don't you think, Tess?"

"Oh yes," but she didn't elaborate.

"I just asked her why she had said that to me yesterday."

"So what did she say?"

"That I seemed to have got hold of the wrong end of the stick. I demanded that she stop playing games. Then Tess accused her of fancying Dan and told her to lay off." Mal immediately looked at Tess.

"No, Tess was trying to help," I defended. "I'm glad you were there. But Jules just seemed as though she was enjoying the game." I returned my focus to Mal. "She said, 'Why should she?' But then she lowered her voice, adding that it wasn't as though Dan wouldn't eventually get over me."

Momentarily I drifted before refocussing my attention on Mal. "I demanded that she stop all of this. That's when she slapped her own cheek and started crying. I didn't understand at first, at least not until I saw Dan appear from up the stairs. Then it all made perfect sense. He had obviously heard what she had wanted him to hear. She accused me of slapping her. That's it really."

"Isn't that enough?" Tess added, looking directly at Mal. But he didn't answer her straight away.

"He just took Jules's word for it?" he asked.

"Yeah. I don't blame him. I suppose from what he had heard, she was the injured party."

"How can you say that, Nic?" Tess demanded.

"Tess, just let her finish, please," Mal urged.

"He only heard what she wanted him to hear, and I walked straight into the trap. She had obviously managed to get him around there, thinking that I would want to have it out with her about what she had said yesterday, and she gauged my reaction exactly right."

"And what was Dan's reaction to it all?" Mal asked.

"He wanted to know what had happened, and she told him that I had slapped her. Said she didn't know why I had done it. Tess tried to defend me, but he wouldn't have any of it. I told him I hadn't laid a finger on her, but he just told us to go, and he put his arm around her and closed the door on us."

I could feel my tears welling up again. Tess sidled over to me and put her arm around me.

"You definitely didn't do anything, right?" Mal asked.

"How can you ask something like that, Mal?" Tess asked disapproving.

"Tess, I just need to be absolutely sure."

"It's all right, Tess," I reassured her, and I returned my attention to Mal. "No, I didn't. I didn't do anything."

"Good, but I don't understand how Dan would be so easily taken in," Mal puzzled. "He knows she's got the hots for him. He knows you as well."

"Obviously not as well as I thought," I answered.

"Well, we've got to do something about it," Tess demanded.

"Well, obviously, but going in there and throwing accusations all over the place, you're just compounding what Dan probably already thinks."

"What do you mean, 'probably already thinks'?" Tess demanded.

"If I know Dan, Tess, he'll still be mulling it all over. He won't be absolutely certain about what happened. He'll want to try and get it straight in his own head."

"And all the time she's there, putting the boot in for Nic," Tess responded angrily.

"Yeah, all right, I'm sure that's the last thing Nic needs to hear," Mal berated.

"It's okay," I said.

"No it's not, Nic, I'm sorry. Mal's right; it is the last thing you need to hear, but we'll get all this sorted out. Right, Mal?"

"Yeah, we will," he assured me.

Chapter Twenty-Three
Unite

Mal and Tess stayed most of the afternoon with the promise of Mal returning later to let me know what was happening with Dan. My mum stayed out of the way while they were here, and even though they were gone for only half an hour and my mum kept me company, I felt more alone than ever. It just seemed as though everything Dan and I had been through had all been for nothing.

"It'll be all right, you know."

I smiled weakly at her attempt to try and cheer me up, but my moroseness returned with a vengeance.

"I don't think so, Mum. You didn't see him. He looked so angry at what he believed I had done. He actually thought I had slapped her."

"Well, he's stupid then, if that's what he thinks, and you're better than that. I wish you would let me go over there and have a word with her."

"No, please, Mum. It'll only make matters worse."

"Um, it would make me feel better though."

"It's Dan I'm more bothered about. I should have known better where Jules was concerned, but I really thought he knew me better than that."

"What time's Mal coming back?"

"He didn't specify a time. He just said later. I suppose it depends when Dan returns to the flat. That's if he does, he might end up staying with her."

"Oh, stop it, Nic! You're just crucifying yourself more by thinking like that."

"It's possible though; even you can't deny that."

"I don't deny that Daniel Trennan isn't on the list of people I like at the moment, but I don't think even he is that stupid. He'll go back to the flat, and even though there's been no word from him he'll be questioning why you would do something like that and whether you actually did do it at all."

I hoped she was right, but I seriously doubted it. Jules was popular. All the guys flocked around her, and maybe now Dan would be joining them. I took my phone out of my pocket, wondering whether he had even tried to contact me. My spirits lifted, seeing an unread message there.

"Why are you bothering with that?" my mum asked. "You'll only make yourself feel worse."

"There's a message. It might be from him."

She didn't say any more. She walked back out to the kitchen. Alone, I turned my attention back to my phone and to the message awaiting me. But my spirits plummeted again seeing it was only Tess.

Hey Nic. Coming around in an hour with Mal. Hope you're okay x

"How could I have thought it might have been him?" I said to myself, unaware that my mum was standing in the doorway and had clearly heard me. She came and sat on the sofa beside me.

Without saying a word, she wrapped her arms around me. My tears began to fall freely, unhampered and vocal.

I don't know how long I was there, but I must have cried myself to sleep again, because the next I knew I was still on the sofa, only my mum wasn't. It was light out in the hallway as well, making it dark in here. I looked at the clock on the mantelpiece before me. It was seven thirty. I wondered what had happened to Mal and Tess. I was sure they were due about six. I was still trying to work it out when my mum walked back through.

"I've got you some soup. I thought you might be hungry. You haven't eaten all day."

"Thanks," I answered uninterested. "Have Mal or Tess rung to say they can't make it?"

"No, they've been here."

"Why didn't you wake me?"

"I didn't have the heart to, Nic, and neither did they. We all agreed you had been through enough and that you needed to rest. Sorry if we did the wrong thing."

"You didn't. I just don't like what's happening."

"I know, but for now there's nothing you can do about it."

"I'm not sure I ever will."

"It'll all seem better in the morning."

"Aren't you supposed to say that when you're tucking me in?"

"Do you want me to?" We both laughed. "That's better. Now get that soup down you."

I did as she said, but my mind just kept drifting back to Dan. What was he doing? Where was he? Who was he with? With every question my mind asked, the same answer came back… Jules.

"Thanks for that, but I'm going to bed. Do you mind?"

"Sure you don't want tucking in?" And my mum smiled.

"I'm sure." And I stood up to make my way to the stairs.

"Oh, I forgot to tell you. Mal said they would both come over again in the morning, with you being asleep when they were here earlier. I'll be at work. Do you want me to wake you before I leave?"

"Please." I headed up the stairs to bed. Had they got something to tell me? Had anything more happened? I slumped on to my bed, pleased to be alone at last, but I felt more empty. I wondered what was going through his head. Had he thought about me at all? I quickly checked my phone again, but there was nothing there. I lay there for a minute before I climbed in, closed my eyes and willed sleep to come, but the only thing that did was that image of Jules. Had I fallen asleep? The image I was seeing suddenly switched to her and Charlotte. She smiled but retained her distance from Jules.

"What is it? What's wrong?" I called out, feeling her reticence to move any closer to her. Jules seemed completely indifferent, but could she actually see her? No, she didn't even know either of us were there. In my sleep I turned again to Charlotte.

"Please, tell me. What is it?" But she just looked at me. Tears were beginning to fill her eyes, and she shook her head. What was it? Didn't she want to tell me, or couldn't she? But before I could question any further, she turned and walked away. I made a move to follow. I had taken no more than a couple of steps when she disappeared from view. For a short time I felt different, whole almost, but the emptiness now returned with a vengeance, and it was more consuming, like I was spiralling out of control. The darkness was closing in, enveloping me. I looked up into the faintest chink of light, but that emptiness remained, goading me from the depths of despair that now engulfed me. I jumped, feeling someone's touch.

"Ssh… It's all right, Nic. It's only me… It's Mum." And her arms felt warm around me.

Instantly I felt safe again. I wiped my eyes; I'd been crying. I felt worn out. I wanted to let go and have someone else look after me, but my tears came again, more torrential this time, until sleep took me once more.

I woke to the sound of birds singing outside. I couldn't gauge what sort of time it was, but it felt quite early. The sun was out. I could glimpse it through my curtains. I remembered my clock on my bedside table. It was five past six. I fell back against my pillow with a groan. Dan instantly came to the fore and with him all the pain and tears that had spilled out of me last night. I lay there, thinking. Everything was rushing through my head. Tess and Mal were coming over this morning. For a few seconds, my spirits lifted before Dan overtook them again. Where was he? Had he stayed at the flat last night… on his own? I couldn't seem to think of anything else. He filled every thought that came my way. I hated myself for the way he affected me. Why couldn't I just forget and move on like he obviously had? I looked at the clock again; it was six forty-five. I thought again about Mal and Tess. I figured they would probably be over here in another few hours, and I needed to shower, so I made a move, but I only got to the edge of the bed. Even that one act was proving a challenge. I didn't really want to do anything; lethargy was fast becoming my best friend.

But with a massive effort, I managed to get through to the bathroom.

Walking back into my bedroom, my mum followed hot on my heels. I didn't really feel in the mood to vocalise what I was feeling yet again. I just wanted to be left alone to ponder whatever my mind managed to latch onto, and that wasn't a difficult one to grasp. There was only one person in there and numerous scenarios, all bad.

"How are you feeling this morning?"

"All slumbered out."

"Yeah, you've certainly slept well over the last twenty-four hours."

"It's not quite that, is it?"

"You know what I mean. Anyway, I didn't expect you up quite so early."

"Like I said, I'm all slumbered out. I wish I could have stayed in there longer but — "

"Heard anything from Mal or Tess?"

"No."

"Okay. I'll leave you to it. See you downstairs."

"Okay." I had every intention of making short work of getting my hair dry and getting changed, but all I wanted to do was sit here. By the time I managed to move again, my hair was almost dry, so I left it, and instead I got dressed. I just managed to get a slice of toast down, due only to the fact that my mum was watching everything I did, eagle eyed. I was thankful when a knock came at the door and I heard Mal and Tess's voices. Although it was only nine thirty, I was glad to see them.

"Right. I'll leave you all to it. You'll be all right, won't you, Nic?"

"Yes, Mum. Go!" She looked straight at Tess. She nodded as though she were conveying some unspoken assurance that I would be fine, which only succeeded in making me feel resentful for feeling so inadequate.

No one spoke until we had all heard the front door slam shut, signalling my mum's departure.

"So how are you, really?" Tess demanded.

"Yeah, I'm all right," I replied.

"Liar."

"What do you want from me, Tess? I've just told you, haven't I?"

"Whoa... Are you two forgetting what good friends you are?" Mal asked. "We've come over to make sure you're okay, Nic. There's no need to bite Tess's head off!"

I looked over at Tess. He was right. There was no need for it just because of what had happened to me. After all, she *had* tried to help me.

"I'm sorry, and you're right. I'm not dealing with the fallout from Dan very well. My mum ended up coming into my room last night because of a dream I'd had."

"Want to share it?"

"It was about Charlotte and Jules."

"You don't have to tell us if you don't want to," Mal remarked, mistaking the slight pause on my part for a resistance to tell.

"No, it's fine. I'm just trying to figure out how to begin. I tried to get to sleep, but all I could see was an image of Jules, and then Charlotte appeared, and she seemed careful to keep a distance between herself and Jules. I kept asking her what it was, but she wouldn't answer, like she couldn't. I saw tears rolling down her cheeks, and then she walked away and disappeared. Her leaving like that made me feel even emptier and the next thing I remember, my mum had her arms around me. I had woken up crying, again."

"But it's just a dream, right?" Tess sort of suggested, but I still wasn't sure, and the mystery of that letter disappearing from the drawer in Greg's office had resurfaced in my mind, and I still hadn't said anything of it to Tess. But Mal was here. Oh, what the hell! It wasn't as though I could talk to Dan about it now, was it?

"There's got to be more to them than just dreams, Tess," Mal said. "How many times has she appeared in them?"

"Quite a few." I looked at Mal. I knew he was aware of one or two but no more than that.

"I've had many dreams since she died, Mal, where she's entered them, and I just think there's something that maybe she's trying to tell me. Don't look at me like that. I know how crazy it sounds, and I think it's going to get worse when you hear what else I've got to tell you."

"Okay, you've got my attention, and I don't think you're cuckoo, all right?"

I smiled tiredly at him. "I would postpone that judgment until I've finished, if I were you."

"Dan's the crazy one!" Tess blurted out.

"What's this?" I asked them both.

"We'll get to that later. You've already started, Nic." And he threw a disapproving look at Tess.

"All right. But this goes back to before Fran's funeral. Dan and I made the excuse of needing to work in Greg's office because of having to do extra work for college to catch up. It was when we were looking for something to do with his adoption."

"Yeah, I'm with you."

I looked at Tess, who also nodded.

"Well, it wasn't just his birth certificate that we found. There was a letter in the table drawer that stood alongside the wall to the back of his desk, but it was locked. Finding the key, we opened it, and there it sat, just one letter. Nothing else."

"What did it say?" Tess eagerly asked.

"We didn't read it. Dan saw that it was addressed to Greg and that it was in Fran's handwriting, so he refused. He said it was obviously personal and meant only for Greg and that it just didn't feel right for him to read it, so he put it back."

"You want to go back and get it, don't you?" Mal guessed.

"That's just it. I did."

"What? When?" Tess quizzed.

"That day we went to the funeral directors, we went around there afterwards. Remember?"

"Yeah," they both concurred. "But you didn't say anything about it at the time," Mal answered.

"I didn't even say anything about this to Dan."

"So you've got it on you?" Tess asked.

"No... Let me just explain. I had a dream that night before about being in that house. When we walked in there, Dan wanted to go straight through to the back, where we had found Greg's body. I think the purpose was just to lay a ghost to rest, and we stayed in there for a while. Then we walked back towards the front, and he said something about wanting to go upstairs. He wanted to go up there on his own, so I stayed in the hallway by the front door. I wasn't comfortable in there anyway. But as Dan stood on the stairs, ready to go up, I saw a light hovering around him, but it disappeared as quickly as it had appeared."

"Was Dan aware of this?"

"No, Mal, he didn't see anything, and as he disappeared from view, the light reappeared and seemed to expand and grow; it was Charlotte. But that's not the worst of it. It was just as it had been in my dream the night before."

"Christ, that's weird. Did it creep you out?" he asked.

"Yeah." I smiled, remembering. "It did a bit, but she kept her distance and instead moved towards Greg's office, disappearing into it. I just stood there. I couldn't move, and believe me, I wanted to. It seemed only seconds later that she reappeared, holding something. She smiled and looked back towards his office and disappeared again. It was then that I remembered the letter, the one Dan wouldn't open. I wanted to go in, but what would I say to Dan? I knew how he would react. He'd been definite last time. But I knew he could also come down at any moment. But it felt like she wanted me to get it. So then, quietly as I could, I made a move towards it and opened the door. I knew where the keys were, so I managed to negotiate that fairly quickly and turned the lock of that drawer."

"And?" Tess said impatiently.

"Well, that's just it. It was gone."

"What?" Mal said, shocked.

"And where it is now is what I've been puzzling over ever since."

"Didn't you say anything to Dan?" Tess asked.

"No, I didn't feel as though I could. It was addressed to his dad from his mum, and they're both dead now. I've been wanting to talk to you about it, Tess, but when I got the opportunity, something happened, or the time never seemed right."

"So you think Charlotte wanted you to get it. Why?" Mal questioned.

"Why indeed, Mal. What could possibly be in it?" I said to them both.

"A confession?" Tess suggested.

"A confession about what though? She died of cancer. What would she possibly need to get off her chest?" I asked.

"Clear her conscience, you mean?" she corrected me.

"Well, yes," I agreed.

"Maybe she did something she was bothered about, something really bad. Do you know anything about Dan's real mum? Did you manage to find anything out?"

"No, with everything else that's happened, looking into finding her has sort of been shelved. I did mention it a while ago, but he said he couldn't think about it at that point."

"Well, at least, we know one thing," Tess said.

"We know nothing, Tess," Mal contradicted.

"Yes, we do. We now know there's a letter that might point us in the right direction."

"Yes, a letter that's disappeared somewhere, and we don't know who with."

"Well, I hate to state the obvious, but Juicy Jules Harvey has got to be in it right up to her makeup-plastered hairline!"

I laughed at Tess's very individual assessment of her."

"Don't ask?" Mal warned when I raised my eyebrows questioningly. "It's her new favourite nickname for her.

"Anyway, that's what I wanted to tell you. What about you two?" I asked. For a minute, neither said anything.

"I'm sorry, Nic," Tess apologised. "I don't know what else she's told him, but he's as mad as hell with you."

"That's not really a surprise though, is it?" I responded.

"No, not when we know how devious she is," Tess added.

"What did he say then?" I asked.

"Well, he ordered me out of the flat. I was just trying to stick up for you, Nic."

"What?"

"Sorry but he's losing it… completely!" she said, turning to me and Mal.

"Sorry, Tess, I meant about ordering you out of the flat." And I waited for them to elaborate.

"When he told Tess to get out, I took her back home," Mal said, taking over. "I wasn't about to let her just go on her own. Anyway, when I got back, he was just sitting there, not doing anything particularly. I had wondered whether we'd be joined by Jules at some point, but thankfully she stayed away. I asked what the hell had been going on and why he had spoken to Tess like that. His answer was simple. His opinion is that Tess has always disliked Jules and that this situation with you has just compounded what Tess already thinks."

"But that's just stupid," I retorted. "Like Tess said, she was just sticking up for me."

"I know – I think the same as you, Nic, but I've got to be careful that I don't push him further towards Jules."

"So he obviously thinks even less of me?"

"I think it's just the case that she's more convincing."

"But he hasn't even given me a chance to explain, Mal."

"I know that. Do you mind if I tell him what you saw in his house – about the letter and, more importantly, the dream you had last night, and then seeing Charlotte and her wanting to distance herself from Jules?"

"What's he going to say when I've spoken to you two and not him?"

"Well, like you've just said, he's not giving you chance, is he?"

"No, I don't suppose so."

"So… Can I?" he repeated.

"Okay, but can you tell him I've got nothing to gain from this? That I don't hate Jules, never really have, but that I can't say she didn't say that to me when she did?"

"I will, but we need to get you two talking again. Nothing's going to get resolved if you're not talking, is it?"

"Okay." But I felt so powerless. I turned to Tess.

"I'm sorry you've been dragged into all this."

"I dragged myself into it, Nic, not you. And Dan will see that when he stops being such an arse."

"Anyway, it's almost lunchtime, and I need to get back. I can come around again Wednesday afternoon if you want; it'll give me time to try and talk to Dan. What do you think? And I could call for you on the way if you want, Tess." Mal suggested.

"Yeah, that would be good. Thanks."

"You coming then?" Mal asked Tess.

"No, I'm going to stay with Nic a while longer," she responded.

"All right, see you both Wednesday… And it'll be all right, Nic. You'll see."

I nodded, grateful that I at least had Tess and Mal watching out for me..

Chapter Twenty-Four
Action Plan

"Thanks for staying back, Tess. I'm grateful to Mal as well. I probably don't deserve it."

"What? Don't be stupid. We're your friends, Nic. Jules Harvey's the one who's in the wrong here. I was there, remember?"

"I know. I just can't get my head around it. Why can't Dan see it?"

"Mal will talk to him. He's been spitting as many feathers as I have over all this."

"Maybe that'll be one more thing he can hold against me. Ugh... I should have talked to him about seeing Charlotte at his house. I just didn't know whether he could handle it. I tried before, remember, the night Charlotte went missing, and he didn't really want to know then."

"He will. I've got a feeling Mal will make him see sense. Anyway, do you want to come over to my place for a bit? You've been holed up here for too long."

"I don't know, Tess. It would mean us going past Dan's, wouldn't it?"

"Um, except that he doesn't live there anymore."

"'Course. I'd forgotten that."

"So what's it to be?"

"Okay, yeah. Why not? You're right. I have been stuck in here too long, and I'm not thinking about anything other than Dan."

"I'll wait here then, while you get ready." She always made me feel better.

Tess and I walked away from my house in silence, and I was beginning to worry we would remain devoid of any conversation for the rest of the way to her place when she started.

"What we need to do is figure out where that letter's disappeared to."

"There's no way of finding out though, is there?" I questioned.

"I don't know. There's got to be some way. The most logical person to have taken it would have to have been Greg," Tess replied.

"But why would he take it from there when he must have put it there in the first place? And he wouldn't have done that unless he was sure it would be safe."

"Did he find out that it wasn't?" Tess wondered aloud.

"Maybe," I shrugged.

"That's got to be it," Tess said excitedly. "You said he was suspicious, didn't you?"

"Well, I don't think I said that exactly. He did seem strange towards me after we came out, like he knew what we had been looking for," I corrected.

"So all we need to do now is find out where he moved it to."

"Tess, I know you're trying to help, but isn't all this a bit much?"

"Do you want Dan back or not?"

"You know I do. But don't you want Jules to be seen as the villain in all this?"

"Of course, because she is." I sighed, knowing full well I wasn't about to win this round.

"Have you heard anything more from the cops?" she asked.

"No, the last I heard from Dan was that they were still looking into Charlotte's death, but they were treating Greg's as an accident. They weren't looking for anyone in connection with that."

"So could Charlotte's death have anything to do with this letter then?"

"How? Aren't we going off on a bit of a tangent?" I responded.

"Well, either her death was an accident as well, or maybe she knew something."

"Tess, this is all sounding a bit too weird." Her excitement had been gathering momentum, and with one comment from me, her expression spectacularly dropped. "Oh, look. I'm sorry. I didn't mean it like that. It's just that there are too many if, buts, and maybes for any of it to have any real substance."

"You think I'm getting too ahead of myself, don't you?" she complained.

"Not exactly. I think you've come up with some good points, but we need to sit down and weigh them up properly."

"Well, we haven't got much further to go." And she abruptly stopped.

"Why?" But I knew without finishing as I looked across the road; we were standing opposite Dan's house on Morsley Road.

"Why have we stopped here?"

"Do you want to have a walk around the back, see if we can get in?"

"No!"

"Why not? It's not like Dan's going to be anywhere near here, is it?"

"Even so, we can't," I argued.

"Sure we can." And she started to cross the road.

"Tess," I pleaded.

"Come on, Nic. We're here now."

Reluctantly I followed, keeping careful watch in case anyone was watching our advance. As quietly as we could, we tiptoed our way over the pebbled driveway and around the side to the gate. Tess turned the knob to allow our entry, but it wouldn't budge. She tried again, pushing against it.

"It's locked," I informed her.

"Yes, I know." And she promptly began to try and scale it, but was getting nowhere fast.

"Oh, let me." And with Tess's help to lift me up a little, I managed to haul myself over. "I can't believe we're doing this," I grumbled as I slid the lock to the side and opened the gate.

"It's all for the greater good," she happily assured me. "Right. Just keep an eye out for anywhere we might be able to get in, maybe a window or something."

I seriously doubted there would be any open windows. There was certainly nothing where we were standing behind the gate. We quietly followed the path around to the back, fully aware that the neighbours might spot us if they were in. Keeping fairly close to the house, we looked up, but none were open, as I'd suspected. The utility, where they did all the washing was at the back of the garage, which jutted out a little way into the garden, with the outside door leading into it. I tried that door on the off chance, but it was locked as well. I turned to say so to Tess.

"No," I whispered as hard as I could. She put her hand on the French door to try it. There was an alarm on that where there hadn't been on the utility, with there being another locked and bolted door leading into the main house.

"Hey, it's not locked." And she opened it. I squirmed, waiting for the alarm to belt out its deafening shriek, but to my shock, there was no sound. Only Tess.

"Come on, quick!" I sneaked in after her, just pulling it to without latching it. "Right. Where do you want to start?"

"To get out of this room for a start!"

"Oh, yeah. Is this where you and Dan found him?"

"Tess!"

"I was only asking."

"Anyway, one of us needs to stay downstairs to keep watch."

"Okay. Do you want to stay down here?" she offered, remembering what I'd said about this place the last time I had been here with Dan.

"Yeah, thanks. Do you want me to have a look in Greg's office again?"

"No. If it wasn't there last time, it's unlikely to be there now," she answered.

"Okay, I'll stay here, but don't be long, yeah?" I had no desire to stay in here any longer than we needed to.

"Don't worry. I won't." And making quick work of the stairs, she disappeared. I stood in the same position as before and kept watch, though I was careful not to be seen. It felt cold in here and unhappy, and I was expecting someone to appear. It seemed like a very long time since she'd gone upstairs, and I was beginning to get jittery when I heard her making her way from one room to the next. I was relieved when I saw her at the top of the stairs again.

Sweeping down the staircase, she looked as comfortable as though she were a welcome visitor.

"I know you haven't been gone long, but it felt like ages."

"I know my way around this house, and I know a few of the hiding places as well."

"Did you find it?"

"Nope. If it is here, it's somewhere I don't know of. Come on. Let's go." And she led me back through to the French doors at the back. Closing the door behind me, I was just about to question what we should do about being unable to lock it. She bent down by a few loose bricks by the outside of the utility room and retrieved something. She held the key up like a trophy.

"I thought you would have known about this," she said.

"You knew all the time we would be able to get in?"

"They always left it there."

"What about the alarm?"

"They rarely switched it on," she said. "Anyway, we'd better be going just in case."

We walked back around to the gate. Allowing Tess through, I closed it again and bolted it from my side. Positioning my feet on its frame, I climbed over easily.

"Right. Can we please go straight to your house?"

"Sure." She smiled.

Arriving at Tess's, we made our way straight to the kitchen, where her mum found us.

"Nicola, it's good to see you again. I am sorry about you and Dan. Tess was telling me, weren't you, Tess?"

"Yeah," she said and looked my way. "Sorry, Nic."

"It's all right. It's his loss, eh, Mrs Brinham?"

"Absolutely. I don't really know this Jules. Is that her name?"

"Yes, Mum."

"Yes, well, I don't really know her, but I personally thought you two were good together."

"Thank you, Mrs Brinham."

"Do you both want a drink?"

"Please," we both answered. While she was doing that, Tess caught my eye. "Sorry," she mouthed and pointed outside, indicating that we should go out there. I nodded, and when Mrs Brinham gave us our drinks, we made our escape.

"Oh, before you go, Nicola, are you staying for dinner?"

"I would like that. Thank you."

"Just make sure you let your mum know, okay?"

"Will do," I shouted back.

Outside, we both settled ourselves on the grass. I was just about to question Tess about what her mum had just said, but she beat me to it.

"Well, at least we now know where that letter isn't."

"That letter's the last thing on my mind. Since when had Jules become Dan's girlfriend?"

"She's not."

"That's not the impression your mum was giving."

"It's just because of what I said about Jules trying to get around him and pushing you out. She's come to her own conclusions about them."

"You're not just telling me that to spare my feelings, are you?"

"No, Nic, I'm not. We both know she'd like to be his girlfriend, but she's not, at least not yet."

"Oh, thanks. That gives me hope."

"Well, you've got to fight for him, if you want him."

"But he's the only one who can figure out whether or not I was lying. I'm sure Jules has laid it on thick about how horrible I was to her, probably you as well."

"Well, I think Dan telling me to get out of the flat answers that one." And we both laughed.

"Do you really think it's possible that Charlotte knew what was in that letter?" I suddenly asked, thinking back to what she'd said earlier and the paper I had seen in Charlotte's hand when I saw her in my dream in Dan's house, which we'd trespassed not an hour ago.

"Yeah, I do. She was close to her dad, but it depends on what was actually in the letter, and we're not going to know that until we find it, and I don't know how likely that is, if at all." I wanted to know more, to ask more about Dan and Jules, but her mum called us in, cutting me off.

All through dinner, the subject of Dan and Jules was thankfully kept out of bounds. Tess's dad concentrated on his dinner throughout, and her mum kept up a steady stream of safe questions for me, which I'm sure Tess had hastily dictated. After we finished, I made my apologies, and with Tess accompanying me down the road, I said goodbye.

"Sorry about that, Nic. She was a bit transparent, wasn't she?"

"Your mum was just being kind like she always is," I assured her. "Go back. I'll be fine. The walk home will do me good."

"Ring me when you get back, yeah?"

"As soon as I get in," I promised.

"I know Mal's not going around to your place until Wednesday, but I'll see you tomorrow afternoon, right? And we'll talk some more. And hopefully on Wednesday, Mal will have some more to contribute."

"See you tomorrow," I called back. I slowed down and looked back to see her disappearing around the corner of her driveway. I wrapped my arms around myself, suddenly feeling a shiver. I wasn't sure whether it was me or the air that felt a little chilly. I turned back and set my pace. All of a sudden, I was eager to get home. I quickly made my way on to Morsley Road. I had walked about halfway down it when I saw Dan and Jules on the other side. I quickly lowered my head in readiness for their advance. Though my stance retained a resolute compliance to the path ahead, my eyes defied me and darted to where they were walking on the other side of the road.

"Hi, Nic!" she shouted over. I half looked and saw Dan watching me. I nodded without meeting Jules's stare and walked on falteringly, my nerves jangling with every step. I wanted to look back to see whether Dan was still watching me and whether they were holding hands, but I was sure that as soon as Jules had caught a glimpse of me, she'd grabbed hold of him anyway. But I resisted, and instead I quickened my pace. I wanted to be away from here as quickly as possible. I was only just managing to keep my tears at bay.

Putting the key in the lock, I opened the door and ran straight into my mum, who was hovering.

"What's the matter?" I asked, a little irritated.

"I just wondered where you had gone."

"I told you I was staying at Tess's for a bit."

"All right. Are you coming to sit down?"

"No, I'm tired." And I feigned a yawn.

"All right. Do you want me to bring you a drink?"

"I just want to go to sleep, Mum." I knew I'd used that excuse too many times already but I couldn't think of anything else and I needed to get away from her and be on my own.

"Okay." And she made the way clear for me to climb the stairs. By the time I had managed to close my bedroom door, I couldn't hold back the tears any longer. I flung myself down on my bed and cried for what seemed like hours. I know what my mum must have thought; I'd already thought it myself, but I just wanted to be on my own. I didn't feel as though I was much good to anyone considering the way I felt at the moment.

I must have been crying so hard that I didn't hear my phone, and I'd forgotten all about ringing Tess as soon as I walked in through the door. There were five missed calls on it. I really did feel tired now, and I certainly didn't feel like talking to her, so I text her instead.

Sorry forgot all about ringing you, see you tomorrow afternoon x

I climbed into bed, hoping that would be enough and that she wouldn't reply. I had enjoyed my time at Tess's, and for a while, I'd even felt better until I saw Dan and Jules. And now all I could think about was them as a couple, holding hands… I thought about Charlotte again and the funeral for her and Greg. That was only a few days away now. Would he want me there after all this? I figured I could probably talk to Tess about it tomorrow afternoon. I was sure Jules would be there, playing centre stage. But it wasn't just me, was it? All this affected Tess as well, and she had known Charlotte the longest – apart from Dan, of course. He might not want me there, but surely he wouldn't tell her to stay away.

Chapter Twenty-Five
Familiar Face

Just as she had promised, Tess came over and stayed for most of the afternoon, eventually leaving around four. I was grateful, but as she herself had said, what else was she going to do when she wasn't welcome at the flat? I, on the other hand, had lain in bed most of the morning, same as I planned to do this morning. Mal and Tess weren't coming until after lunch, so there didn't seem much point in getting up. I looked over at the clock on my bedside table just to check. I shot up with a start.

It was half eleven already, and with thoughts of them arriving any time after twelve, I dove in and out of the shower with lightning speed. I managed to get my hair dry and piled it up on top of my head without interruption. I pulled on some jog pants and an old T-shirt. I wasn't going anywhere, was I? I remembered the last time I dressed like that, Dan and Mal had turned up. That wasn't happening again, was it? Shaking myself out of the self-pity I'd allowed to settle, I made my way downstairs and made a cup of tea and some toast; then took them through to the sitting room at the back. I was glad for the solitude while I ate my breakfast, and by the time I was done, there was still no sign of them, so I took my pots through to the kitchen to wash.

With everything done, I wandered over to the window to see whether they were coming, but there was still no sign. Barefoot, I walked back into the sitting room and fell back onto the sofa. I had been there for about ten minutes, which seemed endless, when there was a rap at the front door.

"Hey," Tess said breezily.

"Hi... I thought you were coming earlier."

"Well, it's only... What time is it?" she shouted back to Mal, who was just walking away from his car.

"Er, ten past one. Why?"

"Nic thought we'd be here earlier."

"I thought this was early," and he smiled.

"It's okay. You're here now."

"Are you all right?" she asked.

"Yeah," I lied.

"No, you're not. What is it?"

"Come in and I'll tell you."

"Mal, will you make us all a cup of tea?"

"Oh, yeah, that's all I've come for, isn't it?" he grumbled.

"Don't go all girlie on me." She smiled, seeing his irritation. After Mal had sloped off into the kitchen, she turned back to me.

"You've got some talking to do. I forgot to ask yesterday. Why did you just send a text?"

"It can wait until we're all sitting down." And I quickly snuck through to the kitchen to help Mal.

Returning with all three teas, I set them down on the coffee table. "Didn't take long, did it?" I said, looking straight at Tess.

"Yeah, yeah, now come on, spill."

After sitting down, I began. "When I left your house yesterday, I managed to get as far as Morsley Road. It was there that I saw Dan and Jules down the road from his house."

"Oh my God! What did you do?" Tess questioned.

"I tried to keep my head down, but Jules shouted over, 'Hi, Nic,' and I mimicked her tone."

"I hope you told her where to go," Tess responded.

"The only thing I wanted was for the ground to open up and swallow me. It was humiliating. I sort of nodded and kept my head as low as I could, though I did catch Dan watching me. He didn't look particularly pleased to see me there."

"I had a chat with him last night again," Mal responded.

"He told you, didn't he?" I guessed.

"You knew all about this, and you said nothing?" Tess accused.

"I prefer to leave the gossiping to you, Tess. This is our friend we're talking about."

"I know that, and I don't gossip!"

"Yeah, right."

"Come on. Leave it out, you two... What did he say about it, Mal?"

"Just that they had seen you. She doesn't come around the flat, you know. She's tried several times, but he won't have it."

"Are you trying to make me feel better?"

"Is it working?" he asked.

"No... Yes, I don't know. From what you're saying, he still spends his time with her outside the flat. Still speaks volumes, doesn't it?"

"Well, it might have done, but she must have seen you a second before he did, because she grabbed hold of his hand. He thought it was to make you jealous," Mal explained.

"It's none of my business," I told him, but I was secretly pleased, and I had wondered that at the time.

"But that's just it, Nic. He pulled his hand away. That's probably why she called out to you, figuring she'd try to make it look like they were together."

"It still doesn't really alter anything, though. He still believes I hit Jules."

"Wrong again, Nicola!" Mal said smiling.

"You mean, he's finally coming to his senses?"

"Not exactly, no. But he is beginning to question things. The way Jules acted when she saw you has made him think again," Mal explained.

"Have you told Mal where we ended up yesterday?" I asked, turning to Tess, who had remained suspiciously quiet.

"This sounds interesting," he said, curious.

"We went around to Dan's house on Morsley Road," she answered.

"What for?" he asked.

"We – I mean, I – thought it might be worth a look around the house to see if we could find that letter, seeing as the drawer in Greg's office was empty. We thought it might have been moved elsewhere, didn't we, Nic?"

"Er, yeah," I reluctantly agreed.

"How stupid are you?" Mal angrily retorted.

"What do you mean?" Tess demanded.

"You broke in!"

"No, we didn't. I know where they used to keep the key to the French doors, and lucky for us, they were still there. Actually, we didn't need them to get in. The French doors had been left unlocked, so from our perspective, we didn't break in at all. In fact, it's lucky we were there really. When we left, we were sure to lock the doors."

"I wouldn't go that far. Did you find anything then?"

"Nothing, and I knew where to look, but it's good to know you're interested, Mal."

Ignoring Tess completely, he turned to me.

"Well, I told Dan about what you saw that day, Nic – Charlotte, I mean, and the dream you had that involved Jules."

"You did tell him that I've got nothing against Jules and that I didn't hit her, didn't you?"

"Yeah, I told him all that. Don't worry."

"So what did he say?" Tess questioned.

"Not much until I told him about the letter Charlotte was holding in her hand and said that you thought she was trying to tell you something. He didn't say much about it, but he wanted to know everything that had happened while he was upstairs. I told him you went into Greg's office and opened that drawer and saw it was empty."

"Oh, God! Was he annoyed?"

"No, not at all. Jules rang him later and wanted him to go around there, but he put her off straight away. He said he had a lot on at the moment and that he'd be in touch. I can't imagine she was very happy about it."

"Do you think he's having second thoughts about Nic?" Tess asked.

"I think he's realising what an idiot he's been – that you didn't hit her, and neither would you have done."

"I would like an apology as well!" Tess added, disgruntled.

"One step at a time, Tess." But a knock at the door stopped our conversation dead.

"You expecting anyone?" Mal asked.

"No," I answered, getting to my feet. "I'll get rid of them." But I recognised the silhouette straight away as I turned into the hallway. The remnants of toast I'd had for breakfast were jostling for a position further up my throat, making me queasy, and I felt hot as well. Uneasily I opened the door.

"Dan," I greeted. Tess shot around the doorway hearing his name from where we'd all been in the sitting room.

"What are you doing here?" she asked.

He opened his mouth to answer when another demand came from behind him.

"Yes, I would like to know that as well!"

"Mum?" I said.

"Well?" she demanded.

Dan turned to face her. "Mrs James, I... I know I don't deserve it, but could I just have a few minutes with Nic? I just want to talk to her and then I'll go." And he looked back at me. I looked at my mum who was still standing behind him.

"Mum, it's fine. I'll talk to him."

"You don't have to, Nic."

"It's fine, really," I assured her.

"Excuse me," she hissed and pushed her way past him into the house. "I'll be in the kitchen," she said to both of us.

"We'll all be in the sitting room, okay?"

"All right." And she disappeared without another word.

I led Dan into the sitting room, where Tess had returned and Mal remained.

"Tess. Mal." He nodded, but Tess completely ignored him.

"Sit down," I offered. He did but he seemed really uneasy. "How are you?"

"Are you for real, Nic?" Tess questioned. "He took her side, and you're asking him how he is?"

"Tess, shut up," I said. "Let him speak."

She sat back against the sofa and folded her arms across her chest defiantly in Mal's direction.

"I'm sorry, Nic – you as well, Tess. Has Mal told you we spoke last night?"

"Yes, he has." And I smiled reassuringly at Mal.

"I've treated you very badly, and I'm sorry. You didn't deserve it. You didn't either, Tess. I should have known better."

"What's brought all this on?" I asked. "Do you know that I definitely didn't hit her? Did she tell you she was lying, or is this just the conclusion you've come to?"

"I started to think more about everything after I saw you on Morsley Road last night and after I spoke to Mal. He told me about the dream you'd had, about Charlotte and what happened inside the house. Why didn't you tell me?"

"You had loads on your mind as it was, Dan. You didn't need me adding to it, and I wasn't sure you could cope with more talk of Charlotte. You said yourself that you were trying not to think about her."

"I wish you had because it wasn't until Mal told me about the letter that I remembered." From out of his pocket, he produced an envelope looking distinctly like the one from the drawer and, from my dream, the one Charlotte had been holding.

"Is that it? Is that the letter?" Tess asked excitedly. "Where did you find it? Or did you move it?" she questioned. But Mal immediately hushed her.

"Let Nic get a word in," he said.

"Where did you find it?" I repeated.

"Remember when I went upstairs? I said I wanted to spend a little time up there in Charlotte's room alone."

"Yes."

"Well, I just sat on the bed thinking. It all got to me a bit, and I started crying. I held on to the bed near the base, and my hand brushed against something. I pulled it out from beneath the mattress and just stuck it in my pocket. Maybe it was what was in my head, but as soon as I had shoved it away, I forgot about it – that is, until last night." And he handed it to me.

"You've read it, right?" I asked.

"No. I still can't see what good it'll do, but you're welcome to read it. That's partly why I came around – to bring this and of course, to apologise."

I'd taken hold of it before I realised what he said. "No, Dan. I can't read it. Greg was your dad. It should be you who reads it. No one else."

"It's fine. I want you to read it."

"No, I'm sorry. I can't." And I handed it back.

"I'll read it if no one else is going to!" I looked at Tess, warning her to back off, not to say another word. I just hoped she wasn't about to blurt out that we'd been there the other day, searching for it.

"Oh, for Christ's sake, someone read it. This is what we've been after, Nic." Tess reasoned.

"What?" Dan asked, puzzled.

"Oh, we've just been talking about it," I said. "I was telling Tess and Mal how we came to find it in the drawer that first time when we'd said we were doing college work." And I glared at Tess.

"Okay, give it here," I said. "I'll read it, but stay at least until we've been through it, and you'll know exactly what it's about."

"All right, thanks."

Taking the letter from the envelope, I unfolded it and began to read.

My Darling Greg,

I'm so sorry I've had to write to you in this way. You've given me so much that it feels cowardly that I should decide to say this in the form of a letter rather than speaking to you as you deserve. Since finding out about the can...

"Dan, you should be reading this. It sounds too personal."

"No, please, Nic. Carry on."

I looked to Mal and Tess, who both smiled encouragingly, even though they too looked unsure. Looking back at the letter, I continued.

Since finding out about the cancer and my time left to me, I've thought about the past more and more. Despite the heartache of your past liaisons, you have given me two perfect children.

I stopped short and looked at Dan again, but he just nodded for me to continue.

I know our daughter, Charlotte, is only truly mine, but your affair with Paige Ellison brought a wonderful little boy into both of our lives; and for that, my darling, I thank you from the bottom of my heart.

I heard a sharp intake of breath from Tess as she realised what all this meant.

I said, "Dan, I really think — "

"No, I don't want any more secrets. Please carry on, Nic."

I dipped my head in answer and returned my attention to the letter still in my hands.

All of this time you have maintained the pretence that Daniel was adopted, and in doing so protecting me as well as him as you promised to do. This sadly brings me to what I must tell you. You see, Paige Ellison returned. Daniel was only three at the time, and he was my world. She had no right to expect to be able to take him back. I made her realise that she couldn't, that I wouldn't allow it. I have to tell you, Greg, that I threatened to expose what she was should she ever come back. I know you loved her and that broke my heart but Daniel was everything to me. I knew she didn't deserve to be treated in that way and I wish with all my heart that I had acted differently. I write this to you, Greg, in the hope that you can forgive me. Although I offer no excuse for my actions, there can't be any, but what I did, I did because of my own fears of losing our son. I know I don't deserve it, but I ask again, if you can find it in your heart, please forgive me. It is also time that Daniel knows his father.

Please make this right for both your sakes. As I've said, you promised him protection, but the time is approaching when he must be told the truth of who and what he is.

With my departure from this world, I hope you may finally begin to know one another – and Charlotte as well to know her half-brother.

My love always,

Fran x

"Wow," Mal uttered. "I didn't expect that."

"I don't think anyone did," Tess answered.

I was watching Dan. "Are you all right?"

"I don't know… No, I do. It feels like my whole life has been draped in deceit."

I handed the letter back. "Before you do go, Dan, can I ask one thing of you?"

"Of course. Anything."

"With everything that's happened, I wasn't sure whether you would want me at Greg – your dad – and Charlotte's funeral on Monday. I would like to be there. Would you mind?"

"Of course I wouldn't mind. I had hoped you would be, and thank you again for allowing me to speak to you." And he closed his hand around mine before getting up. He finally turned to Tess. "You too, Tess. I'm sorry, again." And he turned to walk away.

"I'll drive you back," Mal offered. "Tess is staying for a bit, if that's all right, Nic."

"Yeah, of course it is."

I heard him relay his apologies to my mum again before walking out the door. I wondered what she had actually heard because her initial anger had completely evaporated.

Her appearance was silent and forgiving. Her mood seemed to match perfectly what Tess and I were thinking.

"Did you hear me reading out that letter Dan brought with him?" I asked her.

"Yes, I did."

"Did you know any of it?"

"No. Together they did a very good job of burying everything that happened. I didn't even know this Paige…"

"Ellison," I finished.

"Paige Ellison," she repeated. "Like I told you before, Nic, he had many affairs, but this one obviously bore fruit for her, and it was only after that that they realised she could actually have children."

"But I had known them since they were very young. How did I not know something was amiss?"

"You don't always see what you're not looking for, Tess," my mum answered.

"And none of us saw that, did we?" I said to her.

"I feel bad now though," Tess commented. "I said some awful things to him at the flat before he told me to get out."

"He apologised to you, Tess. I'm sure he feels just as bad."

"Yeah, but what about you, though? What are you going to do now?" she questioned.

"What do you mean?" my mum asked.

"Well, with him going on about how sorry he was," Tess said. "He should have known you would never have done anything like that – hitting Jules, for one."

My mother said nothing in response; she merely looked at me and walked away, back into the kitchen.

"There's nothing I can do, Tess. I'm glad he knows I would never have done that to Jules. Like Mal explained to him, I don't hate her. If she is the one he wants, there's nothing I can do about it. I don't know whether I want to either. He should have known straight away that I wouldn't have done that; he shouldn't have had to think about it."

"I don't believe you, Nic!"

"Look, Tess. If Jules is that determined to come between us, what's to stop her from doing something else?"

"You have to fight for him. Since when did you give up so easily on Dan Trennan?"

"But he made no attempt to fight for me, Tess, while he was here, did he?"

"Nic, he came to apologise." And her voice trailed off to a whisper. "And besides, your mum was here, and she was furious with him. What was he supposed to do – express his undying love?"

I laughed at the absurdity of the scene I was conjuring in my head.

"She would have loved to have booted him out," Tess whispered, laughing along with me.

But in truth he was still on my mind; he was always on my mind.

Chapter Twenty-Six
Not Forgotten

Since Dan had come around that afternoon, I saw him twice more at his and Mal's flat with Tess trailing behind me. And unlike Tess's prediction that he would be falling all over me, trying to convince me to give him a second chance, this had so far come to nothing. Apart from Dan, my thoughts returned to college and the new term, which would begin again in just over three weeks. But not today. Today belonged to Charlotte and Greg. The hearses, as Dan had told us, would be leaving from their house on Morsley Road, and Mal had been around there all of yesterday, helping him get the place ready, freshening it up a bit with it being empty.

Tess and I popped in, but when we saw Jules there, we made our apologies and a quick exit.

All three of us assured Dan that we would be there, at the house when the hearses turned up, and that we would follow the car that had been set aside for him to travel in, and in which Jules had predictably muscled her way in yet again to travel with him. Mal and Tess were coming around at twelve which would give us plenty of time to get around there and be with Dan. I had wondered whether he would return to sleep there after the funeral was done and out of the way, especially after getting the place ready, but when I spoke to Mal early last night, he was quick to dismiss that entirely. They were merely sorting things for today, and he was careful to assure me that Jules wasn't helping out.

Why he had felt the need to tell me that, I wasn't sure, because I had already gone to great pains to try and make him and Tess understand that Dan and I were just friends now, and that was the way it was going to stay. Over the following days since Dan's unexpected arrival, the conversations my mum and I had shared had started to convince me that maybe Dan and I were better off this way.

Maybe the way I was with him told me in ways that had no need of words that we couldn't go back to the way we'd once been. He had certainly allowed room in his life for Jules, so who was I to question that? He believed now that I hadn't done anything to her, so the fact that she had lied obviously hadn't bothered him that much.

We had all kept a close eye on him and Mal, with them living in the same flat. Mal had told me about some of the conversations they'd shared about Greg. Dan hadn't been able to figure out why Greg hadn't said anything. Why had Greg still been so against Dan after Charlotte died? He'd known Dan was his son. Why hadn't he opened his heart to him instead of so unceremoniously throwing him out that day?

And what of Jules? She still hadn't mentioned anything about Greg or Charlotte that could help him. As far as I was concerned – and I told Mal this – I still believed she had ingratiated herself with Greg and Charlotte just to get to Dan. Mal had instantly agreed, but what could any of us do until Dan was ready to accept that fact? I hadn't mentioned anything either about going to social services. That particular subject seemed to have sunken without trace, never to resurface again. Tess and I had spoken of it, but there seemed no point while Jules was playing such an integral part of his life, even if Dan was oblivious to it.

My mum shouting from downstairs shook me from my thoughts. I suddenly realised I hadn't even dreamed of Charlotte of late, at least for a couple of nights. Had she finished what she had come to me for? Had she come to me just because of what the letter contained? No, I was sure it hadn't just been that, though it was definitely part of it. But in my dream where Jules appeared, Charlotte had been careful to keep her distance from her, and she had begun to cry as well. Why? I wondered. My mind was already chewing over several possibilities. Even now, we all remained in the dark as to where she had been that night we found Charlotte.

All she had said to any of us, including Dan, was that she had been with Greg.

Had they really been involved? But my mum shouting up to me again swept any more thoughts out of reach.

"Come on, Nic. You said you wanted to be up early!"

"Coming, Mum." But I stubbornly lay there, mulling over what had just occurred to me as those thoughts settled once more. Was there anything in them, and how was I going to find out?

One final round of bellowing from downstairs did the trick, and I jumped out of bed. I looked at the skirt and top I had chosen last night to wear today. They looked suitably sombre, which would match the occasion perfectly. I thought back to Fran's funeral and Jules's attire and the inappropriate way her face had been made up. In a totally selfish way, I rather hoped she matched that look today.

"Are you coming down for some breakfast, Nic? It's on the table?" my mum called.

I didn't bother to answer; I was so ravenous anyway that I made my way straight down.

"What have you been doing up there?"

"Nothing, just thinking."

"About today, yes. I hope everything goes well for him. Give him my best, won't you? It's quite a feat that he's going to have to endure."

"Yeah, all of his family's gone, and he didn't even know Greg was his father until after he was dead. Can you imagine living with that and not even having the slightest inclination to say something to Dan?"

"Well, that was Greg Trennan. He obviously didn't feel the same way for Dan as he did for Charlotte. Maybe he could see Dan's real mother in him. Maybe he saw him as an irritation, that Dan was the reason she had to leave and that maybe he hadn't wanted her to."

"I hadn't thought of that, but that still doesn't make it right, does it?"

"No, not at all, and for goodness' sake, please don't say anything like that to Dan. But that's the way some people are, Nic. There wasn't any blood connection between Fran and Dan, and yet she was prepared to do whatever it took to keep him."

"I can't understand that. Why would Paige Ellison not come back and fight for Dan even though Fran had threatened her, as she'd confessed in her letter to Greg? She was his mum. I would have fought for him. I'd never have allowed someone else to dictate what was to happen to my son."

"Well, the gift of hindsight is a wonderful thing. You weren't in her shoes, Nic. How can any of us understand what was going on with her? From what you read in that letter, she was obviously very fearful of that exposure, whatever it was?"

"Well, that's the first that I had heard of it, Dan as well, I think."''

"I don't know. It could be anything. I think the most important thing is to be the best friend you can be to Dan. That's what he needs at the moment, his friends."

I couldn't argue with that, and I was determined that I would be, without any strings attached.

"What time are Mal and Tess picking you up?"

"Twelve, and yes, I'm going to get ready in a minute."

"Okay." And she held her hands up defensively. "Who else will be there?"

"I don't know. Probably quite a few of Charlotte's friends and Greg's, plus family, but I'm not sure who. The funeral director did mention about putting a notice in the paper. I think it was in Friday's paper about the time and venue. It's at St Thomas's, the same as Fran's." And I left her to it in order to go and get myself ready.

Standing in front of the mirror to double-check that I looked okay, I thought about Dan again.

Maybe I could text him just to let him know I was thinking of him. I reached over for my phone. I wasn't sure that I'd do it at all if I didn't do it straight away.

Hi, Dan. Hope you're okay and everything goes as well as it can x

He texted straight back.

You are still coming, aren't you? x

I wanted to say that I would be there for him now if he'd have asked. But I was sure Jules would have that one covered. So instead I kept it simple.

Yeah just wanted to let you know I am here and thinking of you x

His reply was immediate, though a bit of a let-down.

Thanks x

I was determined to try and not read anything more into it. I had done well over the last few days in distancing myself in my own mind. The last thing I needed now was to start dredging all that hurt back up. I looked at the clock beside my bed; it was eleven forty-five. I put my phone in my bag and made my way back downstairs to wait for Mal and Tess.

"Um, you look lovely," my mum commented. "You'll impress anyone dressed like that."

"It's not designed to impress anyone," I told her, feeling defensive. "I'm going for Charlotte and to support Dan."

"I didn't mean it like that. Just that you look nice, and I'm sure he'll appreciate it." I was just about to add that I was sure he would when there was a knock at the door. When I opened it, Tess flew into my arms. She was already in a flood of tears.

"What's wrong?" I demanded, sure that something more had happened.

"She was like this when I picked her up," Mal explained.

"This seems so final," she sobbed.

"Come and sit down," I urged.

"I know you probably think I'm being stupid. We haven't even got to the church yet, but it's all I've thought about all night."

"It's all right," I told her. "It affects us all differently." And I handed her a tissue my mum had just given me.

"Can you fetch some more please? I've forgotten to put any in my bag," I asked my mum.

She nodded and disappeared, leaving me to focus on Tess again.

"Do you feel a bit better now?" I asked.

"Yeah, I'm sorry, Nic. I'll try and hold it together a bit better." And she took another couple of deep breaths.

"This isn't going to be easy for any of us, least of all Dan," I said.

"Which reminds me," Mal responded. "We'd better get going; I told Dan we would pick you up and go straight over to Morsley Road." I nodded before turning to my mum, who was holding out a wad of tissues. Taking them, I said a hasty goodbye and hugged her before following Mal and Tess out of the door.

The drive over to Morsley Road was mostly quiet. Once we were settled in the car, I asked Mal how Dan had been last night after they returned to the flat. He relayed how petulant Jules had been when Dan refused to let her go back to the flat with them.

Instead, she had told them in no uncertain terms that she would be at the flat bright and early, just in case they needed help with anything.

"I told her we wouldn't, but you know what she's like."

"He's keeping her at arm's length then?" Tess questioned, having regained her composure with talk of Jules.

"Yeah, but she's hoping his arm's going to relax somewhat."

"Well, we'll just have to put her in her place," Tess responded.

"Not today you won't," I warned. "This is Charlotte and Greg's funeral. They, as well as Dan, at least deserve us all to act with some dignity, even if Jules doesn't, right?"

"Yes, all right," Tess answered huffily.

"Nic's right, Tess. We're there for Dan, Charlotte and Greg. No one else matters today."

"I know that, but— "

"No buts!" Mal finished.

"Actually, Mal," I began, "I thought you said that Jules wasn't helping out last night while you were at Morsley Road."

"She arrived there unexpectedly later on, hoping Dan would say she might as well come back to the flat, but like I said, it fell on deaf ears."

"Oh, right." But I caught Tess eyeing me curiously in the mirror set in the sun visor before me.

"I just wondered. That's all," I said in answer to her.

The rest of the journey was made in silence, and as we made our way along Morsley Road, it became more apparent, as we drew closer, that we weren't the first to arrive.

Getting out of the car, I pulled the seat forward for Tess to get out.

"You okay?" I asked, knowing full well she wasn't happy with what Mal had said to her.

"He needn't have said that to me. I know who we're here for."

"Jules will try to take centre stage. That's all he meant. Don't drag yourself down to her level, and I'm not just saying that to you. It applies to me and Mal, as well, okay?"

"Okay."

But even as I had said the words I could see Jules making her way towards us, and she didn't disappoint. Her make-up was just as overdone as it had been last time. I wanted to say something to Mal, who was behind us, but there wasn't time.

"Tess, Nic. It's good that you could both make it," Jules gushed.

Tess said, "We're not— "

I squeezed her hand to stop her from saying any more.

"We're not at all happy that we had to come," I interrupted. "Far better that Charlotte and Greg had been here in person, but that wasn't to be, was it?"

"No, quite." And she looked bewildered at what I had just said, as had Tess but I couldn't let Tess carry on with what she was about to say.

"It's a sad day for us all," I added.

"Yes, it is," she agreed, and I then saw Dan also making his way towards us. He came straight over to me and hugged me warmly, kissing me on the cheek. He lingered slightly, and I just caught Jules's eye. I smiled at her before returning my attention to Dan, a seriousness returning to my expression.

"I'm so glad to see you, all of you. Are you coming in?" he offered.

"Okay," I answered, and I grabbed hold of Tess's hand to make sure she followed.

"I'll be in shortly," Mal said.

"All right," I answered, but I just caught sight of him reaching out to Jules to pull her back. I looked at Tess. She had seen him too.

Inside, a few people were milling around, so Dan led us through to the sitting room at the back where we had both discovered Greg's body and followed him out into the garden.

"You're both coming back after the funeral, aren't you?"

"Yes, of course we are," Tess confirmed, leaving me to add that I agreed. We didn't have chance to say any more with Jules's presence by our sides once more and Mal close on her heels. He smiled in our direction. I wondered what he'd said to her, though my mind was doing a very good job of putting forward suggestions.

"Do you want a drink before we go?" he asked us all. But then I felt myself squirming as Jules put her hand on Dan's arm and rubbed it reassuringly.

"Actually, Dan. I think they're here, the cars," she relayed.

"Doesn't she mean Charlotte and Greg?" Tess whispered.

"Yes, I'm sure that's what she means," I answered quietly.

"I'll see you all back here then," Dan answered.

"Yeah, we'll be here," Mal answered, and he walked back to the front of the house where both hearses had pulled up in readiness for their final journey to St Thomas's. We followed behind. I could have heard a pin drop from the silence that had descended with the arrival of both Charlotte and Greg. Both hearses had an abundance of floral arrangements and one very poignant wreath for Greg, which spelled out 'DAD'. In the other, a wreath spelled out 'SISTER'.

I wanted to rush up to Dan and throw my arms around him, but again, Jules already had that covered. Instead I made a move to put my arm around Tess, but Mal stepped in between us and put his arm around both of us. Tess was making no attempt to stem her tears, and mine were threatening to engulf me, not just for Charlotte and Greg but for Dan. In a matter of weeks, he had lost everything. He had no one left, not one family member to speak of, except maybe his real mum, but where was she?

He suddenly turned back to us.

"You're following, yeah?"

"Yes, mate," Mal answered and ushered us back to his car as everyone else was doing, leaving Dan, accompanied by Jules, to get into the car supplied by the funeral directors. He lingered by both hearses before walking on to the car behind, the driver of which was waiting to transport both him and Jules to St Thomas's.

After Mal parked in the field beside the church, which was once more doubling as a car park, we all got out silently. Walking through the side gate into the church grounds, I was struck by how many people were gathered there.

"I think we ought to go in," Mal suggested.

"Yes," I agreed. "If we wait out here much longer, we may not get in at all. Come on," I urged Tess, who seemed oblivious to the conversation between myself and Mal. I guided her in ahead of me but behind Mal. I figured this time she might need help from both of us to get through this. After all, she and her mum and dad had known the family the longest. We managed to get seats together about three-quarters of the way back on the right-hand side.

Sitting down, I looked around. It seemed impossible that many of those outside would even get seats. Maybe those who didn't would just stand at the back.

"Are you all right?" Mal asked, leaning forward from Tess.

"I'm fine." But I looked at Tess and then back at Mal. He answered me by putting his arm around her. I nodded and smiled. She needed that.

More people started filing into the church, alerting those inside that everyone was being ushered in for the funeral service to begin. The shuffle of shoes slowly died down, leaving only silence. Then the organ struck up, prompting us to our feet. First Greg was carried forward down the aisle, followed by Charlotte. As she was carried past us, Tess's tears welled up again and flowed freely; she made no attempt to stem them. I followed suit, my thoughts straying to that night when we'd found her below the stage. I heard the vicar begin, "We have come here today..."

That was the last I heard. My mind drifted just as it had at Fran's funeral. But my attention snapped back as the pallbearers were getting ready to raise the coffins onto their shoulders to carry them back out into the afternoon sun and the graves that awaited them.

Behind them, Dan followed, accompanied again by Jules, who had her arm firmly entwined around his. I felt Mal's hand squeeze my shoulder. I looked back and smiled resignedly.

"It'll be all right," he whispered. I wasn't quite sure how he meant, whether it would be all right in terms that I would get over him or whether it would be all right, meaning Jules would go away. Either way, I felt as though she was taking every opportunity to rub my nose in it, even though it was completely inappropriate given the situation. That didn't seem to matter at all.

Allowing them to pass, we waited to take our turn to exit the pews. Both Mal and I guided Tess back into the aisle and out towards the doors. As we walked out, the sun momentarily blinded us.

We followed everyone else, almost as if we were in a trance, and took our places a respectful distance from where the coffins were to be lowered into their respective graves. Of course, Jules maintained her place by Dan's side, but he suddenly looked back.

"Please," he said and urged us to take our places beside him and Jules. I looked at Mal, who immediately pushed me forward. Standing beside Dan with Tess next to me and Mal on the other side and the vicar, who had positioned himself on the ground between both graves, began.

"We have entrusted our brother, Gregory, and our sister, Charlotte, to God's mercy, and we now commit their bodies to the ground. Earth to earth, ashes to ashes, dust to dust."

And again my mind wandered. Instead of the vicar, all I heard were the sobs of those at the back of us, united in grief as we were, around the gravesides. But something suddenly caught my eye. Just as I had seen her in the shop in the middle of Furham, I now saw her standing only a short distance away to my left, past Tess and Mal. Tess was too wrapped up in her own grief to notice my wandering eye, but Mal did. He followed my gaze. He looked back at me blankly. I shook my head, hoping no one would notice, but everyone's attention was firmly fixed on the graves. She was gone almost as soon as I'd noticed her.

"I'll tell..." But the words came out louder than I had intended. I looked around. Tess and Dan were oblivious, but others, Jules included, hadn't been and glared at me as though I had committed a mortal sin. Only Mal squeezed my shoulder again comfortingly, but he would demand to know what had happened, what, or rather who, I had seen.

Chapter Twenty-Seven
Repeat Performance

If that had been the main course laden with questions, I knew Mal would be demanding afters and the answers that came with it, and it wasn't long in coming. Before leaving the graveside, I turned quickly to Dan, expressing my condolences. He hugged me and said he would see me back at the house. After speaking to Mal and Tess, who was still beside herself, he turned his attention to others, who were now patiently waiting to be spoken to.

Pulling me aside, with Tess still in tow, Mal led us to a quieter spot away from those still milling around. "What was all that about?"

"You wouldn't believe me if I told you," I said.

"Well, you were looking way past me, Nic. You saw something, someone, didn't you?"

I nodded, confirming it. "It was that woman, the one we spoke about, the one I saw in that shop when I was out with Tess."

"Do you think it's the same woman," Mal questioned. "Did she have light-brown hair?"

"Her hair was lighter, yes. But I only saw her fleetingly."

"So do you think she's the same woman?" he pressed.

"I don't know, Mal, but I don't think it's a particularly good topic of conversation for right now. We'll have another chat about it after the wake, yeah?"

"Okay," he agreed.

Tess had contributed nothing during our exchange, and I could understand why. Her attention had been focused on what was before her, Charlotte. She had been... was... her friend. Mal turned to Tess, realising she was strangely quiet.

"Are you okay, Tess?"

"Yeah," she answered. But she wasn't. Mal placed his arm around her.

"Come on," he encouraged. "Let's go back to the car and make our way back to Dan's. It looks like the masses are moving away as well now." Leaving Mal to usher Tess away, I duly followed.

The short distance it took us to drive from St Thomas's to Morsley Road was done in total silence. I think each of us just wanted to reflect – not only on the service but on what had been said about Charlotte as well, though I'd taken virtually none of it in. And when we finally pulled up alongside the kerb some way up from 115, Mal turned back to speak to me.

"So was it the same woman we both saw?"

"I don't know, but didn't we agree to talk about this after the wake?"

"Yeah, but what if she's here?" he quizzed.

"She won't be. Let's just leave it for now," I suggested, seeing people passing by on their way to the house.

Walking into the driveway of their home felt like I was being herded along with the gathering number of people who seemed to have congregated around us all of a sudden. Mal must have sensed my unease because he took his place between us again and slung his arms around us, comfortingly.

"Are you all right?" he asked. "You seem a bit reticent, like you did last time we came here after Fran's funeral."

"Yeah, I'm fine," I assured him, feeling a little easier with him by my side, but that feeling didn't last long when I saw Jules appear yet again by Dan's side. Mal squeezed my shoulder as a show of support.

"Don't take any notice," he said. "That's all on her side, not his."

I nodded, but my emotions were growing darker where Jules was concerned. When we reached them, Mal's reassuring arm dropped from my shoulder and Tess's as he moved towards Dan, giving him a hug.

"We'll go straight through to the garden, mate," Mal said. "Come out and have a word when you get chance."

"I will," Dan responded and turned his attention to Tess, who had begun crying again. He took her in his arms and held her there.

"She thought the world of you, you know?" he comforted.

She nodded and smiled stiffly, unable to add anything. Turning to me, he did the same. I caught a glimpse of Jules, whose focus remained doggedly fixed on me.

"We'll talk in a while, yeah?" he promised.

"Dan, people are waiting to speak to you," Jules interrupted.

I nodded and quickly shuffled off a few paces to where Tess and Mal were waiting.

"Whoa, her grip isn't loosening, is it?" Mal stated once we were out of earshot.

"No, she wants me well and truly out of the picture, doesn't she?"

"Um, seems like it. Anyway, come on. Let's not worry about her. Dan won't let her go too far." But I wasn't so sure. Jules was quite formidable when it came to getting what she wanted.

Since I had first got to know her, rarely had I seen her not get what she wanted.

"Mal, I'm just going to get some food, I'm starving."

"We'll see you outside then," he answered.

I told him I would be straight out and headed for the kitchen on the right of the hallway, where I had been standing.

Picking out a few things there, I suddenly felt someone's presence by my side, openly invading my space. I instinctively turned, feeling wary.

"Jules," I greeted.

"Nicola," she answered. "I didn't think you would bother coming," she said in little more than a whisper.

"And why would you think that?" I responded. "Charlotte was my friend as well as yours." In fact, more, I wanted to add, but I figured that would just inflame the situation I desperately wanted to flee from.

"Oh, I was very close to the family... and still am," she whispered, moving in closer, if that was even possible.

"Well, I would love to stay and chat, but I really should get back to my friends." And I made my escape, dodging between those who were milling around and talking about their own memories of both Greg and Charlotte. I had made it through to the room where Dan and I had discovered Greg's body without being stopped. As I walked out into the afternoon sun, relief swept over me. Seeing Mal and Tess, I quickly made for them. They were sitting on some garden chairs that had been dotted about, and they had saved one for me.

"Is that all the food you managed to get?" he commented. "I thought you were starving."

"Er, yeah, I was... am," I corrected. "I had company though."

"Who? Dan?" Tess asked.

"No, Jules." And my features contorted.

"That bad, eh?" Mal questioned.

"Yes," I confirmed. "I think she wanted to put me straight."

"About Dan?" Mal guessed.

"Yeah. She was surprised to see me here. When I said Charlotte had been my friend as well as hers, she said that she was very close to the family and still was, obviously meaning Dan. I told her I would love to stay and chat but that I really should get back to my friends. Actually, Mal, that reminds me. Whilst we were here before we left for the service, you pulled Jules back when Tess and I walked into the house with Dan. What did you say to her?"

"I just warned her off."

"How do you mean?"

"I saw the way she was watching you when Dan hugged you and particularly when he kissed you on the cheek. She didn't look very pleased. I just thought it would be an idea to have a friendly word, like I said, to warn her off."

"I don't know why she's being like this then," I responded. "She's got Dan. What more does she want? Or does she want to make my life thoroughly miserable while she's at it?"

"She hasn't got him. That's the whole point. His mind's been so full of finding out that the man he thought had adopted him was actually his real father. And if that wasn't enough, he's still trying to deal with his and Charlotte's deaths. He hasn't said anything to me or her as far as I know, but his head's as full of you as it's ever been. I know him, Nic, and he always mentions you in conversations when we're on our own. Why are you still so hell bent on allowing her to muscle in, to work on him?"

"He's right, Nic," Tess agreed.

"I don't know. He's my friend again, and to me that's the most important thing. But I didn't do anything in the first place. You know that, Tess."

"I know, but he came round, didn't he? He apologised, and he did bring that letter when he needn't have done."

"Yeah, all right, but I really don't think this is the place to be discussing it."

"Um, maybe," Tess muttered, looking beyond me.

"Hey."

I looked around sharply, recognising Dan's voice.

"Come on. Sit here, mate." And Mal vacated the seat opposite me.

"How are you doing?" Tess asked.

"I'll be glad when all these people have gone and I can get back to the flat," he replied.

"Do you want us to stay behind and help you clear up?" Mal offered.

"Would you mind?"

"No, 'course not. You'll stay, won't you, Tess, and you, Nic?"

"Er, yeah, 'course," I answered for us both. "Where's Jules anyway?"

"Around somewhere, playing hostess." That suddenly confirmed how painful this really was going to be.

"We'll just hang around here then," I said. "Come and get us when everyone's gone, and we'll get started, yeah?"

"Yeah, thanks. It's great that you're all staying."

"You been doing the rounds?" Mal asked.

"Yeah, Greg's family have been asking what's happening with the house. But as his sole heir that's not a question any more, it's mine, everything's mine. A lot of Charlotte's friends came back, but they're all drifting off now."

"There were loads of people at the funeral, weren't there?" Mal stated. "Some were even standing."

"To be honest, I didn't notice, Mal," Dan admitted.

"I think that's normal, Dan. You were focused on those who really matter: Greg and Charlotte."

"Definitely Charlotte anyway," Dan responded.

I was just about to say that Greg mattered, too, but Jules's arrival stopped me dead in my tracks.

"Nic, Tess and Mal are helping to clear up," Dan informed her.

"Oh, good," she smiled and made it more pronounced as she looked in my direction.

"So I was thinking," Dan suggested. "Why don't you have a break this time? You helped me and Mal to set all this up, and I'm really grateful for it." For a split second, her face looked like thunder until she carefully masked it again.

"Oh, that's really sweet of you, Dan, but I wouldn't dream of it. It'll be nice, us all being together again." And she looked straight at me. Why did she dislike me so intensely? As they both walked away, I aimed that very question at Mal and Tess.

"She feels threatened by you, as we've already said," Tess answered. "You're obviously not taking much notice of the way Dan looks at you."

Mal disappeared off into the house to go and get us all something more to eat. With Jules so much on my mind, food was the last thing I could think about.

"Don't take any notice of her, Nic. She's losing the game, that's all."

"It's not a game, Tess."

"It is to her. Didn't you see her just now? Her face dropped and for a second she looked like she might explode when Dan suggested she might as well go home."

"Yes, I did notice. She looked like she hated me."

"Well, I'm here, so she can't do anything, right?"

"Right," I answered, and I leaned forward to hug her.

I almost jumped out of my skin at the sound of his voice. I hadn't expected him back quite so soon.

"What's this then?" Mal demanded, carrying a plate overloaded with sandwiches and cakes.

"Oh, I was just telling Nic that while we're here, we won't let Jules do anything, will we?"

"Absolutely not," Mal concurred. "She hasn't said anything though, has she?"

"No, she hasn't. Now can we forget about it?" I asked. "And it looks like everyone's beginning to leave."

"Yeah, there are only a few people left in the house now," Mal agreed. "Once we've eaten these, we can go in, if you like, and make a start."

"Yep, the sooner the better, I think." But Jules was still weighing heavily on my mind. The sooner I got out of here and either went back to the flat with Mal and Tess or even went home, the happier I would feel. I didn't feel comfortable here at all.

"A penny for them?" Tess prompted.

"Um, sorry… What?"

"You were miles away."

"Oh, I was just thinking the sooner we get started, the sooner we'll be finished."

"And you can get out of here," she guessed.

"I wouldn't put it quite like that." And I smiled uneasily. "But yes."

"Come on then. Help us eat this lot, and then we'll start." Tucking in, I had forgotten how hungry I had been.

All three of us began collecting discarded paper plates and rubbish people had left behind when Dan came walking out with a black bin bag, Jules trailing after him.

"Whoa, you've made quick work of it out here."

"What else needs doing?" Mal asked.

"Well, we've started clearing the back room. The front needs doing, and the plates that the food was on need to be washed up, and that's about it. Then I can go home and relax for the first time today."

"Oh, are you going straight back to the flat?" Mal asked.

"Yeah, why?"

"We were going back as well. Do you mind?" he asked.

"No, 'course not."

"We're all going back then," Jules confirmed.

"No, I was going on my own, Jules. I just want to lie down and relax. Get my head straight. It's been a long day."

"Oh, all right," she responded grudgingly. "I'll go through and start washing up before I disappear then. Do you want to give me a hand, Nic?"

"Er, yes, all right."

"I'll help as well," Tess offered.

"No, that's okay. Nic and I can manage, can't we, Nic?"

"Er, I don't mind Tess helping if she wants to," I commented.

"Good, that's settled then," Mal beamed. "Dan and I can sort the rooms out and bring any pots through that need washing."

"Sounds good to me," Dan agreed.

So Tess and I followed Jules into the kitchen. She took over the washing up, while Tess set about clearing the table, and I waited to start drying. Jules let the hot tap run to get enough water to do the pots. Obviously deciding it was hot enough, she began filling the bowl. Standing where I was near Jules, waiting to begin drying the pots, I was just about to say something to Tess when I suddenly heard Jules screaming and crying. I spun around to see what was happening.

"How could you?" Jules wailed loudly. Tess also rushed over from the table on hearing her before I had chance to react.

"Quick, Nic! She's burned her arm. Run the cold tap!"

Only seconds had passed, but by the time Dan and Mal rushed through, Jules's wailing had reached fever pitch.

"She pushed my arm under the hot water!" she yelled. "Why would you do something like that?" she demanded through very well-orchestrated tears.

Mal came forward and took over from me and Tess.

"Keep your arm under the cold tap," he instructed. Dan turned to me.

"I promise – I didn't do anything," I said. "I was just standing here, waiting for her to start washing up."

"Yeah, she was," Tess confirmed, daring him to challenge her.

"How would you know?" Jules said. "You had your back to us!"

"Is that how you know I wasn't watching?" Tess accused.

"I could hear you clanking the plates!" And immediately turned to Dan. "Can't you see what they're doing? They're trying to make this look like I'm making it up."

"Well, there's no harm done, is there, Mal?" Dan asked.

"No, it looks all right now. I can nip you home if you want, Jules."

"No, I'm fine here!" she snapped.

"No, I think it's better if Mal takes you home, Jules," Dan agreed. "I'll ring later to make sure you're okay."

"Oh, all right," she conceded and sidled up to him. She gave him a kiss and walked away without saying another word.

He then turned to me. "Are you all right?"

"I didn't do anything," I repeated.

"I believe you. While Mal's taking Jules home, we'll clear up here, yeah?"

"Okay," we agreed and Tess and I set about sorting everything out. After he'd left the kitchen, Tess brought some more pots over to be washed.

"Looks like she's upping her game. Be careful, Nic."

Chapter Twenty-Eight
Second Chances

Within an hour we had finished at Dan's house. Mal picked us up, and we were back at their flat, worn out.

"I just want to say sorry... again that I didn't believe either of you when I was at Jules's flat that morning," Dan apologised again.

"What were you there for anyway?" Tess asked.

"She rang early that morning, really upset. In fact, she was hysterical. She said you had said something to her at the flat, telling her to stay away from me. Of course, then when you and Tess went around there, it sort of confirmed what she had been saying. And with that happening with the tap... Exactly how did it happen?" he asked me.

"She was running the hot tap, hot enough to wash the pots, and the next thing I knew, her arm was under it, and she was shrieking. In that instant I was just about to say something to Tess, so I wasn't even facing her. I didn't touch her or knock her or anything. What did she say when you were driving her home?" I asked, turning my attention to Mal.

"Nothing much. She was just concerned that you might turn Dan against her. I reminded her of the conversation we had outside your place, Dan, before we all left for the church."

"Which was?" he asked.

"I just had a friendly word to warn her off Nic. You didn't see the look Jules gave Nic when you hugged her and kissed her on the cheek," he said, seeing Dan's puzzled expression. "If looks could have killed, mate, I'm sure they would have. She's obsessed with you."

"Then I must apologise again, Nic," Dan conceded. "I seem to be doing it a lot at the moment, don't I?"

"You can't be held responsible for what's in Jules's head, and please don't apologise any more."

"But I haven't helped matters, have I?"

"You're listening to what's being said now. That's what's important."

"Fancy going for a walk?" he asked me.

"Actually, I really ought to get back."

"Yeah, me too," Tess agreed.

"Okay, do you want me to run you both home?" Mal asked.

"Please, Mal. That would be great."

"All right, what about tomorrow then?" Dan asked. "Would you come around again, or could we meet up in town?"

"I'll come here. What about you, Tess?" I asked half hoping she would come as well.

"Yeah if I'm invited?"

"Would it make a difference if you weren't?" Mal quipped.

"No!"

"Then I guess we can safely say you'll be here as well," Mal commented. And she unceremoniously stuck her tongue out. "Well, it's good to see we're getting back to some semblance of normality," he answered, laughing.

"Are you warming to him again then?" Tess asked as soon as we got into Mal's car. I laughed easily for the first real time all day.

"He believes me. That's a start."

"Good, at long last."

"I didn't say it was a done deal, Tess, just that it's a start. We're friends again, and we've started talking, and I'm glad."

"I bet he'll ring Jules while I'm gone," Mal commented.

"And say what?" Tess questioned.

"He's gonna have a right old go at her for lying the way she has been. He knew what she wanted, but it was only ever one sided. He was as mad as hell at you, Nic, when he thought you were having a go at her, but he never stopped caring about you. Never stopped asking about you either, like I told you earlier."

"You never told me," Tess berated.

"I don't tell you everything!"

"Well, you should have. It would have saved Nic a lot of heartache."

"And maybe if I had, we wouldn't be in this situation now, where we know exactly what Jules's game was."

"I still think Nic needs to be careful of her," Tess said in all seriousness, "especially if Dan rings her and tells her exactly what he thinks of her."

"Yeah, I wouldn't disagree with you there, Chubbs."

"I've told you before, Mallory. Don't call me that!"

"I wouldn't have to if you didn't eat so much."

"I don't! And where's all this coming from anyway?"

"You didn't eat half of what was on that plate that I brought outside for us all then."

"I was hungry!"

"I rest my case." And he stopped just outside Tess's driveway. Completely ignoring Mal, she turned her attention to me.

"Are you getting in the front, Nic?"

"Yeah, and I'll see you about eleven tomorrow at the flat," I said, getting out of the car. And more quietly I told her not to take any notice. "He's only playing with you."

"He'll be sorry," she promised. "Anyway, see you tomorrow." And she pushed the door shut.

"Does she have to slam it so hard?" Mal whined.

"Just stop it and drive, Mallory."

"She loves it really."

"No, she doesn't. It irritates her like mad, and you know it."

"It's good to have you back again, Nic."

"It's good to be back." And we drove the rest of the way in silence.

My mum was at home waiting, as I walked in through the door. Calling out a cheery hello, I walked into the sitting room.

"You sound cheerful for having attended a funeral."

"Not really. It was really sad, especially with it being a double funeral and burial, but something good has come out of it."

"Don't tell me. You're back with Dan, aren't you?"

"Actually no, I'm not, but we are friends now, and I want to keep it that way."

"Um, why don't I sound convinced?"

"Isn't it enough for you to be happy that I'm doing what's best for me?"

"That's what I worry about, Nic. Anyway, come on. I don't want to argue. Tell me about today."

"Well, we went straight to Morsley Road to wait for the hearses carrying Greg and Charlotte's bodies, and then we followed them to St Thomas's. Jules was her usual charming self. We stayed back to help Dan clear up before going back to the flat, and as Jules was beginning to wash up, she stuck her arm under the hot tap and promptly accused me of trying to burn her."

"What? And he believed her?"

"No. Mal offered to take her home. Dan wasn't very happy about what she'd done and subsequently accused me of but he did apologise to me, again."

"Well, I'm glad to hear that."

"I'm going over there again tomorrow. You don't mind, do you?"

"No, Nic, I don't as long as he treats you right. That's all I care about. Do you want anything, or have you already eaten?"

"Yeah, Tess and I had a load of stuff at Dan's place."

"What's happening about that anyway? It'll be his now, won't it?"

"Yes, that's what he was saying, with being Greg's only surviving child."

"Well, I suppose that's one good thing to have come out of this sorry mess." We remained like that pretty much for the rest of the evening, though it had been late enough when I arrived home. I had already made my excuses and escaped to my bedroom when my phone bleeped, signalling that a text message had come through. It was from Mal.

I've got to go out in the morning. Do you want a lift to our place about eleven?

I was quite looking forward to a stroll over there, but if there was a lift on offer, I guessed I would be a fool to refuse. I replied,

Okay thanks.

I wondered whether Dan had spoken to Jules yet. Maybe there was a link between that and Mal asking whether I wanted a lift, but I inwardly laughed at the direction my thoughts were heading. But something else occurred to me as well; he hadn't said any more about that woman I had seen at the graveside. I made a mental note to remember to talk to him about it tomorrow when he picked me up.

I lay in bed for long enough, hoping sleep would suddenly overcome me. I tossed and turned for what seemed like hours, but eventually it came. Sinking down, I experienced a willingness to succumb to an unseen force, slumbering into the dark abyss. But that peace didn't last long. It opened up to a clear, if yet crisp, morning. It felt late, and again Charlotte was my guide, though my sleep had seen nothing of her for days. She smiled as she had always done. We were outside, and I seemed puzzled somehow, because whenever I had seen her in my dreams or visions in my waking hours, she had always been inside. But it felt good and the air was fresh. We walked for a while. As always there was no conversation between us, but none was needed.

Anything I did have need of was right there with her. Every weight I had been carrying had been lifted from my shoulders; I felt light and carefree. I looked up into the sky to breathe in this newfound freedom I felt within me. But dark clouds were heading our way, closing in. I looked to Charlotte, questioning why they were there, when the air and the warmth of this late morning were surrounding me with such peace and serenity. She smiled knowingly but with an air of finality as well. She turned in the direction of the road, heading up from where we were standing. I could see a car in the distance. It seemed familiar, though I didn't know it.

As it drew closer, it seemed to accelerate, speeding down the hill. Still I watched it, horrified that they wouldn't be able to stop at the bottom where others were, cars and people alike. It didn't seem as though there was any intention of stopping. I held my breath, praying for those caught in its path when the car suddenly veered from its course. It was heading for me.

My heart was racing, matching its speed. I wanted to run, throw myself from its path, but nothing within me would move. The closer the car's advance, the more surreal the moment became. A split second before it ploughed into me, I saw its driver clearly; it was Jules. Then everything around me blacked out. There was nothing; though in the distance there was something. I could feel it: strong and desperate... tears. I could hear them. My eyes shied away from the light. I looked around; they had been my tears.

"This has got to stop, Nic. You're frightening me."

"It was just a dream, Mum," I assured her.

"One you woke yourself up from because you were crying so hard. What was it?"

"Just a re-run of yesterday," I lied.

"The funeral?"

I nodded. "I'll be all right, Mum. Really."

"I hope so but you're really frightening me." And she hugged me; I could feel her fear. Her arms felt good though, warm and safe, unlike the dream I'd just been a participant in. Mal's offer of a lift went through my head again. Jules wouldn't think of trying to run me down; not in my wildest dreams would I ever have thought that. I had come to realise she was a bit unhinged but not that much, surely.

I lay there for the remainder of the night. I vaguely remember the light beginning to break through, and then I must have succumbed – and thankfully without any reappearance from Charlotte or Jules. Waking did bring it all back though, stubbornly

332

lodged in my mind, and I sifted through options open to me. But I openly laughed. Why would I need options? It had only been a dream.

"Nicola." It was my mum again. What did she want now? "Nic, you up there?" That voice wasn't my mum's.

I sat bolt upright. Mal. Oh, God, what time was it? I looked at my clock. It was ten past eleven. Stumbling to the door, I opened it a fraction.

"Give me ten minutes. I won't be long."

"Really?" he replied.

I ignored his jibe and set about jumping in to the shower.

"Um, that was a long ten minutes." He laughed, but when he saw me, his tone immediately changed. "You look awful. Bad night?"

"Yes," my mum answered before I had chance to.

"It was just a dream," I told him.

"One you woke up crying from, and you were sweating!" my mum announced.

"That good, eh?" Mal replied. "Anyway, we had better get back, or Tess will have made herself at home and eaten all the food."

"Stop it," I warned. But it served only to make him laugh harder.

"Come on then. 'Bye, Mrs James," he shouted over his shoulder.

"Will you be here when I get back?" I called from the door.

"Yes, but ring me, please."

"Okay, see you later." And I pulled the door shut.

"So what was the dream about?" Mal asked as soon as we got into the car.

"Can I ask a question first?"

"Sure. Go."

"Did Dan put you up to texting me to see if I wanted a lift this morning?"

"No," he said after a slight pause.

"Liar."

"My question. What was the dream about?"

"You didn't give me an honest answer."

"Okay, he did. He was worried about you."

"Why?"

"Why all the questions?"

"Because he rang Jules last night, didn't he?"

He looked at me strangely. "What's all this about?"

"I'm just curious. That's all."

"No, you've had a bad dream, and it's spooked you, hasn't it? So come on, Nic. What was it about? Jules by any chance? I'm not leaving here until you tell me, and then you can explain to Dan why we're so late."

"Okay, yes, it was about her and Charlotte."

"And?"

"She was in a car. She was coming down a hill fast and then veered off, ploughing into me. That's it, just a dream."

"Well, I can see why that would spook you, but what about Charlotte?"

"She was just there. I figured she was waiting with me until it was all over."

"Wow! But there is one good thing about all this."

"What?" I questioned.

"Jules hasn't got a car."

"Good one, Sherlock. You're not going to say anything to Dan about all this, are you?"

"No, 'course not. I'll leave that for you to do."

I sighed and waited for him to start the car. That was the last thing I needed – for Dan to be stressing about it, and I knew he would.

"Hey," both he and Tess called out as we walked in through the door. They both seemed pleased to see us. But Jules was still on my mind.

"Did you manage to get hold of Jules?" I asked tentatively because Mal hadn't actually answered my question about her.

Dan looked sideways at Mal.

"What?" he responded. Dan turned his attention back to me.

"I told her that I didn't like the way she had treated my friends... and my girlfriend. Sorry."

"But I'm— "

"Not my girlfriend anymore," he finished for me. "I know how stupid I've been, Nic, but I would like us to try and get back to where we were, if you'll allow us to?"

I looked at Tess and Mal, slightly embarrassed at being thrust into this conversation so publicly.

"Can we go for a walk?" he asked, sensing my discomfort.

"Er, yeah, I think that would be a good idea." And before I'd had chance to sit down, I was heading for the door again.

"I'll get a cup of tea ready," Tess offered.

"Thanks," I responded.

Neither of us uttered a word until we were out on the pavement and had begun walking.

"I'm sorry; I know I shouldn't have said that," I began.

"It's not you, Nic, who should be sorry. It's me who should be apologising for putting you in that position," he said sadly. "I shouldn't have said anything until we were on our own. But I was scared that if I had left it until now, you would – you are going to say no, aren't you?"

"Dan... Look, don't you think it's better that we just spend a bit of time together, talk things through before all of that?"

"Is that just another way of saying no?" he asked again, dejected.

"No, it's not. It's just that so much has happened."

"You don't trust me, do you?"

"It's not so much that, although you're right. You did think I was lying where Jules was concerned – at least that first time."

"I know, and I'm sorry."

"But that's just my point. We're still skirting around it all."

"Okay, let's talk honestly then," he offered.

"All right. Why did Jules manage to get between us when you knew she had a thing for you?"

"That's not quite the way it happened, though, is it, Nic? I got pushed into meeting her to try and find out what she knew about my dad's and Charlotte's deaths."

"All right. I accept my part in that, but what more did we find out? Nothing that I can think of, and still she managed to worm her way in."

"The only answer I can give you is that I don't know, really. She was having a fling with my dad, though she didn't say that in so many words. She did say they were very close. I do think she got close to Charlotte in order to get to him and then close to him to get to me."

"Do you think she had anything to do with their deaths?" I asked pointedly.

"I don't know. Maybe... No, why would she?"

"I don't know, Dan. It all just feels a bit uneasy." We carried on walking, and he slipped his hand into mine. When no reaction was forthcoming from me, he squeezed it as if to confirm his intent. I couldn't deny it felt nice, more than nice, to have that closeness again, but for how long if that dream had any substance at all? I wanted to tell him, but now wasn't the time. It was Tess I wanted to discuss it with. I pulled him back and began to speak, but he mistook my intention and kissed me so fast it caught me off guard. Every fibre within me wanted it so much, and yet my head was fighting it, and when he drew back, he knew.

"Oh, God! I'm sorry. I've done it again, haven't I? I've gone too far." I smiled both inside and out for the first time, I think, since all this trouble Dan and I had been plunged into had spiralled out of control.

"Hug me just so that I can feel you're here." He did without question. I belonged here just like this, and I hadn't realised how much I had ached for it.

Still holding on to me, he whispered, "Come on. Let's go back."

"No one will come between us again, will they?"

"Never," he promised and he led me back towards the flat.

When we walked back in, Mal and Tess smiled at the relief that was so evident in Dan's show of affection.

"We're all back to normal then?" Tess smiled.

"Yeah, I think so." And I looked at Dan, who gave my hand another squeeze.

"Good, I'm glad to hear it," Mal joined in. "He's been unbearable lately!" I looked over at Mal's smile, but as his eye caught mine, he raised his eyebrows, asking an unspoken question. I knew he was asking for me to now tell Dan about the dream I'd told him about. I shook my head very slightly so neither Dan nor Tess would notice and prayed he would say nothing. Too late, I realised.

"You've got to tell him," Mal said.

"Tell me what?" Dan asked, confused.

"Nic had a dream last night, mate. Didn't you, Nic?"

I sighed. "Yes," I admitted, "and it was exactly that – just a dream, Mallory." I turned to Dan. "And besides, you haven't even told me how Jules took what you said to her?"

"Not very well. She told me it wouldn't last, that you weren't enough."

"Um, that's nice. What have I done to her for her to dislike me so much?"

"You're with Dan," Tess answered.

"Which brings us back to your dream," Mal stated.

"I've told you what she said," Dan replied. "Now please tell me."

"Okay," I said to him, Tess and Mal. "I don't know where I was, but I was standing at the bottom of a hill. Charlotte was with me. The air felt really fresh, and it was warm too. But as I looked up, there were dark clouds gathering, heading our way. I looked back up the hill again, and there was a car. It was speeding downwards. I remember worrying about any people at the bottom and any cars it might career into. It drew closer, but suddenly it veered off course and was heading straight for me... It was Jules in the car, and then everything blacked out, and I woke up."

I waited for Dan to say something or even Tess, but they just carried on staring at me.

"So?" I said.

"I don't know what to say," Dan confessed but he looked horrified. "I don't want you going home on your own any more."

"That's stupid, Dan. It was just a dream." And I laughed.

"Maybe. I still don't want you taking any chances though." I rolled my eyes and looked at Tess. I knew she would stick up for me.

"Sorry, Nic, but he's right. You can't take any chances. I said yesterday to be careful around her."

"But even you told me, Mal, that the one good thing about it was that she didn't have a car, or is there something else that none of you are telling me?"

"We're not keeping anything from you, Nic," Dan promised.

"Well, it feels like it," I stated.

"We're not, honestly. I just don't trust her, Nic," Tess said, backing Dan up.

"Well, wouldn't it be better to try and talk to her?" I suggested.

"I don't think she'd listen," Mal answered.

"But it's still worth a try, surely."

"Maybe I could go and talk to her," Dan offered.

"Do you think that's a good idea? To go on your own?" Mal asked.

"Come with me then," Dan responded.

"What now?" he asked.

"Why not? You two could stay here, couldn't you?" Dan asked me and Tess.

"You bet," she answered. "I don't want to go anywhere near her, not after hearing about the dream Nic's had."

"I've already told you. It was just a dream. I only dreamed about her because she's been on my mind, probably."

"Well, we won't be long." And Dan walked over to the sofa to kiss me goodbye. This time I didn't object.

Chapter Twenty-Nine
Left Unsaid

On my own with Tess, I began to relax a little. I wondered what would be said and, more importantly, left unsaid.

"It'll be all right, you know," she reassured me.

"How do you know that?" I asked.

"You're worried about that dream, aren't you?"

"I'm a little uneasy," I admitted. "But don't you dare say anything about what we're talking about to Dan or Mal. Promise me, Tess."

"Only if you promise me that you'll be careful."

"I will." And I smiled. I knew what Tess was getting at – that I would make sure someone always took me home and picked me up if I was going to their flat. But how was I supposed to keep that sort of thing up? I figured it might be better to wait until Dan and Mal came back before making any judgments. "Maybe they'll be able to make her see sense where me and Dan are concerned," I told her, sounding more upbeat than I really felt.

"I think that's pushing it a bit, but we can always hope. Anyway, it is good to have you back in the fold."

"It's good to be back," I told her, and it was. It was only this dream hanging over me that bothered me, and Tess knew it.

"Just forget about it now. The dream is probably just the result of you worrying about her, like you thought."

"Yes," I agreed. I thought about Mal again. He hadn't mentioned any more about that woman I had seen at the funeral, the same one he thought had been hanging around here and who had been at Fran's funeral. We had agreed to speak more about her after the wake, but with everything kicking off the way it had, she had gone clear out of my head and Mal's too, I was sure. But

I still wanted to talk to him about her. More importantly, who was she? As far as I was aware, we were the only ones aware of her existence. I just didn't want to mention anything more to Tess in case we were completely off track. And I was the only one Mal had told. But could my dream have been related to her?

Even though Tess and I were the best of friends, I couldn't tell her this. It was clear from talking to her that Mal hadn't mentioned anything.

"They're taking their time," I said instead.

"They won't be too long now. He just wants you to be safe, Nic." I knew that, but Dan couldn't be with me every minute of the day, could he?

"Maybe all she needs is time. Her feelings for him were strong, weren't they?"

"Yeah, you can say that again!" Tess huffed.

"Tess, please don't say anything to Dan or Mal, but what if that dream I had was a premonition?" I said, scared that it might actually come true.

"It's not. You've just been worrying about her, that's all." But that wasn't all. This had been going around inside my head since I had woken from the dream. It had seemed so real, and Charlotte had remained by my side the whole time as if she was waiting... for me.

"Look, she probably doesn't like you very much because she's so fixated on Dan, but murder..." She'd spoken the word I had been carefully trying to keep out of my head.

"Why not? It's not as though you or any of us didn't think about it where Charlotte or Greg was concerned, did we?" my voice shakily relayed. She thought for a minute, sifting through the possibility I had tossed her way.

"But why would she go that far?" she questioned.

"Because I've put myself in her way again where Dan's concerned." And the more I thought about it, the more sense it made. I just hated thinking this way, but even I had to admit that maybe she did have something to do with the deaths, and I said as much to Tess.

"But surely the cops would have picked it up by now, Nic. They've never been back to see her, have they?"

"How do we know that? Maybe they just haven't got enough evidence. It wouldn't be the first time that sort of thing's happened, would it?"

"Um." I could tell she wasn't convinced and it was a bit of a turnaround, but our attentions were suddenly diverted when the bottom door slammed shut.

"That's probably them now," I said, but my stomach had already started churning as I wondered what had happened between them all. I certainly hadn't expected them back so soon. I remained where I was, with Tess next to me on the sofa. My thoughts had retreated inward, and I guessed Tess's had too, because as the door was flung open, we both jumped out of our skins, even though we were expecting them.

"Hey," Mal greeted as he walked in through the door.

"Well?" I urged.

"Can we get inside first?"

"Yeah, sorry. I just want to know what's been said." I felt alone in my unease; even Tess seemed laid back in comparison.

"Well, you'll be pleased to know that nothing happened," Mal informed us.

"She wasn't there then?" Tess guessed.

"Yeah, she was, though I think she was a bit surprised," Dan told us.

"So what did you say to her?" I responded.

"Just that I wanted to know she was all right and that I was sorry I couldn't give her what she wanted. That it was you I wanted and that had always been the case. I just wanted her to accept that you weren't at fault over any of this, Nic."

"Wow, she couldn't have liked that," Tess commented.

"Well, if she didn't, she was putting on a bloody good act."

"Do you think that's what it was, Mal?" I asked.

"Well, she seemed genuine enough, didn't she, Dan?"

"Yeah, she said she would apologise to you when she saw you."

I felt Tess's eyes rest on me.

"That's not much of a consolation considering the dream she had last night, is it?" Tess pointed out.

"I'm sorry, Nic. I didn't think," Dan apologised.

"It's okay. It was just a dream – just me going over events, I suppose." But Tess glared at me. I averted my eyes, ignoring her.

"I'll take you home later, Nic," Mal offered.

"No, it's all right. We're walking," Dan explained.

"Well, I'll be walking home. I thought Nic and I would walk part of the way together," Tess told them both.

"Actually, I'm going home around four, and I'm walking, so that would be nice, Tess," I said. "Thanks."

I had made that part up on the spur of the moment, hoping it would appease her, but both Dan and Mal looked at me like I was mad.

"What?" Dan demanded.

"Nic, we just want to make sure you stay safe," Mal replied.

"I know you do, but there's really no need. I'm not in any danger."

Dan looked at Mal. He just shrugged.

"Leave it for now. Let her do what she wants," Mal urged him. Knowing he wasn't going to win this one, he relented.

"I'm making a cup of tea. Anyone want one?" Mal asked. Both Tess and I accepted gratefully, leaving Dan to walk over and help. They were hunched together, going on about something, but Tess demanded my attention, taking my focus from whatever they were whispering about.

"You're all right with walking down the road with me later, aren't you?"

"Of course. Why wouldn't I be?"

"I don't want you to think I'm keeping tabs on you with what we were talking about earlier."

"I don't, Tess. I think I just got carried away earlier. I just want to get on with things now. I know they mean it for the best, but they want to wrap me up," I whispered, looking over at Mal and Dan.

"They're just concerned about you, that's all." But I didn't get chance to add any more, because they walked over with the drinks.

"Right. What about heading out somewhere once we've had these?" I asked.

"Where?" Mal questioned.

"I don't know, anywhere. Just going out for a walk would be good. We're always cooped up in here."

"Oh, cheers!" Mal grumbled.

"I didn't mean it like that. It's just that we haven't been out anywhere in ages together. There's been so much stuff going on around us lately and none of it's been good. I just think it would be an idea if we got out for a while, do normal things, have a bit of fun, you know?"

"Yeah, it's not exactly been a barrel of laughs over the last few weeks, has it?" Mal concurred.

"I think it's a great idea as well." And Dan slumped down on the sofa next to me and kissed me. "We've been miserable for long enough!"

"Speak for yourself, Trennan. What about you, Chubbs?"

"Oh, yeah, thanks, Mallory!"

"Why does she always call me by my proper name when she's mad at me?"

"Because you annoy her when you call her that," I reprimanded.

"I'm only playing." And he laughed, but Tess's face was still fixed.

"Come on, Nic," she said, standing up, tugging at my arm. I allowed her to pull me up, and we walked out of the flat, leaving Mal and Dan to catch up.

We stayed out for several hours. We walked for long enough, preferring to spend time in Avery Park, where it had all begun again for me and Dan. The outside air seemed to release and cleanse us of the last few weeks and all three funerals Dan was still trying to work through, as well as the fact that Greg had turned out to be his real father, something he'd been keen up until now to keep to himself. Mal had told me that Dan had spoken very little of Greg. He'd broken off from the rest of us and wandered off down towards the stream that wound around the edge of the park. With the early afternoon sun of late summer warming us as we sat on the grass, I made my excuses to Dan and Tess and made my way over to him.

As I neared him, I could see he was crouched down with a stick, messing about with something in the water.

"A penny for them," I uttered. He jumped at the sound of my voice and looked around.

"Hey, Nic! I was just thinking."

"So was I. We've not spoken any more about that woman I saw at Greg and Charlotte's funeral, have we?"

"We must be thinking alike because I saw her again when Dan and I went over to see Jules. She was on the other side of the road from our flat."

"What?"

"Yeah, a bit weird, eh?" He looked back to where Dan and Tess had been sitting. "They're both coming. Let me drive you and Tess home later. We can talk more then." Knowing he needed to talk but at this point was unable to, I agreed.

"I'll say I've changed my mind about the lift, yeah?" I suggested.

He nodded.

"We were just wondering what you were both up to," Tess quizzed.

"The thought of the water drew me." I smiled.

"And I was just messing about in it, Chubbs," Mal lazily added. She looked genuinely hurt by his comment.

"Apologise, Mal!" I warned. He looked back at Tess.

"I was only joking, Tess. Don't take any notice. I'm sorry, all right?"

"Okay," she answered grudgingly and sat down again. I moved over to where Dan was standing.

"You okay?" I asked.

"Yeah, do you want to come for a walk?"

I turned back to Tess and Mal. "We won't be long," I said, and with his arm slung over my shoulders, we sauntered back across the grass to the path that wound across the park in all directions. For a while, neither of us spoke. I think we both just wanted our closeness to bond us back together. It seemed so long since we had last been this easy with one another.

"Feels good, doesn't it? The way we are again." And he inclined his head, giving me a quick kiss. I smiled.

"Yes, I didn't think we would ever get to this point again."

"We never allow this to happen again, yeah?"

"Never," I echoed.

"I just wanted a little time alone. Mal and Tess have been great, but it hasn't been just you and me for ages, and I've missed that." And I allowed him to guide me further away from them.

"You've never said much about Greg," I said, wondering whether he would open up to me now.

"That's probably because I haven't really sorted it out in my own head yet."

"Sorry, I'm prying."

"No," he answered. "I just don't know how I feel, Nic. They both spent eighteen years of my life lying to me. Even after Fran died, he still didn't say anything. Why? Why wouldn't he want to tell me he was my real father? And that I wasn't just someone they had taken into their family? Even Charlotte was my half-sister, and he didn't think that was important. I'm not sure there's any way to think about him. I don't think I care about him any more than he obviously cared about me or Charlotte. If he had, wouldn't he have told her about me and me about her? He was selfish, pure and simple."

"I never realised. Sorry, Dan, I never thought."

"Why would you? It certainly puts into perspective why they were never interested, why they would ignore me when I asked about my real parents. They both knew who my mother was and obviously who the father was. I was the product of a fling, end of!"

"But Fran wanted to keep you. Surely that means something."

"Only because she believed she couldn't have more children."

"But she loved you, even after Charlotte."

"But don't you see, Nic? By finding that out when neither of them cared enough to tell me, the truth makes all those years such a lie."

"No."

"Nic, Charlotte didn't even know I was her real brother, well, half-brother."

"She must have, Dan. You found the letter in her bedroom, didn't you?"

"Yeah, I did, but doesn't that make it even worse?"

"I don't know whether it makes things worse like that, but it does raise other questions, at least for me," I told him. "Had she said anything to Greg or even to Jules? After all, by Jules's own admission, she was close to Charlotte near the end, wasn't she?"

"Yeah," Dan agreed. "I hadn't thought of it like that."

"Come on. We had better get back. They'll be wondering where we are. We'll talk about this again. There's plenty of time to sort through it, isn't there?"

"Yeah," he repeated, but I could tell his thoughts were still deeply entrenched, and I doubted he would surface from them any time soon.

Arriving back at the flat without any prompting, Dan brought up what we had been talking about in Avery Park.

"Do you think Jules had something to do with Charlotte's death then?" Tess asked.

"I don't know," Dan answered. "But what I am saying is that Charlotte must have known that Greg was my real dad. Whether he knew she had that information is something else entirely."

"But he must have known, Dan. It wasn't in the drawer, was it? And it would explain how withdrawn Charlotte became and why he kept her away from us," Tess argued.

"Maybe Charlotte confided in Jules and she, in turn, told Greg," I reasoned.

"Yeah, that's a good point," Tess agreed. "But where do we go from here?"

"I don't know," Dan admitted.

"Shouldn't we take this to the cops?" Mal suggested.

"What? And have them question us all over again?" Dan asked.

"It was only a suggestion. Jules isn't going to admit anything to us, is she? Look how she was when we went around there. She's still playing games," Mal stated.

"I don't know. Let me sleep on it, and we'll all talk again tomorrow, agreed?" Dan looked at all of us in turn.

"Yeah, sounds okay to me," Tess agreed.

"Yep. Me, too," I told him.

"And I'll be here," Mal said.

"Okay, great. So we'll decide tomorrow." And then he turned to me. "It's past four, Nic."

"Actually, could I scrounge a lift from you, Mal?" I asked, like we had agreed at the park.

"Yeah, 'course. What time are you going, Tess? I can drop you off as well if you want."

"Okay, it'll save me walking."

"Come on then. I'll take you both now."

"I thought you might stay a bit longer with Mal taking you home," Dan responded.

"I did say I was going at four, and it's way past that, like you've already said. I'll be back tomorrow."

"Do you want me to pick you up again?" Mal asked.

"No I'll be fine. I'll set off about ten, just so you know." He kissed me goodbye. It felt familiar. It felt like I was home already.

"Ring me before you leave," Dan said.

"Okay," I called back from the door.

Mal dropped Tess off first and then carried on towards my house but stopped down the road before we reached it. He turned to me.

"Right, yesterday at the funeral, you saw that woman just as I saw her today across the road."

"Want to tell me about it?" I asked.

"I don't really know what to say. I just noticed her out of the corner of my eye, watching from across the road, and then she was gone, as suddenly as that. At both funerals as well. It's creeping me out a bit, Nic."

"It said in that letter that his mother had come back, didn't it?"

"Yeah, something like that. Why?"

"Well, what if she's come back again?"

"You think this woman is Dan's mother?" Mal asked. "That means she's watching him."

"Well, it's not beyond the bounds of possibility, is it? Think about it. Fran threatened to expose her and now she's gone and there's nothing keeping this woman from him."

"Only that she hasn't made herself known to him." But he still didn't sound convinced.

"What did she look like?" I asked.

"Probably about your height, light-coloured hair... lighter than I had initially thought, maybe dark blonde, something like that anyway."

"But what did she look like? Anything like Dan?" I prompted when his expression remained blank.

"I don't know. I didn't get that good a look at her."

"Are you going to tell Dan?"

"I don't know what we'd gain by it. It's not like we know who she definitely is, do we?"

"But surely he's still got a right to know."

"And what if she's just some crazy?"

"Oh, Mal. If she was just some random woman living near your place, she wouldn't have turned up at both funerals, would she? She must have known the family."

"You want me to tell him, don't you?"

"That's up to you, but if you don't tell him when you get back I definitely think we should tomorrow…"

"Fair enough. We'll tell him together, but can you make it earlier, be at ours for ten?"

"Okay."

Taking his attention from me, he turned the ignition on and pulled away, driving just up the road from where we'd parked. Pulling up outside Chievely Terrace, he turned to me.

"Actually, Nic, wouldn't it be easier for me to pick you up again in the morning?" I knew what he was thinking, but I was adamant. I wanted things to get back to normal as soon as possible. All this fuss was making me wish I hadn't said anything about that dream at all.

"No, I'll walk. I'm quite looking forward to it." And I climbed out. "See you tomorrow," I said and waved as I walked away.

Chapter Thirty
In Shadow

I called out to my mum as I walked in through the door, seeing the light blazing out from the kitchen.

"Hi, Nic. Good time?"

"Yeah."

"Dan's all right, is he?"

"Oh, yeah, he's okay... Actually, Mum, we talked and we agreed to give it another go. You're okay with that, aren't you?" I asked uneasily. I wasn't sure how she was going to take it.

"Do I have a choice?"

"W-what?" I stammered. I knew she'd been angry at him the other day when he'd come over here, but I thought she'd calmed down.

"Oh, don't look so scared, Nic. No, I don't mind. Like I said last night, as long as he treats you right." I walked straight up to her and threw my arms around her.

"All right, don't go too mad." And she held me away from her. "It is good to see you smiling again, though. No more dreams, eh?"

"No, I hope not," I agreed, remembering the effects my dream from last night had already had on me.

For the first time in days, we both settled down to dinner and we really talked. I went on endlessly about the woman Mal had initially noticed at Fran's funeral and then again around where he and Dan lived. I also mentioned that I had seen her when I'd been shopping with Tess and at Greg and Charlotte's funeral.

"She could be anyone connected to the family," she explained. "Maybe somewhere along the line, there has been a falling out that Dan hasn't been aware of."

"But that wouldn't explain why she would be hanging around the flat, would it?"

"You think it's his mum, don't you?"

"Paige Ellison," I said. "Well, it would make sense, wouldn't it?"

"Yes, it would, but so would a number of other alternatives."

"Well, we're going to tell Dan about her in the morning. I'm going over there for ten."

"Just be careful about the way you tell him," she warned.

"What do you mean?" I asked, a little taken aback at the way she'd said it.

"Just go easy with the information you both have. Just tell him you've noticed a woman hanging around as opposed to the fact that you've seen a woman hanging around and that you think she could be your mother – you know, the one who deserted you."

"I wouldn't come out with it like that anyway!"

"I know you wouldn't, Nic, at least not intentionally. Just go easy – that's all I'm saying." I knew what she meant. I would never hurt Dan, but if there was any chance that she could be his mum, he needed to know.

"How is he coping anyway? Has he spoken much about his father?" she asked.

"We all went to Avery Park this afternoon, and Dan and I went off on our own for a while. He opened up a little bit. He's not doing so well, as far as the subject of either Fran or Greg are concerned. He can't understand why neither of them told him the truth, and he thinks the fact that they didn't makes his life a lie. He thinks he's just the product of a fling."

"Well, he was, wasn't he?"

"Mum!"

"Well, he was, Nicola. There's no other way I can see to dress it up. Maybe he wasn't in his mum's mind – none of us can know that for sure – but certainly in Greg's? As I've said to you before. He wasn't a particularly nice man or father, as it turns out, was he?"

I certainly couldn't disagree with that. My experience of him, especially in the last week or so, had been strange to say the least which brought me back to Charlotte. At what point had she got hold of that letter? Had he checked it days afterwards, found it missing, and immediately blamed us? But he never said anything... Or had he checked the drawer as soon as we left the house and found it was still there? Maybe Charlotte saw him in there and went back later, curious to find out what was in there."

"You look lost in thought," she muttered, catching my attention.

"I was just thinking about Charlotte."

"All this must be having an effect on you as well. Is that what all the dreams are about, do you think?"

"Maybe." Sometimes – and this was one of those times – I felt like I wanted to tell her everything that was going through my head, but something stopped me; something always stopped me. I don't know why. I don't know whether I thought she might think badly of Dan or think I was in too deep and ground me or something, but I just couldn't get it out.

"I'm going to bed, Mum. I've got an early start, so..."

"Yeah, yeah, I know. You've got to go to Dan's."

I smiled apologetically and walked over for a hug. "I love you."

"And I love you," she replied as I pulled away.

I walked out of the room without saying another word. I think I was too shocked at what I had openly admitted. I know she was my mum, but I just wasn't given to such open affection.

Those sort of words meant nothing to me.

Other people always said them with such an air of indifference, like it was the easiest thing in the world to say without attaching any real emotion. To me, it was the deeds that others performed that spoke volumes – of people caring enough to stick around. But maybe that was just me.

Reaching my bedroom, I felt strangely emotional, and I cried for reasons I couldn't comprehend. Were my tears the result of the endless weeks all of us had been made to endure after finding Charlotte and Greg? Were they the result of being mercilessly questioned by the police or Jules's ruthless actions towards me with the sole intent of gaining Dan's affection? Or maybe it was just the fact that all these emotions had just built up and needed to be released. But as the tears lessened, I climbed into bed and lay there. Closing my eyes, I was unable to hold back my exhaustion any longer. My mind drifted along on a sea of calm, my senses recalling nothing.

Lazily stretching from my sleep and disturbed by nothing, I yawned contentedly. I remembered nothing. For once my sleep had been happily uneventful. I glanced at the clock… It was eight. I lay there for a minute, feeling happy. It seemed strange that only hours before I had fallen to sleep amid tears I couldn't explain. But today was different. It felt like we were finally going to be able to get somewhere with the deaths of Greg and Charlotte. All the pieces seemed as if they were slowly coming together now.

After showering and getting dressed, I made my way downstairs to the smell of something good wafting out from the kitchen.

"I thought you might like a more substantial breakfast this morning," my mum offered. Lately, most mornings I had left the house without so much as a cup of tea, so I relished this: scrambled egg on toast and it looked good.

"I enjoyed last night. It seems a long time since we just sat down like that. What time will you be home, Nic?"

"Around six."

"I'll have some dinner ready, okay?"

"Yeah, that'll be great. Thanks, Mum. And I enjoyed last night too."

"Don't be late!"

"I won't be," I assured her, grabbed my bag and made for the door. "See you at six," I repeated before pulling the door shut.

Outside I began walking with purpose, my eyes searching out each woman who passed me, wondering if she was the one Mal had tried unsuccessfully to describe. Dan and I were properly back on track as well, and with the way I felt, it seemed that life couldn't possibly get any better than it was right at this moment. En route I must have cocooned myself, my thoughts unintentionally blocking out everything and everyone around me, because hearing my name being called behind me made me jump out of my skin.

"Didn't you see me?" Tess asked, a little disgruntled.

"Sorry. No, I didn't expect that you would be on your way this early either."

"Well, I've been waving like mad. I thought you had seen me."

"Sorry, no," I repeated. "I must have been in a world of my own."

"Okay, got any gossip?"

"No," I answered, wondering whether Mal had said anything about that woman.

"That wasn't very convincing," she replied. I weighed it up. She was going to find out anyway when we told Dan that Mal had seen that woman a number of times.

"Well, are you going to tell me?" Tess badgered.

"Mal's noticed a woman hanging around their flat," I told her. "But it's not only that. The first time he noticed her was at Fran's funeral, and then I noticed a woman at Greg and Charlotte's funeral. The same one I think I saw when you and I were shopping. Remember?"

"Nope," she answered vacantly.

"Well, we think it's the same woman." She went quiet for a minute, obviously mulling over what I had said.

"So who is she?" she questioned.

"We don't actually know. But it seems strange that she's been hanging around their flat and that she must have known his

355

family well enough to have gone to Fran's and then Greg and Charlotte's funeral."

"You think it's Dan's real mother?" she guessed.

"Well, that's the logical conclusion we came to."

"Why didn't you say anything to me?"

"Mal mentioned it that night he took me home after Jules made that remark to me about not getting too attached to Dan. To be honest, my head was so full of Jules that what he did tell me went straight over my head, and then whenever it did occur to me, the time never seemed right. It was only yesterday, when he gave me a lift home, that I remembered to ask about her again, whether he had seen any more of her. We certainly weren't trying to keep anything from you, Tess."

"Okay, but I'm guessing he has seen her again more recently?"

"Yes, near their flat, like I've just told you, and that's why I'm on my way there now. Have you spoken to Mal?"

"Last night, he said you were going around about ten and asked me if I wanted to get there around the same time, but he didn't say anything about what you've just told me."

"He kept it quiet for Dan's sake, that's all. I'm not sure whether it's going to be a shock for him or not."

"Well, it'll be up to him then, to do what he wants." And with that final statement, we carried on in silence. I just hoped he didn't think the same as I was getting from Tess, that we had been keeping this from him.

As we neared the flat, we walked past several women around the age Mal had gauged her to be, somewhere around her late thirties early forties. I tried to take notice of anyone who looked vaguely like my mum – age wise, that is. Although she was nearer to forty, she looked much younger.

There was one particular woman who caught my eye as we turned into Risely Road; she watched me as we walked by, and she had fair hair – maybe a little darker, as Mal had said. But she looked at me strangely, like she knew something about me.

"What was she looking at?" Tess questioned when we were out of range.

"Search me... Maybe that was her." She laughed like I had just told the best joke ever.

"Go and ask her?" I challenged. She stopped in her tracks.

"Okay." And she turned to walk back to catch up with her. "W-where's she gone?"

"I don't know." And I stood there, looking as well. There was no way she could have disappeared that quickly, was there?

"Come on. Let's get to the flat," I said, a shiver suddenly running through me.

The welcome we heard from Dan when we pressed the buzzer to their flat couldn't have been in sharper contrast to the way that encounter had left me feeling.

"Come on up," he replied brightly and buzzed the door open. I looked back at Tess, who was still waiting for the woman to reappear.

"Come on," I said, holding the door open for her.

"We did see her, right?" she said, not quite believing what we had both seen.

"Yeah, we did," I answered.

The door was already open when we reached their landing. I waited while Tess caught up before walking in.

"Hey," Dan greeted, planting a kiss on my lips as I walked in, pulling me close.

"Oh, please!" Tess said, walking around us. "Can't either of you wait?"

"No!" he replied but promptly let me go. "Thanks for ringing me. I asked you yesterday to ring before you left home."

"Oh God, I'm sorry, Dan. It completely went out of my head." He turned his attention straight to Tess.

"And what's the matter with you?" I surreptitiously stole a glance in Mal's direction and nodded, letting him know that Tess knew about the woman we had spoken of yesterday.

"Nothing," she told him.

"Anyway, mate. Sit down. We've got something we need to tell you," Mal announced.

"Sounds ominous."

"It's not so much ominous as intriguing," I said. "But before we say anything, I just want to say that we didn't tell you this until now because we weren't really sure how to, right, Mal?"

"Yeah, absolutely, mate. You see, I've noticed this woman ever since your mum's... sorry, Fran's funeral. I've seen her around here and more recently at your dad and Charlotte's funeral." Mal seemed to mentally back away and went very quiet, waiting for Dan's reaction.

"You think it's my real mum?"

"I don't know, mate."

"What about you, Nic? What do you think?" he asked.

"Honestly, I don't know either, Dan. But I suppose it could be. She must obviously have known Fran and Greg, and Charlotte to some degree, for her to have wanted to be there at the funerals."

"And you, Tess?" he prompted.

"I didn't know until we bumped into one another on the way here." She looked sideways at me.

"What?" Dan asked, catching the questioning expression aimed at me. I nodded, signalling her to tell him everything.

"We saw a woman outside. She watched us as we walked by, well, as Nic walked by actually. Once she was past, I commented about the way she had been watching you, Nic, didn't I?"

"Yes, and you thought I was joking when I said that maybe that was her, so I told you to go and ask her." And I turned to Dan. "Tess turned around with the intention of doing just that, but the woman had disappeared. In those couple of seconds, she just vanished."

"So what are you telling me?"

"Well, I think it spooked both of us, didn't it?" I said, turning again to Tess. "I'm not sure whether she was watching us or not. It could just have been a coincidence." But before I could say any more, he rushed out of the flat and bolted down the stairs. A few minutes later, we heard the door slam and his footsteps ascending the stairs. He walked back in through the door, looking crestfallen.

"No one out there?" Tess asked.

"No, I thought she might still be there even though you'd said she'd disappeared."

"Well, let's leave that for now," Mal said. "You wanted to sleep on what we were talking about yesterday, Dan, about going to the cops with what we pieced together about the letter and Charlotte, Jules and Greg. What do you want to do?"

"There's nothing concrete in anything we've got. That's what they'll tell us."

"Maybe. But what if they've got the letter in front of them and you tell them where you found it? Aren't their deaths, then, more suspect?"

"Yeah, and they might think that I then had cause to do Greg harm. You're forgetting how he was with me after we found Charlotte, Mal, and that was in front of the cops... Then finding me with Greg dead in my arms. No, I think that's the last thing I want to do."

"But what does that leave us with?" Mal asked.

"Face Jules ourselves... but all of us this time," Tess suggested.

"I don't know whether that's a good idea either," Dan responded.

"Well, we've got to do something, mate," Mal commented. "We can't just leave this as it is."

"Fine... Have it your way. We'll go and see Jules Harvey. See what she has to say about it. Not quite yet, though. A bit later, yeah?" And he searched our faces. Both Tess and I agreed straight away, but Mal held back.

"Don't you think it would be easier to go and tell the cops, let them sort it?" he asked Dan. "I hear what you say but it might be best," Mal added.

"No, I've already told you why."

"Okay." And he held his hands up defensively. "But if I get the slightest inkling that she's had any involvement with either Greg or Charlotte's deaths or both, then I'll be going straight to the cops."

"Fine," Dan responded, and suddenly everything went very quiet. I looked over at Tess, wondering what to say.

"Anyone want a cup of tea?" she asked, filling the void.

"Yeah, but can I have coffee, Tess?" Mal answered.

"Thanks," Dan answered quietly. I went and sat down next to him.

"Come on, Dan. At least if we all talk to her, we'll be able to gauge whether she knows anything, at the very least."

"I know that. I just didn't want to have to see her again."

"What can she do?" I questioned.

"Um... Maybe you're right."

"Of course I am." I snuggled into him, more to try and put him at ease than anything else. It was plain for anyone to see how uncomfortable he was with all this, and Mal didn't look much happier.

"Do you want to ring her to make sure she's in?" I asked Dan.

"No, not really, unless I'm forced to."

"Yeah," Mal readily agreed. "We would only be giving her time to get out of the way."

"Thanks," Dan said finally.

"I don't think anyone here really wants to go over there, mate, but if the cops aren't an option at this point, we haven't got a lot of choice."

Dan nodded. "We'll have these teas and then make a move, yeah?"

"Yep, that sounds good to me," Tess replied, setting them down.

Chapter Thirty-One
Reactions

Sitting around with all three of them felt good; it felt comfortable, like I truly belonged. All the trouble we had collectively faced over the last few weeks seemed like a world away as we sat around, drinking our teas, though just lately, in Mal's case it was now coffee. I don't think there had been anyone – Dan, Tess, or Mal – who I hadn't upset at some point during this summer, but we had all come through for each other; and going over to see Jules seemed like the last push before we could all properly get back to some normality.

"It seems a long time since we've been like this, just sitting here without anything else going on, doesn't it?" Tess commented, mirroring what I had been thinking.

"Well, something's going to happen soon," Mal responded. "Are we going over there in my car?"

"Yeah, it would get it over with a bit sooner, wouldn't it?" Dan agreed.

"Are we heading straight back here?" Tess asked.

"We can. I haven't got anything else going on, and I don't need to be back home until six," I remarked.

"Oh, I was going to ask if you wanted to stay tonight," Dan said, "but I wasn't sure whether it was a bit soon."

"I'm sorry, Dan. I can't. I promised my mum, but maybe I can tomorrow." His face brightened up.

"Really?"

"Really," I repeated. As he smiled in response, his whole demeanour seemed lighter and far less troubled in that moment.

"What are we waiting for then? Come on." And racing to finish our drinks, we jumped up and made our way out through the doorway Dan was impatiently holding open.

As we piled into the car, our moods changed just as quickly as Dan's had in the flat. I think back there we all felt brave about facing Jules again. Now though, the atmosphere felt thick, weighing heavy.

After we pulled in by the roadside a few houses up from her flat, Dan sighed, he'd drifted back into a melancholy mood.

"I felt charged up back at the flat about coming here, but now we are here, I'm not so sure it was a good idea."

"It'll pass, mate," Mal told him. "It's probably just a bit of apprehension about how she's going to react to us all turning up like this."

"Yeah, you're probably right." And Dan reluctantly opened the car door. I looked at Tess, who had been observing proceedings.

"He'll be all right when we get in there," she reassured me.

"If she's home," I answered.

"She'll be in there, feeling sorry for herself, because she lost out."

"Well, I just hope we can get over this and at least be civil with one another again."

"That's not gonna happen, is it?" she responded.

"Why?" I asked.

"Well, if you don't know by now, Nic, it's not worth me saying."

"You mean, Dan."

She leaned over and whispered, "Exactly. She's not going to forget that. She's the one person at college, Nic, who has guys buzzing around her like bees around a honey pot, and you managed to get in her way."

I pulled myself up to get out as Dan pulled the seat forward, but Tess's words stayed with me. I wondered again what her reaction to my appearance here would be, though I knew I wouldn't be waiting long, if she was here. After Tess rejoined me, we followed Mal and Dan. We waited just to the side of the door, allowing Dan and Mal to take the lead. I noticed Dan take a deep breath. Did that mean Jules was in and he could see her approaching? Yes, she was, and she was opening the door. I stayed as still as I could, as did Tess who was still beside me.

"Dan... Mal," she added less enthusiastically. "Oh, and you've brought Nic and Tess with you as well."

"Can we come in, please?" Dan asked.

"What's all this about? I thought everything had been said the other day."

"It would be better if we could come in, Jules; we just want to have a chat, that's all."

"Be my guest." And she held the door open for each of us to pass through. Tess ushered me in ahead of her, probably to prevent Jules adding any more bile out of anyone else's earshot. I kept my eyes averted as I passed her, but I could tell she was watching me. I heard Tess address her as she passed, but it was just met with a wall of silence on Jules's part.

Once we were all congregated in Jules's flat, Mal seemed anxious to take charge.

"So what can I do for you all?" Jules asked, following us in.

"It's about a letter Dan found in Charlotte's bedroom," Mal explained.

"This sounds like it has to do with Dan. Is he unable to explain for himself?" And she turned to him.

"Yeah, it's all right, mate. I'll take it from here."

"Like Mal's just said, Jules, I found a letter in Charlotte's bedroom, and it explained a few things. I... We," he amended, "just want to know whether you knew anything about it, whether Charlotte confided in you. I know you've said before that you and she were very close in those last weeks. Maybe she was worried about it. I know she was very withdrawn, even from me on occasion, and at the time, I couldn't understand why. Maybe this could be the reason."

"So what was in the letter?" she asked. But I got the impression she already knew, and I think Dan did too.

"Surely if you were that close to her, she would have told you," Dan prompted.

"I'm not sure. She said many things to me, but she never showed me a letter," she explained.

"Did she say anything about Dan?" I asked. She looked over at me, her expression full of contempt.

"Well?" Mal demanded.

"Was I talking to you?"

"No, but you weren't exactly about to answer Nic either, were you?"

"Yeah, she talked about you, Dan," she said, completely ignoring me, though she didn't say anything else either.

"And said what?" Dan continued.

"She told me she had read a letter that said Greg was really your father, but she swore me to secrecy. She said Greg didn't know that she had read the letter and that he'd be really angry if he found out she had gone rooting around in his office at home."

"And did you pass this information on?" Dan questioned.

"No… 'Course not." But there had been the slightest of pauses, and I had certainly noticed it, as had Mal and Tess, and I was sure Dan had as well.

"You're lying," he said.

"I didn't say anything, Dan."

I quickly left the sofa where I had been sitting with Tess and took my place beside Dan with Mal on his other side.

"It's time we were going, Dan," I said.

"Yeah," Jules scoffed. "Go and do as your girlfriend says, Dan."

"Shut up, Jules!"

Her attention shot straight to Tess who'd said it. "Get out of my flat, all of you!"

I reached out for Tess, who was just getting off the sofa, and ushered Dan towards the door. Mal stayed back, following Tess.

"I hope you're proud of yourself," he commented. "You could have made this a whole lot easier for Dan."

"It should be Charlotte being blamed for this, not me."

Tess heard her and rounded on her. "How dare you? She's dead! You were supposed to care about her," she screamed at her.

"Come on, Tess," I responded. "She's not worth it."

"You got that right, Nic. She's not!"

"I meant you." And I ushered Tess away towards the door.

"We'll see what the cops think about what you've said; maybe you won't be so full of yourself then!" Mal shot back before joining us.

Out in the street, I tried to calm Tess down. She was still crying uncontrollably. I held her close.

"Don't take any notice. She only said all that for effect," I told her.

"No, she didn't," Dan cut in.

"No, she didn't," Mal agreed. "And I think it's time we went to the cops."

"Please, can we go back to the flat first?" I asked.

"Yeah, Tess isn't in any fit state to go anywhere at the moment," Dan reasoned. With that decided, we made for the car and home, Mal and Dan's anyway.

"Are you both all right?" Dan asked once we were safely in the backseat.

"Yeah, I am, and Tess will be," I said, though she was still very quiet. What Jules had said about Charlotte was unforgivable, and though Dan had shown no emotion at the time, I was sure it had affected him just as powerfully as it had Tess. I put my arm around her; she needed that.

Dan would wait. Tomorrow night he could command my attention as much as he liked.

"I can't believe what she just said," Mal said to no one in particular.

"Please, Mal, can we just get going and get away from here?" Dan asked.

"Sorry, mate." And he turned the ignition.

The drive back was filled with silence; all our thoughts no doubt centred on two subjects, Jules and Charlotte. We all knew Charlotte's death had been a terrible waste. I think we had all wondered what she had been doing at the theatre. She must have been there with someone or meeting someone, at the very least. Had it been Jules or maybe even Greg, if, in fact, Jules had said something to him. But why her dad would have wanted to meet her anywhere other than at home was a complete mystery. If he had wanted to say anything to her, surely he could have said it anytime while they were both at home. I realised as well that Dan hadn't said any more about the woman Tess and I had seen earlier on. But so much more had happened since then; there wasn't really any wonder that he hadn't.

Parking, we all piled out as silently as we had piled in. Nothing was said until we had climbed the stairs and walked back into the flat.

Leaving Dan and Tess to go and sit down, Mal and I made ourselves busy making drinks. I felt at a loss to know what to say.

"Do you think it might be better to leave it until tomorrow to go to the cops?" Mal asked me.

"No, I would go today. Jules is aware now that that's what we're going to do, isn't she?"

"Oh, God, yeah. I told her, didn't I?" he said, remembering.

"You didn't say anything the rest of us wouldn't have, Mal."

"Thanks, Nic."

"Give them both an hour... Actually, Mal," I continued, keeping my voice low, "I'm a little concerned about Dan. He hasn't shown any reaction to what Jules said, but I'm sure he's feeling it equally if not more so than Tess."

"I'm sure," he echoed. "But don't worry about him. He'll be all right. I'll keep an eye on him tonight." I just wished I shared his optimism that he would be all right, or maybe he was just saying that for my benefit. He really loved Charlotte, even when he believed they weren't actually brother and sister. Finding out she really was his sister and then having to listen to Jules spewing

366

out her bile could tip anyone over the edge. I just worried that after all he'd had thrown at him, this would just be enough to tip that balance.

"Okay, we'll have a drink, and then I'll broach the subject of the cops, yeah? Nic... Nic!" And he nudged me.

"What?"

"I said okay to having a drink and then broaching the subject of the cops."

"Er, yeah," I agreed.

"Do you want to take Dan's then?" I looked down at the cups full to the brim. When did that happen? He moved mine and Dan's over the worktop slightly towards me.

"Okay," I responded and took hold of them and deposited them on the coffee table. I sat down on the carpet at Dan's feet, leaving the chair free for Mal. For a few minutes, my mind wandered until Mal's voice shattered my peace.

"Would it be an idea to make our way to the cops once we've had these?" he asked Dan and Tess.

"To inform them of our suspicions about Jules?" Dan asked.

"Yeah," Mal answered. Dan shuffled around and reached into his back pocket. He pulled out a folded up piece of paper.

"I decided to take a copy. I figured I might need it when we went around there. Maybe Jules's loss will be their gain, eh? I used your printer, Mal. You don't mind, do you?"

"No," he responded. "We'll drink these and then go." I glanced back at Dan. He smiled; nothing seemed wrong, and yet everything was.

Draining the bottom of my cup, I placed it back on the coffee table, followed by everybody else's.

"Right. I suppose we had better go then," Mal urged. Getting up from the sofa, Dan pulled Tess to her feet and then turned his attention to me.

"We'll go to the cops and then drop you both off. Is that okay, Mal?"

"Yeah, that's a good idea." And we tramped out of the flat with just that one thing on our minds. Following Dan out of the bottom door, Tess and I walked straight into the back of Dan, who was just standing there.

"What's the matter?" I asked, wondering what he had seen. That woman was my first thought until Dan spoke.

"Where is it?" he demanded.

"What?" I questioned as Mal closed in behind us.

"What's up?" he asked, making his way to Dan's side.

"It's your car," he replied. "It's gone."

"It can't have." And Mal laughed until he looked to where he had parked it and saw the vacant space it had been occupying. He then looked up and down the road. "What the hell... Where's it gone?" And he looked to Dan, who just shrugged.

"You did lock it, didn't you?" Dan asked.

"What? 'Course, I did," he snapped.

"Well, then you'd better ring the cops," he said and turned to me and Tess. "I'll walk you both home."

"No, stay here with Mal. We'll walk together as far as the bottom of the hill. We'll both ring as soon as we get home, if that's okay with you, Tess."

"Yeah, but what are you gonna do now, Mal?"

"Well, first, I'll have to ring the cops and report it stolen." And he reached into his pocket for his phone.

"I didn't hear anything up in the flat. Did any of you?" Dan asked. "There is an alarm on your car, isn't there, Mal? I'm sure I've heard it going off before."

"Well, yeah."

"But I didn't hear it this afternoon," I responded.

"Well, I'm still ringing the cops," he retorted. I turned to Dan.

"Stay with him. We'll be fine. I'll ring you as soon as I get in," I assured him.

"I'm not happy about this, Nic. We were going to the cops together."

"You need to sort this out, and then after that, you and Mal go. If they need to speak to me and Tess, we can go there tomorrow."

Tess dipped her head in response. "Yeah, it won't be a problem, Dan."

"That's settled then." I gave him a quick kiss goodbye, but he pulled me back. In his arms, he kissed me long and hard. There was an urgency there and a stubborn refusal to let go.

Pulling away, I smiled.

"We'll be fine. I'll be fine, honest."

He smiled falteringly before fully releasing me. Reaching for his hand and in barely more than a whisper, I said, "I love you." He was about to say something, but I put my finger to his lips and shook my head to stop him. I walked away with Tess, our arms linked. Shouting our goodbyes to Mal, I turned my attention to Tess, but not before I stole one more glance back at Dan. He looked like he had the weight of the world on his shoulders, probably stunned by my declaration of love. I wasn't even sure why I had blurted it out. That was the second time today. What was the matter with me? I inwardly berated myself. I looked back, stealing one final glance. He was still watching.

Out of earshot, Tess wasted no time in casting aspersions as to who might have stolen Mal's car.

"They must have known what they were doing, whoever it was," I responded.

"I didn't hear his alarm going off either."

"No, don't you think that's strange?" I replied. "I'm sure I've heard it up in the flat before."

"Maybe it was someone who knows Mal," Tess wondered. "Hey, what about that woman, Dan's real mum?"

"What?"

"Well, stranger things have happened."

I laughed. "We don't even know she is Dan's real mother. It could all turn out to be a complete coincidence."

"It could, but I don't think so. Do you?" Tess asked.

"I don't know what I think." The fact that I hadn't heard Mal's car alarm going off still bothered me. "Do you want me to ring Dan to let him and Mal know that we've arrived home without incident?" I asked.

"How about you ring Dan, and I'll ring Mal," she suggested.

"At times you two have seemed a bit closer. Anything you want to tell me?" I teased.

"I wish," she replied.

"Well, one of these days, he might surprise you, Tess Brinham."

"Do you know something I don't?"

"No, but from what I've seen, he does seem to be warming to you."

"I think that's just wishful thinking. Besides, the only thing that'll be on his mind right now is his precious car."

We had been talking non-stop since we left, and I hadn't realised just how much distance we'd covered. We were almost at the bottom of Tanners Hill.

"Well, we had better say goodbye now. Are you going to ring Mal as soon as you get in then?" I asked.

"Yeah. Just make sure you ring Dan. He's really worried about you."

"I will, but there's no need." And we hugged one another before she crossed over the road and headed home. Standing near the kerb, I shouted to her.

"Tess, I'll see you tomorrow, yeah?"

"I'll ring you later." And she carried on walking.

I smiled to myself. How come I had such good friends around me? I don't know why but I stole a glance back up the hill before making my way home, but something kept me there. It was quiet. I looked up at the sky; the sun was still warm, but clouds were gathering to my right.

I looked back up the hill, there was a lone car. I don't know why, but the woman Tess and I had passed near Mal and Dan's flat suddenly popped into my head, as Tess had mentioned. I hadn't seen any more of her, and again, I smiled to myself, shaking off an unease that had unexpectedly settled over me. Though it was still some way off, the car did look familiar; it was black just like Mal's. No, it couldn't be. I shook my head, remembering my dream from last night, again berating myself for actually giving it any serious thought at all.

I turned and started to walk in the direction of home, but something again made me turn back. The car was closer; it had sped up. I looked around me. Whoever was inside the car seemed like he or she had no intention of stopping, and they were going to hurt someone or worse. But then its tyres screeched as its course was forced in my direction.

Visions of last night suddenly flooded my brain, my fear rendering me still, rooting me to the spot. Everything slowed down; like you hear from people who have had a major accident or something. Even the car seemed to glide, synchronizing with my movements to perfection. In that moment my fear ebbed away with the appearance of Charlotte, who, one last time, was tugging at me. I stood my ground though, and instead I looked at the driver, more intent on recognising who was behind the wheel, but there was no recognition. It wasn't Jules, as she had been in my dream. I didn't recognise who it was though I caught sight for the briefest second.

In that moment of time being suspended, nothing seemed to matter; everything seemed calm, serene even. But then it swiftly resumed its normality as the car, only inches from me, ploughed headlong, accompanied by an echoing chorus of piercing screams that resonated through me from somewhere in the distance. Was I dying? As my senses faded, I remembered only Charlotte standing beside me.

Lightning Source UK Ltd.
Milton Keynes UK
UKHW011453110920
369746UK00003B/171